BY EZEKIEL EVERSAND

Kingfall – Book One

Spellblade – Book Two

Greyfire – Book Three

Goldfyre – Book Four (coming soon)

Ashenwave – Book Five (future project)

KINGFALL

The Neverborne Series

(Book One)

EZEKIEL EVERSAND

Kingfall is a work of fiction. Names, characters, places, and incidents either are the product of the author's imagination or are used fictitiously. Any resemblance to actual persons, living or dead, events, or locales is entirely coincidental.

First published in 2020.

Library of Congress Control Number: 2020909656

ISBN 978-1-7342737-2-4

Book Cover Art by Soós Gergő @deviantart.com/random223
Book Cover Design by Lance Buckley @lancebuckley.com
Map Illustration by Cornelia Yoder @corneliayoder.com

Printed in the United States of America

2026 Content Revision Edition

CONTENT DISCLOSURE

Let this serve as a notice to the story's intended audience. The reader should understand that this work is a novel of mature content that would be considered rated R, with certain topics mentioned that may be found offensive. Reader discretion is advised, as this book may be inappropriate and unsuitable for younger audiences.

DEDICATION

To my father, my biggest fan, and the prime motivation for why I write. To my mother, who has been my rock of peace in my journey of interesting peaks and hard valleys. To my older brother, Sean, for introducing me as a young child to this endeavor that is the endless realm of the fantasy genre. To my younger brothers and cousins who spawned many of the character concepts and encouraged the evolution that has become The Neverborne Series. This is for you, Ty, Kirk, Micah, and Justin – beyond "the Box." To my most loved thing on earth, my dog, Hero, for saving me when I needed it the most.

INTRODUCTION

Kingfall is the first novel in *The Neverborne Series*. The direct follow-up of the plotline and POV characters from *Kingfall* is the third novel, *Greyfire*. The second novel in the series, *Spellblade*, takes place simultaneously as the story in *Kingfall*, although in different parts of the realm with an entirely new set of characters whose trajectories will collide with the *Kingfall* characters. Sequential novels may have similar plotline development.

There are several annotations and maps available in this novel to help with references when needed. It is encouraged to visit the maps when geographical points are mentioned to better come to know the world of Penthara. The Pentharam System, the Racial Descendancies, the Geographical Demographics, the Powers and Organizations, and a Word Glossary are included in either the front or the back of the book to browse at your leisure.

Penthara is a world of two main races: the humans and the elven. Among the two, they have many subcultures, all differentiated by their elemental descendancies – tairan, fire, sky, shadow, water, or mixed lineages. Elven have impowers which enhance them with special abilities granted from their elemental lineages. There are also evolved versions of the races such as the umbran, quasi, and animayan for the elven, and qindrid, mages, and hyperi for humans. There are even halfkinders and more to be discovered.

Each of the five elements of the realm correlate with one of the five seasons. The Dawning is to Spring, which is to tairan (earth). The Sunder is to Summer, which is to fire. The Reaping is to Autumn, which is to sky. The Umbra is to Winter, which is to shadow. The Torrent is a unique season to Penthara, which is to water. Each novel in a whole is intended to cover an entire season, which is five months long.

Italicized phrases are inner monologue from the point-of-view characters. "*Italicized phrases in quotations*" indicate translations of dialogue spoken outside the Civil universal language.

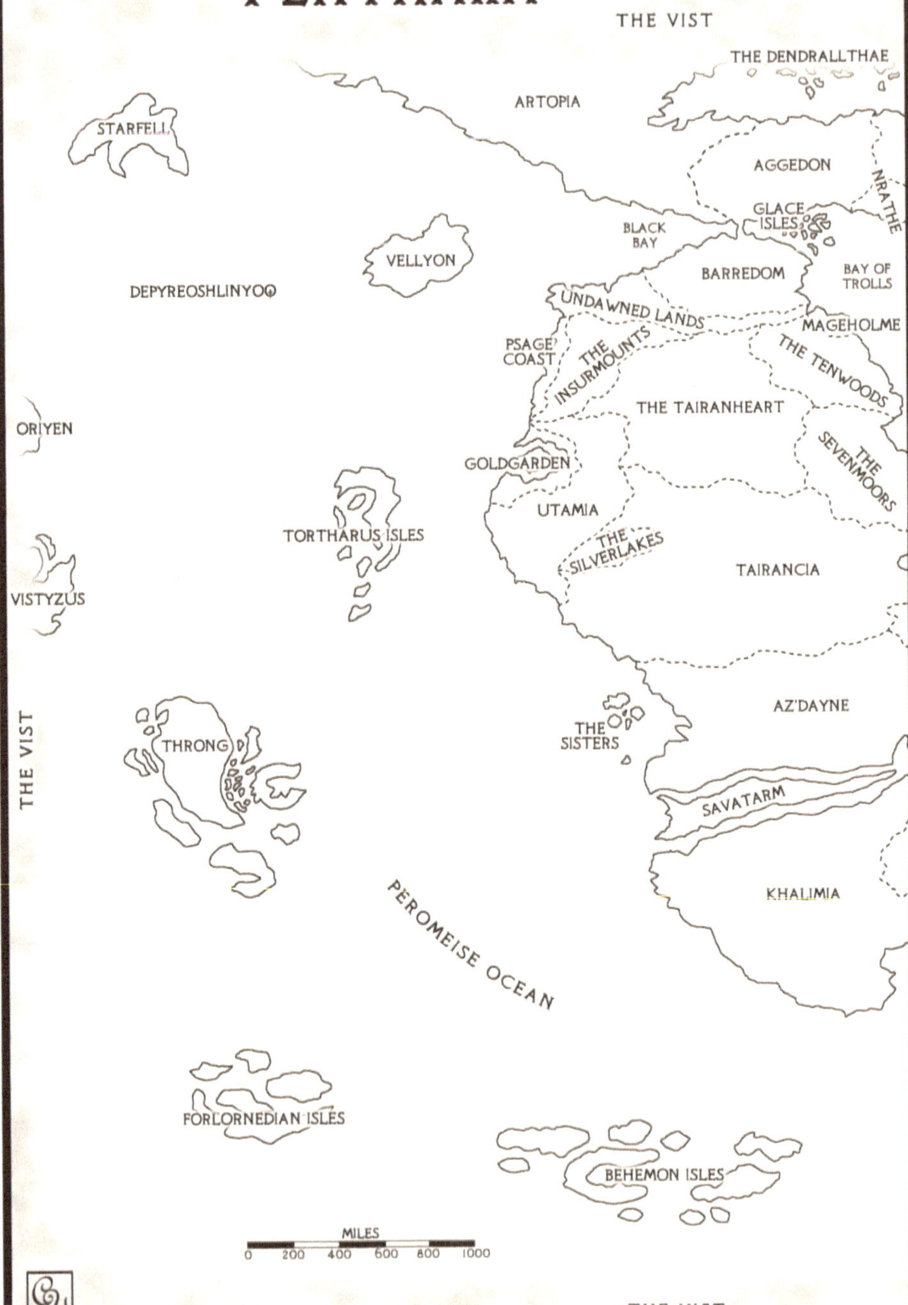

THE LANDS AND SEAS OF
PENTHARA
THE VIST
THE DENDRALLTHAE
ARTOPIA
STARFELL
AGGEDON
NRATHE
GLACE ISLES
BLACK BAY
VELLYON
BARREDOM
BAY OF TROLLS
DEPYREOSHLINYOQ
UNDAWNED LANDS
MAGEHOLME
PSAGE COAST
THE INSURMOUNTS
THE TENWOODS
THE TAIRANHEART
ORIYEN
THE SEVENMOORS
GOLDGARDEN
UTAMIA
TORTHARUS ISLES
THE SILVERLAKES
TAIRANCIA
VISTYZUS
AZ'DAYNE
THE VIST
THRONG
THE SISTERS
SAVATARM
KHALIMIA
PEROMEISE OCEAN
FORLORNEDIAN ISLES
BEHEMON ISLES
MILES
0
200
400
600
800
1000
THE VIST

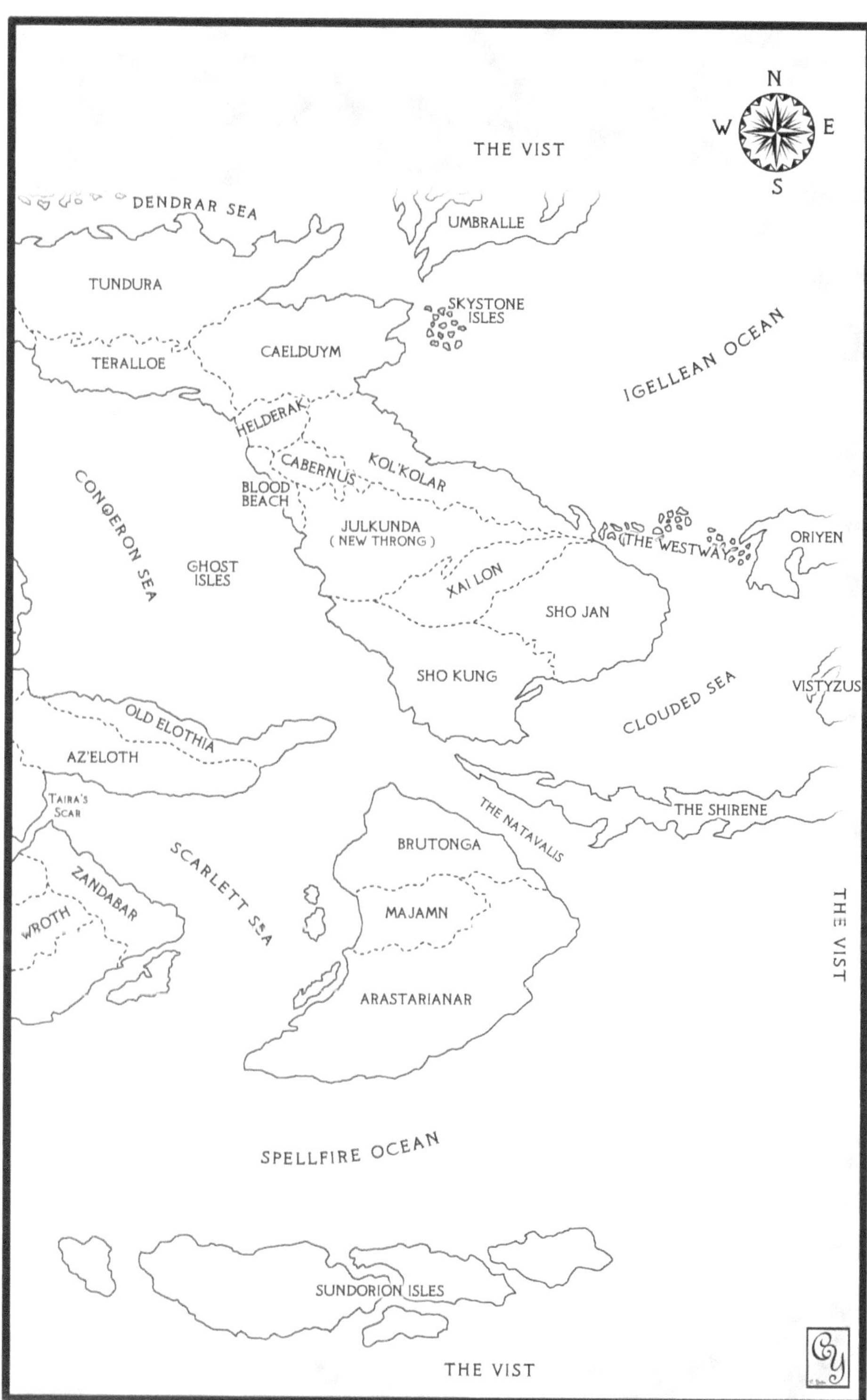
N
W
E
S
THE VIST
DENDRAR SEA
UMBRALLE
TUNDURA
SKYSTONE ISLES
CAELDUYM
TERALLOE
IGELLEAN OCEAN
HELDERAK
CABERNUS
KOL'KOLAR
CONGERON SEA
BLOOD BEACH
JULKUNDA (NEW THRONG)
THE WESTWAY
ORIYEN
GHOST ISLES
XAI LON
SHO JAN
SHO KUNG
VISTYZUS
CLOUDED SEA
OLD ELOTHIA
AZ'ELOTH
TAIRA'S SCAR
THE NATAVALIS
THE SHIRENE
BRUTONGA
SCARLETT SEA
ZANDABAR
WROTH
MAJAMN
THE VIST
ARASTARIANAR
SPELLFIRE OCEAN
SUNDORION ISLES
THE VIST

THE BROKEN CLAN LANDS OF AGGEDON
AND THE KINGDOM OF BARREDOM
N
W
E
S
THE VIST
THE DENDRALLTHAE
DENDRAR SEA
LEGEND
CAPITAL CITY
CITY
TOWN
VILLAGE
KEEP
FORTRESS
RUINS
CAMPS
TOWER
POINT OF INTEREST
ROAD
WALL
COLD HARBOR
HROGANYN'S HORDE
NORTH PASS
PYTALON
THE WARRENS
THE HUB
SOUTH PASS
HROGANYNDALE
UR DYNELENOX
ENTRANCE TO ZSOLINDAL
RUEN'IR
GOREGUN HILLS
DOBATHENA
RUENATHA
THE ICEWAY
AGGEDON
RUINS OF REDDENBARK
NORTHAVEN
THE GREAT GREY WALL
OSTUNJORN
TAIRUMBRA
LILEALAHN UPLANDS
UR SULBOROL
RUINS OF THALVOSKA
ROKMOR
USELJAK
LAUSTDALE
AEPESS RIVER
AEPOX
RUINS OF FARANGA
GREYBONES
EASTERN DEADPLAINS
WESTERN DEADPLAINS
HAVVENPORT
HAVVENDALE
HAVVENVAL
AKAYDIS COAST
RUINS OF NRATHE
RUINS OF CRICKCROAK
KARLOHR VILLAGE
TWO TOWNS
RUINS OF SYLVOR
HUNTRESS ROCK
ARKAERYKA
WOLF ROCK
WOLVERINE ROCK
WARRIOR ROCK
RITUAL ROCK
TRADETREE ISLE
THE FOURTEEN
CONTINENTS' KISS
ENTRANCE TO ZSOLINDAL
BLACK BAY
RAPTOR ROCK
BEAR ROCK
TUSKED ROCK
TROLLBANE TOWERS
DEFIANCE
THE DAEGONS
THE GLACE ISLES
FORWOKEN MONASTERY
BARREDOM
THE ELDENVALES
FISHER ROCK
BAY OF TROLLS
THE HIGHLANDS
WHALESTOWN
GAHOANAN MTS.
SEAGRAM'S KEEP
ICEBATHED
FROSTDALE HILLS
OTTICUS RIVER
MOUNT KOMAK
FROSTDALE
CASTLE BAYN
RUINS OF TROLLTOWN
KOMAK KEEP
HALL OF FINAL LIGHT
ROTHLANDS
THE LOWLANDS
MOUNT MERRIDAN
MILES
0 50 100 150 200 250
VELHAUST
LAKE LOCKEHART
EBONSTAR VILLAGES
LOCKEVILLE
KEELTOWN
UNDAWNED LANDS
MAGEHOLME

PRONUNCIATIONS

CHARACTERS

Tsunosoto: SUE-NO-SO-TOE
Ryleohk: RYE-LOK
Nhoenathor: NO-EN-ATH-OR
Honorah: ON-OR-AH
Ebrielle: EE-BREE-EL
Aerik: AIR-IK
Lilealah: LIL-EE-AY-LAH
Kyson: KYE-SUN
BrKomak: BR-KOH-MAK
Khomo'Jhuvonus: KO-MO-JSHEW-VON-US
Jrulthun: JRUEL-THUNE
Zuulzin: ZULE-ZIN
Jhukamwi: JSHEW-KOM-WEE
Kavajin: KOV-AH-JIN
Tristostopher: TRIST-OST-OH-FUR
Sorovronus: SOAR-OH-VRON-US
Sriyah: SRYE-YAH
AeriAllyse: AIR-EE-AL-LISS
Thymarius: THY-MARE-EE-US
Agendwar: AG-END-WAR

PRONUNCIATIONS

PLACES & THINGS

Barredom: BARE-UH-DUM
Aggedon: AG-ED-ON
Zsolindal: ZOL-IN-DOL
The Dendrallthae: DEN-DROL-THAY
Khalimia: CALL-EEM-EE-AH
Tairancia: TAIR-AN-SEE-AH
Caelduym: KALE-DOOM
Xai Lon: ZYE LON
Ichean: EYE-CHEE-AN
Karlohr: CAR-LORE
Hlsyonya: HLUH-SYE-ON-YA
Hroganyndale: HROE-GAN-IN-DALE
Qaegons: KAY-GONS

Wyldenar: WIELD-EN-AR
Terollar: TEAR-OH-LAR
Shiniryn: SHIN-EAR-EN
Ibyssai: IB-ISS-EYE
Qindrid: KIN-DRID

Saiyenai: SYE-EN-EYE
Glazjhendun: GLAZ-JSHEN-DUN
Lilealytes: LIL-EE-AY-LITES
Pentagogue: PENT-A-GOG
Oathemic: OTHE-EM-IK

Animayan: AN-EM-EYE-AN
Crystalyte: CRIS-TAL-ITE
Tribesven: TRIBES-VEN
Mortali: MOR-TOL-EE
Wyrmway: WORM-WAY
Wyrefire: WEER-FIRE
Yharl: YARL

CHARACTER GUIDE

BARREDISH HUMANS

Honorah Bayn: *the Royal Inquisitor of Barredom, mother of Ebrielle and Aerik Blackendale, widow of Lucas Blackendale*

Ebrielle Blackendale: *daughter of Honorah Bayn*

Aerik Blackendale: *son of Honorah Bayn*

Aerik Roth: *King of Barredom*

Ondrew Roth: *only legitimate male heir to King Aerik Roth, founder of the Norther Knights*

Broc BrKomak: *second in command of the Norther Knights, a highborn yharl of Barredom before he denounced his lands and titles*

Randon Roth: *younger brother of King Aerik Roth, General of Barredom*

Mathias Oreville: *Captain of the Eldenvale Rangers, now part of the Norther Knights, after the death of Lucas Blackendale … also a scarred survivor from an encounter with Jrulthun*

Datron Ackhill: *the youngest of the Norther Knights*

Snowden & Sheridan Shaw: *two brothers that serve as scouts for the Norther Knights*

Thade Karway: *Scoutmaster of Northaven*

Nathahn BrKomak: *Commandant of Northaven*

Henrick Brigannor: *cousin to Ebrielle and Aerik Blackendale, son of Tomas and Elsa*

Tomas Brigannor: *brother-by-law to Honorah Bayn, uncle to Ebrielle and Aerik Blackendale, former Eldenvale Ranger and blinded survivor from an encounter with Jrulthun*

Elsa Brigannor: *sister of Lucas Blackendale, sister-by-law to Honorah Bayn, and aunt to Ebrielle and Aerik Blackendale*

Barys: *Grand Artificer of Frostdale*

BrKaim: *warden of the Frostdale Deeps*

OTHER HUMANS

Kyson: *the unofficial leader of the Timberhands*
Sarin, Ryder, Jonthon, Tarance, & Caldwell: *the other five Timberhands with Kyson, of Tairancian lineage*
Aramgar & Odemnar: *two Vellyans released from imprisonment to serve with the Norther Knights*
Tristostopher Boldandgold: *Captain of the Boarneck Cavaliers, a group of cunning mounted mercenaries out of Goldgarden hired by General Randon Roth to help win the war in Aggedon*
Annison Roth: *Queen of Barredom, of Daynish descent*
Vaximus Az'Ampion: *Daynish male dominarch of the Az'Dayne Dominadom*
Sriyah Az'Ampion: *Khalimishe female dominarch of the Az'Dayne Dominadom*
Nominus Vlo: *a Psage human Umbra mage who is closely tied to Tsuno's quest to discover the cure for the Qindrid Curse*
Haelyn Rook: *Archon of the Silverlakes*

UNKNOWN LINEAGE

Soro: *High Chancellor of the Frostdale Council*

QINDRID

Tsunosoto Akazi: *alias "the Westwalker", a skyborne qindrid from the region of Sho'Lon, working as a bounty hunter for the kingdom of Barredom*
Landron Thalbear: *a stoneborne elite henchman for Lilealah*

ELVEN

Ryleohk: *the Westwalker's companion, a Wyldenar rogue-elvan*
Khomo'Jhuvonus: *an infamous Terollar elvan warlord, the King of the Glace Isles and the Chosen Troll, renowned for his three bloodrime axes*
Jrulthun: *Alpha of the Glace Isles, a brutish Terollar elvan warrior*
Zuulzin: *"Kind-Eyes", the youngest son of Khomo'Jhuvonus, suffers the Aging*

UMBRAN

Lilealah: *a Wyldenar umbran, the origin maker of who transformed the humans of Aggedon into stoneborne qindrid centuries ago*
AeriAllyse: *one of the Shiniryn umbran who transcended Tsuno from a human into a qindrid, now in captivity in the Dendrallthae*
Thymarius: *the other Shiniryn umbran who transcended Tsuno, lifemate of Aeri-Allyse, who was slain by Tsuno's son, Hirotai*

THE DAWNING SEASON

PROLOGUE

"To the trees!"

The voice of Timance bellowed out as the marksman led the way into the Ichean. But his cohort didn't even have to say the words aloud. Landron's sprint was already faster than his seven hunters could follow. He took up position beside the archer in pursuit of their prey. None could hope to match his ardent pace.

The rhythm of his breath harmonized with the march of his boots as he descended the rocky hillside to enter the forest outskirts. This was his purpose. He was a chosen warrior of his revered master, and this was the bounty that would propel him into her eternal esteem. Every clansman in Aggedon would remember his name. He dared not let his bleeding prize out of his sight as his entourage trailed.

The Wyldenar elvan known as Ryleohk had been a prime nuisance to the western clans for several cycles. An elusive assassin, the rogue was recognized for working alongside the Westwalker, a dangerous foreigner who had been commissioned by the soldiers of Northaven. The two had been the nemeses of Landron's ambition for countless seasons.

Wyldenar and Terollar were the native elvan races of Aggedon's regional borders. Both species remained unique in their unnatural abilities. Ryleohk would gain ground as they entered the thickening brush. Nature's hindrances did not slow or obstruct the Wyldenar elven.

Landron's breath pounded with each step taken as his endurance prepared to be tested. He and his men had long ago transcended into qindrid, beyond the mediocrities of the average human. Through the

Transcendence, they had become the stoneborne of Aggedon, enhanced by impowers to the tairan and shadow element. Their grey skin was as thick as hide armor, and their strength was far superior to that of their human enemies. They were ageless, sleepless warriors. And he refused to allow fatigue to creep in.

"Clear through the brush! The rogue gains no ground!" he roared to his bloodthirsty hunters.

Timance clearly had the elvan bleeding from his initial arrow, finding its mark in the Wyldenar's side. The fresh crimson could be seen on every piece of high underbrush Ryleohk grazed as he desperately fled the inevitable doom at his heels.

Landron had hoped the wound would hinder the Wyldenar's momentum, but he was surprisingly incorrect. The foliage before the elvan's feet simply parted as he fled. He watched as Ryleohk's feet did tricks, finding the sides of trees at the bottom and jumping from trunk to trunk, where there appeared to be nowhere to gain traction. The elvan's leaps took him higher into the copse, between branches that seemed to bend in his favor. Landron shouted to his bowman. *"Timance!"*

His archer stopped and knelt. Landron halted beside the marksman to watch the kill Timance was about to take from him. The anticipation must have been an hour's worth of a few seconds as the arrow was nocked and aimed at its condemned target.

That was when the voice of Aldor cursed it all to the Vist. Landron's eyes grew in fury and curiosity as his henchman called, *"Where's your Westwalker now, wylde?"* As if a sudden jinx of fate were there to curse him, Aldor's ill-timed remark prompted a trap to be set off.

Landron looked back to see Brom wailing as his left leg fell through a thin veil of ground into a small spike trap, designed to impale the ankle upon attempting to retract it from the snare. If that wasn't enough to put Brom out of the pursuit, the swinging scythe blade that sprang rapidly from around the nearest tree, cleaving through his neck, surely ended the job.

Time had seemingly paused, and everyone forgot about the chase as they watched the blood sputtering from their gurgling comrade. Only Brom's brother, Eredis, screaming in garbled rage, could be heard over the man's dying sounds. And the sound of Ryleohk still running.

Ryleohk. "Forward!"

Eredis was the first to push past everyone, taking point just behind Timance. They pressed on, seven strong now, nearing the clearing. The elvan hit the meadow and never slowed one bit. Landron's eyes must have deceived him, however. The Wyldenar dived to the ground for cover, obscured by the waist-high, thin-bladed grass. Eredis darted straight into the clearing, hacking away at loose vegetation beneath him to carve a path, intending to shear off the enemy's head in the same manner that had taken his brother's life. Timance skulked behind him into the meadow with his bow drawn, seeking its death mark.

Landron held up his hand for his remaining men to stay within the cover of the trees. He felt a slight pang of guilt from intuitively knowing he was about to witness Eredis take the next trap. It wasn't just about Ryleohk now. The Westwalker was undoubtedly present as well. This prize was too unreal to be true. The elvan already wounded, and one of the foreigner's traps already triggered. How many traps could the Westwalker have had time to set? And there were still seven of his men versus the two of them. Was he really willing to just sit and watch Eredis die so that he could claim this unparalleled victory, instead of devising a more tactical plan? He knew it was against his mercurial code of honor, yet he stood as silent as a corpse and watched the predictable fate of Brom's brother.

"Step into the demise," came a ghostly whisper on the wind, the thrown voice of the Westwalker in the Civil tongue upon each of their ears. And it was Timance who took the blow instead.

Timance dropped with a thud into the undergrowth with a crossbow bolt to the side of the head from the east of the clearing. Before Landron could make a sound to shout, the mechanical clang of a turret crossbow clicked again. Just as Eredis turned about to look back at his dead companion, both qindrid in the meadow fell to the Westwalker's precision.

Ryleohk appeared again, rising from the tall grass to sprint into the trees. As a shadowy glimpse in the day's break of clouds cast, the shrouded figure, which could be none other than the Westwalker, backtracked into the woods as well, leaving his preset turret, built with two crossbows mounted atop a swivel platform. Landron had to choose quickly. *"Michayle, Yalen, Thuros – on the Westwalker! Stick to the tree line, but do not be lured by the trapmaster! Aldor, to the wylde, on me!"*

He and Aldor raced across the vulnerable meadow, keeping as low as possible to the grass with their senses tuned to the left for any signs of the marksman assassin. He would claim Ryleohk's life today, even if it meant all his men saw the grave. He prayed to his matriarch, Lilealah, for the forgiveness of ill thoughts toward the fate of his men and for the good fortune this destined hunt presented to him.

They reached the trees once more and took after the rogue-elvan, still in sight. Ryleohk was guiding them back in the direction of the Westwalker now. Landron knew he had to close in on his kill. The elvan took a methodical trek through the skirt of the tree line, all the while barely touching the ground. A low branch here, the side of a tree there, even when it seemed his weight couldn't possibly be supported. Nature bent to him as if he were its king. It was an awe-inspiring feat to behold, one that he would retell in his saga to his people after he returned with the elvan's and trapmaster's heads. Aldor's labored gasps of pursuit beat with his own as they dared forward to make history.

The death wails of one, or maybe two, of the others broadcasted throughout the unseen vicinity. *Michayle, Thuros, Yalen … which of you? Someone stall the Westwalker until I finish the wylde.* Ryleohk would taste his blade soon, and they could take the Westwalker by numbers. His men were on their chosen ground. This was their stage. What a fitting place to bury them.

And there, the opportunity. The elvan leaped impossibly far from the base of a tree, but no cushioned ground was there to save his stunt this time. Ryleohk tumbled and collapsed awkwardly, lying there at the edge of the mantle of leaves over the soft soil. Six more steps, and Landron's sword would cleave through the Wyldenar's neck. The head of Ryleohk was his.

But there were no fallen leaves during the Dawning season. This wasn't natural. The leaves had been placed here for a purpose. And Wyldenar elven never landed in any way but gracefully. Even if he could have commanded his own defiant feet from the thrust of the pursuit, his misfortune would have remained the same. Aldor came blazing onward for the glory blow, and their weight together plunged them into the depths of the sinkhole trap.

Landron saw the ground around him become rising walls as he

fell helplessly. His hands frantically searched for loose roots to save him from the lengthy wooden pikes reaching to take his life. One of the stakes found its home deep inside his right thigh, piercing through, even though his augmented stoneborne skin was far thicker than that of the human northmen. It was one of the skinnier branch pikes fashioned in the pit, and as it skewered his leg, the upper tip snapped completely off, with femur and branch perpendicular to each other. He landed, bizarrely, still standing, face planted against the side wall of the cold dirt. Rage kept him from collapsing, and either fear or defiance kept him from looking down at his leg or back at Aldor. He paused only for an instant, not even enough time to curse. He didn't have time to curse death. He had two lives to claim yet.

His hands found a root system in the soil wall, and his enhanced strength dragged him to the rim of the ditch. His sword was found at the edge before the fall, replaced back in his readied grasp.

Landron peered down into the pit, into the dead eyes of Aldor staring back up at him. Aldor's body was impaled through the lower spine on one of the many pikes driven into the sinkhole trap. Landron clutched at his crippled right leg, avoiding looking at the piece of wood protruding from his thigh for fear that the mere sight of it would amplify the pain.

His back found a large boulder next to the pit, and his eyes frantically probed the woods before him for any sign of movement or form that would prove to be the elvan or the Westwalker. Nothing came. His breathing pattern and heartbeat were heavier than a war drum. And still nothing came. Blood drained freely from his leg. His hand that clamped the wound was now drenched in red.

His intuition levels were rising. The crows overhead were evaluating their feast below. His ears heeded the cold wind whistling through the thin-leafed canopy above him. He could smell his own sweat slowly freezing to his grey skin. He could see every detail of this pressing woodland tomb that was attempting to claim him. He could feel himself rising to his feet, challenging the pain in his leg and rebelling against all logic to remain hidden. Landron was a hunter of Clan Thalbear, of the original stoneborne qindrid of Aggedon. He did not hide from death.

"Step into the demise." Again came the whisper on the wind of the Westwalker's famous line.

"Coward!" he heard himself blaring to the unseen ghost, resorting to the Civil tongue to match his enemy's. He now stood several paces away from the pit and the massive rock, in a small brushless clearing between several trees. "The legend is true! The Westwalker is a coward!" He bellowed his taunts as he slowly spun in a limping circle, hoping to provoke the nefarious strategist into a one-on-one advantage. "Come, Westwalker! To my face! To this ground in front of me! I challenge you!" Landron's sword stayed drawn, pointing it to each tree and then the next.

"I played your game. Now play mine, cowa—" A small crossbow bolt thudded into the back of his left hamstring, buckling his leg and forcing him to his knees. The sudden surprise forced him to look at the new wound, and then impulsively at his right thigh. It was worse than he had expected. All his brave nerve retreated inside him. He allowed himself a second to hope that at least Michayle, Thuros, or Yalen had survived, a futile idea that maybe a hero would rise. Instead of fear or tears, he found himself looking to the sky of crows, and involuntarily he began to chuckle at his inevitable dismay.

"Survivalist," came an unknown stern voice behind him. He would have turned to look at whom it came from if he could have, but he didn't need to. He could hear its owner slowly circling around in front of him.

Landron grunted as he tried to turn and see his attacker. He thought on the lone word, utterly confused. "Eh?" was all he could intelligently manage, however.

Again came the firm foreign voice, thick with an accent not of this country. "You said 'coward.' It's 'survivalist.' You see?" And finally he could see him. The Westwalker was before him, at a safe distance, near the trees. "Valiance and honor are for heroes, but heroes simply die. I am no such hero."

Landron stared down his executioner, taking in every detail as time itself seemed to slow in his last moments. Even if he lived to survive this encounter, none of his clan would believe that he had come face-to-face with the Westwalker, living to tell the tale.

The Westwalker was armed with two exotic handheld crossbows, both built with a clip of sorts above the stock, which had been engineered in such a way as to allow him to repeat several shots, though as to how many per weapon, the gossips varied.

Across his back was his infamous bow, crafted of the white

wraithwood of his eastern homeland. It was the most outlandish machinery Landron had ever seen on a weapon. The longbow held some form of perpendicular centric magazine that extended long enough for a full draw of the string. The narrow compartment was known to fit special-sized long-bolts, not arrows, that allowed the Westwalker to release shots repeatedly. The unique contraption acted as a barrel for the bolts to accurately project from, as well as aiding as a sight guide for improved precision. The master engineer had a name for himself that he was the one who designed and constructed his own weaponry, including his traps.

Not much could be seen of the small foreigner, since he was covered from head to toe in camouflage garb. He decked himself out in thickly layered clothes, blended into the contours of the many wooded terrains of Aggedon's stretch. His face was hidden by faded woolen wraps, leaving only his mouth, nose, and sky-blue eyes open to the elements.

His barely exposed skin shared the same grey hue as that of Landron and his doomed entourage. The Westwalker was indeed also a qindrid. But while Landron was from the local Aggedon region and of the stoneborne Transcendence, the Westwalker was known to be of the eastern skyborne, hailing from half a world away. His pale blue-washed eyes were altogether alien to look into, more of a squint and slant than the northmen's, with a different intent in his resolve far from loyal to the Aggedonians.

His enemy stared into Landron's transparently glass-glazed eyes, crystalline-clear, like those of all stoneborne. The skyborne engineer was a being of unwavering confidence and impeccable calculations, having played this game before, time and time again. He and Ryleohk were not the prey; they were "the hunters of hunters," just as the saying went.

The dismal quiet seemed to last an age. The Westwalker was allowing the defeat to sink in, and the psychological sport began.

"What do you want with me, foreigner?" Landron growled lividly. "You have already baited my men to their deaths!"

"Should have taken heed of the tales of your camps, then, Landron Thalbear. It is we who hunt the hunters. And you know what I came for." The trapmaster revealed that he even knew his actual name. Of course he knew. The Westwalker always studied his prey before he brought them "into the demise."

The Westwalker whistled a signal into the trees, and immediately his obedient steed came into view, striding up beside him. His exotic horse was just as foreign as he was, nothing like the breeds of Aggedon or Barredom: piebald, with black dominance and white splotches throughout, and an extravagant faded-blond mane that matched its lavishly long tail. Around its fetlocks and hooves it sported the feathering aspect seen only on the stallions of the eastern realms. Most bizarre, however, was the otherworldly semblance the horse possessed in its eyes, wisp-like orbs that faintly glowed green. There was a story of another life within them. This was no normal animal, but something more.

Landron could have described the Westwalker and his horse in the finest detail on the yestermorn, even though it wasn't until just this instant that he had seen the famous two so close. Every qindrid and human in the wide north knew the tall tale of the Westwalker and those he companioned with.

"The missive. You want answers, and you must have learned I had it on me. Should have known Northaven would be sending their submissive pets to strip it from me," Landron fervidly taunted. "You kill your own kind, Westwalker, and side with those who use you like a dog. They'll dispose of you as soon as this war is over!"

His disciplined rival ignored the provocation and instead simply cocked his head curiously, as if he were a professor schooling an inept child. "I am qindrid through and through, but you stoneborne of Aggedon are not my kind," the skyborne contended winningly with no sense of pride in his defense. "This war is over. I already know that the entirety of the Aggedonian army has mysteriously vanished, and I have an idea how so. The humans of Barredom just paid me to find out why, and where to. Everything I need to know is on that scroll you carry. I am nothing more than a glorified bounty hunter, just like you, Landron."

Nothing more than a privileged prisoner, more like a fool. I am a chosen of my maker, while you are a deserter of yours! Landron kept his hostile thoughts to himself. He could no longer feel the pain from the bolt that had struck his leg, nor the excruciating throb from his injured thigh. He felt paralyzed from his waist down, yet somehow he was still poised on his knees. The Westwalker's bolt was undoubtedly tipped with some sort of numbing toxin that had already taken effect. He decided to enjoy the euphoric numbing while it briefly lasted.

Landron stammered for an avenue to survive this encounter, as some had before him. "Wait." He tried to shout it, but it came out much quieter than intended, and much softer. The hemorrhage from his thigh and poison in his veins had made him weak. But poison did not last long in stoneborne blood, and he knew he would gain his resolve back any moment. He removed his helm of rank among his clan, revealing his bald head and bare face.

"Negotiations, then? I have heard the Westwalker is reasonable in a parley," Landron murmured, tentative of the rumor. Landron knew that the wise trapmaster had already deduced the answer behind the disappearance of the Aggedonian qindrid army the human northmen so desperately desired clarification of. The Westwalker did not need to read the missive to know the truth. The purpose of the skyborne acquiring the scroll was to plainly prove validity to the General of Barredom, the Guardian of Northaven, Randon Roth.

"Negotiate?" The Westwalker sounded curious, pulling down his cowl, which had hidden half of his face. He was definitely no northman, an obvious product of his people, who hailed from the far east, never seen in the regions of Aggedon or Barredom. "I have been known to do so."

"Am I to become your prisoner now?" Landron demanded, ready to be done with the charade of false diplomacy. "To be tortured? To Northaven or the Frostdale Deeps, then?"

"Prisoners and torture? That is just not my way. As I said, we both know the war is now over. You have nothing more of value," his enemy divulged. Landron's eyes went mad for reasoning, but his throat caught the words as the Westwalker resumed his sentencing. "You see, there is just one larger concern for you."

The Westwalker moved from his position, pulling his steed by the reins. There, at the tree base behind him, stood Ryleohk, covered in blood on his left side, from arm to leg, and as feral-looking as ever, seeming more beast than elvan at the core of his soul.

Ryleohk's skin was grey, like his own, with ashen-colored feral eyes. His knotted hair frayed down across his upper back in a mesh of various stone hues, twisted into random tresses throughout. Ever wild as he was, his mane looked as if it had never known a wash. The young elvan's beard ended in a small braid on his chin. His pointed elvan ears were longer than the norm, turning outward instead of lying flat against his head. Though of Wyldenar descent, Ryleohk had been born a rogue-elvan, imbuing him with certain cosmetic alterations, including the grey features, like those of the qindrid.

The shirtless rogue was unarmored above his waist. Tattered leathers of off-white furs covered his legs down to his bare feet, Wyldenar being as near-immune to the cold as stoneborne and skyborne were. One hand held his prominent oversized throwing axe, while the other held the carcass of a dead tundra rat, and his dark eyes were seething with dedicated hate.

Landron's visage grew just as malign as Ryleohk's, now realizing the entirety of the ploy. Timance had never struck Ryleohk on the hill. The elvan had never been injured. He had cut open a fresh rodent kill and covered himself in its blood to bait them into the Westwalker's forest-trapped gauntlet. With his anger consuming him, he switched his aversion to the Westwalker to slay him with one final oath.

But it was the Westwalker who spoke instead. "Ryleohk never negotiates."

The last sound Landron heard was the ear-piercing whistle of the elvan's axe cutting through the air.

WESTWALKER (I)

THOSE OF THE GREY

Tsunosoto rode on his exotic horse, Nho, as he watched the north-bred steed to his right carry his lone surviving prisoner. He kept his face unshielded by his cowl but his head still covered. The padded bindings snaked around his neck like a scarf as protection from the elements during the gust-chilled ride across the Western Deadplains.

At least they would have, if he had not already become near-immune to the cold due to the state he transcended into long ago. Now his many-layered choice of camouflage garb served a single purpose for concealment. There was an age when he had openly yearned for the breeze on his face and the wind at his back, but that was once upon a distant time. The windy element still clung to him like a relentlessly reminding curse, the anomalous effect that enveloped those under the skyborne transmutation.

Aggedon was one of the most northerly territories of Penthara. As a civilization that had taken its entire population under the qindrid Transcendence centuries ago, Tsuno should have felt at home among his element-bound ilk, but these were not his people. The qindrid of this region were of the stoneborne, not the skyborne. Furthermore, the Aggedonians and Barredish were northmen, entirely foreign in histories and great in differences from his own distant culture.

He hailed from Sho'Lon, far to the central east. It was a lush but harsh realm of rolling highlands, strong winds, and great mountain cities. Long ago, the empire was the first nation to suffer through the calamity of the qindrid takeover. It had since stood divided between two civilizations in perpetual strife: the human kingdom of Sho Jan, which remained loyal to the ways of old Sho'Lon, and the nation of Sho Kung, which was populated by the skyborne qindrid.

Tsuno had left that life as a human several decades ago, sixty-five years ago to be exact, though he still possessed the youthful presence he had in his thirties. This month was a significant one, marking him officially a century old.

The ritual of Transcendence, which a human could undergo in order to mutate into the path of a qindrid, was mostly a voluntary decision. Only those of specific descendancies could take to the turn. Many made the choice in zealous reverence to embrace the element of their lineage, to infuse it into their very being. They would become blessed with specific impowers of their bloodline's element and become near-ageless, sharing the lifespan of the masters who turned them. But they could never again know sleep, for better or worse. And it followed with the irrevocable curse of forsaking one's place in the Godslands for a possible afterlife, along with losing the ability to reproduce altogether. Longevity as an augmented, sleepless, infertile mortal, or a normal life, in hopes of passing seed and carrying on a legacy, and the belief of an afterlife among loved ones and ancestors—such was the choice.

Tsuno's doomed decision to become skyborne had cost him the fate of his own wife and had ultimately caused his only son to disavow him as a father and name him an enemy. His family was all he had ever held dear, and all that had been done had been executed in the foundation of the protection of his loved ones. Yet in the end, it had rapidly paved the course to the subsequent separation from anything he had ever cared about. The love of his life was dead, and in decades past, Tsuno had eventually come to learn that his son had passed as well.

Such eternal regrets as embracing the Transcendence and failing his family were now but faint remnants that he still clung to. He buried them deep inside, with a constant internal struggle to refrain from revisiting them as best as his resolve allowed.

It was no longer just about his condition, or his soul's redemption from his betrayal of his loved ones lost. It was now something much more vast.

He had hiked the long walk west, from Xai Lon to Aggedon, pledging himself to a lifequest to seek out the alleged cure for the

Qindrid Curse. Such had never been recorded as being found throughout the annals of history, but his unique sources were prophetic in that he would be the one who delivered the remedy to the realm. Tsuno had remained unyielding for timeless seasons foregone in accomplishing the clear mission laid out before him: to heal his homeland from such a needless, power-craving affliction that had caused nothing but eras of unending strife.

He was now feared as a legendary bounty hunter by his local qindrid enemies but shunned by his subtle alliance with the Barredish humans. He considered himself alienated and alone in his pursuits. There was only one individual he could now call friend.

The enduring Wyldenar could be seen over half a mile west, in the direction of their hike to Northaven. His rogue-elvan companion did not take to a horse and never had. As was customary, Tsuno allowed Ryleohk's keen senses to play scout for them in the lead, while he trailed behind at the elvan's pace.

They were in no particular rush to rejoin civilization, if the one Barredish garrison in Aggedon could be called that. Northaven was a stone-walled keep that housed a contingent of four thousand men in its protection, under the command of their pragmatic and famously grim general, Randon Roth. The Roths were the commanding house of Barredom and its capital of Frostdale. Randon's elder brother, Aerik Roth, had been the standing king of Barredom for the last fourteen years. And only recently, in the past two years, King Aerik had become subject to the rule of the ever-powerful Az'Dayne Dominadom, in the southern mainlands. The unexpected decision seemed to have sown much discord among the Barredish royal houses. But none of it affected Tsuno. He kept out of human and qindrid politics alike.

They had been at a casual canter for three days, but with little stoppage for true rest, and still the silence hadn't been broken since he had taken his prisoner. His bound enemy slumped in exhaustion, but the clansman's eyes were fixated in revulsion, ever awake. His captive had been successfully stubborn in avoiding any form of communication, much less eye contact.

The stoneborne qindrid was the first to initiate the needless courtesies of banter to familiarize themselves with each other. "*Westwalker,*" he seethed in his native Norspeak tongue. "*So it must be me to break the silence? If you seek answers, ask them, but do not bring me to*

Northaven. They will send me to the Frostdale Deeps. I know what happens to our kind there." Even though they were but a few paces away from each other, the prisoner had to amplify his voice into a yell just to pierce the interjecting wind segregating the two steeds.

Tsuno just shot the stoneborne a wicked grin. He was going to enjoy the brief company of this fiery clansman. The Aggedonian vehemently continued, *"Speak, then! You obviously chose to spare me only to seal me into a fate of torture. I will know what you will of me, and let this farce be over with!"*

Tsuno analyzed the nervous clansman a bit longer and forced the dialect back to the Civil tongue, despising speaking in the Aggedonian language. He coolly replied, using his skyborne impower to throw his voice into the wind to be heard clearly in his typical, nonchalant tone. "Perhaps you may not even have to see Northaven. You do seem to carry less misfortune than your recent peers, Michayle."

The injured stoneborne looked straight ahead with clear, colorless eyes narrowing in irritation. "Aye, and you know my name? And what is your name, *Westwalker*?" He emphasized Tsuno's northern alias. Not a one from the region had come to learn his true name, and he was quite agreeable with that. "Westwalker" was the derogatory slang used to identify pilgrims found in the western lands who came from the east, from Sho'Lon or Oriyen. It had suited Tsuno to remind him of where his roots still lay.

"Calm now, stoneborne. We can converse cordially." Tsuno couldn't help but laugh at Michayle's growing frustration, maintaining an amused sneer as he explained. "We have been following your party for a pentday. The demise I planted in the Ichean has been there for more than a month. I already knew each of you by name and skill before the hunt began."

The baby-faced clansman appeared to be in his mid-twenties in years, but one could never tell the true age of a qindrid by cosmetics alone. Michayle was decked in the same white furs as his slain comrades. The snow-bear hide armored the leathers that covered his legs and torso, down to his boots and gloves. His head was naturally bald, just as all stoneborne became hairless after they succumbed to the Transcendence.

"The demise? I heard that is what you call it, the scheme of traps you set to lure your prey," Michayle hissed. "I was simple game in your baited hunt. Know that I will not pretend to be idly friendly."

The Westwalker shrugged innocently. "It seems you have no other friends around. Perhaps you could use a new one."

"I have none other because you killed them all!" Michayle jabbed back in Norspeak, hawking out phlegm toward his captor, only to have the wind snatch the spittle and shred it into the wild gales of the dead prairie.

Tsuno retained his imperturbable conduct and reminded him, "Only two by my hand. *He* killed Landron." Tsuno pointed nonchalantly off in the direction of Ryleohk. "I am fairly certain the rest of your friends were felled in the woods on sticks and such somehow. A tragic and unheroic end for all of them, really."

Michayle growled, "A true traitor to your own ilk—killing us without honor, and siding with the humans!"

"The words of a naive fool," Tsuno dispassionately scolded. "We are human. Never forget that. Not all qin remain puppets to those who turned us long ago. You sound like every other qin I meet in this region. You will find much diversity among the skyborne in my country. Not all of us forget our roots."

"Human." Michayle's voice drifted on the word as if it were a foreign, long-lost term, almost seeming in sudden sadness. "What we once were, that we may never return to. You live in a past life. You still kill only our kind. Why?" His rabid exchange dimmed down to a more puzzled tone.

"You are not my kind. I am not 'my kind.'" Tsuno peered to the star-littered night sky as he elaborated. "Does humankind not war among other human nations? Do they not murder for greed, lust, power, or take life for any other of various reasons? It goes without question that this is simply their nature. Just as it should be for us who are still human in the core of it all. By what right is it judged that we of the qindrid blood must unite behind the umbran who turned us and be their pawns until our days are ended?" He looked Michayle straight in the eye. "I am a slave to no master. I have my own lifequest I follow."

"What is this quest?" he demanded, but Tsuno's irritated glare quieted the man, letting Michayle know that the verbal joust had played its course. They both stared off to the ruins of some long-abandoned Aggedonian village, where the Wyldenar had stopped.

Michayle yammered on. "Crickcroak. The elders say the place is now haunted, that all elven, humans, or qin who enter come out cursed if they pass through it."

Tsuno muttered for Nho to take him into the village, unwavering in the face of superstition. "Then it is a good thing we are already cursed for life," he answered. "We rest now."

The stoneborne's tone was clear with worriment. "But we do not need sleep," he blurted.

"No, we do not. But he does." Tsuno stated the obvious, nodding at Ryleohk. "Besides, I said 'rest,' not 'sleep.'" The wounded qindrid seemed to be keen on the idea, keeping hushed on that account.

The two horses brought them to the silent elvan, who had chosen their sanctuary for the gathering nightfall. They strode through the ghastly streets until Tsuno came to a particular home. He had done this many times before. He tethered the horse that carried Michayle and made a sound to Nho to let the exotic steed know he was free to do as he pleased.

Michayle shot another sharp attempt at directionless chatter. "You know, you never tied me up. Not once each day except to make camp for brief respites. You even gave me a swift steed. I could have gotten away with him a league away, and the wind too strong for that shot-bow of yours, or whatever you call that thing."

"Wraith." Tsuno looked back over his shoulder to his notorious mechanical design, complexly handcrafted from wraithwood, not found in these parts of the realm. The white repeater bow was probably his most feared tool, he surmised, even more so than his traps or poison-bolted miniature crossbows. "It's called Wraith."

Tsuno motioned, and the barbaric Wyldenar muscled down the mouthy hostage, slamming him against a single pole that stood in the yard of the house Tsuno had chosen to stop at. The grey elvan began forcefully binding Michayle's hands by pulling his arms behind him to hug the mast with his back against it. Ryleohk was savagely rough, even with the clansman's lack of resistance. Tsuno knelt in front of the prisoner and smirked, calmly assuring him, "I do encourage a good hunt. Haven't you heard, hunter? Quiet now."

Tsuno left his captive and Ryleohk to vanish inside the broken abode. He removed his quivers and the belt that held his hand crossbows, tossing them in the corner by his pack and other tools. He took his cowl off and let his roaming hair breathe once again. Laying his back on the familiar bed, he rested Wraith across his belly and stretched his arms behind his head. His fingers interlocked as his hands cupped beneath the pillow. The roof was missing just above the headboard, where one could lie and view a glimpse of the heavens with the compromise of subjection to the raw cold whistling through. It was why he had chosen this battered home time and time again on his many exploits.

The stars were out in full in the open black sky, with no hindrance of cloud, as it always was in this country at twilight. He noted to himself that it may have been that lone detail of splendor that preserved his sanity in this forsaken land.

Regret and remorse were infections of his past, and he oft defied allowing those feelings to fester back to the surface. But tonight he did want to feel again. He wanted to remember why and how it had all started. He focused in on his favorite cluster of stars and permitted himself a reverie, the best consolation for sleep his body could comfort him with. He had lost that ability long ago, to know what a true dream felt like.

Yoshira, he whispered in his mind as he slipped into his distant trance, allowing him out of the hard façade of his alias back into who he was from the beginning: Tsunosoto Akazi. The memory of his sweet wife came back clearly to him in that instant. He recalled the very day they had met and the time of his youth before that.

Tsuno's mother passed to illness when he was but a boy. His father, Hirotai, followed a darker course of rage, after which he led a rebellion in Sho Kung to inspire the humans residing there to conform back to the old ways of the original Sho'Lon Empire, against the spread of the skyborne qindrid. A year later, his father was assassinated by conspiring loyalists, betraying him in the end to adhere once more to the creed of Sho Kung. Tsuno was given a one-time choice: he could have vengeance and exile if he chose to battle a son of his father's murderers in honorable combat, or he could join the neutral monk brotherhood of the Saiyenai in Xai Lon. Tsuno did not choose retribution and chose to join the monastery instead, as all fatherless boys of noble bloodlines were expected to do.

Xai Lon was the territory north of the divided Sho'Lon Empire, impartial to the civil war's politics. The Saiyenai monastery trained its young orphans into specialist warriors in a variety of select skill sets catering to their personalities and capacities. Tsuno himself was honed in mechanical engineering, wilderness survival, and advanced reconnaissance.

The monastery held strong on traditions of giving its brethren a life of normality outside its walls. At the age of twenty, Tsuno was allowed to choose a wife in a ceremony of selection with his fellowship. The rite of choosing required one to wait an entire Dawning season before laying claim to a wife, but for Tsuno, it was Yoshira the instant he met her. She was the only love he had ever known and ever would know. They were married and granted a home in the hills off the monastery grounds, which he was sanctioned to visit intermittently between his obligations within the order.

Two years later his son was born, named Hirotai after Tsuno's own father, in commemoration. Years passed in relative peace and fruition for him and his family as Tsuno became distinguished within the Saiyenai for his innovations with weapon schematics and trap mastery. His designs became highly sought-after by battle officers in both Sho Jan and Sho Kung. The Saiyenai began to take profits from either side, who paid for the secrets of their masters.

Tsuno attempted to turn a blind eye to the growing corruption within his order as each season passed, but eventually, it was too late. The Saiyenai ultimately sold themselves to the expanding power of Sho Kung and the skyborne qindrid. Any brethren of the monastery who refused to undergo the Transcendence were offered a swift and merciful execution for themselves and their immediate family. Tsuno was a survivalist. He chose life for him and his family.

The act of his transmutation to qindrid did not create any goodwill between him and his wife and son. Hirotai, at just thirteen years of age, ran away to join an activist group on the outskirts of Sho Jan, against the powers of Sho Kung. Yoshira became more estranged each passing year, depressed into a hermit-like state. Their relationship became stale and mute as Tsuno stayed true to his duty for her protection.

The Saiyenai grew from a monastery of desired war-tactic specialists into an assassination guild of the skyborne elite. The monks of the order were commissioned by the masters to eliminate problem targets that went against the Sho Kung power base, to further the expansion into Xai Lon territory and partisan sects. Over the following years, he was sent on several hunts to take down leaders of uprisings against the Sho Kung agenda. His reputation became flawless in his trade. Tsuno's political favor flourished among those in the highest authority of his region.

In the end, the Saiyenai decreed, by law of the aristocracy of Sho Kung, that all immediate family members of shared households undergo the Transcendence, because of the increasing number of insurgencies. All wives, sons, and daughters of the monastery brotherhood had a year to commit to voluntarily forgoing being human and become qindrid. Yoshira did her duty, as her husband bade her.

He could never consign to oblivion that haunting day in all its heartrending detail, as if it had just happened on the yester. It wasn't even a year after her forced Transcendence, fifty years ago, exactly half his life in the past, that Tsuno had found his wife dead. She had consumed sleep poison under the very tree where Hirotai had been conceived. Yoshira had surrendered to suicide due to his continuous cowardice in remaining a victim of fear to his order and the masters who had turned him.

Surviving had taken on a new meaning for him that fated day. He had lost his parents, his wife, his son, and all his pride. He had lost each and all due to one single enemy in his entire existence: the qindrid and those who were responsible for the Transcendence. His lifequest had begun in effect that very eve.

Ruminations of his long-dead love and the fate of his son engulfed his reverie to subconsciously force a numbing effect of emotionless determination back into his mind. It was a callous defense mechanism that half a century of time had tried to perfect. Tsuno's focus on the contrition over his doleful saga was a weakness he could not afford. And so he became the Westwalker once again, the calculated killer with an unbreakable purpose. His past was all a slipping silhouette, fading in the perpetual sunrises and sunsets as time gluttoned away on the remnants of bittersweet memory.

HONORAH (I)

THE DEEPS

The declining slope into the dungeon of the Frostdale Deeps had always seemed an insufferable passage and an annoyance that Norah would stubbornly keep to herself. She was the Royal Inquisitor, and these halls of anguish were her macabre playground.

They were halfway there, nearing the second set of cell halls. The arduous hike wouldn't have been so strenuous if the warden had opted to make their stroll anything less than what seemed to be a half gallop on heels. But this was the most anticipated day of her life. She could hardly breathe from the news of the account reported to her. Her most significant enemy was finally in Barredish incarceration.

Norah looked to her daughter, Ebrielle, next to her, trailing from the lead to show due respect. She knew this was not the life Ebrielle would have chosen for herself, if such a choice had even been permitted at all. It was the path of an aristocrat, all duty and no such fantasy as choice, bestowed upon one from birth.

Her daughter had dirty-blond hair, the same as hers. She styled it alike as well, in a thick braid that came around to rest across the front of her right shoulder, as was customary when in the castle's court. Ebrielle had been a prize to obtain for lords young and old, near and afar, since her ninth cycle of age. Norah could choose any of them at any time, if such a unity was her priority. But it was far from it. There was precedence in the prisoners instead. And there always would be.

Eleven cycles and three seasons, she remembered explicitly in her head—Ebrielle's current age. Norah was still not accustomed to the modernized decreed measurement for age, as dictated by the Az'Dayne Dominadom. Only since their king, Aerik Roth, had recently resigned sovereignty over to Az'Dayne had Barredom been mandated to use the old Tairancian system. The Aggedonians, the Thrench, and the Sho'Lonese still measured age in the traditional counting of years. But the Dominadom's strict governing policy would adhere to cycles and seasons instead.

With five days to a pentday, or pent, and five pents to a month, and fifteen months to a year, each of the five seasons lasted five months, entailing a daylong intermittent furrow between each. A complete seasonal rotation comprised of a total of twenty-five months, with the furrows, which ended up being six hundred and thirty days, with always three seasons and their furrows to a year. Beginning with the Dawning, to the Sunder, into the Reaping, followed by the Umbra, and concluding with the Torrent, a full cycle consisted of the passing of the five seasons, from the Dawning through the Torrent.

And so we tread deeper into the Kingfall. Each upcoming cycle was named by Psage prophets upon the latter half of the prior cycle's Torrent. Superstition infected every kingdom across the western continents for whatever the title entailed, believing the name to hold some implication of fated inevitability. Kingfall was the name of the current cycle. And the realm was half its first season in now, over midway through the Dawning, and had already held true to that divination, with the unprecedented grand news of the fall of the Glace Isles king. The Psages were never wrong, it seemed.

Norah numbed out the knee-buckling drudge of downward steps by calculating her own years in cycles to ensure she had gotten it down. *Forty-three years of age, with my bornday on the tenth month. Twenty-five cycles and two seasons? Or is it twenty-six cycles now?* She would need to study the system some more to ensure she did not embarrass herself when speaking with the Daynish dignitaries recently present at court.

"For the qindrid, we have five stoneborne, and thrice that many greyborne. All Lilealytes, from what we can surmise. For the Terollar elven, we counted three score and four. The most we have ever had in the Deeps in all our records." The warden detailed the fresh captives transported from Northaven.

Titled interrogator and esteemed torturer as she was, her predeveloped bias negated her reservations in referring to Terollar elven by anything more than their derogatory alias. Terollar were termed "trolls," and Wyldenar were "wyldes" to all but a few mainlanders.

"Surprisingly, the general's reports show that the elven came willingly. Unheard of for a Glace Isles war party, and most bizarre behavior," the animated warden continued.

Bizarre indeed. But further report does claim that their legendary leader was executed by the alpha of its own tribe, just before the ambush and capture. You left that prominent part out, Norah thought to herself. A few Terollar could kill a contingent of men ten times their number, no matter the seasoning of the soldier. At least, that stood accurate for those hailing from the Glace Isles, in her experience. Terollar were accepted as the most dangerous elven throughout all of Penthara's expanse. Infamous as cannibals who ate their human and qindrid prey, these trolls were ruthless beasts. Norah believed them more fiends than true elven. She bore a special hatred for their kind due to the calamities of her loved ones lost to the brutes.

"You did hear detail of how it happened, I am sure. How the Glace Isles king was killed by his own? I know it is not public knowledge yet, per General Roth's request, but"—the warden's revelation finally came—"we even recovered the three Axes of the Sons."

"I did" was all she retorted with, irritated by the subject. That wasn't the way it was supposed to have died. It had been given a mercy it should never have been afforded. Norah habitually expressed her tone arrogantly and nonchalantly. "I will sort the trolls. Is she still here? The umbran Lilealah?"

Warden BrKaim shook his head and dared a confused peer back at Norah and Ebrielle, seeming surprised. "No, Inquisitor. She was directed right away to an audience with King Aerik. I assumed you were aware of such details."

She was. Norah still hoped to meet with the nefarious qindrid creator before Lilealah was shipped off on whatever clandestine scheme was being produced in the upper court at the moment. The fact that she had not been given the first opportunity to probe the umbran was downright insulting to her court position. Lilealah, formerly a Wyldenar elvan, was said to be one of the original umbran to aid in the turn of the Qindrid Curse throughout Aggedon. And now she was recorded as the last one alive that was still active in western Aggedon.

Umbran were the creators of the transmutation that turned humans into qindrid. Only elven of the mixed shadow descendancy could be candidates for evolution into umbran. The irreversible choice of becoming an umbran was an act of the Taboo, greatly frowned upon by the elvan society across the realm.

Almost all elven on Penthara followed the same universal theology, which they referred to as the Balance. Their creed adhered to absolute neutrality through all facets of life, and the ultimate preservation of nature at its core, paying great tribute to the aspects of each element. Their culture as a whole believed that after an elvan died, their hunder—the elvan's soul—passed into the Beyond, which lay parallel in an ethereal realm outside the reaches of the Vist, which surrounded Penthara's rim.

But not all elven heeded the Balance. There were three forbidden practices an elvan could enact, vastly differing depending on the elvan's elemental lineage. These unalterable paths of desecration of the Balance were known as the Taboo.

Norah knew much about the history of the umbran that had turned Aggedon into a qindrid nation. The Shiniryn elven who had already committed to the umbran path and were responsible for the turn that made the Caelduyans become skyborne had been the ones who converted a sect of Wyldenar elven in Tundura to take on the Taboo also. With the Wyldenar losing the war to the encroaching Aggeans across their territories, this sect sacrificed their relationship with their race to save their homeland. The Wyldenar umbran conquered the Aggeans through a convincing defeat to transcend into stoneborne qindrid, just as the Shiniryn umbran had subjugated the Caelduyans.

No umbran had ever been captured by the Barredish throughout history. Lilealah was the first. The details of how an elvan evolved into an umbran, or even the ritual of Transcendence that turned a human into a qindrid, were sundry, with convoluted hearsay from prior qindrid prisoners. She had to break from her annoyance at not getting the chance to interrogate Lilealah and bring light to the plethora of questions that only an umbran could answer.

"Have any greys broken to confirm suspicions?" She ambiguously queried the warden.

BrKaim shook his head again, visibly disappointed to keep giving his peer undesirable news. "You would have been informed if they had, Inquisitor."

"They will," she directed coldly. *They will all talk. They always do in the end.*

She discerned that they had already navigated well past the third set of cell halls, where greyborne qindrid were incarcerated. *Grey skin, grey hair, grey eyes, and lost souls.* The stoneborne Aggedonians who had lost their umbran makers were severed from their elemental impowers but could again reproduce among others similar. Those born into the qindrid affliction were known as the greyborne. They were still cursed with sleeplessness, were immune to disease, and highly resistant to the cold, but they were similar to humans in all other aspects besides the obvious aesthetics. Their skin was grey like the pure qindrid's, but their irises and hair were also grey from birth. They were just as much abominations to the realm, and their clans had remained a foe to Barredom all the same.

They were now nearing the bottom pits. They weren't stopping to see the qindrid prisoners just yet. Quiet again slipped its way in for the remainder of the sconce-lit march until the stairway found its end.

A plethora of dungeon guards lined this level on the hour. Such was requisite upon the arrival of such an array of new captives. Her curiosity overcame her outward irritation that the warden beneath her rank was partial to pertinent news before she was. "The umbran. To whom is the king sanctioning her custody, then? If I am not properly briefed on these privy details, how can I begin any effective interrogation?"

Warden BrKaim puckered his lips, as if the gesture were supposed to define his sympathy. It only annoyed Norah more. "King Aerik is handing her over to Ondrew of the Norther Knights. Details on why have been made strictly confidential."

BrKaim mentioning such a name forced her to burst out with more disdain. "Ondrew? A leader of nothing but errants! Fallaciously dubbing themselves knights! We would hand over our principal prize to a disfavored mob of sellswords ostracized from Barredom's service?" Saying it out loud made it even more real and immediately instigated a bitter taste to swell in her mouth. She thought she might spit.

The warden interjected sensibly. "Ondrew Roth is King Aerik's only son. The Norther Knights are errants, I agree, but they do not act for coin. I stand beside His Majesty's royal judgment, as his wisdom sees fit."

What a puppet. Her eyes impaled the dark halls ahead, and she sneered to herself about how much she believed she might hate the warden. To be alone with her prisoners was the only cure for the scourge of his presence.

She could now see her destination. The Forlorn was the deepest area of the Frostdale dungeon. So titled just as its name implied, a place to store those meant to be forgotten. Only a rare breed of enemy was ever imprisoned in the Forlorn. And now its abysmal hollows were brimming with almost eighty residents.

Walking upon the view-way built into the stone, the three of them peered down upon the cluster of captives in the pit below. The bottommost ward of Frostdale's prison system had resolved itself into a circular hall that originated from the stairway to the upper levels. Acting as a window for onlookers, it was as large as an average man's torso in height and operated as a stone barrier that separated the free from the captive.

The Forlorn was a deep well of sorts, beginning at the top of the oubliette's uppermost level, burrowing far beyond the prison's foundations. The Forlorn in itself was technically its own dungeon. There was no door at Norah's level to grant access to the prisoners. The only way in was down the winch lift on the inside, currently hoisted to the top level, where the ceiling's trapdoor was locked.

The level of the Forlorn in which the captives were held was some three floors or so deeper into the well than the sentries' observation point, where she stood. The imprisoned only had stone ledges as narrow as the width of two grown men to lie and walk upon. These footholds rimmed the circular oubliette but also crisscrossed throughout the subterranean void in a checkered pattern, making an intersection of walkways. Below the man-made causeways, the black pit appeared to fade into perpetual oblivion.

Twenty men would be an uncomfortable cruelty to detain in the tight confinements of the Forlorn. Seventy-nine was delightfully merciless—a gift returned from Barredom to their historical enemies on the Glace Isles.

Half of the Terollar elven below scurried about like ants, frantic to find a safe place to make their stationary home for the rest of their soon-to-be-arbitrated life span. Some sat solemnly contemplating their fate in a motionless trance to the depths. She had been the king's torturer for over a decade, and her practices were well-known to her nemeses of the north. With her loathing for trolls above all else, she admitted to herself that the maltreated spectacle was already staged for her work to begin.

The half-naked trolls appeared human in likeness, aside from their long, pointed ears, stature, and perhaps their uniquely eccentric hairstyles. Their skin was fair like that of the Barredish, and their hair was of light blonds, with light-green eyes. Remnants of bright green war paint striped their faces and exposed flesh. Most of them had adorned themselves with bone jewelry pushed through their skin, through their ears or nose or lips or chin or various other places. *Primitive savages through and through.* Norah belittled them in her mind.

Norah's intuition levels were high now. She picked up everything. Her specialty was to scrutinize flaws in her victims, to make the once unbreakably strong into the enfeebled weak.

Ebrielle's soft mutter of "Mother?" in appalled inquiry instantly anchored the remorseless fortitude that Norah was recognized for. She ignored her daughter and stared at each elvan in the Forlorn as the trolls now peered up to gawk at their curious new observers.

Terollar of the Glace Isles were the only elvan race known for their exclusively categorized hairstyles. Tribesven were branded by rank and achievement or by vocation from their style of cut. Groomers that practiced this fashion of individuality were known as the mortali among the troll culture, who also played a role as sacred elders and herbalists. Being that trolls were unique in their inherent ability to regenerate, it was the mortali that were gifted in keeping the length and design of hair to a specific placement without it growing irrepressibly long and wild.

To no one in particular, she demanded, "Jrulthun, then? Randon's report states that it felled the Chosen Troll in front of its own tribesven just before the apprehension. Show me this alpha traitor that executed the khomo." She used the Terollar term for the Glace Isles king. In a matter of seconds, she had already discerned the obvious, brutish culprit below, though it wasn't Jrulthun she was overtly earnest to meet.

Warden BrKaim nodded to the elder guard who had been present from the induction process of settling the Terollar in. The veteran sentry readily declared, "That one. The biggest I've ever seen. Treacherous fiends, the whole lot of them."

Norah had identified Jrulthun before any of the others the moment she gazed down. It had to be the biggest troll she had ever seen too. The towering elvan must have been almost eight feet tall. It seemed as wide as the largest horse in the keep's stables, a pure freak of barbaric brawn. Its bright green war paint still clung in patches to its face. Its pale blond hair was braided in tight plaits against its scalp, blending in with its fair skin. Bone rings ornamented the bridge of its nose through the brow to its scalp, with trophy studs jutting from its chin and jawline as well.

Terollar elvan tribes were savages who followed their alphas, like the true beasts such as the vicious ferahn and the Skystone apes, only loyal to the proven strongest. This was indeed the legendary Jrulthun. She inwardly celebrated that the most malicious brute in all the north, responsible for a century of countless deaths, was in her custody. *You stole a great victory from me, Jrulthun, in taking the khomo's life. You will feel regret for that theft soon enough*, she cursed.

"Any others of deduced import? I am told one suffering the aging was taken. That can only mean one thing," Norah coldly continued, still inspecting the elvan array below. This was truly why she was here. This troll was her drive for living.

The lead guard obeyed, pointing to one. "There. We think it may be Zuulzin. None others as of yet, but we haven't begun questioning, as ordered, Inquisitor."

To see an old elvan was unheard of. The cultures of man simply never saw elven when they had succumbed to the aging. It was a known tale in Frostdale that her husband, while alive, somehow managed to find the location of the Glace Isles Grove, in the Teralloe Forest, and sever many lifetrees.

All elven were originally tied to their lifetree and spiritroots. A mother elvan did not give birth the natural way that humans or animals did. The children would be spawned through a cocoon manifested by the lifetree. Upon birth, the newborn and its spiritroot were ethereally tied hand in hand. The spiritroot remained a part of its parents' lifetree until the time came for the elvan to accept its own lifemate. They would grow their own lifetree together in permanent matrimony. Once an elvan committed to a lifemate, it could never choose another to reproduce with. And so long as the lifetree of the two lifemates remained intact, their longevity would stay entwined with the life span of the tree.

Elven who never committed to a lifemate had their spiritroot remain a part of their parents' lifetree, which would become weaker over time. The fable of Zuulzin was one as such. Before Zuulzin's spiritroot was destroyed, the troll was rumored to be quite handsome—if such a preposterous notion could be ascribed to the creatures. The story was spun that Zuulzin was the odd sheep of its tribe, and that it was shunned for never taking on a lifemate by tradition, only attracted to humans, which was a great sin in their culture.

But it was of the blood of the khomo, and so it merely suffered temporary exile. It was during this time that Zuulzin was captured by Vanson Blackendale, father to her now-deceased husband. Vanson had taken his wife, Carah, on all of his exploits with him through his dangerous endeavors as the leader of the Eldenvale Rangers. During its captivity, Carah had come into contact with the troll prisoner and nicknamed it Kind-Eyes. Within the camp, the moniker began to popularly stick because of its innocently downtrodden appeal, in contrast to the ferocious tribesven of the Glace Isles.

But Kind-Eyes allegedly betrayed and seduced her into breaking its bonds, kidnapping her as its ransom, but not before killing Vanson and several others. Some years later Norah's husband, Lucas, taking up the mantle of his father, tracked and nearly killed Zuulzin. After freeing his mother and learning of her physical boundaries being violated by the troll, he declared her tainted by the fiend. Lucas ordered a decree, approved by King Aerik Roth, that all women, imprisoned or free-willed, who had lain with Terollar elven should be cleansed by death, burned at the stake. Norah dared not refute her husband's harsh sentence.

But it was that decision that later yielded Lucas's own doom. On his final expedition into Aggedon, just north of the Glace Isles, the only two survivors of the onslaught testified that Lucas and Norah's youngest brother, Justan, who was a vital part of the hunting crew, were assassinated directly by Zuulzin itself, with the Chosen Troll in their war party. There was no greater foe alive than this very being before her now.

Kind-Eyes? It is it. Why else would an aging troll be permitted in the war party? Her archenemy was finally in her grasp. And it no longer held the miraculous ability of self-healing, like other trolls. It would no longer be ignorant to the sensation of true pain—the true pain it had inflicted on her when it murdered Lucas. Norah tried to maintain her elated yet bellicose resolve in order to focus on the professionalism of her royally dictated task at hand.

"And then there is that one. The only damned troll who won't stop staring and smiling at us. It's all it does!" The guard wrapped up his assessment, sneering down at his target. "We hoped you would start with it. We call it Smiles."

You refer to the troll as "it" instead of "him." We share similar vocabulary, soldier, Norah mused to herself in her racist appreciation. Norah's eyes searched to find the one defined.

An eerie sensation washed over her when she saw that this particular troll was already staring back at her, glaring a hole into her soul, as she had done with its allies. But it did so with a smile. A growing devilish grin, confident to embrace the indubitable torture that smirk just rewarded it with.

This one was of average height for its kind, a foot taller than most Barredish men, but muscularly leaner than its fellows. Like the others, it still carried remnants of the Glace Isles green paint across its exposed flesh. Its blond hair was shaved on the sides and pressed back on the top, woven into a topknot held in place by bone rings. The fiend's features were sharp yet rigid, sculpted with confidence.

She accepted her smug enemy's staredown with an opposing harsh answer of her own. She didn't smile back. She never smiled. She only winked, as she always did before invoking her evil whims. In concurrence with the sentry's request, Norah asserted, "You will get that wish. It wants to talk."

She turned away from the view-way to take her leave back up the steps to continue her assessment on the qindrid she had yet to visit in another level of the cells. Ebrielle and BrKaim clung to the heels of her quickened pace away from the Forlorn.

Keeping her focus on the stairway she had been reunited with, Norah ordered the warden, "Bring me that one. Smiles. Along with the alpha and the aging one as well. This is an era of reckoning, Ebrielle. You will watch me make them talk." Norah icily glared back at her daughter with an absolute promise. "To the Troll Gardens."

BrKaim made some obedient reply of affirmation, but she ignored it all. *They will all talk.* Under her knife, they always did.

WESTWALKER (II)

NORTHAVEN

The glowing dawn beamed over the rim of the hill's summit. The knoll's climb smothered the cries of the wind as Tsuno breached the plateau and gazed across the valley's expanse. And there it stood in all its foreboding glory, nestled against the northern outskirts of the forbidden Artopian Forest.

"Northaven," Michayle whispered from behind Tsuno on the ascent, almost as if he were afraid of alerting the soldiers at the fortress if he spoke any louder. "No clansman sees it and lives."

Tsuno said nothing, letting the Aggedonian absorb the moment in full. On this particular morning, no mirth found its way into his typically blithe demeanor as he poised in consideration of the awe in the stoneborne's glassy eyes.

Michayle took in the wonderment of defensive architecture below, the only Barredish stronghold built on Aggedon soil. His scrutiny slowly shifted to inspect the full panorama of the sinister majesty before him. The clansman's focus shifted and settled, training itself on the lone heap of tinder set to burn atop the primed bed of flammable brush.

The qindrid's logic presumed the dreaded inevitable. "So, what happens now?" Michayle seemed to almost sob in angst to hear the absolute certainty uttered aloud. "A pyre? Is that why you sent the rogue-wylde so far ahead of us? For whose death rites do we prepare?"

Tsuno knew the Aggedonian had ascertained that preordained

doom the moment Michayle observed the feral form of Ryleohk perched with his axe near the unlit pyre. "You will be taken from my hands before we enter the gate. You will be tortured. Rest assured of that. First for a pentday, but likely more, by the prejudiced and battle-starved men of Randon Roth." Tsuno paused only to let his dire guarantees sink in before elaborating. "Then you will be sent to Castle Frostdale, to continue your persecution at the cruel hands of the Royal Inquisitor. Your death will be prolonged piece by piece into the furrow of the next season. You know this truth."

Michayle and Tsuno could have appeared as two of the same to any spying scouts. Both qindrid, though obviously of different heritage, stood side by side as momentary, happenchance companions. "Or?" The morose clansman dared inquire for other dismal alternatives.

"I grant you a mercy," Tsuno sympathetically offered back in the native Norspeak. *"A warrior's death."*

The bold warrior was finally proving to show some form of vulnerability, with visible fear etched on every feature. But Michayle refused to honor the Westwalker with any return of his Aggedonian language, stomaching speaking in Civil, as they had been. Half-barren of emotion as the ultimate reality infected his voice with a choking emptiness, Michayle ventured to softly plead. "Why even keep me alive this far, then? You should have slain me with my brethren in the Ichean."

Because I hoped you were the candidate I have been looking for. I've been told to find a stoneborne like me, a qindrid who wishes to no longer be so. I am to selflessly find the cure for another's people before I am granted the cure for my own. But you simply are not the chosen. "Let us just say because I had hoped you were someone that you are not, and if I told you the detail, you would lie for survival, and I know survivalists better than any," Tsuno conveyed. "So to unravel the riddle, let *me* lie instead."

He paused, looking beyond to Northaven and then back to Michayle, in the eye. "I kept you alive for the pleasant company, of course," Tsuno bluffed before calmly demanding, "Tell me what is not told in this missive. Where are the Aggedonians going, and why? The near entirety of the western population has disappeared almost overnight."

Michayle's eyes scrunched into a detesting glare in the direction of Northaven below. "You believe that we fear the Barredish? Even with their southern alliance?" Michayle scoffed, as if offended at the absurdity. "We have been enlightened as to the true threat. The one that comes to us from the eastern shores, already at the empire's doorstep: you westwalkers. The people of your homeland are likely already dead and butchered."

The stoneborne shot a satisfied grin toward him, but Tsuno ignored any sensitive response back. "Go on," Tsuno insisted, pretending not to waver at the unanticipated, ill-omened report.

"Landron had been instructed to round up outlying villages and hermits, or any of our people we came across, and force them to report to Two-Towns, across from Loch Karlohr. Lilealah calls it the Great Exodus," Michayle testified proudly.

"That does not explain the bizarre disappearances," Tsuno probed for further clarification.

The bold Aggedonian wrinkled his face in hate once again, stabbing back in defiance. "I will not betray my people with any more words. You have your missive telling you where to go. You will find out." Michayle grimaced and briskly walked over to the flat stone where Ryleohk ominously stood by the pyre. "May you and the rogue remain Barredom's eternal pawns, until they dispose of the two of you like rotten harvest." Michayle hocked spit toward Tsuno, glowering at the grey elvan while doing so.

Tsuno looked at the spittle ornamenting his boots. "You have been a hostile delight," he countered amiably.

Tsuno gave the nod to Ryleohk, and the captive qindrid was dropped down to his knees, his neck and torso pressed to the cold rock. Michayle stared at the stronghold of his enemy in his homeland of Aggedon as his last sight. Fury enlarged his crystalline eyes, drowning in a swell of tears as his focus took in his silent slayer.

The six-foot-tall elvan was shorter than the average Wyldenar, but that made Ryleohk no less menacing. Being born of umbran parents meant he was one of the rare rogue-elvan. Rogues were more half-elvan, birthed with no spiritroot, causing them to age as humans did, unlike typical elvankind, who aged slowly, as they were conjoined with the span of their lifetree. They featured the same grey skin and long, outward-turning, angled ears as the umbran as well. As rogue-elven grew older, they gradually lost more of their cultivated sentience and devolved into a more beast-like disposition. Any who met

Ryleohk could attest to this fact having merit.

His famed weapon, the large, custom-forged Terollar throwing axe, now served his hands as an executioner's blade. Ryleohk's inimical gaze narrowed over his victim as he readied the cold edge of his axe against the bare neck of Michayle, slowly rearing it back for the death blow. The elvan's mesh of dirty grey mane draped from his scalp all the way down his wide back to his waist and across his bare chest. The Wyldenar seemed almost part lion, part man, and part something far more sinister in the moment.

The clansman stared, wide-eyed, straight ahead to Northaven one last time, muttering some final, futile prayer to his umbran maker, Lilealah, in his own tongue. Michayle's eyes never blinked. "*Let it be known that Michayle of Clan Thalbear, son of Vargos the Ironeye, died a warrior's death!*" It was the last phrase from the stoneborne as the elvan's weapon concluded its duty.

"*May your lost soul find its way into the stones and trees, nourishment to the great tairan of Penthara,*" Tsuno finished in respect, just before retrieving Michayle's head to add it to the large satchel with the others of the hunt. The deed was done. They hurried the burning of their enemy laid to rest and departed from the pyre.

They approached the gates of the imposing stronghold just as the sun was in its prime. Ryleohk ceased hiking at the wall's arrow range line, aware of the ordinance that no elven were allowed into its sanctuary. Tsuno continued forward, holding the reins of his other steed, which carted Landron's unique armor and the heads of the hunting party in two sacks tied to the saddle. As he neared the gates, they clamored open suddenly in an earsplitting creak that sounded as if a dozen dying trees were falling concurrently.

Five riders trotted out to meet him. He recognized the obvious officer of the company. Commandant Nathahn charged toward him as if he meant to joust, with his four cavaliers circling Tsuno like some unwelcome enemy. Tsuno rolled his eyes to the sun-primed sky and chortled sarcastically at the typical treatment.

"Halt! Greyskin, do you come as friend or foe?" Commandant Nathahn sternly spluttered.

Tsuno went along with the farce, removing his cowl to fully show his recognized features, and glanced back at his renowned repeater bow, peeking high above his shoulder. He sneered and squinted his sky-blue foreign eyes as his straight snow-white hair danced in the wind. Tsuno then replied in a condescending tone, "Is the war over yet, then, that a qin might approach Northaven as friend now? Or has the enemy grown so daft as to charge the gates one at a time?"

Nathahn and his dour men were not entertained by the satirical skyborne. "General Roth made it clear not to allow you passage through until you returned with his demands," the commandant volleyed back, holding his ground.

Tsuno yanked the rope on the two heavy bags that tied them to his companion steed, releasing the knot to allow himself control to hoist the sacks into his grasp. He swung one of the awkward satchels into Nathahn's lap, nearly knocking him clean off his horse. He dropped the other heavy sack at the hooves beneath him. The act did nothing to alleviate the officer's caustic approach.

Nathahn peered into one of the pungent sacks with a squint of disgust at the gory sight and decomposing smell. "This better be the seven that were requested. And what about the missive?"

Tsuno pulled out Landron's note from his glove to display it to his interrogators and replied evenly, without waiting for a rebuttal, as he nudged Nho into pace through the gates. "It's eight. Wise of you to bring these clever men to help you count."

He rode through the courtyard of Northaven with faces of sheer abhorrence mixed with fear stretched across every soldier he trotted by, but none displayed feelings of admiration or respect.

"Westwalker."

"Greyskin."

"Heretic."

Hushed but all too audible, their muttered belittling trailed throughout his canter to the fortress main. He would be in and out of this miserable walled facade of allies as swiftly as possible.

He found his destination at the keep. A guarded escort brought him through the many avenues of the intricate top tier of the lone Barredish stronghold.

Outside the general's door, he waited only for a moment before stepping aside to allow the exit of the audience of officers already within. The elite guardsmen allowed Tsuno into the general's office and were promptly gestured to leave Randon and Tsuno alone.

General Randon Roth was a weathered, battle-hardened soldier decorated with numerous scars across his shaved face. He was a pragmatic and prejudiced man of grim passion, rarely showing sentiment except that which pertained to the dedicated duty toward his country's war.

The general had donned a full suit of splint armor, minus the helm, as if a battle were at the gates. Randon chewed on the side of his cheek as he studied his allied enemy before him. Finally, Tsuno moved first, seeing that the general was not going to speak. He walked confidently to the war table where Randon sat and set down the missive taken from Landron's dead hands, going back to stand in the middle of the room. Tsuno's long white locks remained roaming about as if some breeze had possessed them in the airtight room—a perpetual skyborne trait.

General Roth promptly opened the scroll, seemingly chewing a hole in his cheek as he read. His dull brown eyes scoured each word before he looked back up at Tsuno.

Tsuno and the general had held a fragile forbearance for each other ever since Randon's own father, the former king Tytus Roth, died at the Battle for Northaven. The whole of the north was aware of the great amity between Tytus and Tsuno and the tales of their renowned exploits, which had brought Barredom to the success it was currently enjoying. The Barredish people knew it was singlehandedly the Westwalker who had played the critical role in establishing Northaven in the first place. He had fought alongside the human northmen in victories during the Highlands War and the Second Vellyon War, among others in the civil warfare against House Roth.

After the fall of Tytus and the succession of Aerik Roth, Randon's elder brother had officially conferred on Tsuno the title of Friend of Frostdale, giving him safe passage in Barredish-controlled territories. But throughout the latter fourteen years of King Aerik's rule, Tsuno's delicate rapport with his human allies had seen its share of downsides. Through certain consequences, there had been a time when his badge of haven had been revoked, and he had had to recondition his trust and favor with the kingdom.

Randon did not do politics, like his brother. He did war. And he did it well. The intractable general refused to hide his detestation for and misgivings about Tsuno, never sharing the opinions of his father or King Aerik regarding his worth. The Westwalker was still a qindrid, and they were simply the enemy. King Aerik, however, saw fit to employ Tsuno and Ryleohk as the most well utilized scouts and the most efficient strike team Barredom ever had. The two of them had one of the most formidable reputations in the north. Tsuno knew the Barredish king used them just as much for fear propaganda against the enemy as he did for stories to motivate his men.

Finally, General Randon spoke, not to him but to the closed door of the war chamber. "Nathahn!"

Tsuno grimaced conspicuously at the unexpected name.

The general's underling came into the war room with his armed lackeys to salute their leader in response. "Sire?" the officer inquired.

Randon exclusively addressed Nathahn, never speaking directly to the Westwalker but also never taking his suspicious gaze from him. "Garrison three-quarters of the army. We move on the Fourteen. Just as soon as the heretic and his savage ensure the fortress is vacant of his kinsmen. Tell this greyskin he will accompany Scoutmaster Thade for the survey and rendezvous with the contracted Boarneck Cavaliers for the agenda that will follow."

Nathahn obediently complied, directing Tsuno as commanded. "Yes, sire. Westwalker, you are to—"

"As it turns out, I can hear." Tsuno stared equably back at Randon, smirking in hopes of stoking his ire when forced to parley with a qindrid. "A clever little trick I picked up from being around so many humans."

Randon's eyes narrowed at Nathahn, refusing to meet the gaze of the Westwalker. Through gritted teeth he seethed, "If a word of this missive is true, that the qindrid have retreated from western Aggedon, I want to know why. I want to know where to. We will pull the forces up from Frostdale, with Az'Dayne's backing, and make our march on the east. Wherever they flee, we will scythe their flank with such force as they have never seen."

"You do know that something is strangely amiss here." Tsuno stated the obvious in concern, pointing at the missive on the war table. "The Aggedonians would never leave their homeland entirely. There is something dire in motion. We have to find Lilealah."

This time Randon did look at Tsuno. "Spare me your lessons, foreigner. While you were out toiling for what we had already discerned, I soundly managed to capture her," the general proudly unveiled.

This was implausible news. During countless hunts he had tracked her to no avail in all his time spent in the north. *Lilealah? How did she allow herself into such a baitless trap?*

Lilealah had been one of the last remaining umbran in Aggedon for decades, as most of the others before her had been methodically assassinated by the Glace Isles Terollar, resulting in the rise of the greyborne population at the cost of stimulating the ruin of the stoneborne foothold. "You mean me to believe that Northaven actually has Lilealah in custody?"

Randon assured him, "By order of the king, she has been sent to the Frostdale Deeps to be dealt with accordingly. Her entourage was being ambushed by trolls. Our rescue was timely."

"Rescue?" Tsuno laughed at the ridiculous absurdity of the notion. "Saved from being eaten by the Terollar, to now be tortured for seasons indefinitely by the Royal Inquisitor? Lilealah is oh so very fortunate."

"The Glace Isles king's axes were found among the trolls." Randon wasn't done elaborating on the monumental victory. "My men at the ambush said they saw the alpha, Jrulthun, betray and slay the Chosen Troll just before being apprehended. The remaining trolls have been brought into captivity for questioning in the Deeps. You are bearing witness to the end times of Barredom's strife. The war on all fronts is nearing a triumph. We close on the hour for you to be out of my sight for good, heretic."

Khomo'Jhuvonus dead as well? Lilealah in Barredish imprisonment? The stoneborne army, and every qindrid in western Aggedon, vanished almost overnight? Tsuno buried his instinct to overcalculate how grandly bizarre such incredulous news sounded. He countered smugly, "A final triumph for both of us indeed."

"Commandant," the general barked at his puppet. "See this unwanted ally in our enemy's skin fed and supplied. I'm done with his tongue for a lifetime. He leaves on the morrow's dawn." Randon abruptly advanced from his war table and departed the room.

Tsuno offered a dramatic Sho'Lonese bow to Randon as he swept past him. He ardently embraced Nathahn's eager escort to steal him from these bigoted walls, back into the unjudging wilds.

ONDREW (I)

THE CHARGE

"Osh, osh, oshah!"

A clamored unison of tankards smashed against the tables throughout the feast hall, now taken over by the Norther Knights gang. There were twenty-four of the lively, half-drunken knights errant, joined by a dozen of the hardened Eldenvale Rangers, and two strangers he had yet to introduce to his men.

"Osh, osh, oshah!" The vigorous cheer roared louder as Ondrew stepped from his chair to mount the head of the long table where his loyal crew all restlessly sat. Ondrew had formed the Norther Knights, a zealous band barely two years in the making, the very season his father, Aerik Roth, Barredom's king, had decided to bow down in subservience to Az'Dayne.

The king's decision to succumb to the heavy hand of Az'Dayne was not taken lightly by most of the noble houses. Even though it was an advised resolution to aid in the war effort, coerced by the Barredish Frostdale Council, the citizens of Barredom knew that breaking out of it would mean a war with Az'Dayne itself, which was a fight they could not even remotely hope to win.

When Ondrew refused to bow to the new rule, he was graced, as the king's son, with the leniency of renouncing all of his lands and titles to live his life indefinitely under no house surname. He chose to endure as an esteemed freelancer. His mission was to see justice brought back to the north, without the unwanted patronage from the south and its politics. He called upon any fervent activist of the traditional Barredom nobility to honor him in his quest to end the interminable war with Aggedon. All this was sacrificed so that the southern Daynish rule would dissipate from their borders and crawl back to their corrupt cities in the leagues beyond.

Several men from royal houses had joined his outlawed order when he took up his new banner, all forced to do the same and renounce their birth claims or be branded traitors to the Az'Dayne Dominadom. Some of his enlisted troops were even former Barredom yharls or renowned local champions before they had been sworn into their censured enterprise.

He had not spoken to his father since the last day he was titled Prince Ondrew Roth of Barredom, some two years before. Ondrew was no knight errant at that time. Since his birth, he had been the sole heir to the throne of Barredom, having no other siblings. His uncle, the esteemed General Randon Roth, as younger brother to his father, would be venerated as heir in his stead, now that Ondrew had disclaimed his royal name. Such was the radical price he had paid for honor. And if not for his handful of undeniably loyal disciples, present with him now, Ondrew knew his tenacity would have long ago crumbled into mortifying regret. Being called upon as the king's chosen group for this critical assignment, however, gave Ondrew faith that there was still hope for his father and him to pardon one another for the binding choices that had driven them apart.

"Osh, osh, oshah!" He came to after his daze, realizing they had chanted it four more times after he initiated his ascent to the tabletop, standing above them all like some idol. He mutely noted to himself that he was deeper in his mead than he had intended to be before his anticipated inspirational speech.

Ondrew gazed upon each man before him. "I look around this feast hall. And I see something more than mere would-be warriors. Nay, I see destined champions with legacies for the sages throughout the ages." His even tone was slow and steady as he tactfully navigated between the bountiful, rummaged-through servings garnishing the long table. "Hearts of gold and hands of iron. Forgone by name, but bound by honor."

Walking from one end of the table to the next, he drew his longsword and signified each of his knights as he paced forward. "I see the elite swordsmen of Komak Keep and its former yharl, the legend Broc BrKomak." The highborn men nodded and muttered in concurrence with their leader as they were mentioned.

"I see those who were Lockehart and Bloodmont and Ackhill. There a BrGennie, a BrKeeley. The Shaw brothers, I see you," Ondrew continued, receiving some form of gratitude from the specified house after each reference. "I see the famous Black Brigannor."

When he finished his reverences to his original knights, he raised his tankard in salute to Mathias, the scarred leader of the Eldenvale Rangers, now in his service as well. "Here, to the former Orevilles and our Eldenvale Rangers!" Every Barredish man seated slammed their mugs to the table and brought them back up to their lips for a healthy swill in welcome.

Lastly, he walked to the two outsiders—the only non-Barredish in the feast hall, and no doubt the pariahs of the room. They were Vellyans. Though the western island nation of Vellyon had been at peace in current times, from prior wars with Barredom, their people were still shunned in general prejudice by the locals who clung to the past. Vellyans exiled from their country who settled on the mainland continent were known to become brigand gangs or barbarian clans that filtered throughout the Undawned Lands.

They were brown of skin, dark blue-eyed, black-haired, and taller than the average mainlander, easily by over a foot or so in height. This stood no less true for Aramgar and Odemnar. Ondrew was considered to be of typical height, and still he only came up to the shoulders of both half-giants at best. The two humbled Vellyans had been released from their incarceration in the Deeps into his care the day before as a boon from his father to aid in his escort quest underway.

It occurred to him that his knights had deemed it ill-favored to invite the barbarians into the fold, but even now, none dared show him their distaste for it. He stole up his tankard one final time. "And now to these Vellyans, an enemy of the yesters, but friends of today and the morrows ever forward." Ondrew judged each of his knights for signs of approval but received only still silence and raised tankards with no sips following. *None will protest. It will do.*

Ondrew closed his eyes at the far end of the extended tavern table. He lowered the vigor in his voice even more to grant an ominous significance. "Pray hear me now, knights. The south belongs only in our past, so keep it there. And we do not look south." He opened his eyes once again and slowly turned, facing the north end of the table with his sword outstretched toward the wall as if it were the horizon to Aggedon itself.

"Our focus is to the north. Farther north than any have been." The entire feast hall was at his attention, not just his brave entourage of loyalists. His words came out hushed, almost as if whispered to his men alone. "Destiny is unraveling. The Fives have spoken, and they see a norther path for you, my knights." Ondrew shouted now, pointing his sword to each of them. He hammered his boot into the table so hard half the copious fine dishes quaked onto the floor. "Stand with me, then! Do not forget or forsake your new family, as we are all there is! And it is the Norther Knights whom the king has called upon to end this ancient strife. The war of our grandfathers and their grandfathers before them. Frostdale has not shut her gates to us. It never has. And it never will!"

"Osh, osh, oshah!" The signature Barredish cheer erupted throughout the feast hall, with no other voice as loud as Ondrew's. The Norther Knights all stood with their weapons in the air and mugs drumming and spilling onto the table.

"Drink! Laugh! Feast! On the hour, we march our first steps into our fates as timeless heroes! Meet me at the castle, brothers!" Ondrew looked over to the councilman chaperone patiently waiting for him by the feast hall's inner foyer. "Time to meet our charge!"

Several more cheers ensued as he began his exit. He was pleased his father's advocate had allowed him the necessary respite with his knights, even when time was unmistakably of the essence.

Ondrew nodded to the stranger of the court, but was inwardly irritated that he seemed to recognize none of these newly appointed officials since the transition Barredom undertook into Az'Dayne's growing political envelopment. He noted to himself that he honestly couldn't care less about coming to learn the man's name. The dignitary dressed half his face with the traditional signature masque of Az'Dayne. He clearly wasn't Barredish, which alone was enough to earn disfavor in Ondrew's eyes.

They took to their mares outside and began the lengthy canter without talk. Ondrew and the dignitary hastened through the escalating streets of Frostdale to the palace keep, where the former throne room was based, before the royal seat had been subtracted. That sordid thought reinforced his disposition against these immigrants encroaching upon his home, into the very house he had been raised in.

The doors to the throne room were opened, and Ondrew made

his march across an unrecognizable setting. He assumed a dutiful guise, not to be swayed by insolence while on the precipice of destiny's call. He compelled his furious eyes from the now-golden-painted flooring that blanketed the hall. Barredom's heraldic colors of the Roths, the accustomed green and black, were nowhere to be seen on the tapestries. This was no longer a piece of Frostdale. The pretense had been ignited by the bright orange and flame-red decor of Az'Dayne's hellish appeal.

He impulsively peered onward, looking for the throne he knew had been removed, reminding himself that this was the first time he had been in the royal hall since his father had become king under another sovereign. Ondrew's last time standing before these high ceilings was the very eve he had denounced himself as no longer a Roth, claiming no house to his name in front of his father for all the high lords of the court to witness. He had rarely even visited Castle Frostdale since the time of the transition and had especially never dared an audacious step toward the palace keep until today. He knew his father's clemency for his impudence would not hold a second time.

Echoes of laments accompanied his every footstep as his boots clung to the cold Barredish masonry, refusing to walk on the Daynish carpeting. His visit to the palace court on the same morning had not gone as anticipated. He had hoped to receive the special assignment directly from his father, but the elusive king never made himself known. "Ondrew of no house, founder of the Norther Knights." He had been thus announced when he entered the court. He was handed the assignment from complete strangers, Daynish usurpers and subjective Barredish minions of the new Dominadom, and told his father would remain in his chambers until Ondrew had departed from Frostdale entirely.

It was as if a poison knife had been plunged into his gut and twisted up into his heart. The king was truly done with him. *You are only sending me on this inevitably futile mission to rid yourself of my shame once and for all, are you not, Father? An expedition to slay all of those who denied your choice to bow to Az'Dayne.* Their bodies would be buried in the mountainous tombs of Zsolindal, or in the reaches beyond the horizon of Aggedon's deepest contested territories, never to be seen again.

Ondrew collected himself and checked his wavering resolve as his taciturn escort brought him to the makeshift cell in the recess adjacent to the renovated throne foyer.

There were no Barredish watchmen overseeing her cell, nor any Forwoken monks, whom Ondrew had grown used to as silent sentries for securing politically important prisoners. The infamous umbran had a decem of Daynish paladins outside her door instead.

He found the female Wyldenar utterly bare and chained to a pentacrux. The lone object in the small alcove was the large wooden saltire to which she was strapped, with her wrists chained to hang exactly parallel to the floor. Her ankles were bound together by another shackle that linked a perfectly measured chain to the iron collar around her neck, forcing the hostage to remain wholly upright, with no scope to slump in posture. Such was the exhausting position of torture for the incarcerated who found themselves doomed to endure the Barredish pentacrux.

She was fiercely attractive, in a barbaric sense of sinister beauty. One could never tell the true age of an elvan, and this was especially so for those that had succumbed to becoming umbran. She could have seen a decem of his lifetimes or beyond for all he knew, and yet she still looked as young as he was, possibly mid to latter twenties.

It was known lore that an umbran aged differently from a normal elvan. Elven were tied into the longevity of their lifetrees, which stretched their mortal existence relatively long. An elvan could detach their inborn ethereal spiritroot from their lifetree at any time, customarily only done for the purpose of fusing with a lifemate. If an elvan failed to reattach their spiritroot to a lifetree before the passing of an Umbra season, then the umbilical connection the root had with the elvan would wither and die, affecting their lifetree as well, and they would become sick with the aging.

However, an elvan of mixed shadow lineage, such as the Wyldenar, of tairan and shadow descendancy, or the Shiniryn, of sky and shadow descendancy, would undergo a different effect if they carried their detached spiritroot beyond the season of the Umbra. The elvan's spiritroot would become severed the same, causing their lifetree to die, inducing a period of illness that followed, while a rigorous physical transformation overtook them.

Ondrew was aware that normal elven were slow to cultivate offspring from their lifetrees, only able to produce one child every five seasonal cycles. It was said that the umbran could pass seed and reproduce a new child with their lifemate once a cycle, though, during the Umbra season. How umbran lifemates could reproduce without lifetrees was unknown to him, however, and no savant in Frostdale could ever quite clear up that concept for him. He only knew that the umbran, when paired with their lifemate, carried some possessive power over most humans, and that was how the qindrid Transcendence occurred, through some obscure means of a mythical ritual. No Barredish had ever truly been educated on the particulars, since no captured stoneborne would speak of it. Grueling torture interrogations had always failed in discovering new information on the process. But it was clear that the umbran did not need a lifetree to avoid the aging disease. Instead, their longevity was tied to how many qindrid followers they had.

He had never thought he would see an umbran if he lived all his days out and then some. His imagination could not have conjured the tangible image before him now, with Lilealah in all her exotic magnificence. Her ebon hair was untamed and long, down to the small of her back, matching the black of her sharp, clawlike nails. Her pointed ears breached the thick of it all, drooping more outward from her head instead of slanting up like the typical elvan. The subtle hint of her small fangs could be glimpsed behind her pouty lips. She was cursed with grey skin but without a blemish to be found on her petite yet curvaceous nude body. The remains of any garments taken upon her detainment were nowhere to be found.

His focus inadvertently skimmed by her flawless breasts, then to her tiny waist, realizing he had never seen a naked elvan before. Her otherworldly all-black eyes swallowed him whole, like a beckoning shadow pool, as he entered the alcove.

Her Wyldenar accent was softly inviting as she looked upon him in dared hope. "Are you my champion I called for?"

He looked over to the Daynish usher beside him with a confused glance at the startling question. "Leave us," he commanded, and the royal appointee obliged with a bow and left him with the umbran alone.

"Lilealah. I have always wondered what you might look like. You hear stories, but …" He observed her in full, mesmerized by her aura of palpable evil, assuaged by sheer perfection. Why his father would allow this enemy to arbitrate her own fate was beyond any logical reasoning he could warrant. Almost stuttering, he murmured, "Why am I your chosen?"

With perceptible fatigue etched into her tone, she purred, "I want what you want."

He coerced his noble mind to stay virtuous to that implication. Female umbran were fabled seductresses. All his life, he had grown on the tales of the past and how they bewitched the entire Aggedonian civilization over time. And now here he was, getting lost in her soulless eyes as he studied them. "The leader of my enemy wants what I want? Doubtful." He found his courage once again as he shook the spell taking over him. "I want the qin eradicated for good."

The lethargic elvan offered a supple smile to Ondrew. "Yes, Prince of Barredom. I simply want to take my people on the Great Exodus, to our new home."

She had him at "Prince of Barredom."

"Our migration had already begun just before my capture. But my people need me to lead the departure."

Your people? We are not going into Artopia or Tundura, the realms of Wyldenar elven, Ondrew thought to counter with. But he already knew that the umbran were exiles and even enemies of their former elvankind. The Wyldenar tribes of Tundura, to the northeast of Aggedon, actively hunted them down and slew all qindrid on sight. The reclusive Artopian Wyldenar, westward from the enemy lands, held a pact to never allow the umbran back across their borders, and often dispatched rogue-elvan assassins who sought out redemption to seek out their deaths. "So tell me the meaning of this Great Exodus, then."

"You have heard of the Thrench Empire and of the dreaded Ashenwave, no doubt."

Of all the things she could have said, he would have lost any wager if projecting she would have countered with such an irrelevant theme. "House Emmonost?" Ondrew incredulously asked. The Ashenwave was a reputed alias for the nefarious royal house of the distant Thrench Empire. "Naval marauders who plague the western seas? Those who invade, destroy, and enslave isles of the elven? No threat to the north. Why fear something so far-fetched and far away rather than the immediate enemy at your doorstep, and even more so now with the Az'Dayne Dominadom aiding in our invasion?" He was genuinely lost.

"Some things I am sworn to and will keep privy, but you will not,

Prince. But I will tell you that the Ashenwave has already begun their engulfing tide with invasions through eastern qindrid lands. Helderak and Sho Kung are just the first to suffer the wrath of their wave. Since their breach of the Vist, after founding New Throng, they now have new allies in their fleet. The Emmonost conquests swallow all like the savage seas of the Torrent storms." The look in her eyes and tone in her voice beckoned like a tragic plea. "Once the skyborne of these lands are vanquished, they will next make their assault on Caelduym, and then come for the stoneborne of the north. They already prepare an offense at the borderlands of Blood Beach."

He stood musing, contemplating the many theories about the Vist and how the Thrench Empire ever dared to test their chances through it. For the pious, the magical mist rim was considered a forbidden gateway into the Godslands, and suicide of the soul to enter. It was irreparable sacrilege of one's faith even to try it. In the elvan cultures, they named the speculated realm past its borders the Beyond and believed in a parallel ethereal plane that overlapped it, where their souls went to rest in the afterlife. But allegedly, House Emmonost was shaking religious philosophies across Penthara with a tidal wave of new discoveries. They had taken half of their near-infinite navy through the western borders of the mystical fog and established a new nation in the east, conquering the tropical river lands of Julkunda as New Throng.

Ondrew narrowed his eyes at his captivating enemy and sighed a deep breath, shaking his head in disbelief. "So this Great Exodus is a journey for the Aggedonians to abandon their homeland, the grounds of their ancestors, and hand it over for Barredom's free taking? And join with the Caelduyan skyborne against the Thrench to ultimately save their qin race as a people?"

Ondrew needed to say it all aloud to fathom how this permitted migration might conclude in a peaceful fruition. "How could you possibly have coerced such a movement? What happens to us, settled in Aggedon after you and your new Caelduyan allies defeat the Thrench invasion? It does not bode well for an armistice without war for long."

The enthralling witch returned a pacifying grin, enlightening him with her tranquil voice. "This migration consensus was no flower that blossomed overnight. The idea for the Great Exodus began with a seed of fear, gradually nourished season after season, grown cycle through cycle, until finally the tree and its branches reached across all of Aggedon. It took years, but it has begun. The qindrid majority now follow me and the umbran of eastern Aggedon. Even the greyborne have joined, save for a few stubborn clans."

Ondrew pondered her underlying endgame. His eyes scrutinized her own, judging her thoughts for possible future betrayals, but how could one discern anything through void orbs of total darkness?

As if she could read his mind, she sensually uttered back to him, "I need you to trust me. If you agree to do this, no more Barredish lives need be sacrificed. This timeless war will have an end. Barredom will have Aggedonian lands for new resources. Your father, no more need for a partial sovereignty under Az'Dayne. Through careful politicking, King Roth can arrange a royal marriage to keep his alliance with Az'Dayne to maintain the peace. And you will be the champion of Frostdale who brought this to attainment. The one who led the umbran and all of their qindrid from Aggedon. You will see Ondrew Roth restored as prince, rightful heir to your throne, and your name will become ageless in the annals of heroes for all time." Her lewd enunciations transformed into an inspiring climax by the end of her stirring spiel.

"You spin quite the tale." Ondrew created some distance between them, leaning against the wall. His eyes scoped out her exposed body, and he did not try to hide it this time. "You are accustomed to seducing men with their desires, aren't you? You will now answer me a few truths to gain my trust, then."

"Ask what you will of me, Prince," she teased, perceptibly gaining confidence that she could erotically lure him in like the weaker men she had turned before.

She was still his foe, and she needed to hear in his voice that he felt it. "Your capture. It makes no sense." His tone demanded respect and an urgency to end her farce with the seduction attempts. He stood straight again, close to her face, but this time with an impervious will behind his visage. "Why would you be so close to Northaven with so small an escort in the open? And my uncle's apprehension, almost as if he knew you were among them. This was all arranged, was it not?"

"I knew you would be well educated, but never dared hope you would prove to be so clever. Of course." She shot him a weary grin of satisfaction. "On every journey I made, I had your uncle's soldiers after me, or even specialists, like the Westwalker. And furthermore, every venture in which I strayed from protected lands put me through the Glace Isles king's ambushes, which were always inevitably waiting for me. It has been an unyielding toil of my enemies. And I am tired, Prince. I knew I could dispose of both enemies by getting word to your father to orchestrate my safe capture and lead the Terollar into an ambush of my own."

"You mean to have me believe that the Chosen Troll of the Glace Isles was among the Terollar taken in the ambush?" Ondrew was far more astonished by that paramount revelation than when she had first mentioned the outlying Thrench as her people's most eminent threat. "This is a critical testimony! Why has this news not been brought to the heralds?"

"I saw him fall, executed by beheading, a willful killing by his alpha, Jrulthun." The fatigue-beaten temptress closed her eyelids, flickering on the verge of fainting from the numbing drain of her limp upper limbs. "He knelt as his Glazjhendun encircled him. He accepted his loss as his final fate. They ritualistically burned his body before the Northaven soldiers could make it down the hill. It was almost as if it were all meticulously premeditated." She drifted off again but this time seemingly in pondered skepticism.

"But then again, decems of attempts have been made on his life by his own tribesven, including those of his own roots. His axes were recovered, and his son, Zuulzin, seized with the rest. Your Royal Inquisitor has been informed."

Khomo'Jhuvonus dead? Even thinking the full name in his mind sent a shudder down his spine. None in Barredom ever spoke the name aloud, for suspicious fear that it would conjure his presence. *Zuulzin, his last son, in custody? And Jrulthun too? Celebrities among trolls in our chains. The war may truly be over on all sides, praise the Five and Five,* Ondrew mused to his faith, astonished at the outstanding news. "A pity the orders are for me to take you this very eve. Our departure is to be secretive. You could do well with Lady Bayn, procuring information from those in the Deeps."

"And end up being tortured myself?" she scoffed with a disapproving chuckle at the ludicrous idea. "All in Aggedon know of your Royal Inquisitor. It was part of my bargain for capture that I would never meet her. My advice to her is simple: Ask no questions. Burn them all and be done with it."

"So, then, let us talk details about your clandestine escort." There was still the necessary facets to debate on how he was supposed to sneak the most precious prisoner ever taken by Barredish hands past the vengeful soldiers holding the northlands, away from additional expectant troll ambushes, and out of sight of the greyborne clans who were against the umbran loyalists. "It seems the Norther Knights have been assigned as smugglers to move dangerous contraband out of Barredom and through Aggedon unseen. And that contraband is you, witch."

"Please, call me Lilealah." She finally formally introduced herself. "Unchain me, then, Prince Ondrew Roth, and I am yours. I will tell you all that you need, and why this is the only way."

Ondrew took the key given to him and did just that. He unlocked the shackles and delicately eased the naked prodigy down from the pentacrux. He held her limp body to brace against his shoulder and the wooden cross behind her.

"Begin, then, Lilealah." His tone altered to one of great grief and shame. "But know that my name is no longer Prince, nor Roth."

"We will change that," Lilealah promised.

EBRIELLE (I)

MY DIVINE

The twin royal mares of House Bayn propelled the silver-leafed coach through the cobblestone drive of Castle Frostdale's promenade. Upon both doors to the carriage was engraved the Blackendale coat of arms, a dead green tree against a black shield. Her father had taught her that it signified the truth that all things patient find a way to survive and heal, even throughout the coming Umbra.

Such was the lineage of Lady Ebrielle Blackendale, only daughter of Lady Honorah Bayn, the Royal Inquisitor. Her father, Lord Lucas Blackendale, had been an illustrious huntsman and decorated Barredom soldier before he had been reported as slain by Terollar from the Glace Isles on the cusp of her seventh bornday.

She sadly reasoned that she hadn't been able to visualize his face for years, but it was the smell of the musk on his armor and the strength of his paternal embrace before departing with the army that she would ever evoke from memory. A jolt from the wheel passing over a missing stone in the cobbled path shook the reminisced apparition, and she was all the more thankful for the flawed street afterward.

Ebrielle sat alone in the concealed coach cabin traveling down the rocky pavement of Frostdale toward the city's main gates. She had dressed specially for this occasion, as suitable for a lady as she had in months. She had festooned herself in an elegant silvery corset dress trimmed with dark green lace and matching openwork on the hem of the skirt. She had adorned her meager collar line and wrists with her mother's jeweled fineries passed down. Her blond hair had done away with the braid she was mandated to wear by her mother in court and was styled properly in a fashionable Barredish bun up high to accentuate her slender neck.

Today was the day she reunited with her brother. He would no doubt be with her cousin and uncle and aunt, with whom she was accustomed to staying as her guardianship family who had raised them after their father's death. Only since the town crier had declared the announcement of the apprehended in Northaven's newest victory had she been called to the castle's court by her mother. Ebrielle much preferred the quiet grace of her uncle Tomas's countryside estate to the undesirable pandemonium of the city keep.

But she was keen for its aromatic delights and charming curiosities. A fragrance trace whiffed through the carriage window, coercing her to draw the veiling curtain, hiding the outside world. An exotic Khalimishe smoke tent neighboring a Tairancian perfume shop passed by her coach. She involuntarily turned her head to watch the outlandish sensations fade in the opposite direction to her passage.

"The troll king is dead! The troll king is dead! All rejoice! The troll king is dead!" broadcasted the town crier. It was a day of celebration throughout all of Barredom's cities and villages.

A troupe of multicolored jugglers and fire dancers swaying against the esplanade's citizen path meshed with Barredish revelers and gleeful drunkards. Daynish noblemen and ladies pranced in the city streets alongside, each in their eccentric and unique identifying masques. The Castle Frostdale she had grown up to know was not the one she beheld now. Az'Dayne had brought with it so many foreign wonders and tasteful appeals since the conversion to its sovereignty.

Ebrielle remembered a year ago, when the unspeakable deed was done by the king, in a way that seemed like more than half the citizens would fall into mutiny and rebel, or even murder the poor relegated monarch. But that front had withered fast, and now one could spot no such revolutionaries, excluding possibly the Norther Knights.

Az'Dayne was thick in Frostdale now, with its mix of capital citizens from its metropolitan realm, and with it the neighboring allies from many countries in its ever-far-reaching clutches.

Ebrielle knew, however, that such an exhibit of splendid outlanders within her walls was for but one purpose. Az'Dayne had announced, in honored veneration of Barredom's new allegiance, to hold the new cycle's Paladin Trials in Castle Frostdale this year, commencing within the pentday.

As she neared the castle's main gates, her excitement practically shoved her from the guided coach. Her brother, Aerik, and her cousin Henrick would be joining the Trials to become paladin initiates as official royal invitees. Her carriage was nearing the drawbridge waypoint for the scheduled arrival of her brother and family. And there she saw them. Ebrielle shouted to her coachman, and she bounced from her enclosed perch to tackle her brother from his high steed. "Aerik!"

Her brother burst into laughter and met her embrace with an instant dismount from his horse. Her uncle, aunt, and cousin, all shortly behind, joined in on the reunion. Only two months, but two months too long; she hadn't seen them since the beginning of Kingfall, and that was a far stretch for their devoted bond. If only she could have felt the same relationship with her own mother, she lamented as she hugged her family.

Aerik looked her over and shook his head in disapproval, never dropping the genuine smile from his face. "Oh, Brie, and here I thought Mother dressed you in Frostdale! Have the dungeons made her go blind, to let you out so? I fear I'll be striking down an improper lord or two before the Trials even begin!"

The flattery from her younger brother made her blush, since she secretly loathed her mother's mundane wardrobe. She had never truly known how her mother could have seduced her father in their time, unless he had pursued her for her royal name. She jested back in full honesty, "One never knows what knight a fair lady might attract at the Trials, Aerik. You must swear your first oath to your sister that you will introduce me to your new friends!" She smiled and innocently kissed her smooth-faced sibling on the cheek.

Her younger brother, barely over a year her junior, had been preordained for great things from his bornday. On the year that Aerik Roth had become king of Barredom, fourteen years ago, her brother, at the age of three, was brought before the new king by her father, and with the sovereign's blessing, Lucas changed his son's name to that of the king—such was not an unheard-of practice in Barredom among rich lords who owed favors to the crown. Ebrielle was too young to have remembered such a ceremony, but simply knowing that she had indeed been there, in those regal halls at the time of her brother's royal blessing, was all she needed. She would forever lend support to Aerik to do grand things. They were both fated for a tale far brighter than the one their mother intended to paint for their future.

They leisurely traversed the bustling promenade with carriage and steeds in tow. They made small talk during their stroll through the bazaar, sampling foreign cuisine and fingering baubles as they lightly exchanged stories of the past and current gossip.

As they went deeper into the marketplace, an approaching melody broke their train of conversation. The unified trot of the six riders swelling the streets behind them came across just as harmonious as the song they played. The beat of the horse hooves against the cobblestone pavement was as if the mares were trained for the circus, their iron shoes acting as drums to the variety of instruments playing.

The six were each armed differently: a long tabor, a tambourine and some shell-shaped device unknown to her, a lap harp, some form of shawm, a flute, and a lute. The others were all shadows on a wall compared to the striking, red-haired light of the troupe member who played the lute as he sang:

You, sir, there,
Here we are, the unfinished.
Do you hear me now?
Destiny's cry ... say dare we try!

The six minstrels sauntered directly beside Ebrielle and her family, near the pastry house where they stood on the patron terrace. She investigated something explicitly peculiar about this group of seeming troubadours. The five men and one girl all retained a large, identical longbow paired with a full quiver across their green-cloaked backs. All were young, perhaps slightly older than Aerik and herself. These were not just minstrels.

The impossibly handsome singer continued his heavenly ode. His piercing, fire-kissed eyes found hers and locked on as he slowed his troupe and sang to her.

O'er here, my lord,
We've yet come so far.
Do you see me now?
Sun in my sky ... oh, it is aye!

He was noticeably startled and annoyed by his flute-toting companion's smack of the instrument pipe across the back of his neck. The young girl in the group, remarkably unattractive, Ebrielle thought to herself, interjected with the interruption performed by the one with the flute. "Oh, Kyson, so we gonna be takin' her with us, then?"

Kyson countered with but a slow trot daringly closer to her. His perfect smile was spellbinding, and she felt herself dizzy with a flush of heat to her forehead and sweat building in places she had never felt it before. She could feel her protective brother and cousin shifting behind her, but the streets of Frostdale and all its ambience had faded into a blur. Only Kyson and herself existed in this castle of theirs.

Another anonymous impatient from his group spoke up to sever their dreamscape. "Southland's done made us late by nearly a pent by sidetrackin' us through Frostdale! 'Twasn't even on the way, and we've hearin' the Norther Knights moved on four moons back!"

Her newly fated love broke their trance with an overly dramatic frown and shot back behind him, "Aye, our first time through Frostdale, and likely your last. Sightseeing and joyriding and taste-touching is all we'll bring with us out of this cold world. And I enjoy seeing such sights. The joy of a good ride. To touch. And to taste."

She thought she may faint or explode but wasn't sure which one first. A clutter of questions invaded her fantasy. This man was obviously a divine not of this realm.

His horse loomed directly over her now, and his exotic amber eyes stared down into hers. She could feel Aerik's firm hand on her shoulder and see the silhouette of her brother at her side, but he was still a faint illusion to the reality of Kyson so near to her.

Kyson plucked a silver arrow trinket from his vest, half the size of a pocket dagger, and gifted it softly into her grasp. Her mother had her well versed in six languages, but all it took was this one man to make her forget them all, as no words found their way past the lump in her throat. Her heart was beating so heavily, she was sure Kyson was about to strike her dead with a kiss. She would not survive it.

His gentle touch slipped from her hand as his steed trekked backward to his troupe. And at last he spoke to her, his gaze never leaving her own awestruck stare. "Until I return, my divine."

Kyson graciously bowed from atop his horse, and the six strangers departed from her perfect daydream down the streets. She heard one or more announce the same thing: "Make way for the Timberhands! To the Norther Knights we go!"

You sir, there,
Evermore, the unfinished.
Can you feel me yet?
Death's kiss, but why ... is this goodbye?

Her lover's sweetly celestial voice paled into the promenade. She held on firmly to the silver arrow token and was immune to any attempt at family banter for the remainder of the day. She could not be cured until she saw him again.

WESTWALKER (III)

THE FOURTEEN

A ghostly fog combatted the mouth of the great isthmus, feebly attempting to devour the archaic structures that posed beyond it. This was the entrance to the world-renowned land bridge that served as the contested boundary between the two warring countries of Aggedon and Barredom. Continents' Kiss stretched across as over fourteen leagues of frozen stone and ice that connected the land masses of North Taira and Central Taira.

From his vantage, he could see it now through the futility of the cold mist, the Fourteen in all its foreboding glory. Titled to honor the original clan chieftains that founded the nation of Aggedon, the formerly impervious fortress had secured the nickname from its southern enemies.

In ancient times, the whole of the northern region, with the land bridge at its center, was recognized as Aggea. But after the stoneborne takeover, the clans that acceded to become qindrid remained north of the Kiss, claiming it evermore as Aggedon. Those who defied the turn took to south of the Kiss and united with neighboring kingdoms for aid, which subsequently became hailed as the country of Barredom.

The union of the fourteen clans that transcended into stoneborne came to be called the Aggedonian Alliance. And as such, in regard for their history, the Aggedonians constructed fourteen enormous statues to sentinel the south end of the elongated stronghold in idolization of the founding chieftains. Those same elaborate monuments were later erected across the northern mouth of the Kiss as well, after Barredom's establishment of Northaven on Aggedonian soil.

Four of the fourteen monuments made themselves visible to the small reconnaissance team at the peak. The field in their forward proximity had always been recorded as being rife with enemy soldiers. The bulk of the main Aggedonian forces had been stationed at the Fourteen, both stoneborne and greyborne, and all loyal to Lilealah. But now only the wailing of banshee winds from the Kiss made a pretense of life.

Tsuno flashed a glance to Ryleohk and the Barredish men next to him. Scoutmaster Thade had been steadfast in his resolve to remain at the camp a day's ride back, under strict orders to await the Boarneck mercenary company. But after a pentday and still no sign of the cavaliers, Tsuno's initiative to proceed without them had gone unchallenged.

The scoutmaster had brought with him nine other specialist rangers, though two of the youths had been left back with the horses at the cave camp in hopes the Boarneck Cavaliers would decide to finally join them and proceed with their paid contract. Tsuno knew each to be as proficient in survival skills as he was, but none of them were honed engineers of death. They were esteemed scouts but not warriors. If any presence of the enemy remained, it would be up to the Wyldenar and himself to defend against any true threat.

All could see the colossal pyramid ornamenting the core of the fortress several miles back with the aid of the latitude descent of the land bridge from one continent to the next. Many might argue that it wasn't the legendary statues or the stronghold's gargantuan stretch, but it was the pyramid alone that gave the Fourteen its menacing reputation. The pentagonal behemoth was fifty floors of otherworldly awe.

"So, this is it, then," came a whispered interruption to the dreadful silence among the group. Tsuno hadn't registered the name of the scout who spoke, but he did regard the response from Thade that sharply returned.

"The dreaded Fourteen. Unless we are now ghosts of the fog, none of this makes sense. We should have seen remnants of the qin by now," Thade quietly explained, more to himself for reasoning the conundrum than to anyone in particular.

Tsuno offered the answer he was sure these men already well

knew. "They are gone."

Thade and the other scouts stared upon Tsuno as if he were some street priest with all the solutions to life's questions. Tsuno kept his scrutiny ahead, dissecting the obscure terrain with his eyes, piece by piece. A grin eased onto his face, and he continued. "They are all gone. And so is Ryleohk."

Tsuno sprang up from the snow trench the group huddled in and jogged straight toward the fortress. He knew the rangers would be too befuddled to move, between registering where Ryleohk had disappeared to and the foolhardy act he had just brazenly darted into.

If there remained a skeleton contingent of the army on lookout, it was too late now. Tsuno knew he was a dead man, already past the outer palisade. But his self-assuring intuition told him otherwise, that no perils would be found on this excursion onto the Kiss.

His perceptive eyes never lost track of the stealthy rogue-elvan who had successfully slipped from the rangers in the trench. Tsuno endeavored to find a trace of footsteps to mirror his companion. But he felt all the fool for the futility in his attempt, quickly appreciating the nature of his unlikely ally. Wyldenar left no footprints, of course. The snows behind Ryleohk's wake were utterly virgin, as if not a corporeal soul had denatured its unsullied icy skin.

On his jaunt through the perimeter defenses, his route brought him before one of the grand statues. The others stretched away in parallel ranks, each uniquely sculpted in honor of a founding chieftain.

"Erod Thalbear, the South Slayer." The inscription was carved into the monument's base. The figure towered at least fourteen men high, painstakingly fashioned to immortalize the revered overlord as he had stood in life. Tsuno recognized the name, though the man had died decades before the Westwalker first set foot in Aggedon.

Clan Thalbear. The same as Landron and Michayle... and those I dispatched in the Ichean.

This was farther into the Fourteen than Tsuno had ever ventured. Ahead, an open gateway waited without a lowered portcullis or guarded barbican. The abandoned fortress seemed almost inviting, daring intruders through its lone northern entrance.

Even stripped of its defenders, the Fourteen's scale was staggering. Layered walls, towering watchposts, and broad killing grounds stretched across the width of Continents' Kiss, all engineered to funnel invaders through this single approach. It was a fortress built with the certainty that no enemy would ever breach it. Without siege engines or climbing equipment, there had never been another way in.

Ryleohk casually poised at the opening to the corridor, holding a peculiar parchment. The elvan passed it over, and Tsuno scrutinized it while Thade and the other scouts made their belated jog to catch up to them. "A map of the Fourteen in detail."

By the time Scoutmaster Thade and the other rangers caught up, Tsuno had already begun studying it.

Thade frowned. "Why would the greys leave a layout where anyone could find it?"

Tsuno traced the north chambers with a finger. "They didn't."

The scoutmaster looked unconvinced.

"This section isn't meant for an enemy." Tsuno pointed to the first halls beyond the entrance. "It's for their own people. Greyborne born into the Qindrid Curse, who never chose transcendence for themselves. These chambers teach them what it means to become stoneborne before they are permitted deeper into the fortress."

Thade considered the revelation before ordering two rangers to remain near the statues as messengers should the party fail to return—or if the Boarnecks finally arrived. The rest split into pairs, advancing in staggered formation. He returned the map to Tsuno and together they entered.

According to the map, the sprawling complex ahead was simply called the Maze. The Maze introduced newcomers to the five elements—water, tairan, fire, sky, and shadow—and the role each played within stoneborne doctrine. The architects had built these halls less as defenses than as a pilgrimage.

Aggedonians and Barredish alike descended from the ancient Aggeans, humans born of tairan and shadow lineage. But centuries had divided their beliefs. The Barredish had embraced the wider civilized world, while the Aggedonians had surrendered themselves to their umbran masters, becoming ageless stoneborne. Here, their elemental ancestry had become religion.

Massive columns divided the first chamber into broad aisles. Every wall was covered in pictographs and runic carvings arranged with deliberate purpose, recounting stories, lessons, or perhaps both.

"What do they say?" Thade asked quietly. "You're qindrid. Is this your tongue?"

Tsuno barely concealed his irritation. "It is not my alphabet," he answered flatly. "I am more foreign here than you."

Beyond the chamber waited fourteen doorways, each marked by different pictographic symbols. Following Thade's plan, the scouting party divided. The scoutmaster led one pair to the right while the others explored the center passages. Tsuno and Ryleohk chose the left.

They entered a long hall whose pictographs required little interpretation. Snowstorms, white bears, ice whales, and frozen corpses gave way to depictions of disease before the sequence concluded with symbols of darkness and shadow.

The adjoining passages converged into the next tier of the Maze. The moment Tsuno stepped onto the black stone floor, a familiar chill reached through his body. Though no longer vulnerable to the cold as he had been as a human, he still felt its presence.

The chamber had been built entirely from *ebonice*. The walls, floor, and low ceiling gleamed with the mirror sheen unique to the unnatural substance. Ebonice was a phenomenon found only in select northern waters during the Umbra season, a solid black ice that could never melt.

Four plinths occupied the center of the room, though only one still held its intended relic—a solitary tome.

Green flames burned steadily atop enchanted candles arranged around the displays. Tsuno recognized them as *wyrefire*. The candles were fashioned from wax secreted by insects that fed upon the elven of Teralloe Forest. Their wax retained traces of the Terollar's supernatural regenerative properties, passing them into the wick itself. Such candles were exceedingly rare, worth fortunes in the greatest cities of the realm.

Ryleohk spared the chamber barely a glance before moving on.

Tsuno remained behind long enough to open the book. Written in Norspeak, it explored the shadow element through the nature of cold, recounting how Aggedon had embraced winter itself as its greatest weapon against southern kingdoms. It spoke at length on the importance of the Umbra season to their people.

He closed the cover thoughtfully. *Why leave this behind?*

The next chamber stood open to the sky, its high walls admitting shafts of morning light while deep shadows still pooled across the floor. Empty shelves circled the room, broken only by meditation blankets surrounding another lone podium.

Another surviving tome, Tsuno noticed. This one spoke of concealment, darkness, and the properties of shadow. It also recorded every known Wyldenar umbran to have existed within Aggedon. Again, the relic remained untouched. The pattern unsettled him.

Rather than lingering in every chamber, Tsuno and Ryleohk pressed deeper through the Maze. Libraries stripped of nearly every artifact, meditation halls, and abandoned sanctuaries blended together, each devoted to the same doctrine. Everywhere, the stoneborne celebrated cold, shadow, immortality, and absolute devotion to their umbran masters.

One chamber alone differed. It was part library and part laboratory, it housed dozens of surviving books beside sealed specimens of diseased animals preserved in glass. Blood still stained an open dissection table.

Tsuno leafed through the largest volume. It detailed the transformation into a qindrid, explaining how transcendence forever freed stoneborne from sickness and disease. This was nothing new to him. Skyborne, stoneborne, and greyborne alike shared that blessing.

Beyond the archive, the Maze opened into a central pentagonal crossroads connecting the surrounding routes. Tsuno continued left, following the course he had begun.

The final passages led through a burial crypt honoring revered stoneborne. Each tomb bore only a brief inscription recording its occupant's title, greatest deed, and glorious death before the halls opened into the Chamber of Enlightenment.

Tapestries filled the vast triangular room. One depicted the Rite of Transcendence, showing a human surrendering to an umbran to become qindrid. Another portrayed the ageless immortality granted by the bond. The third celebrated the stoneborne's freedom from sleep itself.

Had Ryleohk possessed more patience, Tsuno might have returned to study the abandoned archives more carefully. Instead, the rogue was already waiting at the exit. Moments later, fresh air replaced the stale stillness of the sacred halls as they emerged from the Maze.

The map placed them between the sacred halls and the North Keep. A narrow passage east led toward the northern camps, the only approach into the keep itself. High corbels jutted from the towering walls, while machicolations replaced the parapets above, allowing defenders to rain death upon any force that reached this far.

When they arrived among the deserted encampments, Tsuno stopped Ryleohk. "I am not fond of the Barredish either," he said, "but this mission is different. Search the tents for anything of value. I won't proceed without the scoutmaster."

The grey elvan answered with little more than an irritated huff, casting a glance toward the distant homeland he had long ago forsaken before disappearing among the tents.

Tsuno watched him for a moment. He knew Ryleohk understood the Civil tongue. What he had never understood was why the Wyldenar refused to answer in any language at all. As expected, no reply came.

Barely half an hour later, Thade and the remaining scouts emerged from the Maze unharmed.

"I thought you would be ahead," the scoutmaster admitted, still visibly shaken. "Those tapestries..." He struggled to meet Tsuno's eyes. "Is that truly what you endured?"

Tsuno dismissed the thought before it could awaken old memories. "Did anything you found explain this place?"

"Our route centered on the tairan lineage of the stoneborne," Thade replied. "Their gifts...their beliefs."

Aye, and mine was centered on their shadow descendancy. But that was not what concerned his curiosity. "The books?"

"Yes. I opened those I saw. That is what took me so long to reach you. I have so much more" —Thade seemed almost nervous to be in Tsuno's presence—"admiration for you, Westwalker."

More like fear of me. I can see it in each of your miserable faces. You are scared of me. Tsuno ignored the compliment.

"They left them. The archives. Their histories. Their teachings." Tsuno's gaze swept over the silent fortress surrounding them. "These people treasured their doctrine above all else. Why abandon it for their enemies?"

The scoutmaster offered no answer. Tsuno doubted he had considered the question at all. Thade had been brainwashed into merely being a reconnaissance tool for Northaven. He would report what he saw and nothing more. This country was full of mindless soldiers.

"Leave it for now." He unfolded the map. "Send two rangers to inspect Black Bay Port. Northaven reports it abandoned, but we confirm everything ourselves. They can wait here for our return."

Thade immediately relayed the order, and the remaining party advanced through the North Keep.

For the first time since entering the Fourteen, the architecture resembled a conventional fortress. Murder holes overlooked the entrance passages, barracks lined the inner courts, and training grounds stood deserted, their practice dummies and exercise frames left exactly where soldiers had last abandoned them. Beyond them spread rows of stone-and-ice dwellings, all silent beneath the endless northern wind.

Everywhere they walked, the same impossible truth confronted them. An army had vanished.

The four continued south, skirting the prison compounds before reaching Troll Port, whose harbor overlooked the Bay of Trolls. Tsuno and Thade approached the cliff's edge. Below, the harbor lay utterly empty. No ships. No movement. Only crashing waves and drifting frost.

A sudden blast of icy wind slammed into the scoutmaster, knocking him backward onto the frozen stone. Tsuno merely smirked and offered him a hand. The negative effects of wind no longer held dominion over him.

Gathering once more around the map, they identified the final landmarks. The great pyramid dominated the center of the fortress, surrounded by the North-Central Keep, reserve camps, prison compounds, southern defenses, and both military ports. Even amid the immensity of the Fourteen, the colossal structure commanded every eye.

Again they divided. Two scouts departed to survey the surrounding districts. Tsuno, Ryleohk, Thade, and Lionel crossed through the North-Central Keep toward the elevated bailey that cradled the legendary pyramid.

The monument rose before them in the form of a perfect pentagon, its northern point facing directly toward Continents' Kiss. Four of its faces had been fashioned from pale stone. The fifth was something altogether different. Forged entirely from flawless ebonice, the northeastern face reflected the muted daylight like polished obsidian, throwing the dim northern sun back across the fortress in shimmering black light.

Broad steps encircled the structure, climbing toward a single entrance set within the ebonice wall. Tsuno led the ascent. At last, the reconnaissance party crossed the threshold into the most sacred place in all of Aggedon.

There were no elaborate corridors, no additional flights of stairs to upper levels, no pathways into lower chambers, and no windows to divert the trespassers from the marvel beheld within. It had been so long since Tsuno had witnessed anything like what was before him.

"Fuck me, by all the Fives," Lionel gasped.

"Westwalker." Thade whispered so low his voice was near-inaudible. "Is this a ..." The scoutmaster's query faded before he finished his assumption.

It was as if they had stepped into another region, far away from the frigid north. The whole of the pyramid's vast interior was pleasantly cool in temperature, like that of some Tairancian forest. Two elemental anomalies conquered the capacious bowels of the lair's entirety. Identifiably natural yet mystically aberrant in the same sense, these totems seemed like things summoned only in dreams.

On one side stood a great tree, gnarled and twisted in the most bizarre contortions. The diagonal walls and pentagonal floor plan were conjoined with its live roots, and lush vines intermingled throughout sporadic ore deposits. At its canopy, the tree stretched its crown to shape an archway that merged into another tairan form. The thick branches at the top were infused into a counterarching rock formation, a mass of minerals and mundane gemstones native to the north. The bizarre conglomeration was an impractical phenomenon, but nevertheless, it stood as tangible as the floor beneath them. Together the warped, outlandish tree and the eccentric rock cluster modeled a makeshift doorway of sorts through their arch.

"You are looking at a wyrmway," Tsuno confirmed. "An elemental portal made by the umbran."

It was exactly what Tsuno had predicted. Wyrmways were ancient gateways manifested by the original Shiniryn umbran and the latter Wyldenar umbran.

Each wyrmway could only open during the furrow before the Umbra or the furrow before the season it was built in correlation to. Furrows were the intermittent days between seasons that were unassigned to any particular month—neutral recesses of seasonal transition. Each wyrmway was also only capable of transporting travelers to a single assigned destination, to which the portal was linked. All types of qindrid and umbran could pass through wyrmways when they were open, but humans and elven who had not taken the turn could not.

Thade apprehensively stepped up next to Tsuno, shoulder to shoulder, and whispered, "Can you see the other side? Where does it lead?"

He educated the scoutmaster. "We are midseason during the Dawning. The wyrmway is closed for now. The furrow that it was open in has passed."

The young scout followed with his own concerns. "So that is how the greys have disappeared from the Fourteen. We have our answer. But why did they go?"

Why indeed? An enigma of a puzzle with missing pieces. "That answer is an elusive prey, obscure for now. But I do know where this portal leads."

Thade and Lionel gazed upon Tsuno in complete focus, as if the unnatural oddities had never been present directly in front of them. Ryleohk, on the other hand, began to further investigate the archway portion that consisted of the tree, ignoring the banter as usual. Tsuno continued. "It is said among the qindridkind that four wyrmways exist in Aggedon, just as four also are placed in all of the realms of shadow descendancy, of both humans and elven. Of the human regions, four each are hidden among Aggedon, Vellyon, Caelduym, and even the subterranean Psaegora. In the elvan countries, they have been placed among the lands of Tundura, Starfell, the Kol'Kolar, and underneath Cabernus."

"I always believed they were simply tales of old women for children's fancies." Lionel was awed by the revelation.

"Of course they are real," Thade chastised him. "We are in the presence of the Westwalker. Even newborn babes in the north know that he has used them in the past to get to our lands."

Tsuno looked at his fellow scouts with a coy grin and shrugged, nodding. He pointed one hand to the twisted tree, then the other to the stone mass. "These arches, they are tributes, both formed of the tairan element. You can always tell where the portal will lead based on this. Aggedon is the human country of tairan and shadow descendancy. This portal leads to its mirror in the elvan region. Tundura, the homeland of the Wyldenar elven."

The two rangers were still confused. Thade aspired to clarity. "Lilealah escorted the entirety of the Fourteen's forces through this wyrmway to cross into the wylde lands? What in all the Fives for?"

The answer came with the screaming sound of an axe being hurled through the air. The weapon cracked with a splintering force into the trunk of the tree totem. Ryleohk growled like some feral beast as he ripped his axe free, tearing out a healthy chunk of bark with it. The Wyldenar kept his eyes low and departed from the pyramid without looking back at the others once.

"What's his trouble?" Thade worriedly probed.

"You said the name," Tsuno admitted. "Lilealah."

The scoutmaster was still just as lost. "What does he care if I mention the umbran?"

"She is his mother," Tsuno enlightened him. "And it is his life's destiny to hunt and kill her. A story for another time."

That disclosure silenced the room completely. No more questions were asked. There were many puzzle pieces yet to ponder over as to why the qindrid had migrated such a force into elvan lands, and why they had left behind their important archives. But they had been sent to scout, not conjecture. The job was done. Word would be sent to General Roth that for the first time in history, the legendary Fourteen of Aggedon now belonged to Barredom.

ONDREW (II)

THE TIMBERHANDS

Thirty-eight men stood outside the guild house on the iron-fenced hill, ready and eager to meet the last members of their fellowship who were approaching upon the paved knoll. Upon each of their sword arms, the men wore the green and black of the old Barredom kingdom, represented by a sash tied below the shoulder. Ondrew and his original twenty-three Norther Knights had also armed themselves with their prominent kite shields, each displaying House Roth's coat of arms, a fierce white bear against green pines in the backdrop, cast upon a black night sky.

Ondrew and his men had been waiting somewhat patiently for a pentday for the Whitewood archers. The Timberhands, they called themselves, or so it was claimed by those who endorsed them. They were bastards who had been abandoned to the Greene House orphanage in the Whitewood, leagues south of Barredom, on the edge of the Undawned Lands, the most northern segment of the Tenwoods.

Ondrew remembered when he had first heard of the six marksmen. Four seasons before, the Sunder of the prior cycle, word reached traveling merchants that traded through the Utamian Thoroughfare, Central Taira's principal highway, so named because the trade path stretched from Castle Frostdale in Barredom all the way south to Everdawn, the capital city of Az'Dayne. Traders brought tales that these six grown fosterlings had single-handedly eradicated a warren of ferahn that had reputedly razed several of the local villages. Stories told that the chameleon pack beasts slaughtered two of the small settlements, with not a soul left alive. Over two score of the ferahn fell to the Timberhands' arrows, with the beasts skinned and beheaded for all the villages of the Whitewood to see as proof.

The Timberhand name had grown from there. They were also celebrated for assisting in the defense of a distant fishing settlement in the Undawned Lands against the incursion of one of the taiga's barbarian tribes. They did all of this for what they believed was justice, never accepting monetary payment. Their code of responsibility to their homeland seemed close at heart to the creed of Ondrew and his Norther Knights, if ever he had heard of another.

Ondrew could hear the minstrels' odes ringing down the streets of Defiance long before their horses trotted into sight. *They may even be welcome for morale if they can learn to be on time,* he mulled to himself. The Timberhands reached the Norther Knights' member hall and halted before the ensemble of ardent adventurers. In unison, they took a synchronized bow from horseback, as if they had just concluded some theatrical drama.

Ondrew stood in front of his loyalists and inquired, "The Timberhands, I take it?"

An obvious answer, but courteous formalities were still necessary. They were not of Barredish blood. In truth, some of the bastards seemed of mixed descent, of likely more than one region.

Their spokesman proved to be the one carrying the lute. "We cordially apologize for the interlude in our quest, good lord. Your Timberhands have arrived."

Ondrew noted that he was a remarkably charming fellow, like some paragon found only in a playhouse at Goldgarden, not some village of uncivilized woodsmen. He appeared to be of the common Daynish and Khalimishe descent in his heritage—naturally tan skin and a head full of vibrant fiery locks. Wherever his parents hailed from, it was discernably close to those borders, or possibly the Everdawn capital itself.

Ondrew ignored his better judgment to comment on the delay and opted instead to begin with a commendation. "We have heard of nothing but good deeds of the renowned Whitewood archers. And I officially welcome your proposal to volunteer. But we commission no mercenaries here. We will need you to swear in and be dubbed as Norther Knights. Does each of you consent to this compromise?"

The archers seemed eager to be done with formalities and commence with the initiation. They likely hadn't traveled so far to commit if there were any residual hesitations. The troupe's singer again replied for the group. "And we have heard of nothing but good deeds of the illustrious Norther Knights. Whether we invade Neveril depths, raid the beaches of the Thrench, or assail the heart of Aggedon its very self, you have our song and arrows! So long as the cause ensures the realm bleeds a bit less, tell the Timberhands where to take your oaths, and our word is blood and gold!"

Ondrew noted the irony of his prediction: they would indeed be visiting the Neveril elvan depths soon. He observed that his men seemed pleased with the Timberhands' virtuous intent. "Aye, and allow me to indulge you on that charge. An invitation into your new guild house. Come. Acquaint yourselves first with your new brothers!"

With that, the Timberhands exchanged greetings and names with each of his entourage of knights errant. The two Vellyans were particularly disgruntled in attempting any courtesy toward the archers, for whatever reason. The troupe's orator was named Kyson. The lone female in the group was called Sarin. Each of the Timberhands had taken on the bastard surname of Greene, for the foster house in which they had been raised. He noticed more than one of the archers referred to Kyson by the slang name "Southland," likely due to his visibly interracial lineage of Khalimia.

Over forty strong now, the crew all stepped inside the private guild house. Ondrew escorted the six initiates to the war chambers, where a large map of Aggedon was strewn across a pentagonal table. Different wooden figurines were strategically placed over the map to symbolize the forces of General Randon Roth, or the surmised location of the enemy. Inside sat Lilealah, in all her rare beauty, with her arms chained under the table, sitting at the side across from the table's head seat. She was guarded by Broc BrKomak, Datron Ackhill, and Black Brigannor.

Ondrew stood by the chair at the head of the table and waited for the Timberhands to situate themselves inside the small council room. He motioned to the umbran shackled across from him and made sure he had the archers' attention. "Here sits our charge, Lilealah, the First Umbran of Aggedon. She and her former lifemate were responsible for many of those turned long ago, transforming Aggedon into the qindrid state it now lies cursed in. The collective clans known as the Lilealytes are her direct disciples," Ondrew gravely finished.

The girl in the troupe retorted, "You've brought us a practice target for an archery contest?" A few of the Timberhands chuckled at Sarin's jest. Kyson did not.

Neither did Ondrew. "You will each vow a sworn mandate to protect her at all costs. Your quest is to provide her safe escort to a rendezvous with her people, to allow her the continuance in leading the remaining qindrid followers on their migration out of Aggedon for good," he educated them in a scornful tone.

Ondrew could feel the pleased eyes of Lilealah upon him, but he refused to break away from his grim resolve and gaze back upon her. He knew she could sense the chink in his armor, but she had yet to reach it.

Kyson questioned for more information. "How are they leaving? And why not just release her back if she means to take them away from your borders? You mean to march her into the thick of the remaining enemy and hope it doesn't end in our demise? Elaborate, please, good lord. We Timberhands would know all that you know before we swear our lives to this endeavor."

Ondrew was not done explaining before the interjection. "There is a wyrmway. There, on the map, we have it drawn on the frozen lake bed. These act as elemental gates between this region and another. We must get her back to this portal in time so that she might meet with her people and finish their Great Exodus. If the Northaven soldiers find out we are releasing the head of the enemy, we may have a mutiny on our hands and an ended war renewed. She also has greyborne enemies in opposing clans, as well as the Glace Isles trolls out for her head."

Ondrew pointed about on the map as he continued. "Our Shaw brothers have experience as scouts through half of Zsolindal and have given us a full report on what to expect." He indicated the subterranean entrance on the west side of Continents' Kiss. "Zsolindal is a cavernous old Neveril tunnel system of sorts. Some ancient home to the subterranean elven, long vanquished by the north. We will embark on longships through the Black Bay to this marked entrance at the Kiss. The Shaws will lead us into these half-charted caverns, and we will journey through it to the exit we know to be here, somewhere in the mountains of Ur Dynelenox, near the southern Wyldewoods.

The frozen Iceway will act as a highway that will steer us out of the forest, across the Hroganyndale, and to the wyrmway on the lake. It will be an epic that births legends, worthy of writing songs about through the ages."

Ondrew smiled, hoping he had struck some chord of motivation in mentioning glory to the bards, but the astonished looks on the faces behind Kyson spoke of something else entirely. It appeared the picture he had painted only stirred feelings of doubt.

Kyson teased over a small pause before timidly agreeing. "Indeed. An epic if ever there was one." The lead minstrel looked up from the map to stare down Lilealah ahead of him. He seemed unaffected by her captivating beauty—an impressive feat to attempt, Ondrew mused to himself.

Kyson continued, making sure he had the scheme of the quest correct from Ondrew's synopsis. "So we lead this cocreator of the Barredish enemy back to the coagulation of her reputedly violent people, who hold a special loathing for all those south of the Kiss, with one of two things to become the outcome. One, we meet with this army at the portal, with the fair presumption that she could bring more of these hostiles back through, all in hopes that she does not betray our gullible company with an escort destined for a preplanned rally of her loyal clans to swiftly dispose of us all. And mayhap, if fortune smiles and cruel gods are kind, she only forces us to forsake our Norther Knights' vow to Barredom, ambushing us with more umbran in wait, and ultimately, we become turned ourselves into part of their cursed qindrid legion."

Kyson's eyes were wide in feigned fright as he took a deep breath between statements, and Ondrew's eyes narrowed in a glare at the disbelieving performer. The relentless bard went on. "Or two, at best, we bring her to this frozen lake, miraculously unscathed, across miles of greyborne-patrolled territory, and drop her off before this inevitable army arrives, bidding her farewell in high hopes that she retreats far away with her people indefinitely?"

Kyson's face went blank, barely waiting a second for Ondrew to possibly conjure a rebuttal as the minstrel finalized his prosecution. "Just making sure my merry band understands the unpromising plan and bleak possibilities of survival."

Ondrew didn't know how to respond to the sarcasm and the way Kyson made the entire quest seem like such an absurdity. He couldn't help the flush of anger controlling the scowl he fixed on the man. Just as the heat boiled into his neck and a stammer of arguable defenses quivered on his tongue, only the seething word "You" was verbalized from among Ondrew's furious thoughts.

He thought he might dismiss the six mocking archers from his hall on that instant, but then, unexpectedly, Kyson broke his stony look into the jolliest smile. Kyson raised his arms wide into the air and turned in a circle, keeping his hands outreached as if pleading for a brotherly embrace, and slammed his hands together for a dramatic clap. "Ah, my good lord, all a jest! We love it! An epic indeed, I say! Where do we sign? The Timberhands are ready to be Norther Knights!" Kyson laughed, and his comrades with him dropped their ploy of panic in the background and joined in the mirth.

Ondrew was a bit confused as to how to react, but the warmth did leave his face. He thought he might laugh infectiously, but he was still too muddled to even comprehend what was amusing. Evidently, his three Norther Knights near Lilealah shared his uncertainty toward these strange characters.

"Ye've brought us fuckin' madmen." Broc BrKomak stared at the lot incredulously as Sarin blew him back an inflated kiss for the remark.

Madmen indeed. But maybe we all are for signing up for this, Ondrew entertained.

After the merriment died down, Ondrew regarded the archers over the war table, saying in a serious tone, "All I can offer you is this. My father was ... My father is King Aerik of Barredom. I am his only heir. He accepted an audience to hear her plea, he heeded it, and he trusted in her. And he trusts in me to hold faith in his judgment. He would not send me to die. We will prevail on this quest. The Norther Knights will bring peace to the war-torn north. I trust her because my king does. Now I am asking you to do the same."

The Timberhands took a moment to ponder his earnest words. Kyson responded for them with a sincere look of compassion and support. "And you will have it. We are ready to take our pledge." The minstrel's heartfelt grin following felt genuine enough. Ondrew would need to learn to entrust his life to these new archers.

Ondrew turned to Broc, his burly second, former yharl of Mount BrKomak, and directed the next order of business. "Broc, take our initiates to the feast hall and prepare the ceremony. Our travelers are likely worn from the ride and should eat and drink richly before the pledge."

The salt-and-pepper-haired knight bowed to his former prince with an "Aye, Drew." And with that, Broc and the Timberhands left the war chamber.

Alone in the room with Datron, Black, and his umbran infatuation, he stared briefly at Lilealah. He was pleased to see her in a continuance of restored condition from when he had first met her in imprisonment at Frostdale. A swarm of qualms infected his pensive forethoughts toward the critical quest.

Lilealah broke the silence. "Do you trust me, Prince?"

Ondrew coolly replied, "The moment I no longer do is the moment all of this is for naught, and we fail." His eyes went to both of his knights and then back to her. "We will not fail."

He then turned and departed from the war chamber. His feet did not take him to the feast hall with the others, however. He trekked to the back door of his guild house and exited into the brisk Dawning breeze that commingled with the sunset.

He walked through the training yard, filled with practice dummies and battle gauntlets, to the small iron fence encompassing the hill that housed the guildhall. He placed both his hands upon the thin barricading bars that rose to his torso, and peered out over the rooftops of Defiance.

This had been his home for the past few seasons. Defiance, the most northern town in Barredom, only a few leagues from Continents' Kiss, was more of an icon of hope for all of the northmen than anything else. It was so named not for its victories but as a result of its cyclical defeats. Defiance had been first crushed by the Neveril of Zsolindal long ago. And then marauded again countless times by the Terollar of the Glace Isles. In addition, it had suffered conquests from the qindrid hordes encroaching from the Fourteen. But it always returned. No enemy could ever decimate it completely or cause the tenacity of the northmen to break. With each reconstruction, it came back stronger, with more blood and heart to fill its defiant stones, which refused to surrender and die. This town was the ideal symbol of all that Barredom stood for.

It was his home now. And as he watched the waning light drop down over the horizon, dimming the gables of the terrace lodges over the walled settlement, he apprehended one thought alone. This may very well be his last sunset to gaze upon in Barredom. His Barredom, the kingdom he was heir to.

He elected to skip out on joining in with the celebratory feast inside. He would enjoy this moment a little while longer.

HONORAH (II)

THE TROLL GARDENS

Norah stared at the door directly in front of her now. The boarding below the wooden transom to the chamber gate was so close, she could feel the rebound of her breath gently kissing her nose and cheeks. She had been here for a while now, unmoving, just anticipating her raging emotions and sedating her temperament before going forward. There was an act to play, and she could not falter for impulse. She was the Royal Inquisitor, and she was always in control. The unfortunates who received a visit from her always bent to her beckoning, not the other way around.

But these were not her typical prisoners. This was Zuulzin, offspring of the legendary, now-deceased Glace Isles king. This was the fiend who had killed her husband eleven years ago. And as soon as she opened the door, she would be forced to confront it in the flesh.

Norah opened the door to proceed inside the torture chamber. Located topside, outside the prison complex of the Frostdale Deeps, this detention specifically catered to the persecution of Terollar elvan captives. It had been constructed in an unsullied natural park nearly the size of the castle courtyard, allowed to run wild with an abundance of flora. Rightly named the Troll Gardens, this was not a place for citizen leisure. It served a single purpose—making trolls talk before they died.

With her entourage of armored guards in her wake, they lit the lanterns of the windowless chamber, and the doors were sealed shut. Norah found her familiar torture assistant, Minley, loyally waiting for her to inaugurate the session. Minley was a bit daft, born with a defect at birth and unable to think deeper than a young child, but his raw brawn and lack of intellectual capacity made up what she needed from him.

Norah carried a bottle of Daynish Firebrandy. It was an expensive gift from one of the newer foreign dignitaries on the Frostdale Council, none of whom she was a fan of. And regardless, she despised the brown wines so popular in the south, which were so harsh, it felt like her throat was on fire with just a sip. Firebrandy was an ideal name for the potent concoction. It was supposed to be the new trendy drink for aristocrats who followed the vogues of the Dominadom. That made her hate it even more than the taste.

She made no eye contact with the four trolls chained to the crosses in the middle of the room as she trekked to the long table on the far side of the room, near the heated firepit. Norah kept her focus on the lone wine glass as she reluctantly filled it. She closed her eyes, took a deep breath, and inserted her hand into her "toy box," as she referred to it—a large chest full of all manner of menacing devices of torment. Without looking, she fished out her simple tool of pain.

Armed with an unlit torch in one hand and a chalice of the strong spirit in the other, Norah plainly spoke to the wall. "Today is a very special day for me." She nursed her first taste from the acrid beverage as a test of her resolve and found herself unflinching, impervious as expected. Her mind was ready to endure anything. "Do you know what makes this day so special?"

Still not turning to gaze upon the chain-bound, she extended the torch into the firepit and set the end to blazing before continuing. "Today is the day I look my enemy in the eye and deliver justice to the north. This is the hour I view the foe that stole each of my brothers' lives. It is the minute that I stare down the archnemesis that murdered my husband and his father before him. Alas, I have yearned so long for this moment of righteous retribution. The wrath of Inquisitor Bayn sits over you all now."

Norah did turn now, targeting one specific troll, shackled to the second pentacrux. The wrinkled elvan had its hair shaved to skin on the sides of its head, and the blond hairs of its scalp were fashioned forward across its brow. Its body held scars, unlike other Terollar, proving that it had lost its regeneration capabilities when its spiritroot was destroyed in her husband's assault on the lifetrees of the Glace Isles tribe. Sheer animosity beamed as she inquired, "Do you know who I am, Zuulzin?"

The defeated troll's soft green eyes slipped, downtrodden, into submission, its guttural voice trying in the Civil language with a strong troll accent. "All on da Glace Isles know who be Lady Bayn. D'you be feared, as our khomo be to d'you people."

"Flattery and respect?" She now regarded the other three pentacruxes in the room. Jrulthun, Smiles, and one other random, insignificant troll she had had the warden select braced, exhausted, against their uncomfortable bindings. "Unexpected. Do you believe this should merit my mercy?"

"I accept fate dat waits fo' me. D'you people take 'way only ting I eva' love. An' da only ting dat eva' love me back," Zuulzin murmured in its dejected tone.

"Carah? My husband's mother." Norah already knew but pretended ignorance nonetheless. "You kidnapped her. You defiled her. You may even have cast some shamanistic sorcery on her for all we know," she scolded as she circled the pentacrux Zuulzin was chained to. "But what I do know is plain. She deserved to burn in that cage after lying with you."

The despicable elvan slipped into a silent fit of deviating emotions, from wrath to the verge of tears and then into a state of lifeless emptiness.

"This pains you? Oh no." Norah sadistically feigned compassion. Nothing could please her more than bringing this creature anguish in the most impactful ways. "Not yet. Your true pain has not yet begun, Kind-Eyes." She used the troll's popular alias. "I need you to be much stronger than that. I have so much more in store."

Norah motioned the guard captain a cue for what was next in her premeditated agenda. "I have a guest I brought just for you." The doors to the Troll Gardens chamber opened, and the sentries outside ushered in a blind battle veteran.

"Former scoutmaster Tomas Brigannor for the fallen Eldenvale Ranger captain, Lord Lucas Blackendale. Lucas was my husband, as he was the brother-by-law of dear Tomas." Tomas was married to her husband's sister, Lady Elsa of House Blackendale. He had been a part of her husband's distinguished hunting contingent as their lead scout.

He and one other, Mathias Oreville, were the only survivors of Lucas's last expedition. Tomas and Mathias had been spared to bring back the tales to Frostdale, both suffering horrid scars for life. Tomas underwent the loss of his eyes during the massacre and had lived a retired, quiet life on his farm estate ever since. He and Elsa together had raised their son, Henrick, and Norah's own children, Ebrielle and Aerik, while she kept busy politicking in the dungeons. Mathias, on the other hand, had gone on recently to join the Norther Knights in their clandestine expedition.

"Old acquaintances, it seems, you may all be. This will be a long-overdue reunion," Norah resolved.

Tomas hobbled in, blindly escorted by two guardsmen, and skeptically demanded, "What is this trick, Norah?"

Norah snubbed the insinuation. "No trick. A gift. Tell me again how you came to lose your eyes."

Tomas seemed annoyed by the enacted ploy. "You know how. I won't revisit it to entertain your sessions."

"You know you were summoned here for a reason. And you know you will do exactly that, entertaining at my bidding. I implore you to invoke your memory and enlighten me. Who is the evident widow-maker?" Norah pleaded in a commanding tone.

If Tomas had eyes to scowl, he would have. He was not charmed by the torture charade, and she knew well that he was present against his will, only complying due to her rank in the court. "I am one of the two survivors to live through my brother's last encounter with the Chosen Troll. Mathias Oreville is the other. He was left without a hand and with only half a face, and I had my eyes eaten from my very skull. Lucas and your blood brother, Justan, were slain along with the rest of our ranger company." He shuffled, clearly annoyed by the forced reminiscence.

Norah continued her badgering. "Who took your eyes? Who took the face and hand from Mathias?"

Tomas's face contorted to one of acrimonious detestation. "The Chosen Troll's alpha, Jrulthun. The most ungodly beast in all the realms."

The massive Terollar summoned its strength as rage built, and the veins in its neck began to protrude from its fair skin. Jrulthun's breathing became heavier, building into a clear fury through its manic eyes. The troll growled with obvious intent of murder in its cast glare. Emotion pleased Norah—anger, fear, sadness. She would exploit it all, capitalize on it as a tool to be used, and crush the soul of those she chose to call her victims.

"Name the troll that killed my brother, Justan, and your brother-by-law, my husband, Lucas."

Tomas stood proud on his crutch and answered dutifully. "The aging son of the Chosen Troll—Kind-Eyes. The Glace Isles king subdued Lucas and let his decrepit son have the kill. Justan was slain in the fray."

Norah's anticipation to release her fury had her heartbeat pounding through her chest and her hands no longer steady but quivering with building butterflies swarming through her gut. She pressed on. "You would recognize Jrulthun and Kind-Eyes if you were to encounter them again, would you not?"

Tomas snarled suspiciously, "Norah, tell me you did not dare bring me before them."

She gave the cued nod to her loyal guards, and two of the watchmen grasped her brother-by-law by the shoulders, forcing him to the pentacrux that detained Zuulzin. "You will touch them. And you will confirm it."

"Curse you to the Fives, Norah!" Tomas screamed, as if his flesh would catch fire if he touched a troll. He begged worse than her former prisoners did before she cut them open. "Please don't make me! Please!"

She was the Royal Inquisitor. She ignored begging. Pleading and praying only fueled her ire by habit. "Who is this one?"

"Kind-Eyes," Tomas endorsed. "Zuulzin," he fervidly asserted as his hand was driven to caress the withered troll. "The Exile of the Isles!"

"I know." Norah believed she grinned, but was sure it came across more as a sneer of triumphant retribution instead. "And it will know our wrath shortly. I need you to identify each. Next!"

"No!" Tomas futilely tried to refuse. "No! No! Take me away!" The guardsmen did as bidden and wrestled him toward the beastly alpha troll.

She needed to hear it. "This is Jrulthun, is it not?"

The blood in her brother-by-law's face had retreated elsewhere, and his features were paling in absolute terror. "Norah, what have you brought here?"

She was in full inhumane inquisitor mode now. Kindly emotions were long lost from her afforded capacity. She was a machine of misery and extraction. "Confirm that it is the alpha!"

Two burly sentries manhandled Tomas to touch the bare skin of the enormous troll. Jrulthun just let the petting-zoo farce play out until Tomas's hand reached its massive neck. Jrulthun growled like something far more feral than anything natural, and rabidly began snarling and biting at Tomas's fingers.

"You have him!" Tomas kept resisting his stronger restraints, but his frantic mania was hard to maintain control over. "Jrulthun! You have Zuulzin! I beg the Fives for mercy. Take me away." He slumped to the floor and hugged it as if the air above his body meant instant death. Tomas scurried like a scolded puppy toward the exit wall and began crying hysterically. "Take me! Take me!"

Disgusting. You let them break you this badly. She stared at her legal sibling for a good moment in total disappointment. His horror did not even make her hate the trolls more for what they had done to him; she decided it simply made her like him less. No respect or dignity. "I did not dismiss you," she coldly warned.

His words trumped her disposition on the cruel course she was prepared to take. "I am dismissing myself. Punish me by torture if you wish, but none will match this! Have your guards toss me in the Deeps for all I care. Punish a noble war hero for nothing! Or let me go, Norah! I have told you what you wish to hear!"

The fact that she did not look to stop him, nor make eye contact with any of her city escort, let the guards know they had permission to excuse him. They were well trained in her antics.

"Want my advice?" Tomas counseled with his last words before exiting the torture chamber. "Stop the games. Set flame to them all, and be done with it."

She was growing tired of that same advice. The games would continue. Norah retreated back to her toy box as she let the echoes of Tomas's departing steps fade. She nonchalantly dismissed two of the sentries to ensure a blind man's safety back to his home.

Her eyes became bellicose as she peered deep into the crate before her and taunted those behind her. "Do you want to know why you have each been selected to come to the Troll Gardens?"

Norah pulled out a rectangular glass case covered by a curtain of cloth from the torture chest and cradled it in her hands. She motioned a nod to Minley, and immediately her brutish assistant began to place identical strange devices, which had been stowed in the corner, in front of each troll's pentacrux.

The contraptions were a set of adjustable stands, preset to each troll's height as they were positioned on their crosses. At the top of each iron stand, set at the exact elevation of each troll's mouth, was attached a malicious apparatus that had a screw knob on the end facing Minley, and five leaf-shaped metal petals facing the trolls.

Norah went to stand in front of the nameless troll on the fourth pentacrux to induce her minion into action. Minley pushed the stand as far forward as he could, forcing the point of the metal petals onto the troll's lips. A guard came up behind the cross and held the troll's nose so that it could only breathe through its mouth. As soon as it took a gasp for air, Minley began twisting the handle, protruding the petals into the fiend's orifice and gradually expanding it further open. Minley kept twisting until Norah gave the signal to stop. She didn't.

Not until she heard the first crack of its jaw separating from its skull. Its mouth was ajar now in an unnatural shape, with its cheek ripped, teeth bleeding, and saliva flowing. Minley then reached into his pack and produced a large jar of honey.

Norah then softly presented the glass case to her assistant to signify the finality of what was to become of the prisoner. Minley pulled back the cloth to display the clear box full of raging ants. He placed his gloved hand into the jar of honey, then into the case of frantic insects, and shoved his fist into the forced-open mouth of the troll, and then slid the glove free.

"It is because you cannot die here if I do not allow it. You see." She paused and let the harrowing yowls of the troll swell the ambiance of the chamber. "I am quite merciful. I actually do not want you to die."

Norah flicked her wrist to the door sentry, and the gates of the chamber were opened again, letting in the northern breeze and verdant sights of the lavish garden outside. "I want you to live!"

And as she said so, all could see the Terollar elvan's regeneration powers coming into effect with access to the natural elements nearby. Its mumbled gurgling became recognizable curses in the Terollar language, and its fits were more hysterical in never-ending life. "I want you to live. Over. And over. And over again."

Norah walked in front of the third troll, the one referred to as Smiles. "And that is going to happen." She mischievously winked up at it.

And Smiles indeed smiled on cue. But not in sarcasm nor a taunting humor, but seemingly genuine, like one might to a long-lost friend whose relationship had been detached. "Royal Inquisitor?"

"And the one who I assumed would be the first speaks. Amuse me, troll." Norah stayed her hand to keep Minley back.

Smiles remained grinning cordially, as if no danger or torment were conceivable whatsoever. The troll began in its broken, guttural dialect, heavy with a Terollar accent. "Dat I jus' may. Bein' amusin' is skill I boast." And then it fascinatingly switched its enunciations into a flawless High Barredish accent like her own. "But negotiating is a skill I do far better."

I will not be impressed by a troll. But she incidentally was. She kept her tenacity to show she would remain the one in control. "I will divert, for now. Continue."

Smiles kept up the High Barredish ruse, as if it were some local royal lord with a troll's mask on. "Dare I interrogate a curiosity? Do you only seek vengeance through torture for loved ones lost, or do you also seek answers to questions you have long feared to ask?"

The deafening profanities of the troll on the fourth cross would have deterred any idle conversation for individuals with traditional morality. But the two in an exchange with one another were obviously not of that mold. They continued their verbal joust as if they were toying at a Daynish masquerade with music instead of cries.

"Bold, interrogating the Royal Inquisitor. Risky, enticing me to exact revenge through torture," Norah warned playfully back. It had been a long time since a prisoner was audacious enough to pretend a favorable outcome. She would enjoy the brief sport of it. "But outright dangerous, implying that I fear any of you or any unanswered questions."

"But, Royal Inquisitor, you do have questions. And I have answers. And all I seek is a trade." Smiles grinned in full. "I will tell you what I request. And I will tell you what questions you do have, as soon as we are alone, with just you and us of the Glazjhendun." It used the native term for the Glace Isles Terollar war tribe.

Norah silently called Minley over to her, with the ant container in hand, and stepped to face the oral-expansion gadget. "How can you possibly surmise what it is I wish to inquire about?"

Smiles confidently looked at her as if she were a naive whelp. "You were not ordered to simply torture and kill the alleged culprits in your family's deaths. We both know this. More pressing subjects plague the speculations of the Frostdale Council." The troll said the facts bluntly, though how this peculiar creature had deduced such implications, she had no idea. "Why would Jrulthun kill Khomo'Jhu-vonus by execution with no gain to be made after already being surrounded by Northaven's forces? Attempts have been made on his life before, and many through challenges made by our own tribesven, all failing, dispatched swiftly without mercy. Why would he succumb to a willing death now? You think he feared Lady Bayn? And why did we of the Glazjhendun, the Glace Isles elite, throw down our weapons instead of fighting unto death? Irregularities and inconsistencies and just far too many whys."

Who are you, troll? Why have I not heard of you? Norah quarreled inwardly with her own ignorance. "You are quite the intriguing fiend, troll. Perhaps I will kill you last." But she could not let this overeducated wretch feel any sense of dominance. "Or then again, I may take out your tongue first if you strum the wrong strings on this delicate harp you play."

Smiles was unfazed. Its sideways sneer was still smoothly genial. It was unlike any troll she had ever heard of. "These are the questions the Frostdale Council will want you to direct at us. But these are not the questions you want to ask us, Norah."

"So familiar already?" This could not be tolerated. She set the flame of her torch to lick just under the chin of Smiles. She left it there long enough to smell it char and see it smoke, before moving to the next. She burned the eyes out of Jrulthun and shoved the entire torch inside the open mouth of the fourth troll. And then, with Zuulzin, she set the flame just under its genitals until she could witness a shrieking moan of excruciation, and then she held the fire for five seconds more. "You will never presume to be so again," she proclaimed, and took the torch away to stand before Smiles again.

"Guards! Leave me!" Norah commanded with no room for rebuttal. "You too." She glanced at Minley and waved him away sternly.

"That is not advisable, Inq—" The guard captain tried to offer sound advice but was abruptly cut off.

"Bring me another pentacrux, then, for those that would refuse." She would not be disobeyed. "Out!"

Smiles smiled.

"Still so smug? We are going to have a long day, troll," Norah balefully promised, but the elvan's buoyant grin was unbending. "You know my name. Time that you introduce yourself," she offered on even ground.

The troll tilted its head curiously. "I hear they call me Smiles. Smiles and Kind-Eyes chained in torture." It grinned again and glanced over to Zuulzin, near it. "We vicious trolls do not sound so terrifying to me. Perhaps your people can concoct nastier nicknames if we are to maintain our reputations among the Barredish."

Norah could not grasp an understanding of this elvan's relentless disposition under the circumstances. This was a matchless endeavor for her, to have a prisoner acting more in control than she, and a troll at that. "You have been given the opportunity requested, yet you choose to use it to provoke me. You may have less wit than I gave you credit for."

If Smiles could have shrugged properly on the pentacrux it was bound to, she was sure the troll would have as it casually retaliated. "You made it apparent I cannot call you by your real name, Royal Inquisitor, our so-feared Lady Bayn. So leave it at that, and you can call me whatever title you deem appropriate."

It shook the foundation of her very core to play the trade game with this vile thing. But she needed to hear it. She somehow knew it knew what she knew. Something even she had been too unsettled to speak about with her peers and those beneath her. "I shall allow you a unique kindness. Presume to tell me these questions I have."

"You no longer need to worry. We will protect you, Norah." Smiles provoked her with its biggest sneer yet. She gripped the life out of her torch, pretending it was the troll's neck, and resisted, with every measure of her being, the urge to turn the lot of them into a permanent blaze. "You know Barredom is different now. It has changed. Many are new, foreign altogether. Others look the same, but you no longer recognize them, and they do not recognize you. And still some remain elusive entirely, such as your king and queen. And you are treated with less and less esteem as the unwelcome Dominadom pours into your hearth."

Riddles and rubbish. But this troll is well-informed. It is something important to its clan if even the alpha refuses to silence it, Norah conjectured.

"Bring me the axes of our fallen Khomo'Jhuvonus, and I will tell you what we of the Glazjhendun have discovered." Smiles finally voiced its plea. As it spoke the forbidden name aloud, she cringed out of Barredish habit but refrained from showing a hint of it. "The umbran, Lilealah, is making a fool of you all."

"Ambiguous drivel. Speak your intent, else I think I might just coat you all in honey and bring in the flies and rats," she wearily threatened.

Smiles complied and explained. "The Axes of the Sons, as your people call them, the khomo's weapons, they are sacred relics of our people and should not remain in Barredish custody. Please, we humbly beg of you, bring them to us, to the Forlorn, where we are kept, and choose one of us to return to our isles and make a truce between us. The war between men and elven and qindrid is over in the north."

An absurd notion. "If trolls are still breathing, then the war between us and them will never conclude so long as I can decree it," Norah ardently vowed.

"The answer is simple, and you know it. You see it every day, more and more, season after recent season. There is a new type of qindrid, Norah. And you live among them," it continued without relent. It was speaking what she had already feared but could never say aloud.

Norah had suffered many sleepless nights recently due to growing suspicions of something sinister stirring in the upper court and among the noble houses. Everything and everyone was increasingly off and odd. "You have a loud tongue. I think I may be done with it." Still she countered aloofly.

"They wear your faces. These are not the stoneborne of Aggedon or the skyborne of the east. This is something new. And the realm from north to south is infested with them. We are not your enemy. We never were." This strange troll spoke in all sincerity.

It actually believes its own words. "Who are you, troll? To your people." Her curiosity could not endure it any longer. She had to know its tribal significance.

"I told you, you may call me as you like. But if we must be proper with titles, Inquisitor Bayn, you may call me Master of the Mortali. I have been chosen as the voice of the Glazjhendun, with men, qindrid, and elven foreign to our isles."

"Mortali? I know that Terollar term," Norah revealed with a smirk as she squinted in recognition. "Mortali are the sacred elders of your culture. The unique tribesven that groom and sculpt the eccentric troll hairstyles that define your ranks on the Glace Isles. Herbal shamans and tribe diplomats."

Smiles nodded.

"Know that I will never refer to you as a master of anything." Norah persisted in a condescending tone.

"So the trolls have adapted witch doctors into their choice ambassadors? True primitive tacticians you are. Never send your main envoy or your king as a war party's vanguard. Thoughts of your elaborate deaths have brought me my one peace."

Just then the bells of midday sounded across the city. They continued to carry on much longer than normal on this particular eminent hour. The captain of the guard entered and directed Norah after the bells ceased their song. "Royal Inquisitor, the Paladin Trials begin now. Your son." He referenced Aerik, who would be in the Trial of Melee shortly commencing on the tourney grounds. "You will be late if you do not—"

Smiles interrupted the officer with the wickedest grin. "Bring the axes to the Forlorn as requested, Norah, and I will tell you how Lucas and Justan died trying to become one of them, one of the new qindrid, just like that eyeless heretic Tomas Brigannor you just called in." Smile's grin grew disturbingly psychotic as the troll eyeballed her in a crazed stare.

Peculiar troll. Now why would you go and do that? "Trivial games can wait. Send word to my son that I'm going to be late," she commanded the guard captain.

Jrulthun's eyes had already regenerated. This would not do. "Coat the alpha's eyes in honey and release the ants! Repeat it five times over!"

Norah swiftly pranced over to the toy box and produced a long, curved knife. "Minley! Tongs!" And as her minion did as bidden, her determined gait took her straight to the pentacrux that held Smiles. Minley placed a step stool down for her and began to try to probe out the troll's wagging tongue.

"Don't forget the axes, Norah," Smiles whispered sarcastically as it winked down at her.

"A pity. We were getting along rather pleasantly." She winked back and climbed the stool to sever its tongue from the end of the tongs Minley clamped down on. "You are done talking today," she proved as she walked back to throw the flopping piece of wet flesh into the burning firepit.

"To think I would ever bargain with a troll. You insult me," Norah spat as she watched Jrulthun and Smiles writhe and wail in agony. "Guards, after I leave, you'll keep cleaving its tongue each time it heals back until your shift ends today!"

An intimidated "Inquisitor" followed from several guards.

The guard captain subsequently inquired, "What of Kind-Eyes? I assumed he would receive the worst."

She answered in silence by walking back to the long table, where she had left her chalice, and grabbed the corked decanter of Daynish Firebrandy. She then proceeded over not to Zuulzin but to the fourth troll, who had received the brunt of the torture session.

Staring at its gaping mouth, still forced open by the device Minley had originally used upon it, Norah casually poured herself another glass of the fiery vintage. She cocked her head as if pondering what to do as she investigated the tiny ants crawling in and out of its salivating mouth. Hundreds of welts over its tongue, lips, cheeks inside and out, and all about its neck and face swelled into horrid disfigurement.

She puckered in false sympathy for the troll's pain, proffering the full goblet to its open throat to douse it in the liquid. She then dropped her wine glass and poured the entire bottle of Firebrandy over its head and torso before producing the torch she had wielded before. "I like games. Do you? Let's pretend you are the one who killed my brother, Justan. But in this game, you must be the evil troll that you are, and I must play the righteous heroine. An unrealistic scenario, I know, but . . ." Norah placed the torch delicately inside its mouth next, and all watched its upper body explode in a flaming wave. "You do understand this is simply justice."

She believed its brief screams before death were the best of them yet. "Let it burn and die. You will not let this one heal." The look she gave each of the guards let them know there would be no remorse for any who challenged that order. "Rumor has it that Kind-Eyes never liked its own kind, anyway. Feed it this troll's meat. All of it better be gone by the time I return."

"As you say, Inq—" the timid guard captain attempted, but was interrupted as usual.

"I return in a pentday after the Trials. Another troll dies every five days until I get what I seek." Norah briskly departed from the torture chamber.

The captain of the guard dared, "What do you seek?"

Oh, only the deaths of every troll here, on the Glace Isles, and beyond. No words came from her lips, but the look in her eye as she exited the Troll Gardens confirmed her malevolent and unforgiving resolve.

EBRIELLE (II)

THE MELEE

The crowd in the tourney stands stood in a lionizing cheer as Aerik smashed his opponent down to the ground with his heavy blunted sword. The young armored athlete didn't relent there, however. He returned his sword to his fallen rival's upheld shield, hacking again and again, seeming as if he intended to break the poor man's arm off in his continued beating. And then suddenly the tide was turned as his opponent swept a kick that buckled Aerik's knees and put him flat on the soil.

Ebrielle gasped at the thudding sound of her brother's back hitting the ground as the air erupted from his chest. His opponent found his feet in an instant and pinned Aerik's shield down with a plated boot. It was now Aerik's turn to suffer a spate of sword blows. Her brother frantically attempted to catch each one with his guarding weapon. One. Two. Three. Four. Aerik's sword was getting lower upon each blow.

"Brie!" Sorene grabbed her wrist in empathetic panic, watching the dire turn of events unfold in haste. Her hands found both of Sorene's, and she squeezed the life out of the petite girl's tiny palms.

Aerik slid his pinned shield out from underneath his opponent's boot, upsetting the man's balance just long enough for him to jump to his feet. The cheers that followed were muffled compared to the sound of her own heartbeat drumming in her ears. The two men squared away evenly now, and Aerik spared no hesitation to act on his moment of opportunity.

He feinted with a low slash, then slammed his shield into his opponent's face, bending his foe's helmet to the side. The distraction of the taller boy reaching up to fix his helm was everything Aerik needed to end the fight. Her brother's sword came around so fast she thought he meant to decapitate his rival right there in front of everyone at the Trials. But the blunt edge of Aerik's blade came to a halt on the boy's bare neck.

It took the spectators a few seconds to register what had just happened. But as the boy's shoulders slumped in defeat and the herald ran onto the grounds to raise Aerik's hand as the winner, the racket resumed, none of it louder than her own elated screams. Then came the voice of the herald. "Lord Aerik Blackendale! Son of the Royal Inquisitor, Lady Honorah Bayn! Second victory in the Melee!"

Aerik removed his helmet and thrust it into the air to applause. He was very handsome in the face, she thought to herself, just like the younger image she vaguely recalled of her father. His dirty-blond locks waved in the healthy breeze that swirled through the scattered banners of the tourney.

She noticed her brother's eyes searching the stands near where she stood. Finally he found her, and they exchanged smiles. Aerik then looked at Sorene, and his smile turned into a coy smirk. Sorene squeezed her hand excitedly and giggled away. She knew her best friend and brother had an ongoing infatuation with each other. Aerik's scrutiny then went to the empty seat on Ebrielle's left side, and his eyes went blank, with all happiness dissipated. It was their mother's seat, but she was nowhere to be found.

Aerik had already fought and won twice, and their uncaring mother didn't seem to show an interest in her son's most important aspiration. Her brother was escorted off the field to allow the next contenders to battle before his third match in the bracket of the Melee.

Ebrielle let go of Sorene's hand and surveyed the tourney stands for Norah. Eventually, she did discover her, and in the most obvious location. There the Royal Inquisitor loomed toward the blocked path of an honor guard securing the pergola that housed the king and queen, along with several important Daynish dignitaries, including the exalted dominarchs, Vaximus and Sriyah, high rulers over the Az'Dayne Dominadom. Norah seemed to be raising all kinds of commotion, to no avail. *How long has Mother been over there?*

Ultimately, Norah was defeated in her futile attempt to enter the pergola, and she blustered her way across the stands to the nobility section, where Ebrielle and Sorene awaited her. Her mother huffed in outrage as she slammed down into her cushioned seat, next to Ebrielle. "Preposterous! Unheard-of insolence! His Majesty has never treated ..." An unintelligible grumble of irritated noises trailed away. Her mother looked at her, and then to the two empty seats reserved for her uncle Tomas and aunt Elsa, and dispassionately inquired, "So, what have I missed?"

Ebrielle didn't know how to respond to her angry mother, when, truthfully, she was grieved by Norah's tardy disrespect. Sorene stayed still and silent as a stone. They were both extremely intimidated by Norah. Almost anyone who met the Royal Inquisitor was intimidated by her.

Norah was a woman of frail stature, and her hair was a tarnished blond, faded like it had never seen the light of day. Apart from her mother's cruel demeanor, Ebrielle noted that she wasn't all that imposing a figure. *Mother may just be the most unapproachable person ever to have existed.* "You missed Aerik's victories in the Melee. He has fought twice and won."

"A fool's ambition in that boy. Talent wasted where it is badly needed here in the north. He should join General Randon at Northaven, where I have already secured him a position to be an officer by his twentieth bornday," her mother criticized. She was never subtle about the fact that she despised Az'Dayne politics interrupting the familiar traditions of Barredom. She believed the male paladins and female veritans to be nothing more than overzealous knights policing the already safe streets of Az'Dayne, where no protection of that caliber was needed. Those with fighting talent shouldn't be utilized as glorified sentries but as soldiers, she had long reasoned.

"Henrick's fight is up after this one," Ebrielle elaborated, with no motivation to pointlessly argue back with Norah. Her mother only snubbed the statement with a sneer and a folding of her eyebrows.

Is there any fraction of pleasure to be found in this hollowed husk I was once proud to call Mother? She would rather be back on the hillside estate with her aunt and uncle than suffering through court alongside the most miserably callous woman in Barredom.

The combat below ended in some fashion she didn't quite catch, as she was more focused on her mother's arrival than the tourney battle trials. Her brawny cousin Henrick entered the battlefield next. With his broad shoulders and wide back, Henrick appeared quite daunting when fully armored, Ebrielle assessed.

"You will be joining me after the games conclude, to watch and learn how I deal with the trolls. I made progress this morning. You would have done well to have been there," her mother intervened just as her cousin's fight commenced.

"The Trials, you mean, Mother. They are far from games," Ebrielle dared to argue. She could see Sorene's face whiten in dread next to her.

Norah waved the farcical tiff away with a disapproving groan. "They are games, Ebrielle. Paladins? Veritans? Az'Dayne's unneeded street militia, cloaked in the armor of the Faith. If they are to knight someone and grant them a fancy title, they should use them in the war effort, where a true soldier belongs. Come back to me when you learn the difference, child."

Ebrielle rolled her eyes. "It is the highest honor of knighthood in all the realms to become a paladin, Honorah," Ebrielle returned to her mother.

Norah turned and glared a hole straight through the side of her head. Ebrielle wouldn't dare match her menacing staredown. She couldn't believe she had just called her anything other than her title or Mother. Ebrielle observed to herself that she was becoming dangerously rash. She couldn't help the anger she had felt all these years after her father was slain. Perhaps she had buried it deep and didn't know the level of its roots until she was forced back into Norah's company.

She just wanted to be done with her obligations in the Frostdale Deeps, restored to her dear uncle's country manor, and engaged in her routine, lackluster life.

The slap of steel on steel snapped her back to the gallant vivacity of the tourney grounds. Henrick's heavy blows were deflected by precision parries with hardly an effort from his opponent. Her cousin's sword was averted far and wide and brought back in again, almost like his domineering contender was playing a game to prove his supremacy to the crowd. Just two more quick counters, and the Daynish fighter had managed to disarm Henrick, with his sword flying through the air. She watched her cousin slump to his knees in defeat as his adversary's own sword leveled at his neck. Cheers trailed after the Daynishman's hand was raised.

Her mother seemed to have lost the desire for dialogue, with all of her focus directed to the pavilion area of the king. Delighted at that, Ebrielle took the moment to pull out the silver arrow token that Kyson had given her. She slipped into a daydream far away from there, remembering his voice and every word spoken. The smell of his perfume was still as strong in her nose as the palpable aroma of intermixed fragrances that enveloped the tourney's nobility sector.

Several more fights went on, and still her imaginary musings stayed uninterrupted. Finally, Aerik returned to the fields for his third match in the Melee. Nothing would break her concentration from this fight. The daydream of her lover would have to wait.

In each fight, the aspiring knights-to-be combated each other with a different weapon tactics. The third bout would be with the paladin weapon of the two-handed dawnstar mace, without the spikes, for purposes of safety in the tourney. She had never seen her brother use such a weapon before. Still, to become a paladin, this would become his new, solitary weapon.

His new opponent was the same that had dispatched her cousin with such effortless ease, clad in similar dressings of standard plate armor to what Aerik was forced to don. The man wore a Daynish-forged great helm and sported their colors on a sash around his sword arm. Sheathed at his hip was an overornamented sabre sword, embellished with fine gold on the pommel, fashioned in some shape she couldn't quite discern from the distance. Why they would permit the man the extra weapon in the Trials, she could not fathom, but she did recall him having the same on his hip during his match with Henrick.

The battle horn blew, and the match began. The Daynishman opened in a left-handed stance, with his two-handed mace swung in wide circles as he closed the distance between him and Aerik.

Her brother propelled the heavy head of his own mace toward his contender but received a deflecting bash that bent Aerik's weapon into the soil. A precise kick to the armored sternum sent Aerik reeling backward and off-balance, followed by a vicious hack from his adversary that clipped the face of his helm, sending a gush of blood pouring from both sides of his nose, down his chin.

All three ladies gasped at once in shared panic. Ebrielle looked at her mother's expression of recognizable worriment and took gratification in perceiving at least some portion of despair for her son. She went to reach for her mother's hand in sympathy, to share the distress, but Norah ignored the attempt, her attention too intent on Aerik's match.

Aerik promptly discarded his dented helm and charged through his opponent's whirlwind tactic. The dexterous contender timely sidestepped and let Aerik slide off his chest. Her brother's charge pushed him into a stumble past his opponent as the man tactfully caught Aerik's two-handed weapon and retracted it from her brother's grasp. The bald dawnstar slid from Aerik's control to the ground behind his winning opponent. Helmless and weaponless, her brother looked lost, fully confused about how to retaliate.

Ebrielle looked at Sorene, whose eyes were red and wide, and then back to her mother, whose gaze was equally edged with anxiety. But the bottom half of her mother's face betrayed the upper features with a sneer of rage, as if challenging someone to injure her son.

It all happened so fast and so cleanly, as if no contest had happened at all. His opponent's skill was simply on a level that outclassed his own weapons training. The Daynishman's mace came down to bury itself in Aerik's naked face. Her brother retreated down to his knees with both hands in the air to surrender.

The roaring crowd seemed no less ecstatic with someone from Az'Dayne winning. Ebrielle judged that a revolting act from the pretenders in Barredom, being agreeable with the southern kingdom besting their nobility on the tournament fields. *Thank the Five and Five, at least he was not hurt!*

"Thank the Five and Five, at least he was not hurt," her mother stated, stealing her exact thoughts.

Ebrielle refused to watch the victor's hand being raised and muted the herald's announcement of her brother's loss in the Melee. Sorene and Ebrielle humbly kept their loyal gazes on Aerik as he exited the fields to be discharged from the tourney brackets for the day.

"Power well spent, and coin unmissed," her mother declared, flicking a wink down at her and standing from the benches to apparently depart from the stadium.

Ebrielle wasn't sure she wanted to know the answer she was about to seek. "Coin unmissed? Did you arrange his loss?" Her voice escalated between the queries. The two girls both dared interrogating scowls at Norah, braving where others never ventured.

Her mother snubbed the looks, not returning their futile glares. Smirking at the momentarily empty tourney grounds, she clarified, "You cannot rig the Trials, silly child. Daynish Paladin Trials are far too well governed. I merely filled the purse of the coordinator who manifested the brackets. I wanted to make sure the best fighter contested your brother long before the finals in the Melee."

Ebrielle was appalled. *Treachery against her own blood! Her own son!* "You knew how much this meant to him, Mother! It has been his lifelong ambition to become a knight." Her voice trailed off as she was entirely confounded by her mother's cruel logic.

"Ebrielle, his ambition? Since when do parents of high nobility allow such nonsense into their children's heads? Do you want to see him off to Az'Dayne, leagues beyond our reach, while you stick it out in the cold north, beside me in the wailings of the Deeps?"

Ebrielle had no response to that. Norah always had an unorthodox method for proving her tactless wisdom and opaque compassion. Before Ebrielle could think of anything shrewder to counter with, Norah declined to relent on her elaborations. "Oh, and by the way, soft little girl of mine, enjoy these leisurely amusements. They are fading. My toy box is yours after the Trials. You'll thank me one day, when there comes a time I can look down and smile upon the Barredish lady I hatched and not squawk at the wee bird that trembles to leave her nurturing nest."

Her mother promptly departed from the nobility section, traversing past the royal pergola with a hard stare at its ornamented elevation. All that mustered from Ebrielle's low toned lips was, "Farewell, then, Norah."

Sorene looked at her in matched emotion, as if she meant to vocalize, "Good riddance too," but no sound at all came from her friend. Her mother's terror spread far, even after her presence was long gone, since no one dared risk her ire.

With the brief entrance and exit of her mother, Ebrielle's thoughts slipped back to the images of her father, Lucas. The regal version of Norah had not been so spiteful then, from what she recalled of her earlier years. There had been joy and love in Norah's life, regardless of her position in the court as a magistrate.

She had spent her seventh bornday in mourning for her father, with her mother and brother. Report had come that he had led his vanguard successfully through the frozen waters of the Bay of Trolls, onto the snowy cliffs of southeastern Aggedon. There his contingent met head-on with an awaiting band of Terollar, fully anticipating their landing. Lucas and his men fell fast to the trolls, save for two soldiers kept alive.

One survivor, her uncle Tomas, was the father of her cousin Henrick. Both mangled hunters, Tomas and Mathias, transported their brethren's remains to the capital and conveyed the atrocious tale of slaughter and cannibalism to Norah.

Ebrielle knew that as a child, she had only received the censored version of the grisly ordeal. However, upon her adolescent years, Norah suppressed no vivid illustration of the gruesome details. Ebrielle was raised knowing that trolls had killed her grandfather before she was born, and now they had taken her father's life and uncle's eyes. Such was enough to foster a lifetime of prejudice.

The Melee continued on throughout the remainder of the day. By the final match, breaking into dusk, Ebrielle and Sorene were far too lost in gossip about boys to have possibly paid any attention to the fights. The only deviation from their girlish banter was the occasional disparaging remark about her mother through hushed whispers. Neither of the girls imparted even a remote interest in the fighting, only in the fascination of the knights-to-be if they were to their selective taste. While Sorene must have picked out a half dozen or so of the young men, Ebrielle found herself acting behind a facade just to go along with their typical game.

She had told Sorene of Kyson close to a hundred times in the past two moons, to be sure. Boys that she was certain she would have fancied were now so bland compared with the vivid memory of her fated lover. She found herself fiddling with her silver arrow throughout the tedium of the Trials, often tuning out Sorene.

Cheers erupted again all around her as the nobles in her section rose to applaud. Someone must have won, and she wasn't even of a mind to pay heed. Sorene and Ebrielle stood to expectedly see the champion of the Melee was the same man with the mystery sword that had so swiftly defeated her brother and cousin. Nikayle de'Queur, or something like that, she believed.

As the herald left the field after announcing the champion of the Melee, the horns now blew from the royal pergola. All focus went above to King Aerik and Queen Annison. Absolute silence infected the whole of the grassy arena grounds as the king approached the front of his pavilion and outstretched his free hand to demand the attention of everyone below.

"My people of Barredom! Your king speaks and asks for your devoted attention and open hearts." King Aerik Roth appeared in more confident form than he had since recent reports after the transition of sovereignty.

"I stand pleased, on this fine Dawning day, with the Paladin Trials our Dominadom has graciously honored us with! Foremost, Queen Annison returns to us in favorable health! Blessed be the Five and Five!" As Queen Annison rose, the crowd chanted the conventional invocation to the gods and goddesses, with Ebrielle and Sorene submitting to joining in the contagious practice. *I had forgotten the queen has been absent for so long.* She inwardly chastised herself for being ignorant of important political news.

King Aerik Roth continued with his bolstering broadcast. "All praise the Psages' cyclical prophecy of the Kingfall, for their divinations have spoken! You have heard true, the Glace Isles king is dead! And his elite is in our Frostdale Deeps!" If she hadn't been deafened by the intermittent cheering throughout the Melee before, then she would be unhearing on the morrow now.

"And to my noble citizens of Barredom, all of you, under the gracious power granted by our new sovereign Dominadom, as a first in the histories of our beloved country." He paused to gain momentum in his drama. "I continue with the grandest news of all. The Fourteen has fallen! All of Aggedon west of the Great Grey Wall now belongs to Barredom!"

The triumphant screams were unlike anything she had ever experienced. "Barredish lords and ladies, a brief word from your dominarchs, who have come from afar, all the way from Everdawn! Vaximus Az'Ampion and Sriyah Hazhalah!"

Vaximus Az'Ampion, the standing overlord for the Az'Dayne Dominadom, took his Khalimishe queen and stood beside King Aerik and Queen Annison with joined hands. Ebrielle swore she had never seen anything so regally enthralling as the two dominarchs. They were adorned with golden trinkets and rubies on every finger, and the same was the case for their lavishly bejeweled necks. The two majestic figures seemed more celestial than mortal. Sriyah poised tall beside her husband, with her stylishly cropped fiery-red hair serving as the perfect perch for her imperial crown, wearing a matching orange-and-yellow contrasting gown to pair with her husband's exquisite vestments. Vaximus, on the other hand, maintained his scalp fully bald and kept the sides of his cheeks shaved against his pristine goatee, which hinted behind the masque covering half his face.

Like all royal Daynish and Khalimishe in the Dominadom, both Vaximus and Sriyah bore their matchless half-masques, which signified their station and house, though unique to the dominarchs was the fact that their masques both attached to their imperial crowns. Vaximus's masque was of pure gold, shaped like a climbing, angry fire, covering the right side of his head, while Sriyah's seemed of bronze, speckled with rubies, in the same flame design that veiled the left of her face.

When Vaximus spoke, the world fell silent. "The enemy wane in irrevocable defeat as our growing reach triumphs in such conquests. Bathe in these blessings bestowed on Barredom. The Five and Five have spoken clearly, and they say your prayers are heard. The Dominadom has come to deliver you all into a lifetime of peace for your children and theirs to come!"

She could no longer feel anything in her ears except the vibration of mobs of feet stomping the tourney benches where she stood. In the serenity of her temporarily deafened ears, Ebrielle could hear only one thing: the sound of the end of the war entirely. And it sounded like Kyson's sweet voice singing once more, returning to her.

ONDREW (III)

FROM HEAVENS TO HELLS

A golden sun struck the mirror of the frozen black wall that stood as the western side of Continents' Kiss. The glare from the immeasurably tall land bridge, glazed in an enveloping sheet of ebonice, reflected its darkness back onto the freezing waters of the northern ocean between Aggedon and Barredom. Aspiring blue sea remained a liquid mass of shadow-dark waves. Thus the Black Bay had gotten its name from the sailors who discovered it long ago.

The Norther Knights' eighty-passenger longship broke through the black swells, riding the breakers against the cliff line along the wall of the Kiss. The vessel was not intended for long ocean voyages but was ideal for practical travel between Defiance and the channel that led to Northaven.

But it would not be making its customary journey to Northaven on this trip. The route's first stop was far before his uncle Randon's keep. The sleek design of the vessel was meant to fit into the crevice canal network of the Kiss, described by the Shaw scouts, which led to the secret entrance through Zsolindal.

"So, how many o' those ridiculous trinkets did you hand out?" Sarin laughed accusingly at Kyson.

One of the other Timberhands, Ryder, Ondrew believed his name was, chimed in to his female companion, "I musta saw him buy 'bout ten o' those things from the highway merchant 'fore we ever hit Frostdale! And saw him hand out at least half!" The other Timberhands, all aside from Kyson, laughed at the singer's expense, the inside joke beyond the grasp of the Norther Knights.

Kyson shot them the most pretentious grin and snubbed the jabs, undaunted. He pulled out a few silver arrow charms from his vest and spun them in his gloved hands, back and forth. His exotic amber eyes shot an alluring attempt at the head of the small ship, directly at Lilealah, who sat next to Ondrew. "Perhaps someone else wishes to be entranced by my wizardry."

The incomparably arrogant bard then bent low with an intent to seduce the unimpressed umbran captive. Ondrew felt a rise of annoyance with the man. He told himself it was simply dutiful protectiveness toward his charge, and nothing else. He had been dealing with Kyson and the Timberhands' quips for days. While their jovial demeanor was a delightful hit with most of his crew, it did not strike Ondrew's particular favor to stay in such lighthearted conduct during these dire times.

Ondrew looked to his knights and new fellowmen near him at the bow of the boat, and then glanced at Lilealah, directly to his left side. They may as well have been holding hands, as close as they were, with their thighs touching and incidentally rubbing against each other upon each rolling wave.

Lilealah smiled at the egotistical minstrel. The normally quiet umbran blithely played the game. "A wizard, then? Please tell us more of your power, oh magical one."

Broc BrKomak, holding her chains on the opposite side of Ondrew, retorted with a scoff at Kyson's absurd claim. "Bah, there be no mages round here, boy! An' yer eyes be that o' southern fire. All know mages got the green in their eye. Ye claim t' be a mage, then show yer marks, singer!"

All the Timberhands looked at their antagonizing speaker, eager to hear what tale he was going to spin out of this one. Kyson remained grinning, gladly obliging the banter. "Marks? I have no tattoos. I never said I was a mage, good sir. I said 'wizard.' A grand difference."

Broc and the general populace of the boat in hearing distance looked over at the songster in disbelief. "Pah! Well, there be no such a thing as a wizard! So cast yer tall tales int' the Black Bay as bait fer all they be worth. Catchin' nary a fish in this boat!"

"But of course I am a wizard. I cast spells daily. The only true magic there is, you see." As Kyson attempted to outargue his contender, Ondrew turned to look in the direction of the ship's path along the ice wall. He would not let Kyson see his smirk of acceptance. This archer had the gift of gab and had somehow stolen the attention of all those around him. He could probably say anything next and win the argument. "Music. Song! The only real magic that will outlast it all."

No one appeared to know how to reply to such an unexpected but obvious answer coming from whom it did.

The silence after allowed Kyson to explain himself. "I've seen your faces when I play. I've felt your hearts when I sing. I have witnessed some of you smile on this song and cry on that one. I have seen men and women struck in a daze, unable to move. I've walked upon those seduced by my voice, subjugated to my will. I've had farmers and fishermen fight savages of the Undawned Lands like trained soldiers, just because of song." He broke into a makeshift melody as he sang the rest while strumming his lute.

So listen now, and tell me if I'm wrong ...
We, the Norther Knights, we fight like the Thrench,
By honor to glory, spoils far yond we can quench.
You shall see our mighty Barredom restored,
And see a prince remade of our high lord.
Oh, to each of you, raise thy sword,
Of blood and gold, I so confess my word,
And all because ... of song ...

Ondrew looked around at his men, studying the emotions on their faces. Everyone was awestruck, giving Kyson their undivided attention, other than the two prejudiced Vellyans, for whatever purpose. Evidently, Kyson was not done, since he continued to wrap up his oration.

"Oh, and also because I am a wizard." If the entire ship hadn't burst in sudden mirth, Ondrew definitely couldn't have pinpointed who resisted.

Kyson got up from his personal chest, which served as his seat, like the rest of the crew's, and balanced a few paces ahead to the vicinity of Ondrew and Lilealah. The bard bowed low with one hand out wide in a courteous fashion, and one outstretched to gift the umbran the arrow tokens in his hand. She reluctantly accepted them, as if asking for Ondrew's permission, and nodded politely to the bard.

Kyson stood back up dramatically fast as a large wave struck the ship, nearly toppling him completely over, but he caught himself in a timely spin, dexterously turning the stumble into more of a nimble dance as he regained composure. He then shouted to his new comrades across the longship. "And evidently also because of a few arrows properly handed out!"

Ondrew also laughed this time, joining in with the full ship of his merry men. He had never felt such mixed emotion of inner jealousy coupled with confiding faith toward a single man in his life. Kyson was someone no one could not take their eyes off.

The ever-changing black face of Continents' Kiss was mesmerizing. One could find just about any imagined design in the natural rock face of packed ice and stone. The day declined into eventide, and for the most part, Ondrew remained quiet unless addressed. His thoughts were heavy on what to expect in the legendary unknowns of Zsolindal.

His concentration was often interrupted by allowing his ears to bend toward one of the many selections of chatter around the boat.

On one side, he had the Timberhands hounding one of the Eldenvale Rangers on the most nonsensical of topics. The archer Caldwell pressured the ranger Denson. "So ya mean to tell me, ya gots a knight named Huntley who's ne'er been on a hunt, and a fella named Black who's pale as snow?"

On another side, he could hear the Lockeharts debating with the Orevilles over past land disputes that only their great-grandfathers could likely put any final justification to.

And nearest to himself and Lilealah, he was caught listening to the educational sermon of Broc BrKomak, preaching to the youngest of his original knights, Datron Ackhill.

Datron was relentlessly brave and naive to try to debate with the gruff veteran, but his passion vented nonetheless. "Say what you will. If a troll came at me, I would fight it dead! The Glace Isles tribes still use throwing axes and spears, like primitives, and carry on no swordplay. The sword wins out against all weapons five times out of five. Look at all the human regions of civilization, and tell me why it is, then, that the elven are in hiding and we are not. And if any Neveril still dares reside in Zsolindal, they'll be cut down the same as we would do any troll!"

As much as he desired for each of his men to employ that kind of courage against their enemy, he couldn't help but wince at the eager nineteen-year-old, who had yet to wet his blade in real battle. Broc was the one who took it as his duty to shut the inexperienced knight down. "Ye Thrench, boy?" the former yharl vociferously puffed down at the young knight.

Datron looked upon his burly mentor in sheer confusion, proudly boasting, "Thrench? I'm Barredish through and through! Thought you knew this, Br—"

Broc didn't let him finish, huffing in his rowdy voice back down at his apprentice. "Didn't think ye were Thrench, so that be too bad! Boy, ye've ne'er seen an elvan in yer life, besides this savage lass next t' ye, or maybe in the Bayn dungeon! Ye think this be what they look like? Let me 'splain somethin' t' ye they don't tell ye in squire school, an' I had t' learn the hard way." Broc stood up from his lockbox seat and whistled over to Mathias, who was already eavesdropping on the two knights' dispute.

The marred Eldenvale Ranger leader trekked his way over to the group at the bow. Everyone already knew the haunting tale of the man as one of the only two survivors who had lived through the massacre that felled Lord Lucas Blackendale's famed hunting party many years ago. Mathias had half his face chewed and scarred, from his jawline his right cheek, and was missing his ear on the same side. Where his right hand had once been, a small grabbing claw was fastened instead. Ondrew was eager to hear the actual story from the mouth of the hunter himself.

Mathias exchanged seats with Broc, as the larger man stood and towered over the adolescent in question. Broc blustered, "Look at his face! Show me his hand an' ear. They reside in the belly o' them primitives, boy!"

Datron didn't respond, enthralled by finally looking upon the disfigured features of Mathias without the previous hesitations of doing so out of disrespect.

The brawny knight continued. "Math, tell this poor pup what a troll can do!"

The grim hunter maintained his seated balance upon Broc's chest while the rocking longship cut deftly through the sporadic ambush of waves. His voice was raspy but clear over the thrash of the cold sea. "Your blade is quick, young knight. Quicker than ours. Our skill is indeed marred by age. And by the summit of the day, your stamina plays the victor against those with seasons, who suffer from weary old bones and war injuries unhealed. Can you imagine a soldier with the proficiency of Black, the strategy of Ondrew, the ire of Broc, and the speed of yourself? One would need a lifetime of training to get there, yes? Okay, then, now imagine fighting one of those very soldiers who has lived ten lifetimes or maybe more, and all the same still carries the vigor of your youth. To age as slowly as a tree but live indefinitely in your prime." Mathias continued, building into proving the validity of Broc's argument.

"Now I want you to imagine that soldier with unmatched speed and strength and skill and raw rage. Now imagine that he can self-heal, regenerate. He has no former injuries. And you can give him none new. If you cut him, his blood only sends him into a ceaseless fury as you watch the fresh wound seal before your eyes. As he plucks the very flesh from your skull. As he proceeds to dine on your face while you yet live. What is your move now, bold boy?" The hunter's voice escalated throughout the story's progression, with his clawed hand raised and challenging Datron to say just one more ignorant response.

None came from the stammering young knight. Mathias answered his own questions for him. "You have no move. You die. You die every damn time. Unless he chooses to let you live with your half-eaten face. This is the Terollar. These are the trolls of the Glace Isles. And there is only one proper way to kill them."

Lilealah replied for them all. "From a distance. No man will outmatch a Terollar in single combat. They are blessed with the Blooding. That fleeting frenzy you feel building just before you nerve yourself for battle? It dies after a few moments, just long enough to save you in your time of need, no? Well, for Terollar, it rekindles. Over and over. Through their innate self-healing, they cannot tire or bleed out. They do not lose that crazed rage. It rises the longer they are forced to fight. If you have not seen a Terollar in the full Blooding of battle, you have not seen what the perfect warrior is. You kill him from a distance, or you simply do not challenge him. So why, you reason, do most of them use throwing axes or spears, and not swords? Because they do not need swords. They only need weapons to kill your archers. If they get to you, then you've already lost no matter what is in their hands."

Datron's eyes were awestruck by the reproof that had indeed shut him up. Clearly, the declarations of Lilealah and Mathias had transfixed the entire boat into stillness, as everyone's focus was fixed on the lecturers at the bow.

Lilealah assuaged the visibly apprehensive looks that swarmed the faces of the knights around the ship by stating a hopeful fact. "I can ease all of your woes. The khomo is no longer a threat. He has fallen. And his elite Glazjhendun reside in your dungeons, awaiting execution. The remaining of the Glace Isles will never dare as far into Aggedon as we trek now. And no Wyldenar dwell in these parts, the same as Zsolindal is long empty of any Neveril. I am the only form of elvan you all will see—what little of any elvan that remains within me."

The oars on the right side of the longship were suddenly pulled. The gargantuan divide of the frozen isthmus was approaching to within spear shot at a rapid pace, with the crash of the waves maneuvering the boat toward it. The bottom of the Kiss, at the base of the bay, was white and stone, of typical glacial rock, and not like the blackened ebonice of the higher rise.

The Shaw brothers stood pointing ahead, directing the longship's navigator toward the cavern opening ahead in the Kiss. A stillness from the men encompassed the boat, induced by both the anticipation and fear of entering the unknown. Only the sound of the swells battling the cliffs in an eternal war of sea versus ice could be heard, drowning out the splash of the cautious oars guiding the vessel to its cryptic destination.

"There! The ice tunnel! Zsolindal is through there," Sheridan Shaw, the elder of the two brothers, shouted as he indicated the direction ahead.

Ondrew studied the sky one last time. The sun and the moon were both about, on the brink of dusk. Luminous stars and fading clouds fought for authority over the heavens. He knew this would be the last time he would look upon their celestial expressions for quite some time.

The oared ship grazed through the calming waters of the skinny channel that snaked its way underneath the overhang of the looming land bridge, traversing its way through the icy sea caverns. Light was fading fast.

The transitory voyage under the Kiss gradually brought them

upon the opening to the former home of the nefarious northern Neveril. Dark red crystalytes wreathed the otherworldly entrance to the cave that would lead his men through the southern half of Aggedon undetected. The faint glow of the crystalytes was enough to illuminate the ceiling of the glacial grotto in a majestic radiance that cast an illusion, making the waters appear the color of wine, coupled with a frosty mist that rose from the spiritually eerie lagoon. Humans were not supposed to experience such splendor as the foregone elvankind were teasing him with.

Please let the ghosts be gone from this place. I will not betray my men by leading them into foreign tombs. The nature of the Neveril was unknown to the living in Barredom, except what knowledge had been passed down from ancestor to ancestor. The only human country world-famed for combatting the subterranean elven were the indomitable Thrench.

Neveril elven were oft called "ghosts", just as the Wyldenar were "wyldes" and Terollar were "trolls" in such slang terminology. He was sure no one in his crew, excluding Lilealah, had seen the white-skinned elven in their lifetime, but the mere thought of invading their eldritch warrens prompted a shudder through his bones. He would blame the tremor on the chill of the frost fog if asked.

The longship was rowed directly up to the rocky shore that scaled to the radiantly lit entrance. The Norther Knights disembarked and bade farewell to the boat's captain, who would be returning to the channel to Northaven. If Ondrew and his men came back alive at all, it would not be by the same route. General Randon's contingency plan was supposed to offer them an alternative, to reroute them with the Barredish army. Ondrew was privy to the exact details and decided he would inform his men when the suitable time came.

"Zsolindal," Snowden Shaw whispered to his brother as they all beached, with packs readied to begin their venture. The longship of remaining oarsmen pushed off from the shallow shore and circled around the lagoon to leave them to their quest.

"Zsolindal, we meet again," Sheridan returned to his younger sibling. Named lead scout and expert on the caverns, Sheridan nodded to his liege to call the order to commence forward.

Ondrew took the cue. Guardedly hushed, but loud enough to let his voice be heard by his crew, he decreed across the echoing grotto, "Take your last breath of fresh air, brethren. We follow the Shaws, and we vow to nary a word inside, unless I nod for approval. You all know the chain of the fallen if I fail. But we will not fail." Ondrew pulled his pack open and revealed two bottles of Utamian Sweetmint, the favored alcoholic drink of the union. He had strictly told them all to pack no such hindrances. Nevertheless, he had prearranged the liquid encouragement for them all as a motivating incentive.

He pulled a third bottle from his pack and severed its top with his belt knife. He took the first small swig of the milky, intoxicating substance, then handed it over to Broc to pass down the line. "Our first drink together on our first mission, and my oath that it is not our last! Get the torches ready."

"Osh, osh, oshah!" The original Norther Knights and Eldenvale Rangers joined in on the spontaneous chant, with the two Vellyans and the Timberhands leaving it a bit late to join in the ritual.

Forty-three men, one woman, and their detained Wyldenar umbran began upon their odyssey into the depths of Zsolindal. For every fourth man, a torch was lit and carried in place of a weapon or shield. Even with the recurrent Neveril crystalytes, formed in the abnormal stone walls, producing the radiant dread-red glow, Ondrew chose to trust nothing other than the fiery natural light that was carried by his own men.

Just as they neared the first corner, only moments into the elvan tunnels, the two Shaw scouts in the lead both waved their hands back to halt the group in their tracks. Ondrew ceased movement, and his entourage obeyed his intuition.

Sheridan pointed to the seemingly mundane stony ground at the curve. Ondrew registered nothing out of the ordinary, other than the lack of lighting from the large section barren of any crystalyte formations. Hardly any justification for why he had immobilized the crew. But Sheridan spoke up to explain, shining his torch high to the tunnel's ceiling. "Firetears."

His younger brother, Snowden, pointed at the two elvan runes etched into the stone above their heads. Sheridan further clarified. "Neveril traps. We set the first one off coming through on our initial scout. Snowden noticed the tiny holes in the walls, thank the Five and Five." He shone his flaming light into the cave corner to illuminate the small hollows he had described, half the size of grapes. "Everyone step back."

The Norther Knights all did as commanded. Sheridan searched for a heavy stone, just light enough to be manageably tossed. He threw the melon-sized rock onto the hidden pressure plate that resided underneath one of the runes. An instant hissing spray burst from the holes in the cave wall, shrouding the entire corner in a cloud of orange mist.

"If it gets in your nose or mouth, you're a dead man within less than an hour. At first you'll feel the sting in your throat. Then you'll feel the bleed from your nose and mouth. That's not when you die. It's when you start to feel the tears in your eyes and ears. When the blood turns orange, you'll start the cry. Tears till you die."

Sheridan waited until the poison fully dissipated and finished with one final advisement. "We scouted many exits from these devil halls on our survey, but never the route we're taking. The ghosts have these runes at each egress we came across. Be wary to heed that. Let us keep the lead."

Even with the Neveril long gone from their northern underrealm, this cavernous world would be no less perilous. This was going to be a harsh expedition, thick with dark tidings and deep paranoia—beginning now.

Fives protect us as we say farewell to the heavens above and enter the hells beneath ...

WESTWALKER (IV)

THE BOARNECKS

The enemy cliff line stood in rare form as friendly campfires burned on both sides of the once impassible land bridge. The infamous Fourteen at the northern edge of the Kiss now seemed like nothing more than scenic ruins for southern tourists. Swarms of men scurried in and out of the vacant defenses, and for the first time in history, none of them were stoneborne or greyborne.

What was once an unthinkable territory to approach was now a safe haven of over fifteen thousand tents topped with a diversity of allied sigils. The ranks were filled with the battle-scarred men of Northaven, along with the soldiers of Frostdale and the mounted mercenaries of the Boarneck Cavaliers. Even several of the heavy-armored Daynishmen had entered the fold.

The fields were littered with Barredom's black banners of House Roth, with green pines and the great white bear in the foreground. Throughout, all could bear witness to the Fire Star of Az'Dayne, the symbol for House Ampion, a black dawnstar mace sporting nine spikes, depicted upon an orange background. The tusked brown boar head on red pennants, representing the Boarneck Cavaliers, married with the multicolored emblazonry. Various royal heraldries throughout the Dominadom's reach also embellished the snowy tapestry that covered the formerly forbidden grounds.

Tsuno strolled through the camp by escort of Commandant Nathahn, with Ryleohk directly behind. The snowfall was thin today, with long periods of none at all. The ground had already lost several layers in a matter of days as the Dawning season climbed toward the approaching Sunder.

Today would be his last day at this insufferable camp of reproachful northmen. He had been obliged to tolerate their company for the past couple of pentdays, but being the only qindrid in the mix made socializing futile, particularly when shadowed by Ryleohk.

In scheduled time, they were coming upon General Roth's command tent for their final briefing. One of the scoutmaster's rangers had returned at sunup, bearing news of the eastern reach at the Great Grey Wall, Two-Towns. Nathahn ushered Tsuno and Ryleohk inside.

The tent pavilion boasted a pentagonal war table with a decem seats total in place: five on the corners and five pulled against the sides. Randon Roth sat at the north point of the table, waiting impatiently for the tardy to take their stations. The discriminatory general neglected to censor his scowling visage, turned on the half-clothed, barefoot grey elvan as Ryleohk entered the makeshift lodging of privileged humans.

Surprisingly, Tsuno was offered one of the ten chairs at the table, reserved for the Westwalker, in the far left corner, between Commandant Nathahn and some bearded Boarneck man he did not recognize. Scoutmaster Thade was already sitting in the adjacent corner seat, next to Nathahn. Tsuno exchanged a nod with him before inspecting the rest of the ranked individuals invited to the tent.

In the right corner seat, nearest to the general, was the distinguished Willem Shaw, Commandant of Frostdale, while the officer between himself and Thade was none other than Godrey Lockehart, a young battle hero who had just been proclaimed by the king as the new Commandant of the Fourteen on the yestermoon. Both were famously respected figures throughout Barredom and capable lieutenants under Randon.

Seated closest to Roth was a chosen from the Az'Dayne Dominadom and a spokesman sent from the Frostdale Council. The Dominadom's delegate seemed to be an extravagantly decorated paladin, dressed in full bronze plate, with the signature orange cloak and symbolic tabard ornamenting his armor. A two-handed dawnstar was strapped securely across his back. The high paladin's great helm and emblazonry were customized much more eccentrically than Tsuno had noticed in the attire of the other Daynish knights prancing outside.

Frostdale's appointee was High Chancellor Soro of the Qaegons, an influentially persuasive but arrogant nobody of alleged royal roots in Mageholme bloodlines that none in the high court could ascertain. He had no real surname, and even though he was of northern roots, his state of dress was entirely southern, like that of the exotics in the popular capital territories. He had the same outlandish green eyes, angular face, and shaved scalp as the silent Forwoken monks, who safeguarded the most prominent Frostdale sects and the royal chambers of highest importance. His lofty height was a hand or more greater than any in the room.

His story told that as an adolescent boy, he had been presented to Seagram Bloodmont, Yharl of Whalestown, as the chosen voice of the Forwoken warriors from the Qaegons monastery. Yharl Seagram had been the father of the richest house in all of Barredom for the last two decades. His words and opinions held power in the court. Fostered by Seagram like a son, Soro was pushed into Frostdale as a liaison between Whalestown, the Forwoken monastery, and the council. His political navigation happened swiftly and timely. Shortly after the Dominadom absorbed full sovereignty over Barredom, Soro found that his unexplained foreign lineage aided him even further as he was promoted to High Chancellor, a new position on the council, with more voice than all the other seats combined. The enigmatic man was indeed cunning, with a knack for scheming.

Nine out of ten seats were filled, with the last vacant, reserved for the absent Boarneck Cavaliers' captain, not to Tsuno's remote surprise. The unruly sellsword audaciously made it clear that he did not care for scheduled promptness.

Ryleohk showed his classic trait of disinterest and took a place to squat in, in the corner behind Thade, away from the curiosities of the battle map and as far away from any humans as he could be.

Frostdale's chancellor spoke up after several quiet seconds. "Might we begin, then, General?"

Randon declined in annoyance, chewing on the inside of his cheek. "We wait for one more to join."

The commotion of some raucous individual just outside the tent flap approached, and in stumbled a flamboyantly dressed drunkard. His shirt was puffy in the sleeves and striped like that of a troubadour, in drab green and violet, with the neck of his collar a ridiculously large white ruff. His pants were cloth tights, the brightest red in color, and he was knee-high in black riding boots. Strapped upon his left shoulder was a pauldron made from the head of a tusked boar, with the hide of its skull still preserved.

Enter Tristostopher, leader of the nefarious Boarneck Cavaliers. Tsuno had already had the unfortunate displeasure of meeting him. While he emitted a vivaciously masculine personality, he was not the least bit shy to let the world know he preferred the company of men, with a ravenous fetish to bed a qindrid of each kind before his contract ended in the north. His insufferable dallying toward Tsuno hadn't stopped since the moment they met.

The Boarneck captain burst in with his drinking horn in hand, spilling about as he swerved his feet to his seat between Soro and the other Boarneck representative. As the inebriated mercenary plopped down, the ale from his curved mug nearly splashed on Soro's shoes. He looked around the tent with a goofy smile and tipsy sway of his head.

"Now we may begin," Randon presented in an irritated tone, glaring down the sellsword boss with thorough disdain.

Soro superciliously scoffed at the mercenary's obnoxious entrance as Tristostopher's ale horn casually turned upside down beside the man's seat, with the beverage spreading even more in the direction of the chancellor's feet. "Is this some kind of joke, General?" Soro demanded, frantically kicking his shoes from the spill.

"Soro, is it?" the captain politely addressed him.

"You, sir, are above your place! I do not answer to drunken jesters. Your Boarneck rabble may well be the most preposterous waste of the crown's coin ever endorsed," the young chancellor berated.

Tristostopher smiled fully at the lanky man a few measures from him and took a hearty swill of his horn to finish the pungent liquid inside. He let the makeshift mug go to dangle from the strap around his neck and shoulder. "Always dress and act like a fool, I say! That way, you get the surprise of your enemy and the applause of your ally when you suddenly do something serious." And in an instant, the captain lunged out to clamp Soro's wrist to the table with one hand, and with his dagger in the other, he slammed the blade precisely between the chancellor's fingers.

Soro cursed in fear and tried to pull away, but Tristostopher kept the council member pinned. It was the general who had to bring order back to the room. "Are we finished sizing cocks yet? There will be no more disruptions at my table."

The general ensured he had captured everyone's attention once more after the obnoxious sellsword released Soro. "First, brief introductions for those of you foreign or unfamiliar."

General Randon began calling roll clockwise, languidly pointing to each individual he defined as he went around the pentagonal table. "High Paladin Cederick, delegate of the Pentagogue for the Az'Dayne Dominadom. Willem Shaw, 'the Spear of the North,' Commandant of Frostdale and Castle Bayn. Godrey Lockehart, 'the Purger of Defiance,' new Commandant of the Fourteen. Scoutmaster Thade Karway, overseer of reconnaissance north of the Kiss. Nathahn BrKomak, Commandant of Northaven and second to my delegation in Aggedon. The Sho'Lonese skyborne, aliased the Westwalker, and the rogue-Wyldenar Ryleohk."

Randon paused to swallow, as if engaged in an inner debate on whether to commend them for their recognized achievements in Barredom. The words came out like he was passing a kidney stone. "Commissioned specialists and tolerated allies, by King Aerik's orders, for covert missions involving qindrid bounties."

That wasn't so bad, now, was it? Tsuno amused himself as the general concluded the mentionable.

"Jonan Riveiros, distinguished alchemist of the Boarneck Cavaliers. Tristostopher Boldandgold, captain of the Boarnecks, who leads our two thousand mounted mercenaries. And finally, High Chancellor Soro, voice of the Frostdale Council in King Aerik's absence."

Randon did not skip a beat, disallowing possible interruptions to his momentum. "Now that the niceties are done with, I invite all eyes to the map. West Aggedon is in the jurisdiction of the Az'Dayne Dominadom now, under the protection of Barredom. We have reports of no qindrid as far as Loch Karlohr. And even then, they are few but stubborn stragglers, until you reach Two-Towns here." He stabbed his personal knife into the middle of the Great Grey Wall, segregating the noted towns. "The scoutmaster's men report that a riot of reluctance toward this Great Exodus has amassed at Two-Towns, comprised of not just greyborne and stoneborne." Randon gave a rehearsed nod to Nathahn, across from him.

Commandant Nathahn briefly left the tent to return with the entry guards and a large prison cage on wheels. It incarcerated two peculiar foreigners not found in this part of the realm, but clearly identifiable for Tsuno.

Randon tested the interested lot. "Do any of you know what these are?"

"Skyborne, as I am," Tsuno imperturbably replied. "But from Caelduym, not Sho'Lon. They are our northern neighbors. They were the second to find the curse, centuries before any stoneborne of Aggedon came about. Their culture is far different from mine."

And indeed, though skyborne as they were, these qindrid held perceptible cosmetic differences from Tsuno. Other than their trait of skyborne grey skin, white hair, and sky-blue eyes, they resembled the northmen of Aggedon and Barredom much more than Tsuno did. He remembered their people from his transitory explorations throughout their inhospitable regions. Caelduyans were hardy barbarians of heavy superstitions and crude life.

"Accurate." It was the most Randon had ever vocally agreed with Tsuno. "Our direct enemy has sided with this unknown foe to the east. The Aggedonians' Great Exodus is nothing more than a great ruse to reinforce themselves with a stronger ally, these Caelduyan skyborne, and attempt to invade south! They may even pull his accursed skyborne to us." Randon's rage flared while he death-stared Tsuno with the insinuation.

Fortunately, Tsuno didn't have to defend such ridiculous allegations, as High Chancellor Soro soundly reasoned. "This is cynically conjectured assumption, General. I assure you, we can evaluate every detail here today, and I will bring report to King Aerik to consider what decision to make on this."

Randon did not hide his sheer frustration at the mention of his suddenly scarce brother.

Thade was the first to interject with his own concerns. "How did you come by these two? My men just turned in their report this morning, and you would need an army to get through those gates," he explained, referencing Two-Towns.

Randon's smug sneer said it all about how satisfied he felt about successfully keeping everyone in the dark. "Lilealah. When we saved the witch from the trolls, she wasn't with just her stoneborne or the greyborne. Both of these whiteheads were with her. My men involved were sworn to secrecy." The general looked behind him to judge the detained.

High Chancellor Soro squealed in protest. "Why, then, was the council not informed? You sent the elven and other qindrid survivors to us, even the umbran. Why did you not send report to the king? It is your duty—"

Randon sternly interjected. "It is my duty to aid my brother in winning the war we have been fighting since we were born. The same war that our ancestors for generations have bled for. I say I know my brother's mind better than any of you ephemeral court masters, who shift from season to season."

The general looked about the eager assembly, maintaining complete composure, with eyes grimly set on his caged foes. "If I had turned these over to Inquisitor Bayn, they would be good as dead. But I have further use of them, alive. I will let this one speak of his people's intentions."

Nathahn began translations of the Caelduyan trying in broken Norspeak, obviously not the captured qindrid's inherent language. The skyborne sporting a bare chest was who spoke as their envoy, with the longest hair of the two. *"We of Caelduym entreat them of the Aggedon, by strength of numbers, to wall against our new, great enemy. We have seen the true threat that will drown the mountains and swallow us of the qindrid in this sea of blood. In comes the Ashenwave. Lilealah brings the Great Exodus, and with it comes salvation through her many allies."* The feat of Nathahn translating Norspeak may have been the only impressive thing witnessed from the general's puppet since Tsuno had met him.

Soro consoled the captives, for intended interpretation into the language. "I can assure you, by the imperial command of the Az'Dayne Dominadom, you will get your wish of the sanctioning of Barredom to permit your people continuance in their evacuation. I have papers here, signed and sealed by King Aerik Roth, decreed by the dual dominarchs, to allow the Aggedonian qindrid uninterrupted passage from their homeland. I will see to it that you are released without harm as well, for your cooperation." The chancellor pulled a scroll from his vest to hand across the table to Randon.

Nathahn opened his mouth to begin translation into Norspeak, but his military peer stopped him with his hand. Randon stared at the chancellor with an utterly bored countenance. He did not reach out for the scroll and let Soro place it, untouched, in the middle of the table. "We will do no such thing," Randon dared against the commands of his liege.

Hushed gasps sprang about the tent from seemingly everyone but Tristostopher, Ryleohk, and himself. General Randon elaborated to give his reasoning. "Calm yourselves. They cannot understand our tongue and need not know my intent. You would have me believe my competent yet mysteriously absent brother would simply have me let our timeless foe depart unscathed? To rally with a larger nation of strange qin that may return fivefold after they defeat their present enemy? And this one even speaks of Lilealah having other outside allies. What say you to all of this?"

Soro boldly returned, "I would have you open the parchment yourself and bear witness to your king's command for how to direct the Dominadom's army."

Randon pulled his knife from the middle of the war table and opened the hardened wax, skimming through the order with overt skepticism. "If Aerik thinks me fool enough to submit to this paltry maneuver, then I dare say he should have stripped me of my title as general long ago! We have taken the Fourteen, and we are primed to invade eastern Aggedon. This is the most monumental accomplishment in Barredish history, and still he dishonors me by not even showing his face. He should be here now." His booming tone matched the crash of his fist on the battle map, toppling over several figurines. "I will continue to act on my task as it has been laid out before me, to permanently eradicate every last qindrid from the whole of Aggedon."

"Brother of the king or no, what you speak of could count as treason, to go against the Dominadom's command. You intend to rekindle an ended war," High Paladin Cederick forewarned.

Randon would not yield to the threat of his undesired southern sovereigns. "I do not believe these orders to be in the best interest of Barredom. I believe them to be quite the opposite. Allowing the qindrid to leave unharmed, without pursuit, will be the fall of our realm. This abomination speaks of the Ashenwave. That is a hint of the Thrench invasion from the Emmonost army. Let the Thrench slaughter the Caelduyans while we scythe the Aggedonians in their retreat. The survivors in the middle will not survive past Kingfall," Roth reasoned, seemingly trying to convince himself of the logic as much as his judging peers around the tent. "If I were to allow this demise of Barredom, I would be branded unfit for command when the qindrid return. If my brother wishes me to permit our enemy safe passage, then he can come and tell me himself. He knows where I will be, at the vanguard of the charge!"

A long and awkward moment of silence followed. Tsuno felt completely out of his element. He turned around to see Ryleohk in the same corner, indifferent to the tedious exchanges of humans. His elvan friend's focus seemed to be more on a beetle crawling around on the floor that Tsuno had just now taken note of.

High Paladin Cederick retaliated again, with a candid, compassionate tone. "I sympathize with your position and history in the present circumstances, General Roth. But what you propose will be followed by consequences unless you proceed with the blessing of the Dominadom. I cautiously urge you to consider my words, if we may speak alone after this briefing, before dispensing mandates to the army we still *allow* you to command."

"I will heed your private counsel. But I know my brother's heart and do not recognize these words." Randon threw the scroll down to the floor like it was on fire. "Az'Dayne need not get involved in the finale of a war that was never theirs to begin with."

Randon minded not to make eye contact with the paladin. Tsuno thought he even caught a glimpse of worriment on the perturbed tactician. The general was never one to sway from his determination.

Randon gritted his teeth, gnawing on his inner cheek, as always, and began to move about the war table. He grabbed the boar head figurine and the small grey statuette, placing them on the map near Two-Towns and the Thurowood. "We will not stand idle. The Westwalker and his wylde will go with the Boarnecks. The Boarnecks have brought a weapon that has never been tested on the qindrid."

"Blast salt," the captain confessed as he dramatically sprinkled nothingness with his fingers in the direction of his pyrotechnician. "Meet the chef of my favorite recipe."

The master alchemist Jonan beamed with pride in his anticipated moment to capture the room. "The granules are small, like thick white salt," he vivaciously elaborated. "It is a special compound that, when ignited, expands in a combustion so powerful that one fistful could blow the door and wall off a stone house. The flame comes out pure red, not the orange and yellow of real fire. It disintegrates all that it touches instantly, and explodes with a violent effect."

"And we've brought kegs of it! One hundred to be exact," the Boarneck captain smugly claimed with a crazy eye on the Caelduyans.

Randon particularized the strategy to the assembly. "Two-Towns sits on top of a depleted platinum mine, with its entrance directly underneath the northern wall, near the Thurowood. The Westwalker and a handful of the Boarnecks will pose as greys to infiltrate and detonate the blast-salt kegs under the gate at the mine's base. This will cause a breach point with the collapse and create a diversion to bring the forces to the north side of the town. The Reluctants will be baited to the bonfires lit in the Boarneck Cavaliers' camp, to which they will likely lash out in full offense. Their destination in the Thurowood will already be prelined with traps and readied for the mercenaries to flank on all sides.

"Meanwhile, my forces from the V'Gilan High Road will hit them from the south and wipe out the escapees and the resilient that stay behind. We will use Two-Towns as a base to stage our following advance on Aepox and end their reign in Aggedon. This country will be stoneborne-free before the Umbra season."

Commandants Godrey and Willem looked nervously to Soro, as if for consent in the king's voice, then to High Paladin Cederick, fearing the Dominadom would doom them for overstepping permissions. Nathahn and Thade shuffled uneasily, studying the pragmatic eyes of Randon Roth across the table from them. Tsuno and the Boarnecks just sat back, watching the political spectacle with amusement.

Scoutmaster Thade furthered the justification of his superior. "My scouts convey that there is an escort of greyborne citizens being led from the gates on the east road into Ur Sulborol. But far more than half the city doesn't seem to be moving. Thousands of soldiers fortify the bulwarks, preparing for our expected advance. The defense will be made up of obstinate citizens refusing to take part in the migration, along with the Two-Towns militia, the stoneborne who stayed behind, and several of these Caelduyan skyborne, likely now in the fold as well."

Commandant Willem Shaw agreed in half support of Randon's agenda. "I received the same command from King Aerik as was scribed on that note." He pointed to the scroll on the table, discarded to the side. "I have been ordered to garrison the Frostdale forces for your endeavor, General, up to the Great Grey Wall to secure Two-Towns and rid the north of the Reluctants. But I have been strictly forbidden to aid beyond that."

Randon looked at Willem and to Godrey as if his men had betrayed him by siding with the king over their general. The Reluctants had been referenced, the category for all Aggedonians that weren't choosing to join Lilealah's Great Exodus to Caelduym.

"It seems you have it, Randon." Cederick put his period on the end of the debate of insubordination. "Your war ends at the Great Grey Wall, or you risk much in pursuit beyond, by the hands of your enemy or by the law and justice of your homeland."

Randon chewed so much on the inside of his cheek, Tsuno was surprised a hole didn't appear. His eyes fixated in a glazed look of deep contemplation on Aepox upon the war map for future decisions. He nodded and plainly said, "It is settled, then. Tristostopher, your Boarnecks, the trapmaster, and the wylde leave immediately," Randon finished. "Leave me. I have much to discuss."

Tsuno and Ryleohk fell in on cue, leaving Randon and Cederick to their private meeting of choices and the consequences thereof. Tsuno wondered how all this would play out in the royal court, should Randon ignore political caution and move against the Dominadom's mandate to finish his Barredish core calling. Opposing the imperial behemoth seemed like guaranteed suicide.

Tsuno was already packed in eagerness to be done with the chaotic cluster that now plagued Continents' Kiss. He began the short jaunt to the quartermaster's warehouse. He would be directly impersonating Landron, the stoneborne huntmaster he had recently baited and dispatched. For the sabotage of Two-Towns, he needed to grab the Aggedonian's unique helm and armor for the upcoming ruse.

He was caught off guard when a heavy hand wrapped around his shoulder and pulled him in for an awkward shared stroll. "Fortune smiles! It looks like we will be spending a lot more time with each other!"

Tristostopher had appeared from nowhere, reeking of ale but without any drunken slur. Tsuno cursed under his breath, irritated by his new, burly pest. He reverted to his native Sho'Lonese dialect. *"And I will pretend not to speak the Civil from here on out as well."*

The Boarneck captain did not relent. "And seducing me in your Westwalker tongue? Please continue!"

Quickly defeated, Tsuno switched back to the Civil tongue. "You are going to make this ride unpleasant, Tristose. There will be plenty of unwilling greyborne to fuck in the fields ahead. No reason to catch a stray poison bolt before then."

"Tristose? So familiar already, are we? I like it! And I can promise you the ride I mean to give will be more than pleasant," Tristostopher coaxed just as Ryleohk came up from behind, shoving hard the captain's shoulder, separating Tsuno and Tristostopher. "As long as you leash that territorial shadow of yours."

Ryleohk didn't cease his brisk pace, trekking past the both of them without apology or notice. Tsuno grinned, assuring him, "Territoriality and Wyldenar are one and the same. Speak straight. What will you lend me once we diverge at the Thurowood?"

Tristostopher rolled his eyes, obviously annoyed at the content of their conversation being switched back to business, but adapted to the subject. "Roth tells me you took down eight stones recently, which you will be posing as. I've already begun picking out the seven that will accompany you with the sleds to Two-Towns for the blast. Jonan, of course, will be among them. Still seems like folly to split forces and chance the guard towers picking us off, instead of sweeping their retreat from behind in full," the captain reasoned.

Tsuno laughed at that, knowing the pragmatic soldier's experience very well. "Few question General Randon's strategy game. He knows Az'Dayne will deny him further reinforcements, and Frostdale's appointees just informed us that they won't be joining him beyond the Great Grey Wall. He will be making the charge into Aepox with his forces from Northaven and your Boarnecks alone. Makes little room for casualty risk." Tsuno waded in and out of the bustle of soldiers, all readying themselves for the departure. Ryleohk was carving a struggling path to the quartermaster as best he could through the bedlam of anticipative men.

"With your blast salt, the diversion, and the flank tactics around the town bulwark, have no doubts in Randon Roth. The fewer men fall at the battle of Two-Towns, the more of them he will inspire on his march to Aepox, against the command of their recently evasive king. If Randon lives to see the end of this, he will be the biggest hero the north has ever revered. If he dies, he will become a martyr. His brother and these dominarchs will have no choice but to pardon him to dissuade unrest."

"Well thought," Tristostopher mused. "Permit me two questions, then, before we start, prettyborne, ignorant as I am. Why is a qin helping Barredish kill other qin? How did one such as yourself, and this wylde, earn the trust of the uncompromising general?"

Tsuno only humored the exchange for the welcome banter. "You are more typical than ignorant. It's become the most tiresome query in the rare circumstance of one of you westerners speaking to me."

"Tristostopher Boldandgold is typical? An absurd accusation," the mercenary gasped, seemingly appalled.

Tsuno didn't play coy back. "I am sure anyone south of Frostdale thinks they know what a qindrid is. Some fell-souled, grey-skinned half-human who abandoned his gods long ago and surrendered his spirit to the elements instead. Seduced by the evil umbran to undergo some heretic ritual and become an immortal apostate. An idea of the hopeful afterlife in the Godslands traded away for an ageless real life. Do I have you measured thus far?"

Tristostopher sheepishly grinned. "Well, now, I am as transparent as glass, it would seem." The mercenary captain stared ahead at Ryleohk passing inside the palisade toward the quartermaster's hold. Ryleohk stopped his walk and turned around to his followers, apparently sensing that Tsuno had slowed behind him.

Tsuno paused at the palisade gates of the first looming fortress. He took the uncommon opportunity of someone willingly conversing with him to educate the captain further. "Inferring that all qindrid are allied and one and the same is just ill knowledge, branding from the northern naive," Tsuno elaborated, struggling to ease from his condescending tone.

His reserved insight into the qin as a people seemed to have the captain's attention. "But I am southern." The mercenary feigned a pout at the misidentification. Growing increasingly ecstatic, he exclaimed, "Ah, prettyborne, I would wager all my treasures that you could defeat any bard tale spun in Goldgarden! After this is done, you would do well to come with me and make a fortune in the Monodrome. I'll have you know I am part-proprietor. It's the largest amphitheater in all of Utamia, an enclosed cabaret venue atop the Centron Hill Ward in Goldgarden itself! Spellblade performers, mage prodigies, Psage prophets, and elvan prostitutes. They all visit, yet no qin like you! I will indulge you with the business opportunity on the road."

"This interrogation began with you fussing about my intent with the northmen." Tsuno squinted accusingly toward the mercenary. "I won't be joining you in Goldgarden, nor anywhere south of here. I am here for one reason: to rid myself of the Qindrid Curse and bring the cure back to my people, and rejoin my family before I take my last breath."

Without a pause, as if Tsuno were giving some form of audition, Tristostopher chimed, "You see! It's this kind of enactment that will make us wealthy beyond these miserable skirmishes I am forced to succumb to! I'll turn my company over to a trustee, to still gain the spoils but ensure our—"

"No," Tsuno intruded. His eyes fixed on Ryleohk.

The elvan stood barely over fifty yards from the quartermaster's hold, one hand behind on the haft of his axe at his back and the other twitching on the bone handle of his belt knife. Five men formed a half circle, blocking his path forward. Tsuno could make out their obvious taunts but could not discern the threats at the distance. The only sound Tsuno could hear was the feral rumble emitted by the rogue.

Tsuno closed the gap between himself and his friend. Ryleohk's eyes focused straight at the ground, aimed only at the feet of his provokers. His unruly tangle of grey-shaded hair hung over the front of his face in a way that one could barely glimpse his animalistic eyes. The group of agitators picked up on Tsuno's approach and turned their berating attacks on him.

"Was wonderin' when the husband would come t' rescue! Haven't ye both heard? We be packin' t' finish down the rest o' ye greyskins an' wyldes. Best be gettin' yer head start," one of the hillsmen warned, cracking his knuckles and teasing his hilt.

Tsuno pulled out Wraith and loaded a bolt from the repeater magazine, keeping it targeted downward, at nothing in particular. The same hillsman shouted after a mocking laugh, "Oh, so a grey's gonna aim his bow at us Dish in our own camp? Ye'll be quinted 'fore ye pull the trigger." He cited the popular Frostdale execution method done to noteworthy qindrid.

"No. I think not." Tsuno aimed the repeater bow straight at the speaker's head, causing sudden hesitation among the provokers. "Do you know who I am?"

The man stammered to find the correct words, as if he feared the wrong reply would result in instant death. Finally he stuttered, "West ... Westwalker. Everyone knows o' ye two."

"Precisely. Everyone does know our names. But the wager goes that no one of import knows yours. This fact tells me that you are simply unimportant and that my friend and I are important," Tsuno retorted. He had won this fight before it even began. "I am sure the general will forgive you and your unimportant lot for threatening his important specialists and obstructing them from commencing the mission at hand. Let us all trade names now, to see what my dear friend Randon Roth has to say. Or mayhap Aerik Roth too, his brother, if you've heard of him."

A few of the men took a step back at the insinuated threat, while the other two seemed riled. The leader of the bully pack scoffed and kicked a heap of snow in the direction of Tsuno, falling far short of his mark. "Bah! I'll no waste a spit on yer bluff! Ye'll see yerself in the Deeps when this war be said an' done. You ain't ne'er been a friend o' my Frostdale, greyskin!"

The aggressors stormed off, cursing among themselves, toward the ramparts. Tsuno walked up to Ryleohk and put a kindly hand on his taller friend's shoulder. He could hear Tristostopher casually dawdling up from behind.

The captain chuckled and joined them. "You do know you two have quite a name. Depictions and hearsay are contrived in Utamia and all around the Tairanheart. The Westwalker, his horse and bows and traps, the rogue and his axe—all tales and items of legend." Tsuno shook his head though, unaffected by the goad of southern fancied gossips. "You must allow me to be privy to a spin or two for my own delights."

Tsuno nodded to Ryleohk and made a gesture to continue on. The two departed from the garrulous Boarneck captain to furnish themselves with their last necessities for the mission. He shouted back one last thing before entering through the door of the provisioner's hold. "By the end of all this, you will have your fable to bring back to Goldgarden. Plenty of time for prattle on the road."

"Fortune smiles indeed! We leave on the hour. You and your wylde meet me in the lead," the mercenary cordially called.

They stepped inside and the door shut. Temporary peace. He looked over at his elvan companion and said not a word. *Back to our homes soon, my one friend.*

Ryleohk looked at him with silent eyes, converting his savage gaze into a docile stare. It was the elvan's familiar gesture of empathetic friendship.

AERIK (I)

THE TRIAL OF TRUTH

Aerik stood in the antechamber of the great library of Castle Frostdale. All his life, he had lived in or around the fortress city, but he had never before set foot inside the hallowed halls of its vast archive. Memory served that he must have read a hundred or more of the chronicles lining the walls.

His uncle Tomas had made sure to educate him on all matters of history, politics, and foreign enemies throughout the realm. His mother kept him further fed on volumes that contained compositions in the study of languages, or famous scribes' works on war strategy and battle accounts. Such was expected of him, being the only son of the Royal Inquisitor, Lady Honorah Bayn.

He imagined that his life might be entirely different if his father had still been alive. Perhaps his aspirations in regard to Az'Dayne would never have matured, with a rooted obligation concentrated exclusively on the Barredish cause. He was only six years of age when the report of his father's death had swept through the castle. His uncle Tomas, who had been part of Lucas's outfit, survived but came back blind and badly mangled. Aerik and Ebrielle were sent by Norah to be raised by Tomas and his father's sister. He had only come to know what Tomas had raised him to believe and what his mother had driven him to question.

The last of his auditions under the title of Aspirant in Barredom was now: the Trial of Truth. He stared into the scholars' treasury, where several study tables were supposed to be but none remained.

This sacred library had been altered for him. A lone chair sat in the middle of the hemispheric room. Around it several candles formed different layouts on the ground, toward the bookshelves. *Twenty-five candles.* There was more to the room, beyond the shelves, but no access was granted from entering the door before him.

Aerik had poorly attempted to avoid overanalyzing his loss in the Trial of Melee, but his lack of sufficient sleep over the month proved that he was failing at that endeavor. The man he had fought was unlike any other he had seen. Aerik had been trained by the noble swordmasters of Frostdale, but the victor fought like some timeless weapons specialist.

He thought on what it meant to become a paladin, which had been his lifelong ambition ever since he heard his first stories about the fabled men. The popular portrayal regarding paladins and veritans was of elite knights on vigilant patrol over Az'Dayne's urban utopia, exalted watchers of the one true faith, the Five and Five. But throughout his brief experience in the Trials, Aerik had come to know them as much more than that.

There were no courts or magistrates in Az'Dayne. There was no city watch. There was only the Pentagogue, the order of paladins and veritans. The rest of the ignorant realm had them categorized as venerated street guards in ceremonial armor and cumbersome weaponry. In reality, they were not known as combat connoisseurs. They were accomplished in discovering hidden truths and carrying out decreed arbitrations. They carried out the sentence of the Faith, and they did it in the streets and in the homes of the accused. They were the imperial guard, the Dominadom's detectives, and divine judges all in one. The few that escaped from their justice were subject to a writ that was delivered to Az'Dayne's Oathemic Cabal of revered assassins.

Being his mother's son, his powers of deduction had been sharpened at an early age. Neither his sister nor he could have avoided that tutelage. Of further benefit was the scrupulous nature he had developed in his early years. He was cursed with the maddening habit of counting and taking a precise note of every little thing around him. With a glance, he could determine the number of stone tiles in a hall, the number of specific designs on a distant tapestry, or the exact amount in coins on the surface of an open coffer. His awareness recurrently stretched indiscriminately in the most chaotic and random patterns.

He could only pray that the Trial of Truth would exploit his innate affliction. Faith had him certain he would succeed in it. Aerik took his first step into the library and proceeded to the empty chair placed for him.

Two foreboding characters stood like ominous statues in front of the chair, between the first bookcase and himself. Fully armored in blackened plate from toe to face, only a shadowy crevice in their helms hinted at where their eyes should have been. The left figure wore armor fitted for a man and was much taller, while the one on the left wore armor obviously forged in the fashion of veritans.

Between them both was a golden pillar with a single black dawn-star mace upon it, positioned as if it were some ancient artifact of the great archives.

His calculating savant mind compulsively recorded everything in the hemispheric room. Prepared for his clandestine assessors to begin at any moment, he was startled when the sounds of the door being barred behind him came instead. No trace of life came from the statuesque knights.

A missing book on the bookshelf to his left stood out. His probing eyes found a small gap behind the shelf, just enough for an individual or two to hide, with no discernible point of entry. *Another missing book, third shelf, fifth row, second column.* Aerik's eyes twitched for clues of more hidden space beyond. *Ten missing books total, one per shelf, each a different row or column.*

"Welcome to the Trial of Truth, Aerik Blackendale, son of the fallen Lucas Blackendale and Royal Inquisitor Honorah Bayn, brother of Ebrielle Blackendale, cousin of Henrick Brigannor, aspirant in the Trials," came the sudden introduction in a strong feminine voice from the veritan figure in black armor.

A masculine voice followed from the unmoving paladin next to her. "You have been chosen among those of the Melee to progress in the Trials. This will be your prize, should you pass here, Aspirant." The knight implicated the weapon without moving a hand.

The veritan figure took over from him, as if they had perfected sharing their rehearsed speech time and time again. "You will still be an aspirant if you pass. Your initiation comes with your final tests, which you will receive in Az'Dayne at the Pentagogue itself. Only once the five tests of the Trials have been passed may you be granted the eternal title of Paladin."

Aerik's eyes shot to a flashing movement of something white behind one of the missing tomes. It was gone as fast as it had appeared. "I understand. I am ready to begin," Aerik responded.

The paladin spoke next. "You might wonder why a veritan is here during this phase of the Paladin Trials. A man comes from a woman at birth. He learns many things from her throughout his evolution. And again, as the circle closes, if he chooses to parent children himself, a true man must reunite and learn from a woman. But the paladin must also learn from his paladin peers, to master the Trials and carry out the tenets of the Faith's enforcement. There is a balance between the genders. A judgment between them," he schooled, taking a pause before finishing. "And so goes the balance of the paladins and the veritans. A paladin needs both a veritan and a paladin to judge him, as does a veritan in her Trials as an aspirant."

"Do you understand and respect this balance between man and woman in equal power?" the veritan's icy tone inquired.

A dash of something white came again from one of the spaces in the shelves, from a different column, on the opposite side from the previous one. Aerik's eyes shot to it, but he ignored it as a false phantom. "Yes, my lord and my lady. By what do I call you?"

"We are nameless during this part of the Trial. I am the shadow paladin," answered the man.

The woman trailed after. "I am the shadow veritan. Do you have any other questions before we begin?"

"I do not," he lied with his focus incidentally scrutinizing holes to the room behind to discover the lurking spy. "I do not wish to ask my questions at this time, since they may be answered by the end." He corrected his response, fearing to lie directly to these truth-seers in his one Trial that was about trust and fact.

As if they could read his mind, just as rumor had it, the shadow paladin rebuked him. "It is good of you to correct your lies before we proceed. You will receive a series of questions. Some may seem random and irrelevant. Assume they are not. Answer with logic and wisdom, not emotion and bias."

"Do not lie to us, Aerik," the veritan warned.

Aerik tried to keep his attention on the two judges before him, but his disorder was kicking in.

"What do you keep looking at behind us?"

He was afraid to answer the shadow paladin. Awkwardly he inquired, "Is that the first question?" When no reply came, he decided it best to speak only the truth at his Trial of Truth. "I believe there is someone else in the room."

His concern was ignored, shadowed by the veritan's question that finally seemed like one that pertained to the test. "What is the role of a paladin in the Dominadom? What is the role of a veritan?"

Aerik had prepared for this question since he was a young teen. "Paladins are the male public enforcers of the Faith of the Five and Five. They represent the five gods of the elements: tairan, fire, sky, shadow, and water. They are unbending in the law, masters of intuition, able to read the souls of the wicked. It is the Paladin Order that exploits the Dominadom's vast region to discover those who directly go against the tenets and balance of the Faith."

Three spiders in the room. Two in the upper right corner, shelf twenty-four, column six, one on the shelf left of the center, three cases up. He cursed himself for his damned concentration at the worst of times, but continued.

"Veritans are the female judges who have the power to redeem or damn the convicted. The Veritan Order decides on executions and creates services of restoration for those who have fallen in the Faith but are allowed a second chance. They represent the five goddesses of the seasons: the Dawning, the Sunder, the Reaping, the Umbra, and the Torrent."

The shadow paladin went next. "What is the Oathemic Cabal?"

This was an obscure topic that few were educated in. He was told that even the highest royal houses of Az'Dayne were not privy to the ideals of the secretive faction. He replied with their common reputation. "The imperial assassins' guild of the Az'Dayne Dominadom. They are specialists given writs from the Pentagogue to target and eliminate high threats to the government and theology of the Dominadom. They consist of the best-trained killers in Az'Dayne, and even spellblades and mages."

The shadow veritan brought the next inquiry into very personal subjects, obviously primed for his background specifically. "How did your father die, and why did he pursue that which caused his death?"

Aerik's shoulders slumped, and his gaze hit the carpeted floor. *Eighty-seven swirls on the rug. Such an odd number. That cannot be right.*

His scrupulous nature clicked on like a defense mechanism. "He was slain by tro—" Aerik stopped to correct himself and employ the proper term in front of his exalted peers. "Terollar elven. The Glace Isles Terollar have been an enemy of the Barredish for centuries. The annals of history have it logged that they began the first attacks, and as much as Barredom has focused on their preeminent foe in Aggedon, these elven have proved to be a thorn in the side of our soldiers' progress. My grandfather created a force of hunters called the Eldenvale Rangers, trained specifically for hunting and slaying their kind so that the Barredish army could focus solely on the enemy stoneborne and hostile greyborne clans."

The two knights never showed any signs that his answers could sway their next queries one way or another. It was as if no matter what his reply might be, this was a premeditated interrogation explicitly designed for him, only to record and judge his responses. The shadow paladin did not skip a second after Aerik finished his last sentence. "How do you feel toward the Terollar that killed your father?"

"I do not hold the rage of my mother toward it," Aerik answered truthfully, surprised that it was the way he had always felt. "Perhaps I should. It was war. And in such feuds, sometimes the enemy wins a battle or two before you win the war. The Terollar were my enemy before my father died. They are still my enemy today. No more, no less."

A long pause happened with no reply from either knight. It was the veritan's turn. *Ten seconds? Did I answer fairly or incorrectly?*

"How do you feel about the elven and the umbran?"

"The elven, other than the Terollar, have had little impact on the people of Barredom. There is cordial history with the indifferent Wyldenar, and brief contact with the unwelcoming Neveril of Zsolindal, but other than that, their race has been nothing but a giant's tale. The umbran are the masters of all that we have been born to believe is the enemy. They are the kings and queens of all that we hope to defeat. They are as much elvan as we are qindrid, which is not at all."

As expected, the male knight had a paired question to go with it. "What are the qindrid, and how do you feel about them?"

Aerik nodded, appreciating the session more as it went along. He imagined this interrogation session was going along much more pleasantly than anything the Royal Inquisitor might impose if she were operating the Trials. "I believe the greyborne are cursed individuals eternally paying for the sins of their ancestors. I pity them. The stoneborne and skyborne voluntarily made their choice to become such. I believe them the absolute definition of heretics of the Faith of the Fives. All Barredish are raised to know the color of the enemy is grey, and that is the way it has been and always will be until we are taught otherwise or until this war indeed does end."

"Why are they the enemy?" the veritan asked. "What have they done to you or your known ancestors?"

Finally a question that seemed to reflect his particular answer. *Perhaps it is all still preset for me. I am sure Henrick's Trial will be different.* "It is true, I have not fought them. And my father and his father were slain by elven. But I have lost others to their kind. I have had the fathers or brothers of friends killed by them. They are my enemy because my king has told me they are my enemy." If there was ever a simple and just retort, he imagined that was it. "I will continue to perceive them as such until higher powers tell me that the war is over and that I no longer need to see them in that light. But it has not changed since my birth, nor the birth of every ancestor of mine I can name."

The shadow paladin immediately followed the apparent schooling. "What are the different types of qindrid and their origins?"

Aerik felt confident in his lore of the qindrid. Every soldier and noble in Barredom was mandated to learn it as a child. "The stoneborne, the skyborne, and the greyborne. The stoneborne originated in the fall of Aggea, which is now Aggedon. They were turned by the Wyldenar umbran of the region. There were also stoneborne in Tairancia as well, but they were beaten back and destroyed in the Grey War by the Tairancian kingdoms, with aid from us and the mages. The skyborne were the first of the qindrid. They transcended in far eastern Sho'Lon, from the Shiniryn umbran, and they eventually branched north to Caelduym and south to Brutonga. The greyborne are the unfortunate product of qindrid when both their umbran have died and they regain the ability to breed."

The shadow veritan then proved him wrong, that the quiz was not predetermined and that his answers did have weight on the direction. "You say there are only umbran of the Shiniryn and the Wyldenar. Select Shiniryn, elven of the sky-shadow descendancy, who chose the Taboo and took the turn to transcend into umbran, and select Wyldenar, elven of the tairan-shadow descendancy, who did the same to become umbran. This, then, is all the umbran? No other elvan races of shadow descendancies? You mean to say that the Neveril, elven of the fire-shadow descendancy, cannot take the Taboo to become umbran also? And the Lunaril, elven of shadow-water descendancy, either?"

"I fear I cannot answer that." The white flicker abruptly came again, behind a hole where a tome should have been. He squinted at it, and he thought long on the bizarre notion of such an insinuation in her question. "I have never fathomed it."

The shadow paladin explained, "Shiniryn umbran create the sky-borne qindrid. Wyldenar umbran create the stoneborne qindrid. What if there were Neveril umbran or Lunaril umbran?"

Aerik was entirely confounded by the implications these strange knights were seeming to cryptically convey. "Are you trying to tell me something? Why am I being clued in on such things that could be a realm-wide phenomenon that has never been recorded?"

"How would that make you feel? You have no history tied to the Shiniryn, the Neveril, or the Lunaril. What histories do you even have to hold bias against them?" the veritan plainly inquired.

"I know no Shiniryn. Only what they created. They began the ritual that spread like untamed fire across the north, and it was they who convinced the Wyldenar to turn into umbran and create qindrid in their form. I know not all Shiniryn are umbran or the enemy, and not all Wyldenar are the same." Aerik was almost feeling defeated, utterly unsure in his responses. "But I know of no pleasant stories of the Neveril's behavior toward our kind, and all I have been educated on regarding the Lunaril is that they are all slaves to the Thrench. So you ask me questions on a whim that I have never even considered." *What would they even be considered? Qindrid of the Neveril, fireborne, and of the Lunaril, seaborne? What are they implying?*

"What if you found out today, after you leave this room, that Henrick, your sister, or your mother wanted to undertake the ritual of Transcendence to become qindrid? If your answers are different for each, then speak specifically." The paladin invasively tested him.

Aerik took a deep breath of growing frustration. He knew they could see it in him. His bare knuckles were covered in sweat. *Nine beads of sweat, right hand; seven, the left. Sixteen beads. Sixteen books with blue covers on the seventh shelf. Sixteen steps to the door, nine bolts in the frame.* "For Henrick, I know beyond a doubt that he would not do it. He is too stalwart in his beliefs to side with Barredom, even more so than me on most counts. My sister would only consider it to keep her beauty." He let loose a small laugh to lighten the mood. "And my mother ..." Aerik paused, grinning incredulously. "Have any of you met my mother?"

"That was not the question. Answer according to the scenario I inquired about." They were not having it, the paladin again proving that the test was not rigged.

"I would want to know every detail why. I would inform them that I love them but that qindrid are the enemy, and that I could not love the enemy so long as my nation deemed their race such. I would want to convince them out of the decision, to remain with the Faith in the Fives," he returned to the best of his resolve.

The shadow veritan further enticed the fictitious circumstances. "What if you were presented with it? The option for ageless life, elemental impowers, to never again have to sleep, and to be twice as productive as the normal man. All you would have to give up is the color of your skin and your ability to produce children, along with your faith in the Fives, to embrace the elements of your descendancy instead."

"I will never abandon my faith in the Fives. I choose immortal life in the Godslands after this material realm takes my soul." There could be no wiser riposte to such sacrilege, Aerik decreed.

"Do you know of the Transcendence? If you do, tell so now," the male voice demanded.

"I know of no human alive who knows the details. And even my mother, through all of her interrogations in the Deeps, has either learned nothing or told me nothing. All I know is that we men who share the descendancy of the umbran become unnaturally seduced by them when entering their node, and that we succumb to this 'volunteering,'" Aerik cynically emphasized, "to take the turn into the everlasting curse that is being qindrid."

The female voice followed. "What extremes would you go to in the act of saving your countrymen? Would you forgo your sacred faith to save the lives of your family, friends, and allies?"

"To save my family, friends, and countrymen ..." Aerik thought about how he truly felt versus what these icons of the highest faith would expect him to reply to pass this part of the Trials. He decided they were one and the same. "I would hope the Faith would forgive me if it came to such a choice of sacrifice. I would choose those I know in the flesh, yes."

"What do you know of the Neveril elven? Explain in full," the shadow paladin necessitated.

I recall that I already did, he silently countered but knew it would be an unacceptable retort. "White-skinned, hairless, red-eyed elven. The women of their culture are known to wear bright red wigs as fashion, and the men don red armor of strange metals. They are called ghosts by the human cultures who have been unfortunate enough to encounter them. They live underground and can walk on walls and ceilings as if they were level ground. They see in the dark just as well as in the light, through heat in the living. They are ostracized by other elven and generally identified as enemies even of their own race," he finished, proud of his racial tutelage.

The veritan resumed the tangent. "Would you say, based upon facts given, outside of derogatory gossip, that the Neveril are an enemy of Barredom or the Az'Dayne Dominadom?"

"It should be that the enemy of our enemy is our ally. But I believe the Neveril hold no love for an alliance with any human nation. But then again, I am also young and uneducated on such present matters within their hierarchy," Aerik humbly admitted.

"What do you know of the Thrench?"

The shadow paladin's last question was a subject he would never have surmised to be even remotely relevant. Aerik coerced his mind back to his cultural teachings from his uncle and mother. "They are the most renowned human fighters in all of Penthara. A nation of seafaring super soldiers, trained in extreme methods from a young age. They use a metal called Starfell steel to forge their swords, which has more properties than I have learned of, but I do know that the Thrench fight faster and more precisely than any in all the realm. They are remorseless conquerors that stay out of mainland politics and only conquer elvan territories. They are responsible for the genocides of four elvan races: the Ibyssai, the Tortharan, the Forlore, and the Vistaryl. They are the naval people of the descendancy of water, led by Emperor Djediheth Emmonost."

The shadow veritan then asked her final question. "Would you willingly die today, or in the future, for a vaguely explained cause, without question, if it meant gain for your imperial Dominadom and prosperity for your people?"

"My soul belongs to the Five and Five, while my body belongs to the Dominadom. I am your loyal subject to be commanded as seen fit in whatever advances the cause of my dominarchs' shared vision," Aerik responded without hesitation or doubt.

That answer seemed satisfactory. The shadow paladin pacified him. "Your test today is almost over, Aerik Blackendale. The final part of this Trial will end with you asking us any five questions you desire. Know that we will not detour from the truth."

"And that with knowing some truths comes great consequence. Choose your questions wisely, and decide, before you ask them, if you truly wish to know the answer. Begin. Stand. Ask," the shadow veritan instructed, giving the floor to him.

The two enigmatic knights took to seats of their own as Aerik left his. There had never been any preparation for this part of the Trials. *Yes, indeed, eighty-seven swirls there are on the rug. I was right. Eighty-seven men and women died in the last troll assault on Defiance, the Cycle of Skycrowns. Eighty-seven potatoes gathered by Ebrielle three years ago for the Reapingfeast at Uncle's farm. Eighty-seven ...* Aerik's besieged concentration clouded on anything random to do with a particular, insignificant number, until he snapped himself out of it.

He was ready to ask his first question. "Why was my Trial of Truth almost entirely related to obscure topics about the qindrid? I have been told that the qindrid are not an issue in the southern Dominadom; it is only a racial plague we suffer in the northern realms."

"One," the shadow paladin counted. "The qindrid are not only a topic of the north above Continents' Kiss. They are a realm-wide concern. Know that we enter a new age, Aspirant, as you can see, with everything happening here in the north. The race of qindrid will play a heavy part in your involvement in the Order."

He would have to accept that reply. He looked to the veritan, expecting by ritual for her to answer next. "What are my final three Trials, should I pass today?"

"Two." She counted how many he had asked. "The Trial of Melee is in the past. The Trial of Truth is in the now. The Trial of Choice will begin on the road. The Trial of Five and the Trial of Transcendence will take place at the Pentagogue, in Everdawn."

The Trial of Transcendence? I have only heard that word used with qindrid ... And paladins are known to be an eternal order. What if ...? Aerik shook that absurdity from his musings. He made his next request. "Should I ascend further than the title of Aspirant and become known as Paladin Aerik Blackendale, I wish to vividly know my purpose and who my enemy is. Tell me."

"Three," the expected masculine voice prompted. "You will not be known as Paladin Aerik Blackendale. There are no surnames within the Order. You will take on a new identity, as chosen by High Paladin Cederick. Your enemy is currently all mages, spellblades, races that are in open violation of the tenets that will be explained to you, and qindrid who are in the insurgency against the Great Exodus. Your enemy becomes whomever the Pentagogue deems to be your enemy."

There was no news in that illumination. He only had two questions left. He was saving his most dangerous and audacious for last. His fourth was rather to the point. "Did I pass the Trial of Truth?"

"Four," the veritan tallied as she rose. She grasped the Daynish dawnstar and presented it for Aerik to behold as his own. "Your answers and questions were worthy, Aspirant Aerik Blackendale. This belongs to you now. This tool of the Faith will be carried with you at all times, throughout the remainder of your time in the Trials and while serving the Order. You still have one final question."

Aerik took the heavy mace in both hands, inspecting and revering every detail of it. He was reluctant to dare his final question, but he was almost part of the most powerful order in all of Penthara now. He could fear everything just a bit less. He looked past the missing tomes, and there he saw it again, but this time, it wasn't moving—a ghost in the flesh. *No, not a true ghost, but a –*

"What is behind the bookshelf? Is that a ...?" Aerik's words trailed off unfinished, and he had never felt dread like he bore in that moment.

They both stood now. In unison, the monotonous shadow knights concluded together, "Five ..."

ONDREW (IV)

GHOSTGRASS

Ondrew and Broc stared at their mysteriously entranced umbran prisoner while the remainder of the entourage huddled anxiously around Snowden and Sheridan's recent discovery.

Lilealah stood with her face aimed at the ceiling, her usually black eyes now fully white from pupil to iris. Her mouth remained open and still, showing a hint of her front two fangs among her top teeth. Not a flinch of reaction had come from her since the Shaws halted the group. No one seemed to notice, and Ondrew chose to keep it that way. Whatever spell she was under, he deemed it best not to invade.

Snowden peered through a large fissure in the tunnelway, around the size of a child's torso. An army of stringy vegetation as thin as grass lined the round crevice in all directions, as far back as torchlight could reach. He put his torch to the source area and put a finger to his mouth to hush any preempted inquiries. The white grass instantly withered away into grey ash all around the eerie opening.

Sheridan took control of the group's interest for the party's unexpected recess in a whisper. "Ghostgrass. Whatever it hears, it carries like wind, to all its tunnel ends as far as the grass grows. You speak here; they hear there, wherever it may be that spies await."

Sarin retorted in hopeful security. "Fortune's with us, then, aye, that none be on the other end a-pryin'?" She gulped a swallow of fear, sharing what was seemingly felt by the majority of the crew.

"Other things do exist here now, I fear. Fortune only smiles that I am confident it is no longer the Neveril," Sheridan compromised.

The group subsequently looked back at Ondrew for a response of direction, just as Lilealah was breaking from her meditative introspection.

Ondrew nodded to the scouts and whispered his command. "Shaws, burn all the fissures when you see them ahead. If any of you can view one in sight, burned or not, do not make a sound. Careful with your steps, men." He motioned the group forward.

The Norther Knights set onward, deeper into the cavern system. Snowden and Sheridan kept unseen, far in the lead. The majority of areas on the subterranean highway were lit clearly by the clusters of dark red crystalytes that ornamented the cave ceilings and walls. Upon the more illuminated avenues, Ondrew noticed the occasional white X painted upon the rock face. Sheridan had explained to the group that these were how the scouts marked which territories had been traversed and surveyed, to ensure no one got lost upon a retreat. Some of the markings were weathered, as if they were from prior explorations, while others were fresh and wet from the current journey.

More than a few of the small ghostgrass fissures were passed as the group progressed. Caution and duty enforced absolute silence among the entire lot. It had been a rather unsocial saga to begin.

Ondrew found a moment on one of their brief food respites to address Lilealah and ask what had been gnawing at his curiosity. "I need to know. Your eyes." He kept his voice low. "When you lose yourself in your mind. What power are you invoking?"

Broc, as her guardian, knelt beside them and said nothing while Lilealah explained herself. "An impower of the umbran. It is called cerebration. A means of communion with my followers. Doing so leaves me vulnerable, as all I have turned can briefly know of my location, and so can my living children, if any are still alive. It lasts only as long as I am in the trance. Would you like me to stop?"

Broc spoke for them both, perhaps a little more harshly than Ondrew would have done. "Five fucks t' the shadows and stones! 'Course ye're gonna stop yer schemin', witch!" The former yharl frowned at the prisoner, completely untrusting of her intentions.

Ondrew tried to secure his convictions in her, for the sake of the men. "We need to trust one another. Tell me why this is necessary."

"The ones that were taken in with me, that were left in Frostdale.

They have undergone great suffering in your Frostdale Deeps. They know they will not survive long," she explained in a melancholic mood. "I cannot directly call to them. But I can watch through their eyes. I can pass to them a sensation of empathy, showing them my mood, whether I feel in danger or safe. At times, I also reach out to my people that we are to meet, assuring them of my safety and encouraging them to have faith in my captors. Am I wrong to do that?"

Ondrew stared deep into her impenetrable black orbs. Studying them was futile when nothing was there to be seen. She had an effect on him that annulled his practiced ability to judge another's character and true intent. He was in his early thirties, and by his account, Lilealah had lived for more than a few centuries, mastering the art of manipulating the men of the north throughout her time.

Ondrew gave a subtle smile and offered his hand to help her back to her feet. "It seems trusting you is all I can do," he acquiesced. "But I will know one more mystery before we continue. You mentioned possibility of your children, that is. I have always wondered." He paused, pondering how to go about navigating his lore on elven and umbran. "How can umbran spawn offspring? I have learned you forgo your lifetree and instead carry your spiritroot with you."

"It is called a node." Lilealah acquainted him with the concept. "When an elvan of mixed shadow descendancy takes the Taboo to transcend into an umbran, yes, they forgo their connection with their lifetree, and it eventually dies. But because we carry our spiritroot with us, and it is not weakened in our altered state, we create an aura known as the node.

"As Wyldenar umbran, our elemental node will gradually alter the tairan and shadow ecosystem of wherever we travel, more drastically if we prolong our stay in one locale. A node is more powerful when coupled in the vicinity of our lifemate. Natural environs can rapidly change in dramatic ways from the norm. It is here where new children can be spawned between the lifemates, in cocoons sprouted from the ground, rather than from a lifetree. And it is here where humans susceptible to the qindrid Transcendence might find themselves invited to the outlying aura the node emanates."

Broc spat on the ground beside her and damned her to death with his violent eyes. Lilealah was not a good soul, evil incarnate, Ondrew surmised, but he could allow that she justified herself by following some path of contorted ethics in her own delusional grandeur.

"Your honesty warrants merit. I will grant you that. But on this course, you will never again perform that act of cerebration. Save your fellowship with your people until we meet them in the flesh." He then took back the lead and motivated his crew into motion.

Mind-numbing hours crawled by on the endless march. The paranormal crimson hue offered from the crystalyte glow became nothing more than a drab and depressing reminder that he was that far from home. The tunnels and chambers all looked generally the same, blending in with each other. A variety of stalactites and stalagmites and cave columns were offered, with no majestic sights such as lakes or forests or mountains. In the realm of the underground, there was no such thing even as a horizon to behold.

The occasional glowworm nest, with their azure radiance, rimmed the cavern chamber ceilings or decorated the hanging stalactites. He pretended they were stars and that he was indeed under the blanket of the heavens. But they were fleeting and erratic. Their initial awe of bizarre splendor faded into redundancy like the rest of it. Even the tease of a subterranean stream introduced itself a time or two, offering his men an inviting respite. But the water tasted bitter and foreign, too rich with minerals and not enough spring.

The only life other than the glowworms and ghostgrass were the infrequent albino crustaceans near the streams, and the oversize beetles in the glowworm chambers. A few eyeless white lizards and translucent skeletal fish made their appearances on the dismal tedium of the trek as well.

It was no wonder the Neveril elven were known to be the most malicious race in the realm. He could feel that he, too, would grow mad before the end of the next pent's passing.

A pentday. He wondered how he was even supposed to determine an increment of time in this underworld. Hours and days indiscernibly meshed together. There was no way to judge the passing of moons. *Do the Neveril even measure in time like the top world? Or do they simply exist indefinitely?* His thoughts in the monotonous silence of the march sporadically went to the most random, then back to the duties of his mission.

He was just glad he had instructed Black Brigannor to act as a step counter for at least some form of time measurement. He instructed that no knight was allowed to interrupt him on the march.

Ondrew's mind often inadvertently slipped to melancholic

thoughts on his parents. The day he and his men had departed from Frostdale, a messenger presented him with a secret note declaring that his mother had returned in fair health to the capital. The note was not from her, nor was it an invite to see her. It was simply signed "Anonymous." *I am a failure to both of my parents. Neither cared to see me off, nor cares if I return ...*

He had no way to ascertain how long into their journey it had been. It was likely the eighth or so return of the scouts. Maybe the tenth or eleventh. The reports were almost all the same. He could see the two brothers ahead in the tunnel, waiting for the entourage to catch up, probing an item of interest on the floor.

The Norther Knights thronged anxiously around Snowden and Sheridan, with Lilealah still detained in the rear by Broc and Black. Snowden stayed kneeling, fiddling with a clump of coarse white hair in one hand. He held his sword out far from his body. The end of the blade impaled a half-frozen chunk of dried dung, healthy in size, obviously of some beast larger than a human. Around the feces on the ground was the husk of some meatless cave crustacean.

"Skystone apes. We knew a few were here, but far deeper in. Near the egress," Sheridan informed them. "Could be a scout for their troop. Maybe they are trying to find food or a way out from where they came in."

Lilealah stole his attention when he looked back her way. Her bewitching eyes and soft, accented voice demanded he obey her plea. "May I, Prince?"

"I don't need any counsel on my report, especially not from a witch of the apostates," Sheridan sharply interjected back. His brother flung the ape feces on his blade in her direction through the crowd. Broc bowed his arms up in a threatening stance, as if he thought the boy meant it for his boots instead.

"Let our charge through," Ondrew commanded sternly. "You will let her speak."

Lilealah was permitted a temporary relief from her bonds to inspect the scene. She looked straight into the darkness of the tunnel system far ahead. All stood quiet through the long pause of her expert assessment. "They are fleeing in full retreat," she stated simply.

Ondrew was confused how even an umbran could discern this from such by a pile of dung and by peering down a sinister cavern hall. She was not telling all she knew. "You already knew we would meet with resistance from these beasts?"

"I suspected it," she confessed, seemingly blithe in the face of any judgment. "Zsolindal has many cave openings. But our route leads us into the Wyldewoods, which was their home. Since the Great Exodus, many of the greyborne have not joined with my movement. The other clans have migrated north, to the Hroganyndale. The Horde has been encroaching on the forest hard ever since, for resources in case of a war from your uncle. They selectively hunt the apes for their meat and hides."

Broc again pronounced his opinion before Ondrew could squeeze his own in. "Convenient information t' be leavin' us in the dark on," he attacked her sarcastically. "How many o' these ape-men we talkin' about?"

Ondrew followed his comrade with a more pertinent dilemma. "Lilealah, this is folly. You are leading us into the throng of the greyborne horde, which is loyal to no man, and especially not to an umbran. We may as well reroute to the surface and meet with my uncle. I can ensure you safe passage by safe escort of his army."

"No. I am sorry, Prince, but you can ensure naught," she countered. "General Roth's intentions are not those of his brother. Your father has agreed to peace and allowed us safe passage to leave Aggedon for good. But many still believe our intentions are to reinforce elsewhere and return in stronger numbers. The army above our heads now will never listen. Randon does not want such a truce, and he is undoubtedly bitter in finding out my capture was allowed this leave for the sake of our retreat. He wishes to see all qindrid dead and done. If he is given such a chance again with me, I will find myself executed," she finished.

Lilealah then looked over each of the men. "These beasts will be many, yes. Their troop, perhaps in the hundreds. But it is a lesser risk to chance them than it is to see your war restarted on my death at the hands of the general."

Even Mathias had something to riposte with now. "Skystone apes by the hundreds," the mangled hunter assessed apprehensively. "I've seen them pick up weapons and shields from the fallen and use them. Smartest beasts in all the north."

Ondrew knew he had to quickly assuage the growing doubt building in his crew. "We can hope they will be skittish around men. The greyborne may have done us that kindness. Our presence may be more of an intimidating threat than an enticement for a meal," he tried. "What about these qin at the brink of the Wyldewoods, cluttering our path to your wyrmway?"

"The migration has been underway. No armies will be traveling through the Wyldewoods. They will be heavy in the northeast of the forest but absent in the south, where we will travel. The only person wanting a fight out of all this is your uncle. I have a better chance at amity with the clansfolk. Hroganyn's Horde is completely removing itself from any paths of probable battle. If I see General Roth, I'll only receive the blade," she finished.

Unless the Horde captures you and bargains a ransom with my uncle. Their ensured peace by the end of this war, at the cost of turning you over in chains. Ondrew analyzed every grim scenario that could play out.

Somewhere in the midst of the group, the intermittent sound of a stringed instrument resonated, and Kyson cleared his throat to chime in. Ondrew smirked, half-annoyed but curious about whatever was about to come out of the minstrel's quip-filled mouth. "This may not be a priority, but did anyone bring a change of clothes about my size?" Kyson appeared heartily serious with the question, searching genuinely into the eyes of his comrades for help.

"These are some of my finest, and I didn't expect to get bloody. I assumed this would be a leisurely sightseeing hike. If you are telling me I may have to kill something, well, then." He paused to take a deep, exaggerated breath and pull his bow up around his back. "I just may have to rethink all this."

Broc looked over to Ondrew, dumbfounded, as if he could not fathom how they had accidentally acquired such a fanciful coward in their midst. Before even glimpsing Lilealah's disarming smile, Ondrew knew the archer's intent and had a mind to call him out on it. "I sense sarcasm."

"I see stalling," Kyson answered blankly. His demeanor completely shifted from his enactment to one of all urgency. "And all I hear is prattle." He pointed to the scouts, and then to the cave wall in the tunnel ahead. "I also see some of those ghostgrass holes ahead that they neglected to burn because they were too fascinated by a pile of shit."

Every Norther Knight did as bidden and stared at Kyson's truth. Directly ahead, the ghostgrass swayed back and forth with small vibrations each time someone spoke. How the Shaws hadn't surveyed that priority was an enigma of dire error. Ondrew was well past retiring from this debate, anyhow, and decided to let his voice prove it. "Silence! Everyone! You all signed up for a fight. It was inevitable. The bard is right." He nodded in the direction of Kyson without making eye contact, by flaw of pride.

"Take heed of the presence of the apes. Shaws, keep your scouting at a quarter of the distance ahead you were at, and stagger yourselves. No one splits up. No one talks until I speak first." He snarled his series of firm commands to regain order and snuff out all concerns. "When we hit the open sky, we can worry about whatever else the Fives test us with. Move out!"

Ondrew briskly took the lead before the scout brothers could even register it was time to act. He snatched the torch from young Donal Oreville's grasp and walked straight up to the cavity that housed the intruding ghostgrass. He peered into its twisting depths and wondered what enemy spied at the other end, waiting and ready to exploit the mistakes of his men.

No enemy could have them, he decided. Not one man. He would protect them all. *Five and Five, I pray to you now. Let the ears of my enemy grow deaf and their eyes go blind.* He lit the cave weed on fire and watched it wither away before throwing the whole torch in.

HONORAH (III)

THE COUNCIL

The polearms from the two Forwoken monks clanged together, barring her from going any further. The seemingly mechanical sentries looked straight ahead through their fitted masked hoods, showing no notion of allowing her entry. Her livid look burrowed a hole through their odd green eyes before whipping around.

"You would deny me audience again with our king? It has been countless months since I have spoken with His Majesty, and he is yet to speak with me since we have taken this Dawning's captives!" Norah's words were pure venom aimed at her political nuisances.

She despised each of the strange faces before her on the Frostdale Council, nearly all of whom were newly appointed and suspiciously favorable toward southern politics. Half were Barredish noblemen she had never even heard of. These aristocrat appointees were alleged "cousins of such-and-such house" or "a wandering uncle of another house" or even the elder son of some "ancient, long-dead Barredish war hero." It was all too unreasonably convenient to swallow. Norah hissed in her mind, aggravated by the whole grand scheme of the Dominadom's power play forced on her homeland.

But it was Elderman Agustan who spoke up for the Frostdale Council—specifically, the only one of them whom she had known since birth and even remotely held faith in. Why he had remained a party to this transitional drivel was beyond her. "Royal Inquisitor Norah, if I may?"

He really "may" not, but the impatient, smug look wasn't leaving her face anytime soon, so she allowed the old official to continue. "King Aerik has the Frostdale Council under strict orders not to disturb him. All has been entrusted to your capable judgment with the prisoners, as time has proved. Who better to extract what we desire to know?"

She turned her gaze on Agustan and callously hammered, "Since when does the Frostdale Council put themselves above the Royal Inquisitor's rank with the king? I have been dubbed the final voice of all law since Aerik Roth first succeeded to the crown!"

The young chancellor, Soro, in his ridiculously extravagant deep-orange-and-bright-gold gown, picked up the argument in his snobbish High Barredish accent. "You *were*," he audaciously reminded her.

Barredish accents came in three diversely enunciated variants, depending on which region one was raised in. Contrary to the names, High Barredish–speaking citizens were typically from the Lowlands or Rothlands, while those who articulated their speech in Low Barredish were from the Highlands of Barredom or Mount Komak. Low Barredish tongues were the most unsophisticated of the dialects, all in the broken Civil language with different styles of speech. The Eldenvales accent was a hybrid of the two, of the proper sentences used in High Barredish and the heavy pronunciations of Low Barredish. There was also the Agge tongue, learned by only the elder or the educated, and never used, only kept alive as a homage to their ancient Aggean past.

The Roths and Bayns were examples of lineages who were raised speaking in High Barredish, while most who carried a *Br* in their surname were proved to have Low Barredish accents. The Blackendales, Orevilles, Shaws, and many other great houses carried the Eldenvales accent.

And Soro was the only non-Barredish on the council. Her visage seethed at the chancellor, scanning the rims of his ears, ornamented in an oddity of multiple golden rings. "Pardon?"

"You *were* the final voice of the law, Inquisitor," Soro underlined, "before King Aerik Roth made a seat for a High Chancellor at the Frostdale Council table. Now it falls to me to act as magistrate upon such finalities, and you" —his voice waned to help him better emphasize whatever inevitable insult was in trail— "are now nothing more than a glorified torturer."

If she had retained the ability for laughter, she might have exploded into a fit of it on the spot. Instead, she retorted in the only way she knew how—with absolute vehemence. "While you all sit here and gawk at the war board, arguing over which piece to move or which piece to remove, it is I who resides in the Deeps, carving down the real enemy for you. Take heed of whom you address, outlander. We women in the north don't wear dresses to work, like you flowery men in the south, which you keep pretending to be."

Her verbal adversary appeared completely flustered at the slight of being alluded to as a southerner, having obviously been born farther north than she had been, in the mountains known as the Qaegons. She accepted it as sufficient victory.

The conniving upjump did manage a taciturn response. "You should be wary of referring to the Dominadom's chosen with such blasphemous ridicule." His cold threat was half-heeded. She was wise enough, though, to be guarded against any more patronizing insinuations about her new overlords.

Instead, her dark brown eyes simply bore sheer animosity into the light-green irises of Soro. The only persons in all the realm recorded to have green eyes were the trolls and the mages, and now these new Forwoken monks, which had appeared throughout the court some few seasons back. The chancellor's eyes matched those of her most hated enemy and the voiceless guards barring her way forward. That was more than enough to fuel her ire.

But before any more impudent words could escape her witty mouth, the doors behind her unexpectedly slammed open, and the prohibiting polearms of the Forwoken sentries uncrossed. The two armed monks turned in unison, jutting their weapon hafts to the stone in salute to the queen standing in the doorway.

There stood Annison Roth, formerly of House Whent, the wife of King Aerik Roth. Though of pure Daynish descent, her marriage into the Roth bloodline at the age of fifteen had made none question her Barredish devotion. Prior to the surprise at the finale of the Melee, no one had seen their queen since the king had sent her away a few months before he took the bow to Az'Dayne. Queen Annison and various noble lords in the upper wards of Frostdale had become suddenly stricken with a unique plague. The sickness was unlike anything seen before in the north, and bizarrely not contagious, almost like a strategically placed foreign poison. The disease had taken ahold of her so quickly that King Aerik Roth had decided in haste against contemporary advised methods of remedy. He sent messenger birds directly to a proven source of cure and had received a prompt response from Mageholme.

Mageholme had been an ancient Barredom ally from the time House Bayn and her ancestors ruled the kingdom. The mages were the ultimate supporters, who had helped win the war that beat back the qindrid into turning on their own umbran makers and slaying most of the elven who had turned them. Thus, the greyborne cultures reformed a nation for what they had once been, without their Wyldenar masters. The outcome of this became known in the archives as the Grey War.

These timely allies had come and gone from the allegiance long ago, but Barredom had always remained in detached relations of peace with the forbidden lands. Mages were a dying prodigy of antiquity, with fewer appearing as time progressed. Throughout Az'Dayne and Khalimia, if one were found to be a mage, the individual was forced to join the Oathemic Cabal or be tried for irrefutable execution. In most regions, there simply were no mages to be recorded in the written annals. They were generally scattered throughout the Taira continents. The refugee valley settlement of Mageholme was the one known exception.

Rumor had it that the queen had perished in Mageholme, like so many of the replaced council members, and that it might have been the reasoning behind King Aerik's unsociable adjustment: just a period of bereavement for his beloved wife and for pride lost in submitting to the Dominadom.

But this put an astonishing spin on that apparently fallacious gossip. Queen Annison looked prim and pristine, more than ever recalled. *Clearly, these Dawning mages are wonder-workers indeed.* Her formerly pale skin was toned to an unblemished tan. Her hair now held a sun-kissed brown sheen. Her eyes and lips no longer carried a hint of wrinkled age, without the sag in her chin that Norah remembered so vividly. The queen in her late forties easily appeared a decade younger.

Norah had never been one to desire aesthetic changes, but she caught herself looking at her queen for far too long, from Queen Annison's youth-gained face to her ball-formal, regal green dress. The queen equably looked over Norah's bewildered inspection, addressing her first. "Royal Inquisitor."

Norah's eyes widened, all prior anger absent in her peer's presence. She still could not trust her own sight, nor could she believe that her plethora of spies had failed to inform her prior to the Trials that the queen had returned in good health. How the king's consort had managed such a feat of secrecy was an impressive act she had not believed the Roths capable of.

Her voice came out unsure, which was entirely atypical for Norah. She could feel the shake in her own, lowered voice. "My queen! I am immensely pleased to see you again with us! I was so thrilled to hear the announcement at the Melee, and to look upon your face, looking fairer than ever. The Fives have been kind. Cycle's blessings to them!"

Queen Annison's keen amber eyes were sharp yet pacifying, the same as the tone in her voice. "The cycle's blessings to the Fives indeed. I trust you have been well and busy. That is quite the lot delivered from Randon."

"My queen." Norah humbly struggled to express the lone concern that plagued her. "I have been futile in my many attempts to see King Aerik. Have I disappointed or offended His Majesty in some way?"

Queen Annison's lighthearted grimace should have been accredited to alleviating the mood for Norah, but she lacked the competence to take anything lightly, especially on this occasion. "Is this your supple way of interrogating your queen, Honorah?"

Queen Annison had called her by her full name. *Am I being scolded?* She mustered all the resolve she could rally within her. "I have been summoned to use my methods of questioning on the trolls and qindrid brought in by General Roth. These prisoners are more resilient than any I have encountered before. I feel I have not been made privy to all that I need to be."

Queen Annison sustained her commanding poise, along with her mannered tone. "Well, at first it was in jest, but I see that you truly are interrogating me."

Queen or naught, that wasn't a satisfying retort, and Norah needed more. But before she could muster a rebuttal, the ill-favored Soro spoke up. "Maybe if she took the seat on the Frostdale Council we have stationed for her, she might be informed on such."

Norah looked upon the one empty seat at the long table in the royal solarium and pointed toward the mentioned. "I do not play board games, High Chancellor Soro! I whittle the ill-fated caught in the actual battles! My office is in the dungeons, not some unwelcome seat among strangers that know nothing of my war!" She had done it again, with contempt for the Dominadom she hadn't even realized she was repressing until tested.

Queen Annison placed a hand on her shoulder. Even though unwelcome, it was the touch of her queen. She wouldn't dare flinch in disrespect. "King Aerik is not well." The queen dropped the unanticipated news that shut down all her efforts. "And you will not repeat a word of it. He wishes to be alone during his recovery, which is underway. Honor this, Norah. I will not hear another word of it."

She stood blankly before the queen, waiting for something more solid before she was defeated in her case. It was as if Queen Annison had read her mind and given her the necessary response to stow any further inquiries. "I need you in the Frostdale Council, to do that which you disdain and engage in the politics of this realm for us. Just as they need you to do that which they do not understand and finish this war through the Frostdale Deeps."

And that was the end of that probable dispute. Queen Annison went on to lecture her on her duty. "I will offer clarity and insight on what King Aerik needs from you right now. You must do your best to set aside your aversion toward the Terollar. Your work must be tactful, without so much—" the queen paused to contemplate a delicate term "—passion put into it. Times are critical, and something dire is underlying it all. The staging for Lilealah's capture was premeditated and negotiated by King Aerik. Why these elven killed the khomo and staged a surrender is just oddly auspicious and uncharacteristic for the Glace Isles tribesven. Also, the fact that they tracked the exact location of Lilealah is all too clairvoyant. We believe some of the greyborne captured may be double agents for the Glace Isles. The Terollar working with the qindrid in this manner would be a first as well."

Queen Annison had made it simple enough. Norah responded obediently. "Thank you for enlightening me, my queen. I understand your bidding."

"Begin anew on these interrogations, and know that you have the highest blessings of King Aerik with you. Fives strength to you, Royal Inquisitor," the queen finished with a respectful nod to conclude.

Norah gazed through the mock Frostdale Council and gave a mechanical bow. "Council." She then turned back to Queen Annison and acquiesced as well. "Please tell His Majesty that his loyal servant wishes him the same recovery as my queen."

Norah bowed to her queen and took leave of the council chambers. Her eyes gazed up at the eccentric glass ceilings, displaying the canopy of starry space above her. It was a place of black and ice by night and life and sun by day. The royal solar was a recent construction in the hall that stood as the original throne room of Frostdale, abandoned as a museum of remnants and memory some several kings ago.

There is a new type of qindrid, Norah. And you live among them. Memory suddenly conjured Smile's portentous words. *They wear your faces. These are not the stoneborne of Aggedon or the skyborne of the east. This is something new. And the realm from north to south is infested with them.*

She chose to ignore the last of the implications made by the troll shaman about her former husband. But the reflection of his outlandish claims did involuntarily coerce Norah to turn her eyes for one last look upon the suspicious queen as she put the solar behind her.

It was the interruption of a random messenger that broke her from those tormenting inferences, that she might be sharing shelter with some enemy race unbeknown to all. "Lady Honorah Bayn?"

"What do you have?" She angrily snapped.

"The suitor you requested for your daughter. He has accepted your proposal." The envoy handed over the small scroll, which she opened immediately.

Her only answer was a rare smile of relief.

EBRIELLE (III)

TICK U'TON TOCK

A unison of guttural voices repeated the same familiar ode over and over from behind the door before her. It was all she had heard for the better part of an hour. The chant lingered between their heavily accented Trollspeak and the Terollar tongue.

Tick u'ton tock, tick u'ton tock,
We watchin' dat clock ...
Khomo'Jhuvonus kun roo il dar.

Tick u'ton tock, tick u'ton tock,
Keep watchin' dat clock ...
Khomo'Jhuvonus kun roo il vay.

Tick u'ton tock, tick u'ton tock,
Still wit' dat clock ...
A tick u'ton a tock, tick u'ton tock,
A tick u'ton a tock, tick u'ton tock,
Khomo'Jhuvonus kun dueme amda vay!

They would not stop. Such a haunting song every youth in Barredom learned growing up, intended to inspire fear in evolving delinquents to keep them from bad behavior. Just some harmless threat that elders played upon children, purposed for warning that a monster was out to get them if they didn't watch out.

But this one was sung in the crude Terollar language intertwined with their gruff enunciations of the Civil tongue, seeming all the more fitting, as if it were the way the ancient children's rhyme was meant to be recited all along. The guards around her all knew the translation simply because of their Barredish upbringing and the popularity of the northern tune. But among everyone near her, she knew that only she could also translate their Terollar words.

"Tick and then tock. Khomo'Jhuvonus will come for us ..." And then that he "will come for you." And finally that he "will take all of you." It had been many years since her uncle Tomas had sung the rhyme to her. She noted the trolls left out two important verses at the end—"The khomo has not left" and "The khomo cannot die"—but she was not complaining that they did. The latter lines were probably the most frightening. They even knew to whisper the penultimate verse before the great crescendo of the finale.

Ebrielle looked behind her, through the Troll Gardens' trees, toward the exit of the prison courtyard. *Where are you, Mother? I need you ...* She nervously bit her lip, lost on what to do. The watchmen around her seemed to share in her bafflement, coupled with their gradual build of dread.

It was not like Norah to be late to a torture session, especially one as filled as this one. Over half of the elven from the Deeps had been brought into the Troll Gardens' detention center. Ebrielle couldn't fathom how that many were detained in the small complex, designed for only five prisoners. But she supposed she could barely imagine that many dwelling in the confines of the Forlorn as well, and somehow the Barredom dungeon keepers had managed that feat.

She had yet to open the doors and see proof of the inhumane spectacle for herself. But the recurrent cadence of the beasts inside was taking hold of her avid curiosity. It seemed that each time they repeated the chant, they did so more fervently in desperation. Like a cry to their khomo to come save them. Amid the struggled ode, she insisted she could hear the elven grunting or shrieking in pain. It seemed to shift in intermittent patterns among the unnerving harmony.

"That sound," she uttered, adrift, gawking at the high windows from where the sound emitted.

One of the sentries beside her replied, on edge. "It seems your mother has started without you, my lady."

Another guard returned, voicing his superstition now that his comrades were speaking. "Make them stop! They're calling him to come. Some shaman spell! Do not doubt it, my lady."

She couldn't take any more. She had to go inside—with or without her mother. With no warning to the guards, she rushed to open the doors.

Twice as loud as before, and now all aimed straight at her, as the doors flew open, the blast of the unified ode targeted her in its full, guttural volume.

And then she saw it. The horror behind the hinted wails of agony. Scores of ravenous, freshly plump rats scurried for cover in a frantic craze once the sunlight filled the chamber. Many of the naked Terollar were bleeding from various parts of their bodies. Some had large clumps of meat missing from their calves or bellies, or even their mutilated faces.

After their final reiteration of the sinister song, quiet fell over the small room. Even the gluttonous rodents seemed satiated, now scuttling away to find a shadowy refuge far from the unwelcome radiance of the outside world. Moans of relief descended from the various abused trolls. The sudden view of the lush gardens promptly rekindled their innate self-healing.

She heard one or more of the guards behind her warn, "Lady Ebrielle, no!"

And another shouted, "Your mother will want you to wait on her!"

Her noble upbringing incited her on instinct to hold up a silencing hand. She was not accustomed to being commanded by those below her station, and she was just now finding out how unfond of it she was as well. And it worked. The guards went quiet, and her steps furthered inside unimpeded.

"They are all chained and secured, are they not?" She turned to address her inquiry to the officer presiding over the detention.

"Of course. Every one of them, my lady," he confidently guaranteed.

She had never seen a troll regenerate before. Their open wounds were sealing closed faster than she could have imagined possible. Witnessing it up close and firsthand was all so fascinating. There was no more unease left in her. The power of curiosity trumped the fleetingness of worry. "Then you all need not fear for me," Ebrielle assured him. "My mother will instruct the same. Today was the day I was set to lead the interrogations. If it makes you feel more at ease, you can all await me by the door."

The other watchmen traded unsure looks at their officer for his decision. Hesitantly, after a small moment to think on it, he nodded. "My lady." And he motioned his consent to his men.

Several additional pentacrux restraints had been brought in the chamber. Twenty-five of the grisly saltires cluttered the room now, with little space to move in between. Other trolls were bound to the walls, with their hands high above their heads and their ankles shackled in barely a few links of chain. The last of them, with no room to fit, had had their detainment improvised on stone tables or the firepit in the corner. She counted forty. She presumed the other thirty-something were still jailed in the Forlorn, including Zuulzin, who was nowhere to be seen.

Ebrielle took a deep breath and made sure not to look at any of the elven in the eye. This was all new territory for her. Her apprehension began to creep back into her nerves at an alarming rate. She thought she might faint from anxiety within the minute and hoped none of them could pick up the involuntary quiver of her hands or the beat of her breaths.

She awkwardly tried to appear confident as she strolled over to the table that held the toy box, as her mother called it. Filled with a surplus of a variety of sharp and elaborate torture instruments, the tool crate seemed a thing only the most deranged and vile individual could enjoy using. Her mother's lost soul had traveled down a dark road a long time ago.

Ebrielle took the box and dumped its contents entirely out, resting it upside down to hide all the instruments inside. She made sure the elven saw her do it. *Make sure ... Get rid of ... Clear out ...* She checked her trembling voice inside her head before exposing her fragility by speaking aloud. "Clear out these rats!"

The guards acted on her command and took torches from the sconces to light and scare away the swarm of rodents still in the chamber. "My name is Lady Ebrielle Blackendale, daughter of the Royal Inquisitor, Lady Honorah Bayn, and of the reputed troll hunter Lord Lucas Blackendale." Ebrielle's delicate eyes attempted to spy out Jrulthun, but when she found the bestial alpha, she tautly glanced away. "Slain by those just like you. Which of you wishes to speak to me?" She gradually calmed her voice to politely address the detained group, not eyeing any in particular as she stood her ground with her back to the table.

"Doed ay'brek un vay. Nimin doed caber kray en vayr zumbi," came the deep taunt from the exact pentacrux she had meant to avoid. Jrulthun. Upon his massive shoulder sat the hind end and tail of a dead rat. His mouth, chin, and neck were covered in the rodent's blood. She could only imagine that the poor, starved thing had chosen the wrong prisoner to chew on. Either Jrulthun hoped she didn't know their native tongue, or perhaps he was entirely counting on it. He had just told her that he would speak to her, but only while he fucked the skull of her corpse. She could now sympathize with why her mother had reputedly resorted to crueler methods of punishment.

"I am not my mother, Jrulthun," she replied to the brutish alpha in fluent Terollar. She was a student of her mother's. She was proficient in translating many languages and well practiced in speaking their accents seamlessly. *"That remark will earn you my silence but not the blade. One more, and I walk. I am here to broker a trade. A favor for a favor."*

She paced near the tables absent of chained trolls, keeping her distance. She looked at each individual in search for any compliant faces. One came, only a faint Trollspeak inflection in his Civil tongue. "I will speak to you, little mouse."

Ebrielle recognized the distinguishable elvan speaking, smiling in a fatigued but genuine conduct. The other Terollar decorated themselves with small bones or teeth piercing their ears, nose, lips, or parts of their face, but not this one. His face was bare and not all that unpleasant to look on, she inwardly admitted against her conviction. His blond hair was shaved on the sides and pulled back tight into a topknot. "Smiles, was it?" she conjured from memory.

The charismatic troll chuckled. "As ambassador for the Glace Isles, I have been called many things, yet hardly ever my true name. You may call me as you see fit, as the northmen tend to do."

Ebrielle remained indisputably nervous but intrigued. This was her first time speaking to any trolls in the flesh. Before today they had all been forbidden creatures of the prisons that she was never allowed to go near. However, this one did have some air about him that put her at ease. "Pet names it is, then."

"It seems so, little mouse," he continued to disarm her conception that he was even her enemy. "You see, we trolls disdain being called trolls. If today is kind, we of the Glace Isles proudly go by Terollar." He stated the obvious over the distaste toward the referenced northern slang.

Ebrielle innately felt humiliated for the unintended disrespect, unsure why she feasibly cared about offending these wretched cannibals. "Very well, Smiles the Terollar. Is this not as cordial as can be? What can we do for each other?"

He kept up his congenial demeanor, along with his pacifying smile. As intimidating as he had seemed at first glance, the more he spoke, the more he conveyed a peaceable and diplomatic impression. Bypassing her question, he switched the subject. "Did you like the song we sang for you?"

Ebrielle fixed her palms on the table behind her to secure her trembling hands against fidgeting with each other. She needed to remain confident at all costs during this, if the trolls hadn't already read through her facade. She raised an eyebrow and shot a doubting smirk back. "For me? Your song? That is a Barredish song. I was impressed, though. How you all even know it is worthy of an interrogation in itself. In part Terollar, it was even more fitting. You could probably sell it to the troubadours in an unlikely world where you were free." She was proud of herself. She was good at this witty prisoner banter. *Maybe this is Mother testing me as an interrogator to release me on my own. Future magistrate Lady Ebrielle Blackendale, Blood of House Bayn …*

"Khomo'Jhuvonus. You know this name?" Smiles inquired to the theme of the random new topic.

Ebrielle squinted and nodded. One was not supposed to say that name aloud. But obviously, these trolls did not fear such superstitions. "Every child growing up in Barredom knows that name. An ill omen to say it, unless sung in the ode. Our parents knew it as children from their parents, and so forth. A dark fairy tale with no fairies, only a monster. You can blame him for why Frostdale and its regions have such disciplined boys and girls to fight you back. All the vile children quickly became good for fear that the big bad monster would come to steal them away if they did not pile the stones."

"Big bad monster?" Smiles feigned a laugh, and his grin grew into a sneer. "Not sure he likes that."

Ebrielle shrugged, not really seeing the point. "'Likes'? I am sure you mean 'liked.' Every report tells that Jrulthun was seen executing him before capture." Her finger identified the accused big troll. "And then his body was burned by you here, before General Roth could apprehend the war party."

"Do you know the true story of the khomo of the Glace Isles?" Smiles continued to interrogate her.

Her eyes narrowed as she began to realize she was losing control of the exchange, but she took the bait regardless. "I know the soldiers' gossip, the same as all Barredish hear. Some fiend that can never die. They say he banished his own lifemate, that he slays every alpha who dares oppose him. There's even rumor that he killed two of his own sons. They say he forces you all to hunt us only for sport, for blooding to better fight the greys." Barredom had never been the enemy of the Terollar. The stoneborne clans were. But it had been too risky for the Glace Isles tribes to regularly chance their lives with assault on the elite qindrid. To keep the trolls blooded for battle, the Chosen Troll executed sporadic but methodical skirmishes upon the Barredish for battle training. Killing Barredish was just practice for their real enemy. Ebrielle refused to fathom the fact that her father had been slain and eaten for mere sport. There had to be more to know for her to make peace with it.

"And you hear of the axes that magically return to him when he fights. You even hear he devours the bodies of those he fells. So many versions, but hardly a one from the mouths of those he lets live, because those are few." Ebrielle grew tired of the worthless farce and needed to govern the room once and for all. She was failing miserably. "So what is to be believed? How does this help each of us, debating over folklore?"

The envoy elvan sighed and shook his weary head. "You know far too little yet just enough. You do know of the axes, though. And you spoke of a favor for a favor between enemies. They are here. In this castle. Are you ready to begin the trade?" Smiles enticed.

And just as Mother forewarned. "I was told you would do this. How you even presume to ascertain the whereabouts of such is beyond me." She recalled the quandaries Norah had confessed in reference to the same troll. Apparently, he had an obsession with the weapons.

"What if I told you a dire secret? For the ears of the little mouse only. I will give you this secret and grant you two invaluable favors if you do me this one kindness back." Smiles proposed his trade.

She regained a bit of composure, sure of herself in her reply to his game. "I would listen to you, steal your secret, and pretend that we are making a pact. You are in no position to grant anyone anything." She crossed her arms and impatiently stared at him.

He laughed himself into a small fit as a rebuttal. Her daring skepticism seemed to have invoked a smile from Jrulthun as well. "Too fair," Smiles cordially declared. "Your mother should take some lessons from you! Prepare to pretend, then."

Ebrielle didn't move, leaning back against the table, remaining with her arms folded at her chest. She tapped her foot and waited for him to spill his supposed plan.

"As ambassador of the isles, I would have you bring me these axes of the khomo's three sons. You will release me so that I can return them to the grove where their lifetrees once lay, where the khomo can be remembered and revered. These are sacred to our people and cannot stay here. Do this, and I will tell you what none other knows."

Ebrielle dared away from the table, feeling bold for the first time since she had walked into the Troll Gardens. Her eyes locked on Smiles, and she carefully approached. The guards at the entryway did not exist, nor did the other elven populating the grim room. It was just her and the Glace Isles ambassador in the chamber now. "So you get four great favors? The three weapons of your fallen king, and your life with freedom. Yet I get a simple secret, and three favors yet to be brought to light. Troll bargaining ability is being judged, Smiles. Are you sure you are their best choice for an envoy? You misjudge me as too soft and naive."

The diplomatic troll toyed on with more ambiguous scraps of tantalizing drivel. "I will tell you the favors now, but this secret only when you return to me. And it has to be just you, little inquisitor. I cannot tell you until we are alone and I trust we have our exchange."

"You jest to honor me as an inquisitor today." Ebrielle was close to giving up but still had some fight left in her. "My own prisoner mocks me, forgetting his own role in chains. I would hear some of it now. Tell me the two favors I get, troll," she agitatedly directed.

Smiles huffed in open disappointment, like a master irritated at an apprentice for flunking a trial. "Very well," he settled gravely and closed his eyes, then slowly reopened them to a transformation of his formerly passive visage, altered into an ill-omened promise. "Khomo'Jhuvonus will not come for you."

Not an answer she was expecting. Ebrielle sharply probed, trying to sound unperturbed, but her quaking voice and feet betrayed her brave charade as she tried to chuckle the absurdity away. "The dead will not come for me?" She took one step away from the elven in her audience and found her back, by surprise, against another pentacrux, which provoked the troll prisoner into a feral growl. As soon as her body thumped against the wood, the deep hums began, the wordless adaptation of the haunting rhyme she had suffered through prior to coming in. Every elvan in the chamber, except for Smiles, droned the rising tune in a low baritone.

The formerly friendly troll spoke above the swelling resonance of his allies. "Khomo'Jhuvonus will save you and spare one other. The two favors. The secret is yet to come," he continued on, with more cryptic teasing, exploiting her fear and inexperience.

Smiles's eyes turned crazy, and her demeanor went from semi-confident to outright panicked in an instant. The deep-toned hums of the elven switched to a choir of echoing voices, chanting the ode without the words in place. Her feet backstepped between the many crosses, glancing up at each troll she passed, frightened beyond anything she had ever endured. She expected them to start breaking free at any moment. *We are done here! I will return with the Royal Inquisitor! You obviously choose the path of blade and flame!* She screamed it all in her mind, but her tongue and eyes dared not threaten the beasts, chained or not.

The song was in full throat now. Between the "tick u'ton tock" lines at the prominent chorus points, Smiles chanted after her, "The khomo has not left." She found a scream swelling in her constricting throat, and her feet prepared for flight. He was citing the two missing verses the trolls did not include. "The khomo cannot die," he promised gleefully, wild-eyed at every sentry staring him down.

"Guards!" The scream did come. "Guards!" Pride had been thrown to the rats. Her need for fresh air and to be rid of this place took utmost precedence.

"Bring the axes to the Forlorn!" he shouted behind her, all the while with Jrulthun laughing hysterically and the other trolls keeping true to their eerie hymn. "You will be saved!"

"Lady Ebrielle, come! Quickly!" The sentry officer ushered her by the shoulder while several other watchmen formed up in the chamber. There, in the chamber doorway, she saw her savior.

"Mother!" Ebrielle cried. She thought she could never be this happy to see her own mother, whom she despised so thoroughly.

Ebrielle buried her face into her mother's bosom and burst into uncontrollable tears, weeping away. "Sweet, poor child. Shh now, shh," Norah comforted her, stroking her daughter's hair behind her head. "No need for fear now. You need never do this again."

"Where were you? We waited so long!" Ebrielle pulled away, scolding her mother.

"Securing your marriage," Norah replied equably.

Ebrielle sniffed several more times, wiping away her many tears on the sleeve of her dress. She was confused. Perhaps she had misheard her mother with the loud interruption of chants.

Norah affirmed, "You needn't linger in this doomed north any longer. This was never your place. I see that now. And something does not settle right with it all lately. You will be packing your things to go far from here."

"I don't understand, though, Mother. To whom? I haven't been courted by anyone." Ebrielle had forgotten all about the trolls.

"Lord Haelyn Rook, archon of the Silverlakes, in Tairancia. He is old but not so old that he cannot bring you children of your own. He lost his late wife during childbirth and is looking to remarry. This is the best match for you, Ebrielle, to ensure your future. Away from the failing of Frostdale and Az'Dayne's politics. I fear the worst will soon be upon us." Everything her mother was saying came completely unforeseen. Just days ago Norah was doing everything she could to educate Ebrielle as an interrogator and to keep her brother, Aerik, from going south as well. And now she was being planned away. *What has changed, Mother?*

"But what about Kyson?" She hardly registered that her inner thoughts had been whispered aloud.

"Who?" Norah raised an eyebrow in uncertainty and shook it off, continuing. "We will talk about all of this more later. Run along now, child. You need no longer bear witness to this." She shot her habitual wink before enacting something sinister.

Her mother reached to take the torch from her guard officer's grasp and began forward into the chamber. In a stern voice, she unsympathetically warned and decreed, "Bring your torches inside. Shut the doors. I hope you can all stomach the smell of flesh on fire."

And the double doors to the torture chamber shut. With not a soul in sight, she found herself alone in the Troll Gardens' courtyard, still half-shaken and partly tangled in a mix of emotions. She collected herself as she stood still, now listening to the only sound to be heard: the tormented wails of trolls being burned alive.

WESTWALKER (V)

THE MERCY

Ryleohk weaved up the steep cliff walls in a jocular chase after a pair of skittish mountain goats. The playful sprint provided the main source of entertainment for the march of the mounted Boarneck Cavaliers in tow. The elvan's dexterous feet never missed a step on the loose rock, with a constant of impossible balance. Tsuno was pleased to see his typically barbarous friend actually enjoying himself with the two animals.

Nho took Tsuno back from the scouting lead, through the vanguard, to find Captain Tristostopher and deliver his report. Their trek upon the V'Gilan High Road had gone unhindered and rather swiftly, a few days in. They would be upon the crossroads to take their detour to the Loch Karlohr villages by early nightfall.

He found the flamboyant mercenary leader midstride in some elaborate tale he was torturing Jonan with. As Tsuno approached, the captain motioned him to join in the conversation. "Prettyborne! Come! Feed me something good."

Tsuno pulled Nho by the reins to turn his steed adjacent to Tristostopher and Jonan. He looked up at the midday sun through the canopy of clouds. "We will be upon the Aggedonian villages by twilight, if that whets your taste. Your sword can dip into as much qindrid as it pleases soon enough. Two-Towns is next."

Tristostopher laughed in his overly boisterous, deep voice. "You know me too well! Perfect!"

"Karlohr should be empty. I doubt there are any greyborne remaining that haven't already joined with the Great Exodus, or that haven't retreated for refuge in Two-Towns," Tsuno surmised.

Scout Lionel, whom Thade had ordered to join with Tristostopher and the Westwalker for further intelligence, chimed in. "Some Reluctants remain in the villages. They seemed few—stubborn elders and a few injured, prideful warriors. I know these types. They will accept death before they choose to flee."

Killing old men and crippled soldiers was not part of his arrangement with Randon Roth. Tsuno already knew that he and Ryleohk would not be participating in this inevitable slaughter, but Tristostopher seemed to be a man of hedonistic carnage. The captain grinned hungrily, the whole left side of his mouth filled with jagged gold teeth.

The four sat in silence for a long time with no attempt at exchange. They fixated on the mesmerizing run of the Wyldenar up the vertical hill pass on the opposite side of the high road. The captain took notice of his shared interest in Ryleohk. "Story time! We are about due for his. I would hear it!"

Tsuno narrowed his blue eyes at his friend in the distance, becoming lost in his grace. Ryleohk was a majestic creature of all nature's purity, and the man beside him was a product of urban corruption at its summit. *You do not deserve to know of him. None of us do.* Tsuno knew very little himself, but with what slight detail he had, he understood the fable was a tragic one.

He decided to tell the insistent decadent only half of what he had come to learn, for the sake of contentment, to silence the man for a day. "Ryleohk is a rogue." Tsuno closed his eyes, upset at himself already for feeling he was betraying his only true friend's secrets. "Rogue-elven are different in appearance from the norm of their ilk. Only the rogues have grey skin, hair, and eyes, as Ryleohk. They are like the greyborne of the elven. And you can see how his ears go flat to the side like the umbran's, instead of slanting back like those of other elven. That is also a trait of the rogue." *They are also more feral and impulsive than any others of their kind.* He thought to voice the verifiable research aloud but preserved that factuality.

The unquenchable curiosity of Tristostopher was far from glutted. The captain begged, "His origin, then? When was his little twig cut? That is how they become rogue, yes?" His volume increased question to question, but his gaze never left the Wyldenar on the rolling cliffs.

Tsuno was already annoyed and done with the man. "No. Those that have their spiritroot cut are known to suffer the aging." Tsuno took a long breath and stared at his distant companion as if pleading for permission to continue. "Rogues are those born to two umbran lifemates. They are unique in a curse from the day they break from their cocoon. Being of the umbran, they have no spiritroot and thus age as you humans do from birth. Most are exiles, which is why Ryleohk is here and not in Artopia or Tundura, alongside his fellow Wyldenar. He has never known the long life of his people or the comfort of his tribe or home."

The captain was merrily intrigued, regardless of the tragic tone. "But he is so young! Born of the umbran, then? He is a son of the one who was captured? Am I right? Tell me I am right!"

"Lilealah. Yes." Tsuno hesitated again, cursing himself for the flaw of his need for fellowship. "His patriarch, their word for 'father,' was slain during an interrupted ritual of the Transcendence upon his bornday. His matriarch, his mother, escaped."

"Outstanding!" Tristostopher cheered, malignant to the facts, with not even a sliver of sympathy. "So who raised him? A lone elvan babe in the woods, with a dead daddy and a mommy on the run. I am sure those in the ritual were slain as well, before they took the turn. Who was the culprit of the ambush?"

Tsuno decided this would be the end of this subject for him. He couldn't bring himself to tell any more but one minor inkling of Ryleohk's past. "You have seen the axe he carries. That is not of his ilk. That is a Terollar weapon, with the symbol of the Glace Isles king on it. And his name alone, Ryleohk—that is a word in the Terollar tongue. It means 'rogue.' He was not named by Wyldenar." He directed Nho into motion to take his leave of the captain once more.

Tristostopher began shouting for more fare for his boundless intrusiveness. "Wait, prettyborne! He was raised by trolls, you mean? That is the answer! All so fascinating! You must tell me next how you two came to meet!" The captain's voice tried on as Nho pushed Tsuno safely away from speaking distance.

Tsuno trotted back ahead of the mercenary line. His attention immediately went to Ryleohk, who was now done with his chase and staring back at him. The rogue had both of the young rams beside him, as if they had been friends playing a game all along. Ryleohk was petting one under the neck, while the other nestled for affection against the hair cloaking his back.

Tsuno laughed and nodded to his companion, and Ryleohk started back up on his jaunt into the rocky hills ahead. He was now alone, as usual, left to the mercy of his thoughts and memories. His recollection drifted to the time he had first met the rogue, evoked by Tristostopher conjuring the old subject to the surface.

Ryleohk had never been raised by his own kind but instead by the Terollar, as Tristostopher had guessed. It was a rare thing to say one had met the Chosen Troll and lived, yet the Westwalker had survived that purposed encounter—a tale never told. The one in which he prevailed over the Glace Isles and attained Ryleohk from the legendary Khomo'Jhuvonus himself. No one would believe the true version, regardless. His camaraderie with Ryleohk, by popular consensus, was accredited to his vague exploits through Artopia.

Contemplating the past never tarried on the intended focus, however. His musings inadvertently waded into the somber images of Yoshira and Hirotai, his lost wife and son, and his unseen grandchild, conceivably even great-grandchildren by now.

The mournful nostalgia of Yoshira's suicide overshadowed all else. He compelled himself into the practiced reverie of semiconscious meditation to invoke a fragment of significant reminiscence.

It was the memory of the first time he had brought her on a hunt. His tracking had successfully brought them to skulk upon a lone doe. As Tsuno paused to make his precision kill of the unwary deer, Yoshira stopped him. Whispering, she explained her concern that his shot might not kill the poor animal but had a chance only to wound it instead and cause it suffering. She pleaded with him to only take its life if he could prove beyond a doubt that it would feel no pain. His wife's heart toward beasts and innocent things was so great, Tsuno recalled falling in love with her all over again on that very hunt.

He had acceded to her wishes and allowed the doe to escape on that encounter. Husband and wife, together, they spent the rest of the day harvesting a rare plant Tsuno had discovered in his former wilderness ranging. His masters in the Saiyenai called it the dreambloom, an exotic, spiky leaf with bulbous violet veins throughout. The organic purplish striations were filled with a milky substance that was lethally poisonous by consumption or injection, causing one to enter into an instantaneous comatose state, swiftly followed by the stopping of one's heart. It was proclaimed to be a surefire method for a peaceful fatality if ever there was one.

Tsuno and Yoshira embarked on the same hunt the next day, now with the dreambloom coating his arrows. They trailed the same doe as before. This time the mother deer was beside her buck and fawn, an entirely different scenario Yoshira was not prepared to stomach. Nevertheless, Tsuno was determined to prove to his wife the necessity of the hunt, for individual survival away from the monastery, to prepare for what he had planned for their future.

Judging the severity of Yoshira's sympathy, he aimed his bow on the buck instead of the doe. Just before he released for the kill, she placed her calming hand over his and turned his aim back to the original target. He remembered looking into her eyes to ensure her approval. He realized nothing about the hunt was endorsed by her utter consent. But she was his wife, and she was dutiful to the core of her soul. This was her way of supporting his hard verdicts with a hint of soft advice, showing simple mercies in circumstances where they could be shown.

He made the shot, and the doe died peacefully. The fawn ran away, and the buck stared, confused, back at Tsuno for quite some time, not registering what had taken place. Only when Yoshira and he approached did the beast flee into the unknown wilds.

The irony of it all fell back onto that fated day many years after. Underneath the willow tree, where he found Yoshira passed of her own accord, it was the dreambloom he found in her hand. She had consumed the milk of the death plant to take her own life. Just as the doe died that day on the hunt without much cause, and the son ran away, while the husband stood confused. It all seemed like a humorless reenacted parody.

Tsuno commemorated the dreambloom poison with the branding of Yoshira's Mercy following her death, as he was the only monk in the Saiyenai to appropriate it into his extensive arsenal thereafter. He unfailingly kept seeds of the plant on him throughout his ventures, utilizing it in his methods of swift execution.

Tsuno compelled himself out of the melancholic reverie, back to the numbing reality of mere existence with no sentiment or human history to adhere to.

He was the Westwalker again now. Tsunosoto Akazi had died a long time ago.

His exotic horse ushered him along on the barren V'Gilan High Road. All fell still, except his perception, as the Boarneck contingent neared the crossroads to Karlohr. A dying sun collapsed, vanquished by the rising of the full moon's glory.

The star-strewn night was nearly as bright as the dusk of day, allowing the eye to see all to come on the highway of the seawall. The distant waves crashing below the steep cliff line served as a hypnotizing ambience to the rhythm of the plethora of hooves behind him, drumming against the stone road. The Karlohr crossroad was just up ahead, with still no sight of an enemy spotted by Ryleohk.

Tsuno threw a closed fist up to the company's vanguard to signal space for Ryleohk and himself to begin their investigation of the villages. Gestures were passed back through the line to the captain, and the march was ordered to a halt. Ryleohk and Tsuno were on their own for a small time.

After their full descent down from the hills, and the first sight of the outlying farms were discerned, Tsuno deemed it time to temporarily part with his steed. He dismounted from Nho and hushed a command to him in Sho'Lonese. Nho was well rehearsed and far more intelligent than any normal beast. The beautifully exotic horse set out to shadow, on standby, from a distance.

The border settlements were devoid of all life. Not a qindrid or any livestock remained. The nearer they made their way in past the farms, the closer the houses were structured. Eventually, the paths all merged into the road that led to the fishing village of Loch Karlohr.

Tsuno quietly trailed Ryleohk as the elvan prowled along the dirt of Karlohr's thoroughfare. Tall lantern stands protruded in front of each house, which led from dwelling to dwelling, closely assembled together. None were lit, furthering his confidence that indeed the entire village had been abandoned, like the fortress of the Fourteen.

The two made haste through the derelict settlement, toward the lake. Karlohr was known as a fishing hub for the Lilealytes of the Fourteen and their patrols between Two-Towns. The serene, glass-like lake had long piers all over the entirety of its southern waterfront.

The piers stretched across the lake all the way from Karlohr to Two-Towns, acting as extensively long bridges. The interconnected wharves were set as fishing farms over the southern point of the lake.

They held multitudes of crab traps and uprooted fir trees that were inverted underwater to draw in schools of fresh catch.

Ryleohk stopped in a crouch behind a horse trough near the last residence against the boardwalk. His gaze settled on a single silhouette on the docks. A young fisherman pulled in his last catch of the night. Tsuno crept in beside Ryleohk to watch the man a while longer before deciding what fate he should enact upon him.

The man began towing his heavy net of fish on a sled strapped to his shoulder, oblivious to any danger. Tsuno put a halting hand on Ryleohk's shoulder.

"Out here alone, fisherman?" Tsuno inquired amicably in the local Norspeak as he stood up, no weapons in hand, casually walking toward the boardwalk.

The qindrid stopped, alarmed, and dropped the strap on his sled. He guardedly reached to slip the long knife from his belt. He must have been in his midthirties, by Tsuno's guess. And judging from the grey hair on his head and color of his eyes, it was obvious that this man was of the few lingering greyborne.

The greyborne, who were born into no loyalties to umbran masters, would be the most resistant to joining the Lilealytes and the Great Exodus. The man likely had a family, and this was the home he apparently did not intend to abandon.

"I know who you are" was all the fisherman offered back, avoiding the question. He stood his ground, readied, as if he thought the Westwalker would pounce at any moment.

"Of course you do." Tsuno smiled but squinted his blue eyes impatiently. *"Answer anyway, good sir."*

"I am," the man lied, and stood up boldly. *"It is my home, and I will not flee as a coward, like the rest."*

"A brave fool soon to die, then. Thousands of mercenaries are behind me, and behind them, Northaven's army with reinforcements from Frostdale and Az'Dayne itself. It is not cowardly to survive," he warned, feeling sympathy and respect for the man.

The fisherman's eyes betrayed his words. He frantically looked behind Tsuno to the houses against the boardwalk near Ryleohk.

"Which one is yours? And where are they?" Tsuno demanded.

A window shut and a candle went out one house down from the trough where Ryleohk hid. The Wyldenar's whistling axe went flying into the door with a crash of wood splintering into pieces.

"Cynthiel! Maeson!" The man sprinted forward, ignoring the threat of the Westwalker before him. Ryleohk wrenched his axe free and opened the door to pull a young woman and a small boy from its hold and into the street. The man cried at the top of his lungs. *"Please don't hurt them, Westwalker!"*

"I don't hurt women and children," Tsuno promised gently but sternly. *"But the men on their way do. Take your boat and leave now, fisherman. I will stall them until you are good and gone."*

A surprise disruption galloped in with the most inopportune timing. "Prettyborne!" The worst sound in the world, backed by the clamor of a multitude of horses storming down the streets of Karlohr. "You were taking so long, I just couldn't take it anymore! I can't let you have all the fun!" Tristostopher shouted.

The captain and a throng of his men surrounded Ryleohk and the four qindrid in a circle. Tristostopher slowly trotted by the woman and child and made his way up to Tsuno and the fisherman. He stared down the unfortunate man with wild, hungry eyes, like a starved glutton would a piece of cake. "What have we here?"

"Just a stubborn villager. No soldier." Tsuno reverted back to the Civil tongue while speaking to Tristostopher, quickly attempting a solution to save the poor family. "Perfect to send to Two-Towns to warn them of our imminent presence. This should shake up enough fear in the city to have the militia join the retreat to Aepox."

Tristostopher frowned with an exaggerated pout, unconvinced. "I have to send all three to do that?"

"I'm advising you to send all three," Tsuno counseled harshly.

"Advising? Oh, so domineering of you!" the captain blurted, feigning intimidation. But his devious smiled proved his intent. "But, no." He flicked his wrist to a group of his men. "Take her."

"Cynthiel, no!" The fisherman became frantic and tried to run to her rescue but was swiftly pushed to the ground by the haft of the captain's spear.

The little boy screamed for his mother, *"Mama!"* as the mercenaries stripped her from her son's embrace.

She pleaded for her husband as a few of the men tore her gown from her body to the dirt. *"Paylen, please!"*

"Tristose. You don't need to do this. There will be plenty of skyborne, stoneborne, and greyborne soldiers in Two-Towns." Tsuno was genuinely worried for the family, pleading himself now.

Tristostopher puckered his lips and explained, "I'm not going to do this. My men are. I'm going to do *him*."

More mercenaries dismounted and seized Paylen by the shoulders to forcefully escort him to his house. "*Wait, sir, no! Please, Westwalker, tell him I will do anything! Kill me, and send my wife and boy to spread fear in Two-Towns for you!*"

Tsuno felt for the man's request and beseeched the captain once more in a warning tone. "Let them go, or kill them and be done with it."

"Translate this. Tell him I will not kill his wife. But the two thousand cocks of my men just might. She just may live." Tristostopher started his slow trot behind Paylen to the house. "I'm only going to kill him after I fuck him silent. You can tell the boy to start running. He can warn Two-Towns what's coming for them."

Tsuno went up to the boy and drove him by the shoulder. "*Run, boy. Your parents are not coming with you.*" He rushed him to the boardwalk and gave him an encouraging shove. "*I am sorry.*"

His father, Paylen, shouted back to embolden his spirits. "*Go, Maeson! We will be right behind you. Don't wait! Don't stop until you reach the city!*"

"*Papa, no!*" Maeson cried, weeping in place.

Paylen roared his final command to his son. "*Go, child! Go!*"

The Westwalker looked for guidance from his friend Ryleohk but found no solace there in the eyes of the callous killer. He watched as the boy finally ran in full sprint down the pier in the direction of Two-Towns. Paylen's wife was wailing in defiance as the men belligerently pawed at her and started to carry her away. They bent her over the water trough he had hidden behind when approaching the docks. Paylen was almost to his house now.

He hushed a soft request under his breath, keeping to the respects of the Norspeak tongue. He pulled out both of his hand crossbows, preloaded with lethal poison bolts. "*Forgive me for the mercy I grant you both.*"

A click of the trigger from both weapons, and the precision bolts, coated at the tip in Yoshira's Mercy, found their marks. Paylen and Cynthiel slumped in eternal rest.

The men around Cynthiel's corpse were not quick to sort out what had happened to their promised toy. She collapsed completely into the trough. The mercenaries looked all around for a logical reason for the intervention.

Tristostopher, however, pinpointed the culprit immediately. He stopped in his tracks on his horse and looked back to Tsuno, surprised. His smirk grew gradually but was a guise in front of clenched teeth. "Now, that wasn't very fun, prettyborne. Not very fun at all." He galloped over to his nearest man armed with a torch and rode in a circle around Tsuno. "And here I thought you and I were getting along. You are going to make that up to me. I am not one to forget a debt."

Tristostopher threw the torch onto the roof of Paylen's house and bellowed a command. "Burn it all!"

Tsuno watched as the lackeys all performed as bidden. Karlohr abruptly went up in flames. Ryleohk was now nowhere to be found. Tsuno looked into the flames of the burning house that had once been Paylen's. "The point?"

"Taking your advisement," the Boarneck captain retorted sarcastically. He reared his horse up as if to knock Tsuno over and trample him but landed in the other direction, toward the exit of the village. "Two-Towns will see the flames and smoke from across the lake. Let them know the beasts that are to become their reckoning. Let them dream uneasily until my company arrives. They will expect a good fucking from the army on the road arriving at their doorstep but never see the big Boarneck cock that will rape them in the ass!"

Tsuno came to the final conclusion that he simply didn't care for the Boarneck captain, with no hope for redemption. He turned his head away from the bright fires swarming the village and pondered the bright orange mirror that shimmered across Loch Karlohr. He mumbled his reply in his native Sho'Lonese, knowing Tristostopher wouldn't comprehend him. "*Qindrid do not dream. We stay awake. And dwell. And remember.*"

Whether Tristostopher did not hear or did not care, he returned no response to Tsuno's parry. Tristostopher signaled to Jonan and a nearby group of six horsemen who didn't participate in the village torching. Each of them had a separate packhorse loaded down with small wooden kegs. The captain returned to business in an instant. "We don't rest here. Our flank starts now. These specialists are yours with the blast salt intact. They have their guises and are prepared to help you with your traps. I'll see you on the other side on time, awaiting your signal. We can play nice until it's time to pay your dues back to me."

Tristostopher kicked his steed into motion and departed with his group in a hurry from the blazing village. The Westwalker looked around the fiery scene for any hint of the whereabouts of his elusive companion, but he found no trace, as expected. Ryleohk hated civilization for this exact reason. He would meet him in the woods.

Tsuno concentrated his focus on the young greyborne still running away on the piers. The monsters were indeed coming, and for the first time in a long while, he began to question his own loyalties toward the humans he so often allied with.

ONDREW (V)

WHITE WATCHERS

Hushed chatter jabbed at the monotony of the endless percussion of boots against crude stone. The repetitious tunnel system played tricks on his eyes and memory, forcing his mind to second-guess the time that must have passed. The highlight of the uneventful trek was his participating silence in the game being tossed about among the entourage in his wake. While Ondrew's thoughts reflected on his father and mother, several of his men entertained themselves by counting the number of living things they could find—whether beetle, lizard, or worm, it did not matter. The first to fifty won, and the highest counter was only on seventeen. It was a rather tedious endeavor that had begun what seemed like days ago. Worse, they had been ordered not to talk, so one only knew when another creature had been spotted by a knight holding up his hand with a count of fingers.

Finally, Ondrew did permit limited whispering. The chatter between comrades proved to be an educational sermon on some accounts. Ondrew discovered the prejudice the Vellyans held toward the Timberhands during one of the ranting debates. Aramgar and Odemnar were two of the survivors from the barbarian invasion the Timberhands had defended against in the Undawned Lands. Apparently, the musically inclined archers were responsible for the deaths of most of the exiled Vellyans' fallen clansmen. They were deemed accountable for the Vellyans' capture altogether, to be placed under Barredish custody for sentencing.

Ondrew had been rewarded with the brutish and likely unreliable fugitives, while Aramgar and Odemnar had been cursed in tragic irony, compensated by a false sense of freedom, being sworn in to protect and fight alongside their most recent adversaries.

A fork in the cavern's passage came into view ahead, flaunted only by the sporadic constellations of red crystalytes in the tunnel's fork to the left. An alternative choice of passage branched to the right, much darker, with no tinge of what anonymities it accommodated. A distant flicker of faint yellow light around the bend was the only hint of the path on the right.

Why the Shaw brothers would have deemed it wise to move into the junction without informing the group raised the first flag of suspicion. Ondrew signaled for silence and motioned for Broc, Mathias, and Black to inspect the den.

Mathias pointed out a Neveril firetears trap the scout brothers had forewarned them about at the beginning of the journey. It seemed to be triggered the same way, by a stone pressure plate beneath elvan runes on the ceiling above.

It marked the entry to the crimson-lit path, while the obscure passage on the right furnished no such impediments. Broc pointed out the multiple clefts of freshly scorched ghostgrass in the chamber, hinting of Sheridan and Snowden's presence not long ago.

Black Brigannor skulked slowly, with no torch in hand and his two battle-axes readied for the worst, into the darker of the tunnels, toward the hint of light ahead. All eyes locked on the old soldier, absorbed by waiting for an answer to the fate of their vanished scouts. Just as Black neared the bend in the passage, a feminine voice upset the hush of pending dread.

"Blood," Lilealah interjected. "Blood everywhere. They are dead."

Everyone forgot about Black in an instant to look at the umbran for explanation. More than half of the men's faces were etched with fear. Her insinuation stimulated the group to frantically lift their torches to the ceiling and inspect the den as a whole.

She was correct. Blood pooled on the floor nearest one of the fissures of former ghostgrass. The same fresh crimson spattered down the wall near the tunnel Black had disappeared into.

Ondrew's protective sense toward his men compelled his uneasy, vehement outburst. "Black?" His feet advanced after his fellowman.

Black came around the corner with a torch now in hand and one of his axes still in the other. The yellow glow proved to be the dropped torch of one of the Shaws.

The group trailed behind their leader's anxious feet and came upon the mute soldier's findings. Black shone the torch over a severed, bloody arm, torn brutally from the shoulder socket. The limb had white sleeves and black leather gloves.

"Sheridan," Ondrew whispered, wide-eyed, not sure what emotion he was allowed to display to his subordinate brethren in such a dire circumstance.

"Torches up. Blades out. Follow me. We find and avenge our brothers," Ondrew firmly vowed to his men. Their temporary hesitancy was assuaged by the simplicity of his tenacity.

The short passageway ended rather abruptly, more like an upwardly twisting cave than an alternative route. The warren culminated in a funneled-out dead end, with an excess of crawl spaces dotting the chamber, all large enough for something the size of the Vellyans to scuttle through. In the center of the tunnel's end lay the gory remains of what could have been none other than Sheridan and Snowden Shaw.

Their torn clothes and hair matched those of the two brothers, but only their entrails and small bits of their facial tissue lingered on their freshly picked skeletons. Their swords had been taken, as had their trinkets and ration packs. Whatever had taken their lives had made short work of scavenging anything of value, from meat and organs to coin and steel.

Ondrew had never come across any manner of foe that would do this to its victims. At first he considered the probability of it being trolls, knowing their propensity for cannibalism. But the prior discoveries of Lilealah and the scouts suggested otherwise.

"Trolls," Broc spewed in a growing fury, glowering down every crawl space nearby for any shape of foe to dare through.

Mathias gaped at the bony corpses with a cloudy visage in some detached, nightmarish memory. "These boys were eaten out of hunger. Trolls don't feed like this. They do it selectively, and all for sport."

"The Skystone apes," Lilealah contended. "I already warned you they were here. And they are starved."

Several Norther Knights flashed their fires into the large holes in a hunt for the bestial culprits, to no avail.

Ondrew let slip his own inner thoughts to the group. "They even took the weapons."

"Yes, they will do that. And sometimes use them," the umbran confirmed. She walked over to the corner near one of the empty packs and began rummaging. She pulled the map from one of the pockets and handed it over to Ondrew. "Best that you hold on to this from now on. You will need to choose other scouts."

"He will need t' be mournin' our fallen men, ye heartless soul-sucker," Broc returned in a rage. "Give us half a spit t' burn our brothers proper!"

"We are going to burn bones and bowels?" Kyson retorted cynically.

Before Broc could unleash his ire on the insensitivity of the practical bard, Ondrew took the lead in a pragmatic course of action for everyone. "The rules of respect for our fallen kin do not apply north of the Kiss, my brothers. Heed this. Their souls now rest in the Godslands, with the Five and Five. You all may burden yourselves with a token from them, so that we might honor their memory for their family when we are long gone from these elvan tombs."

Ondrew knelt beside the skull of what he assumed was Snowden. He took the Shaw family talisman from the dead boy's neck and parted with it to Broc, who had just retrieved Sheridan's heritage amulet as well. As he stood back up, he was glad to see most of his original Knights participating in the tender respects to the dead brothers. "No more scouts until we take leave of this haunt. We move as one now."

He didn't have to say it aloud to feel the distress at his back. Sheridan and Snowden were the only members of the party that had ever trekked through Zsolindal before. The map he carried had been drawn by their grandfather and had evidently been matured by them throughout the years of their explorations. He had so many other questions he could have asked the boys if he had sensed such a peril would come so soon.

The Norther Knights took leave of the gruesome feeding pit and backtracked to the den with the fork toward the other tunnel. A broken arm-sized stalactite was used on the trap's pressure plate to release the firetears mist into the hall. The group patiently waited until the poisonous orange cloud dissipated before venturing into the unknown any farther.

The glow of the cavern's unique crystals nullified the need for torchlight. The fortuity was taken advantage of as every man stayed armed. All chatter completely ceased as the party delved deeper into the crimson shadows.

According to the Shaws' map, the actual realm of the former northern Neveril was the approaching waypoint just ahead. The erratic crystalyte formations gradually clustered into a spangled burst across the expanding tunnel's stone hide. The ethereal red radiance induced an otherworldly aura of some illusory realm meant for the gods or lost souls.

The passage finally siphoned them into a vast chamber so large, Ondrew felt as if he had stepped into a hollowed-out mountain and not just the heart of the underworld's expanse. The entire scope of the subterranean lair was lit up by some undiscernible means, with a ceiling as high as the sky, illuminated by a spectrum of colors across the craggy heavens.

And there it was before them: Zsolindal, the city. The underrealm itself was often misinterpreted and falsely titled by name. The Neveril originally dubbed only their colony itself Zsolindal. It was adapted later, when the northerners came to refer to the entirety of the cavernous domain by the label.

"Behold, the City of Ghosts," Lilealah purred. "Zsolindal, lost colony of the northern Neveril."

Ondrew had never seen such ingenuity as the bizarre structure of the exotic metropolis. Stone was impossibly stacked on stone, seemingly carved but with a perfectly natural sense to it all, as if not a single human tool had been used to layer it out. Hundreds of dwellings, all made of rock and gem, amassed as far back as the eye could perceive, in no particular pattern or symmetry. A continuum of large steps careened throughout the colony like some perpetual promenade that led to each tiered domicile.

Enthralled awed whispers tumbled from the mouths of the men as they absorbed the alien panorama ahead. Datron was the only knight to let any words slip out aloud. "An elvan city. No one back home will believe I ever saw one."

"More like a necropolis for the forgotten," Ondrew returned in a low tone. "Life has long fled from this place."

In the distance, atop one of the stone terraces, a lone beast stood and watched the group. Taller than the Vellyans, covered in white fur from head to toe, with a crude spear in hand, it scrutinized the intruders a brief moment longer and then crept back into the shadows through the hole of one of the abodes.

Skystone apes. No one had to say it. His Norther Knights had been spotted. And there would be more than one amid the passage throughout the stone crypt. Ondrew buried his uncertainty and bit down on his devoted fortitude against any fear. He intrepidly led the first steps forward into the City of Ghosts.

HONORAH (IV)

OF TONICS AND TORTURE

The stone tile was level on this floor of the Deeps. Her eyes could afford the recess for a short minute. She found her heavy lids draping down to connect with the bags of wrinkled skin that hung beneath her eyes. The blackness was inviting as her feet took automated control to drive her forward. Sleep had not found her in days, and today would be no different. She embraced any seconds of imaginary slumber that she could in the fleeting moments between her agendas.

Tonight was all about her bluff versus her foes' belief. The past several mornings, and on into the dusks, had entailed dealings with the steward of House Rook, arranging Ebrielle's marriage to the estate's patriarch, Lord Haelyn Rook, archon of the Silverlakes. She had her doubts that sweet slumber would find her before sunrise. One needed to be at peace to obtain sleep. And not a shred of peace lingered in her bones.

One of her shoes did not pick up high enough as it dragged her gait into a mild trip, snapping her back wide awake. She was all the more glad for her exhausted lack of grace when she saw who was down the hall in front of her. *Soro*, Norah hissed in her mind.

Whatever ailment of fatigue had been in her veins before now boiled over with anxiety. There was no reason for her to address the man in hostility, but being that the disfavored councilman had just interrupted her walking nap, the tone and squint in her face proved as much disdain as she could convey. "What are you doing here, High Chancellor?"

High Chancellor Soro was being escorted by four of his green-eyed Forwoken monks, each armed with their traditional spear-like weaponry. At the top of each haft, for the weapon's end, was attached a wide, curved single-edged blade that made them seem rather unwieldy. She had never seen the martial prowess of the warriors from the Qaegons, but stories of merit filled the streets of Frostdale that the mute brotherhood was deadly in its particular style of combat.

The chancellor shot a failed attempt at a disarming grin. "Forgive my ignorance on the Frostdale Deeps prison policies. I was not aware that those above your station on the council were forbidden entrance now."

She didn't reply to that bait. She allowed the unwelcome nuisance to continue.

"Perhaps I took your advice. I am long overdue for a visit to check on your progress with Northaven's captives."

Norah's fire was dim with all of her energy depleted. She could not muster the vocabulary for a proper fight with the man, but she shot back nonetheless. "My work needs no monitoring, Soro. Go back topside to your petty table, where it's safe. Leave the grueling tasks for us Barredish, who have the stomach for it."

The tall man's faint jade eyes studied hers. He must have been more than a decade younger than her, if not much more. His lip curled in a cocky sneer. "Oh, Norah." Soro paused to run his fingers over his bald head and smooth face. "So little you know of me. Remind me to educate you one day soon."

She would rather stay awake another pentday than trade chatter with this lowborn pest. She allowed his entourage to move on without any further rebuttals and continued to her destination to find the warden.

She found BrKaim exactly where she had sent command for him to await her. The warden and his own train of prison sentries stood just outside the cells that had been designated specifically for the greyborne taken in from Lilealah's escort.

Norah glanced at each of the ten guardsmen to see if she recognized any of them, but then came to the realization that she simply didn't care. Her pressing concerns were elsewhere. "High Chancellor Soro," she seethed, "how long has he been present here, and whom did he visit?"

The warden readily divulged what he had witnessed. "The greyborne here. The Forlorn as well, very briefly."

"What did he want with the greys and trolls? What did he say to them?"

"He did not permit me to follow him into the cells. He is far my superior, Inquisitor." BrKaim's focus turned to the stone at his boots, like a pathetic puppy being scolded. "With the Forlorn, I watched him. He said nothing. Just opened the door to the lift and peered down. I let the High Chancellor be. Then he left."

What secrets is Soro privy to that I am not? Why is he now showing an interest in this lot? The warden muttered something, but her conflicted thoughts muffled his voice. Her attention caught the real reason for why she was here: the cell gate in front of her.

The Soro dilemma would have to be postponed. The boy they had been waiting on was being ushered down the hall from where the chancellor had exited. That was the cue to commence the ploy.

"You know your role, Warden. Do it well," Norah warned with a wink rather than encouraged.

"I do," BrKaim guaranteed.

He nodded to the gate sentry to unlock the cell and collect a specific five of the greyborne prisoners. After the chosen were secure and in the hall, the warden initiated the scheduled ruse. "Boy, come! Tell me you have it with you."

"Yes, sir," the shaggy-haired teenager exclaimed. "Truth tonic, as you requested. Authentic and pure, straight from Savatarm!"

The march of the five qindrid, their ten guards, Warden BrKaim, the boy, and Norah had already started in the direction of the door that led to the Forlorn, where the trolls were kept.

"We should keep it on hand here in Frostdale. We are fortunate to be graced by Master Jyon's herbal expertise." BrKaim praised some mocked-up, distant alchemist. "How much do we have?"

"It was expensive," the fake alchemist's apprentice admitted. "The crown's coin paid for two vials, sir. Priciest elixir in all the realm, sir. Will this do?"

Norah knew that there was no truth tonic in the small medicine box the boy carried. In its place were simply two vials of fever potion, staged for intimidation. None of them had ever met a Master Jyon, and this boy was no student of the chemical arts. He was a struggling performer discovered by her spies some few days before, just some peasant actor without a name to be remembered by. He was being paid more handsomely than he ever could have dreamed for this drama.

She had been given the most bizarre order by the queen to refrain from her typically macabre techniques of interrogation with the stoneborne captives. Mercy granted for the five stoneborne was evidently part of a prearranged bargain made with the umbran, that they would see execution at the Hall of Final Light but would receive no torture in the Deeps.

For the remaining fifteen greyborne, however, none of her cruel methods of extraction had proved productive. It was almost as if these particular soldiers had been groomed specifically to withstand severe maltreatment if seized. Their pain tolerance was rather unsettling. They seemed to be fearless in the face of torment and death.

Just the day before, report had been sent to her that two of the greyborne were found dead in their cell. One beaten to death on the stone, while the other was strangled in an apparent struggle. Suspicions of foul play by the guards or their own cellmates had all been considered. No witnesses would come forward.

It was obvious some of them knew secrets that the others did not. But finding out who these agents were had been fruitless with traditional procedures. This act with the false truth tonic was her last resort as time for the sacrificial executions neared.

Norah glanced back at the box the boy actor toted. "It has been a long time since I have used such a potion. A few drops from a vial, and all inhibitions are thrown to the wind. One will say all in one's mind without any reservations. An invaluable commodity for my work."

She thought she saw one of the greys shuffle nervously in her peripheral vision as BrKaim followed up. "And so much less messy than knives and rats."

The street actor went on. "Each vial holds enough tonic for four men, easy. One drop does the trick. I know little of the stoneborne, but I hear—"

"Yes, they are highly resistant to all poisons or inebriations in general," BrKaim played along. "It may take a whole vial on one of them to make them talk."

She was sure of it now. One of them was nervous. She could read a flaw in any creature in her vicinity. Discovering weaknesses was her forte, and exploiting them was her hobby.

Norah looked back through the group at no one in particular. "Which is precisely why we will not waste any on them. The five stoneborne will inevitably be sent to the Hall of Final Light for execution. We are only administering the tonic to the greyborne today. I will endorse the life and freedom of the first ones to confess what I need to know, not under the tonic's influence. I have the king's written word," she lied.

The warden performed his lines on cue. "But you need to bring ten qin for the executions, Inquisitor."

"Do not presume to educate me, Warden," she superciliously cautioned. "There are still thirteen greyborne. Five will be chosen to join the sacrifices at the Hall of Final Light with the stoneborne. That leaves me eight to play with. I could feed five to the trolls and free three if they consent to revive their still tongues."

"I say stick to the torture. This enemy deserves no mercy," BrKaim spat back at his incarcerated enemy.

"Normally, I would agree, Warden. But my methods are not working on this pious lot." Norah feigned a pout and switched her language to Norspeak so that only the Aggedonians could understand her. *"Truly, I must applaud your vain devotion. I am running out of time before the ceremony at Mount Merridan. And King Aerik has spoken. I have been implored to administer the truth tonic and be done with this prolonged charade."*

The actor pulled forth one of the milky elixirs to present it. "Do you want one of the vials now, milady?"

"No. At the door to the Forlorn, ahead. I am feeling rather—" she paused as she noted that they were halfway down the hall now "—ungenerous today. Too many secrets, too much silence. They will receive a choice before I open it."

Warden BrKaim pretended to be intrigued. "And what fates are those?"

"They can be silent and become feed for those below—those who have not been fed since they first arrived. We've prepped them to be kept starved. Fresh, live meat will be their first treat." Norah hinted about the scores of trolls in the Forlorn. "Or these greys can comply with what I wish to know."

Norah nodded to the actor to hand her one of the potions. The boy rushed forward past the prisoners at the signal. "Or take the tonic and tell me anyway," she threatened. "If they truly have no answer after the tonic, then the Deeps will have no more use for them. They can join the trolls."

This prompted one of the greyborne into mocking laughter on the spot. It wasn't the nervous one with an elderly look to him. This particular greyborne was the only one of the bunch she would describe as obese.

"Something specific, grey?" Warden BrKaim inquired with a scowl, deviating from the practiced lines. "Do we amuse you?"

With his wrists and ankles closely bound in chains, the robust qindrid pointed his chin toward Norah and nodded with a dangerous grin. His tongue used Norspeak, as expected. "*She does. She amuses me.*"

"What is he spitting?" The warden demanded translation from his superior while the greyborne never ceased his glare at Norah.

Finally, a reaction. I can work with this. She ignored BrKaim's plea and spoke Norspeak with the prisoner, without looking directly at him, keeping her gaze to the door of the Forlorn ahead. "*One wise enough to talk but unwise in choice of words. Go on, then. You may yet live.*"

The fat qindrid seemed eager to confess. "*I killed the two you found dead. They were the traitors. Agents of the trolls. I am sorry you didn't get to ask your questions.*"

Before Norah could marshal a response, one of the other greys, the long-haired one, fired up in a refutation. "*You lie, Oenayus! I have known Vander and his clan all my life's days. He has manned the walls of the Fourteen since he was old enough to shoot a bow. He was more loyal to Lilealah than any others in this lot! And Torr was just as devoted.*"

And another grey after him concurred with the contender. "*Aye, it's you Akaydis Coasters who are working with the Glazjhendun! We've known it!*"

This was good. Dissension among themselves. Perhaps the mysterious deaths of the two yestermorning would be the undoing of this diverse clan fraternity. Norah was sophisticated in the multiplicity of Aggedonian clans.

Those that hailed from the Akaydis Coast resided closest to the cliff shores of the Glace Isles, south of them. It was they who had waged the most historic strife by battle with the Terollar race. She found it unlikely that any clans from their villages would team up with the agenda of the Glazjhendun.

Scores of strong familial societies existed throughout Aggedon, with more than half that remained south of the territory of Hroganyn's Horde, in the far north, belonging to the faction now known as the Lilealytes, for those fervent with the Lilealah's desires. In theory, each of the qindrid captured by General Roth that were alongside Lilealah should have fitted in that category, but as hints were unfolding, she knew that was not the case.

"*What a delightful trade. Now we are all amusing each other.*" Norah encouraged the debate among the formerly silent.

The bigger greyborne, who had started it all, and whom the others named Oenayus, spoke again. "*What is it you want to know? No need for the tonic. I'll confess it.*"

The argumentative one with the long hair contended again with Oenayus. "*You know no more than we all do! All you can tell this pink bitch is where the wyrmways lead – no more! You Akaydis rots are weak and broken, and probably lie with the trolls like fucked sheep to keep your clans alive!*"

Norah decided she didn't like him. "Silence this one." She reverted back to the Civil tongue to be understood by all. "And by *silence*, I mean 'remove all of his teeth.'"

The entourage halted when she stopped. The nearest guard acted on command. She felt a flush of heat rise in her loins when the greyborne's teeth scattered across the floor. Norah scrutinized each of the qindrid, daring any further dissent with her dark eyes.

This was new ground now, unrehearsed. Warden BrKaim, genuinely concerned, asked, "What now?"

Oenayus and the visibly edgy one, who had yet to speak, stole her focus as she explained, looking upon only the two of them. "You will tell me plainly, who else is an agent of the Glazjhendun? Were the two that were killed in the cell murdered because they were weak or because they indeed were traitors to the Lilealytes? Which of you knows why the Glazjhendun surrendered the way they did and executed the khomo outside of honorable combat? Many have tried at the Glace Isles king throughout history, and now this legendary, fearless, tireless warrior just decided that it was done? Just accepted defeat and death, like that? I say there is an agent among you that knows the truth! These are the riddles the tonic will unweave." Norah winked at the boy with a scowl and snapped her fingers to

BrKaim. "Warden, each gets a drop. Prepare a vial."

Finally the nervous one spoke, surprisingly in the Civil language. "Wait! No! He will hear!" he wailed in absolute dread at the top of his lungs. "He will know who tells, and he will have our families slain!"

Who? Norah wanted to ask, but her words stuck in her throat when Oenayus spoke first, now also in the common language. "You are a fool, Benj."

The look exchanged between Oenayus and Benj made it evident they were in league with one another, which added to her understanding, being that they were both of the Akaydis Coast—tidbits of the few facts she had discovered. Perhaps they were both about to prove her premise wrong from what she had conjectured previously.

"Who will know? Who is 'he'? Do you mean 'she'?" Norah questioned, befuddled by the mentioned gender. She knew that umbran could see through the eyes of the qindrid they had turned and could disclose their location. But Agendwar, Lilealah's lifemate, had been dead for over thirty years, slain by the Glace Isles king himself. And furthermore, these were greyborne, born qindrid, never transcended by umbran, like the stoneborne. No umbran could use this ability on a greyborne. *Who is he?* she repeated in her head. Thinking surely the Aggedonian was simply mistranslating pronouns in the Civil tongue, she voiced the only name she could surmise that Benj meant. "Lilealah?"

"No! Him!" Benj, now in a psychotic fit, cried back in his native dialect, sure of himself. *"He of the forbidden name! He that we must never speak of! Please do not make us take the tonic!"*

Now Norah was definitely perplexed. *This grey is delusional. The Deeps have done their deed on his mind. He thinks Khomo'Jhuvonus is still alive?*

She was far too puzzled, muddling over countertheories. Oenayus barked out to his breaking companion before she could speak. *"You'll die for this. By my own hand before we reach that door."*

But they were already at the door, and she no longer had the patience for this. "Guards, separate them. Bring that one forward. Benj." She allowed the warden to open the door to the Forlorn, forcing out a sudden gust of natural, cold wind from the cave-like dungeon well. The guttural sounds of curious Trollspeak erupted from far below. She started to turn around with her hand outstretched behind her. "Boy, give me another via—"

The unanticipated grunt of a man's breath leaving his body and metal chain links slamming against skin sounded behind her. Before she could complete a turn, her head hit the stone edge of the doorway. She instantly found herself planted on her knees, nearly unconscious, with blood gushing from her brow.

Norah put both hands on the ground to keep from fully losing herself to the enclosing blackness that washed over her. Utterly disoriented, she paddled her arms to drag herself closer to the corner, as if it would save her from whatever unseen demise awaited behind her. Finding her solace in the crook of the doorway, she almost consented to sit and accept her ruin.

The guards were desperately scrambling after the prisoners. One sentry appeared fully unconscious. BrKaim had somehow been locked inside the Forlorn, as there was no handle back out once the door was shut. The feeble boy was on the ground with chains cinched around his purple neck. His throat had been crushed. The killer embracing him was none other than Oenayus. Four sentries swarmed over him as he fought back, to no avail.

The box of tonic was broken on the ground, and the chalky potions were scattered about among several shards. Three of the Aggedonians were fighting the prison guards to attain freedom, while Benj was reaching for pieces of glass from the shattered vials.

Benj began openly chewing on several slivers of the glass and spitting out shards, accompanied by globules of blood and chunks of meat from inside his mouth. His eyes were in a manic craze.

As her hearing returned, she could perceive the crunch of teeth cracking on glass from Oenayus too. He had slipped a hand free to devour the remains of a jagged tonic bottle before the guards could stop him. *What hellish spell is this?*

"What are they doing? Have they all gone mad?" one of the watchmen protested in disgusted disbelief.

She slowly tried standing and had to stop halfway when a cloudy wave crashed over her sight. Norah took a few deep breaths, one hand on her forehead to stop the bleeding, the other braced on her knee to keep her upright. Finally, she stood and fully assessed the damage.

The guards were again in control of the hall. Oenayus was spouting blood and spittle profusely from his mouth. Benj continued to cough on shreds of his mutilated tongue. The long-haired one still fought the watchmen, reaching every which way to grab a weapon or piece of glass. The other two slumped in defeat, praying or grumbling in Norspeak.

Norah had never seen anything like this. These two particular greys feared some dead troll more than anything else alive, as if it were their haunting, undying god.

BrKaim slammed his fist on the door, snapping her to. She looked at the latch blankly while one of the guards hastened to lift it and let the warden out.

"Madness! All of it! That one there started the tussle and killed the boy," BrKaim accused furiously. "How are we supposed to explain this? He was …" Norah had stopped listening, and everything went mute again, as if her ears had given up.

Her eyes glazed over in a trance at the greyborne in front of her. She sluggishly turned her body to face the Forlorn and saunter through the door. She found herself on the winch lift, alone, looking down into the depths, to the stone causeways that detained over seventy starving trolls.

"Bring them to me," she whispered softly.

The warden and ten guards behind her sustained paltry disputes, still in the corridor. They did not seem to pay her any heed.

"Bring them to me!" she reiterated harshly and loudly.

Norah didn't turn around to witness the obedience. She could hear her command being minded straightaway. BrKaim's recognizable voice attempted to reason some wisdom. "Inquisitor, perhaps it is not wise to stand on the lift while we load them on board."

She stormed off the lift toward Oenayus. While his arms were in the clutches of the watchmen on each side of him, she wiped her hand, bloody from her injured brow, and firmly grasped the qindrid's hemorrhaging jaw. "Can you speak?" she shouted through gritted teeth.

"*No,*" he gurgled in mumbled agony.

"Will you speak? Or do I feed you to those below?" she fumed.

"*I know nothing, Lady Bayn.*" His now-handicapped Aggedonian dialect came out half-interpreted but well enough understood.

It would do. *He knows much.* "Bring him to the infirmary! Make sure his tongue is intact when you're through!" And three of the present watchmen came to whisk away Oenayus from the Forlorn.

"You there." She pointed menacingly at Benj, motioning for the guards to bring him in front of her. He was slammed to his knees at her feet. "Can you speak?"

The crazed qindrid aimed his puckered lips up at her face and spewed a mist of blood that hit her straight in the eyes. "As expected. To the below!"

She didn't even wipe her spattered face as she scanned the other three. "Who else can't speak?" Norah questioned threateningly. "I've got three score trolls to feed that like their food alive!"

The long-haired one seemed to speak for all of them, and he surged to his feet as defiantly as possible. "We of the Lilealytes will never speak to the Bayn Bitch of Frostdale, nor any pink lord. Your time is ending soon!"

Her ire was being tested to new limits with this season's lot. She felt her face turning red and the veins in her neck becoming hot with welcome anger. "Very well, then! I owe these trolls an apology for the impoverished attention I've shown in favoring you! I've yet to share the wealth with my poor, true northern enemy!"

Norah looked to BrKaim as she went to stand near the Forlorn's entry door and waved her hand dramatically to the hungry depths beneath her. "Warden, give these trolls their feast!"

The four remaining qindrid were bound even further by rope wrapped around their bodies and positioned to lie flat on the winch lift. Norah signaled to the warden to pull the lever and lower the lift. The old winch groaned into motion as the large gears above turned and dropped it into the Forlorn's vertical imitation cave.

Four guardsmen accompanied the doomed qindrid on the way down. Just one floor above the trolls, the prone prisoners were carefully rolled off, to be caught by the eager elvan assembly waiting on the causeways. She watched the condemned hopelessly squirm in a comical combat with the guards. The anticipative Terollar gathered in a cluster to allow their meal a safe landing.

She watched as Jrulthun singled out Benj and hoisted the greyborne off his feet by his neck, then tossed him into the nothingness beyond. And then it happened. The trolls did feast, all at once, like a kennel of rabid dogs, on the other three morsels of bony meat.

She thought it strange how the sound of her victims' screams was the one thing that brought her peace. Tomorrow she would find her sleep.

EBRIELLE (IV)

RIME OR REASON

There was a brook that stretched out from the lake at the fringe of her bedroom window. The melodic rivulet was a beacon for all things serene in nature. Exotic flowers and hedged shrubberies lined the winding stream that trailed parallel to the park's paved path. Tiny arboreal rodents and vibrant songbirds frolicked alongside each other throughout the lush verdure.

She could hear the soft thunder of the Silverlake Falls in the distance as she stepped out onto her palace veranda. Her translucent pink gown yearned for the warm Dawning breeze. The gentle wind married with the protective shade of the east towers to afford her the perfect solace for her afternoon wine tasting. Her servants had prepared vintages from southern Khalimia to northern Utamia, into Goldgarden itself.

Her personal palace butler pulled up her favorite chair, plush with azure pillows, overlooking the lower terrace and pleasure garden below. Her dearest friend, Sorene, sat across from her. Both patiently waited while the assortment of exotic wines was explained by the itinerant guildsman enthusiast. She chose an extraordinary midnight-blue vintage from Mageholme, while Sorene elected for a plum-colored infusion from their own local luxury vineyard.

Ebrielle dismissed the help, and she and her friend sipped their intoxicating chalices, soaking in the dream achieved below. Her brother appeared down at the stream's end, marching in on his stallion in full Daynish barding, with a train of knights in his wake. Aerik was decked from boot to helm in paladin armor, riding in stride with a mounted escort of the Timberhands, instrumenting his welcome home.

Her cousin Henrick slipped up behind Sorene, paladin-armored the same as her brother. He placed his plated hands on her slender shoulders and bent down to embrace her in a passionate kiss, just before sweeping her up from the chair she sat in and whisking her away through the curtained balcony doors.

Ebrielle sat alone in absolute peace, in a totality of life fulfillment. She could need no more completion for her surreal paradise. But her fantasy had room for more.

A fiery-eyed, red-haired matchless beauty of chiseled masculinity approached from her bedroom drapes in resplendence. Kyson instantly collapsed the rest of her surrounding utopia into the forgotten abyss. She was whole again.

He strode toward her with a seductive gaze never leaving hers. He was her husband, and she was his wife, and his grandiose estates in the Silverlakes of Tairancia was their new merry home.

Kyson drew a regal necklace from his vest, gemmed in extravagant yellow diamonds that complimented the color of his eyes. He knelt before her instead of taking the seat Sorene had abandoned. As he presented his lavish bauble of affection to her, he simply whispered, "Are you with me?"

She smiled, happier than she imagined she had ever been. But no words could form. She couldn't speak. And that worried her. She tried to hide her inner panic, but her face painted all the wrong signs of disgrace. He came again, but not so sweet. "I said, are you with me, my lady?"

Ebrielle opened her mouth, but nothing came out. She prayed for the modest words to simply answer and tell him yes. Her features no longer hid her bemused anxiety as she stood from her chair to plead for help.

Kyson's face turned angry. Her warm, bright world turned to one that was cold and dark. He slammed the necklace down on the table, shattering it into pieces. His divine voice changed entirely, rasping like that of an annoyed grandfather. "Lady Blackendale, with me!"

She blinked for far too long. When her eyes reopened, she was staring out of a murky window overlooking the snow-covered rooftops of the castle commons. She recognized every colorless house and venue below. This was far from anywhere foreign, nor was it close to anything green and lush.

And this was no palace. She languidly turned around to face her reality, in no rush to see that her companion nearby was nothing similar to Kyson. The withered Grand Artificer goggled at her, impatiently waiting on a remark that proved she had landed back in the tangible world, a depressing realm the exact opposite of her constant musings.

"What? I am sorry," she meekly apologized.

"Your head has been out that window since you came in," Barys tersely rebuked her. "I thought you wanted to take this seriously."

"I do," Ebrielle snobbishly huffed, throwing her hands at a loss onto the research table between them. "Please repeat what you said. My mind is adrift today with the news of my brother leaving so soon after passing the Paladin Trials." *And me becoming a wife to some likely ancient wilt such as you*, she silently murmured in disgust at her prearranged fate.

Grand Artificer Barys bowed a half curtsy and offered, "Congratulations are in order for Aerik, then. He will make a fine Daynish knight." The old man stroked his tangled beard and grinned after the awkward silence. She could have guessed what he was going to say next. News traveled swiftly. "And you will make a fine Tairancian wife, soon to be Ebrielle Rook. Why are you here?"

She realized Barys had intended it as a kindness, but still, it was a reminder of what had plagued her every waking moment since Norah forced the trauma on her. "Because it is one last thing I must do. I am of my mother's blood, after all," Ebrielle despondently answered.

The artificer studied her like a barrister in a court, attempting to detect a lie. "Very well, then. Stay with me." He paused in an authoritative tone. "These axes. They are indeed special."

She assumed her intuition for visiting the tower was correct. "They are the Chosen Troll's? The Axes of the Sons?"

But Barys shook his head. "I do not know what those look like. But I do know about bloodrime, and what it does."

"And what is bloodrime? That petrified frost that webs over the weapons?" Ebrielle pointed to the white interlacement of frozen substance enveloping the axes, with not a hint of natural wood, which was possibly suffocated beneath. It was as if the weapons had been forged from the outlandish hardened ice in some marvel that only magic could justify. "Or is it those red—" she paused, not knowing how to describe what she was looking at "—things writhing on the surfaces there?" Veinlike tissue networked itself throughout the anatomy of the axe-heads, sometimes blatantly exposed. Hints of the arteries could be spotted beneath the majority of the frozen top layer. Something was darkly sinister yet strangely alive about them.

She now wondered how she could conceivably have slipped into a musing in their presence. She could no longer avert her full attention. *I think that one just moved.*

Barys gladly explained, "Both. Bloodrime is a poisonous phenomenon that very rarely occurs, and it is said to only be found throughout Teralloe, Caelduym, or Nrathe. If it touches any natural vegetation, it will swiftly freeze it over from the bark to the roots and branches, killing it. If a living being touches it, such as a human or elvan or beast of the wild, it will still the being's flow of blood in a fatal cold that will stop the heart. You see, bloodrime is not actually just a poison. It is a parasite. And it is born unto its host. It gains a perpetual need to be with its host for survival, and will remain with it until its host dies. Removal of the parasite while the host still lives will only make the bloodrime return immediately to what it considers its home and source of sustenance."

Ebrielle inspected the exotic axes closely a second time. Twice the size of a typical Barredish throwing axe, they each were specifically designed and crafted of the parasitical hoarfrost from haft to head. The bloodrime was the only material evident in their forging. They were altogether alien to gaze upon. The weapons appeared to be made of sheer cold, but the icy veins that wove over the complexity of their surface refused to show a hint of sweat from the warm hearth nearby. Even the veneer of thinner rime overlapping the chaotic lattice of the weapons' bizarre vascularity seemed as hard as diamond.

The first axe that took her attention was the double-bitted one. It was less crude and was shaped similarly to Barredish styles, like a smaller version of the battle-axe. Both heads were symmetrical, with the toe parallel to the top, and no hook at all, but the heel had a long and keen beard. No surface was smooth upon any of the axes, even so with this one, but their edges seemed to be fashioned as sharp as the best of swords. The two-headed axe was the only one of the three that had material carved out from its central bulk. Customized like two downward-facing eyes, both heads had one hammered out near where the haft melded into the one-piece weapon. Outward from that, on both sides, were three teardrop-shaped slots angling toward the bottom portion of the axe-heads.

Her uncle Tomas had educated her on many troll tall tales throughout her upbringing. She had surmised that most all of them were ornate exaggerations or white lies for children's fancies. But facts of late were proving to have merit. She conjured his vividly specific descriptions of the Axes of the Sons, to deduce which was which. And it all came back to her like he had just told her that very morning.

This is the Axe of Zuulzin. The only living son.

Another axe had a haft with an inward curve just past where one might grasp the weapon. Its head was slightly raised toward the toe and deep toward the heel, with a flat beard. The edge was jagged and odd, with no mirrored pattern. The butt of the weapon had been replaced with a twisted pick, mimicking a gnarled root turned into a spike. Protruding from the eye at the top of the axe was the exact same. Again the material was congruent throughout, as there were no true separations in the anatomy of the weapon.

The Axe of Jhukamwi. The middle son.

The final axe was probably the most menacing of the three, and she didn't exactly know why she thought so. There was no spike out of the eye, no pick out of the butt, no extra head, but simply something about it appeared heavy and deadly. The size of its single head was quite intimidating, with its hook at the toe extending a bit beyond the top, and its linear beard diverting into five acute edges toward the heel. The head alone gained triangular girth toward the merged shoulder. And the haft appeared as two entities: the bottom, toward the grasp, was rather skinny and wieldy, while the midpoint branched into something abruptly twice as thick as it formed into the head. This particular tool would be a bane to any soldier's shield and could obviously obliterate the hardiest of plate armors.

The Axe of Kavajin. The eldest son.

"They each have their own use. Each their own personality. Their own story as the Axes of the Sons, and the khomo who wielded them." She half whispered her own inferences to herself more than to the old man. "Why bloodrime, though? For poison? I have heard of what you mentioned, about the Chosen Troll's weapons and what they were known to do." She trailed off.

Barys was ready with logic. "They returned to him when he threw them, as the legend goes," he stated rather than inquired. "If these are indeed the Axes of the Sons, as report is leading to confirm, then it would all make sense. You see, while bloodrime might be mortal for a normal tree or a human, it is not always so with others. Under the extraordinary circumstance that this bloodrime is born unto a lifetree in the Teralloe region, this takes on a whole new bearing. Terollar lifetrees regenerate indefinitely, their spiritroots staying forever ageless, just like them. The bloodrime parasite must always return to its host while it yet lives. And since the lifetrees of Terollar do not die, and heal themselves from the toxins of the rime, it will always yearn to seek its host. The elvan that is linked to the lifetree, along with their children, are all synchronized to it."

Rationalization and curiosity were one and the same now for her. She had to know more, fairly positive that even the learned sage could not elucidate. "But what happens to the bloodrime once it is removed from its host, thus unable to return? Does it die off? These weapons seem clearly intact."

Barys stroked his stringy beard in contemplation. "Yes," he admitted worriedly. "Yes, in theory, I imagine it would die off, or at the very least, the parasite might lose its poisonous potency and ability to return freely to its host. However, I admit I have never encountered bloodrime crafted into such as these, forged into exquisite weaponry entirely of the material, and not just in spearheads or knife blades. These are unique. These artifacts may have a date soon to expire or grow null in power, Lady Blackendale."

Soon to expire and null in power? It is no wonder Smiles wants to expedite their return, Ebrielle soundly deduced. "Well, I need them. What must I do to take them with me today?"

The old man rattled his head in frustration. "My apprentice, Emeron, died handling the weapons, bringing them in from the general's confiscation. We were too late to provide him with the correct antidotes." Barys tossed the protective leathers to blanket the axes again. "If you believe I am going to endanger the Royal Inquisitor's only daughter with them, you must think me a fool for self-sacrifice to the Deeps! Your mother would peel the flesh from my bones!"

Ebrielle looked at Barys incredulously in a rise of indignation. "And why not? I am her apprentice! Who are you to know of what the Deeps entail?"

"No one. I am just the keeper of all things sacred and misunderstood," Barys humbly defended. "Only the general, the council, or our king or queen themselves can solicit the removal of an item from my tower."

"But my mother," she began in shock with her mouth fully agape when she was interrupted by the bold sage.

The artificer shrugged. "Your mother is on the Frostdale Council as Royal Inquisitor. If she so wishes, she can petition for what she needs herself. I for one think it a perilous mistake to let these artifacts go free."

Her face flushed with anger and embarrassment in defeat. She was powerless in all aspects of her life. The old man, sensing her vexation, decided to entertain her further. "To whom did you intend to present these?"

Ebrielle saw no harm in exposing her intent. "Some captured envoy of the Glace Isles, with the trolls in the Forlorn. He goes by Smiles. Apparently, a shaman of the Glazjhendun, the specialized groomer of the war party, that acts as their voice and ambassador."

"You believe this troll peculiar in his desires," Barys probed, scanning over the covered Terollar weaponry.

"I do not know what I believe anymore. I do know he is not like the other trolls. And I think I trust his intent in diplomacy." Ebrielle voiced her opinions, which leaned more toward her curiosity about Smiles than the fear of him after their last encounter. "And I think it in Frostdale's favor to make a trade for peace with the troll people—such a timeless, needless enemy."

"I am simply the Grand Artificer. I cannot judge you on your political purpose. But I cannot give you the axes, all the same." He took the hide wrap enclosing the dangerous relics away from the table to take them over to the lock chest and set them on top. Barys half-cocked his decrepit body to shoot a glance her way. "Do you want my advice, Lady Blackendale?"

"Not really." She took to the cloudy window again, and then to the door to leave. She couldn't make eye contact with the useless old man. "I've heard all I need."

"These Axes of the Sons, if indeed that is what they are. This Smiles's urgency to have them in his possession. The parasite and life span it has left within the weapons," the artificer vaguely drifted on.

Her aristocratic arrogance possessed her demeanor once again, coercing her to interject before he could finish. "Am I about to receive another lesson about rime or reason? More folklore about trees? It seems like all I speak to lately wish to bully me with another myth to toss coins into."

"Heed this. Tell your mother to bring the elvan prisoners to the Hall of Final Light. One by one. Surround them by as many guards as can fit, and have them each try to cast out the axes. See which troll the axes return to. That is the only way to find your proof that the Chosen Troll is indeed dead and gone." Barys explained his practical solution.

Ebrielle rolled her eyes, knowing that scenario would fail to see fruition. "My mother's mind is elsewhere, and I will be sent away long before that manner of farce is organized, much less permitted."

"Then tell your mother to do what she should have done in the first place." Barys slammed his hands down firmly on the research table and placed her under a stern gaze.

She was genuinely disturbed by the act. "And what is that?"

"Kill them all," he coldly said. "Give them a troll's mercy. Feed them to the kennels, and burn the remains when the dogs are fat."

Ebrielle found herself nearly tearing up for no apparent reason other than her inability to keep up her bold demeanor any longer. He had to know her dread. "Then I suppose you don't fear the wrath of whom I fear? The vengeful ghost of Khomo'Jhu—"

The Grand Artificer held a hushing hand up before she could recite the full name. "I fear his dead name enough to stop you from saying it in my tower. The axes stay." He pulled a ring of keys from his belt and locked several mechanisms on the chest in which he secured the sacred weapons. He then stormed out of his study chamber. The old man held to the same terror of the Chosen Troll as all the rest.

Ebrielle took one last, bittersweet look through the tower window. At least she would be long gone from anything to do with trolls and cold soon enough.

WESTWALKER (VI)

A REMINISCENCE OF ROGUES

Bristled green cones littered the undergrowth beneath the enormous pines of the Thurowood, where the marks were set. Seven men furtively moved in accord with each other as they meticulously prepared the forest into a lethal labyrinth. Their overseer silently delegated the engineering process of the impending stratagem.

Elaborate trip-wire devices lined the entry to the forest, with inconspicuous twine attached to spiked logs or boulders hidden away in the clutter of brush. Concealed deadfalls and fatal pit traps fell in just behind. A plethora of foot noose snares and body nets mazing in a methodical pattern filled the gaps. At the center of it all was his arena of turret crossbows, fit to single-handedly make a stand against a small militia. The Westwalker entrenched the locations of each in memory effectively as second nature and ensured his assigned minions did the same.

The better part of several days passed to complete the tactician's ritual, filled with arduous toil. Tsuno could see the Boarneck urbanites were not accustomed to the manual labor or the mandatory stealth, likely too habituated to their fancy southern cities.

As the mercenaries finished the last of the trap-making agenda, Tsuno took the initiative to steal away for a respite to locate his elvan affiliate. Ryleohk was indeed the primary collaborator in the construction of the Thurowood's deadly renovation, but the Wyldenar could only be encouraged, never directed or controlled. If the rogue wanted to slip away, he did so without a hint of petition or warning.

But Tsuno knew his friend, and he knew where he would be. He made his way through the trigger-strewn killing field to the tallest pine in the woods. He donned his climbing gear and embraced the tree to ascend to its summit. The massive evergreen rose high above the heights of its surrounding brethren, with a flawless vantage point overseeing the nearby Great Grey Wall, to the east.

And there sat the picturesque icon of all things feral, a hybrid semblance of one's notion of elvan and animal. The inscrutable hunter, a grey exile poised like an ornamented effigy atop the pine's tallest branch. His gaze fixated on the northern horizon, through the dense timberlands of the Thurowood.

The Wyldenar's diversely shaded grey mane crested out of his upper spine and draped all the way to his hips and across his upper torso. His long rogue-elvan ears peeked sideways through his hair. The branch he knelt upon was much too small to hold his weight or maintain his balance, but Ryleohk effortlessly preserved his majestic perch nonetheless. His Terollar-style axe nestled within the strap harness against his back. He appeared more like some mystical barbarian of folklore than anything this realm could prove true.

Ryleohk was obviously aware of Tsuno's presence behind him by now, but the rogue-elvan did not divert his northbound scrutiny to pay him any heed.

Tsuno reflected on the long chain of events that had led to their predestined fellowship, a tale beginning more than three decades before. It was a story of loss, betrayal, and relentless purpose—one that had forged both the Westwalker and the rogue who would one day stand beside him.

His journey began with the suicide of his wife, Yoshira, and the discovery that his estranged son, Hirotai, still lived. Her death forever poisoned what little loyalty remained toward his skyborne brethren. Tsuno vowed that the umbran would one day perish from Penthara, though he knew such vengeance demanded patience rather than passion.

He concealed his hatred beneath unwavering obedience, ascending through the ranks of the Saiyenai until he earned entry into the monastery's forbidden library. There he uncovered an ancient tome penned by the enigmatic Dendrar, describing an untested remedy for the Qindrid Curse. It became the single hope to reclaim both his family and himself.

Soon after, Tsuno manipulated his way into the escort of one of his own umbran makers, AeriAllyse, whose diplomatic journeys carried her beyond the fractured Sho'Lon Empire and into the distant north. Before departing, however, he secretly learned that Hirotai had become a celebrated commander leading attacks against the Sho Kung qin—and that he now had a son of his own.

Unable to reveal himself directly, Tsuno instead sent anonymous intelligence to Hirotai, exposing the location of the vulnerable Saiyenai monastery and revealing the whereabouts of Thymarius, the other umbran responsible for Tsuno's Transcendence. He trusted his son's hatred would accomplish what he himself could not. Though Thymarius's death would weaken Tsuno, it was a sacrifice worth making if it offered even the smallest chance of regaining Hirotai's trust.

While accompanying AeriAllyse through Kol'Kolar, Tsuno experienced his first passage by wyrmway into Tundura, where the Shiniryn sought fellowship with their Wyldenar counterparts. There news soon reached AeriAllyse that Thymarius had indeed fallen. Hirotai had succeeded. The revelation shattered her composure, leaving her isolated within foreign lands while Tsuno quietly prepared for the opportunity he had anticipated for years.

Their travels eventually carried them into the Dendrallthae. The tome Tsuno had studied had taught him much of the Dendrar and their unwavering devotion to the Balance. They regarded every act of Transcendence as among creation's gravest blasphemies. AeriAllyse, blinded by desperation, believed she could persuade these ancient zealots to sanction the mass conversion of the Shiniryn into umbran for the preservation of the elvan race.

Tsuno already knew her appeal would fail. When the moment finally came, he struck. Years of deception ended in a single calculated betrayal. Poison claimed the members of AeriAllyse's expedition, and Tsuno captured his own maker alive before leading her across the frozen reaches of the Dendrallthae to seek the cure promised within the forgotten manuscript.

Instead of the Dendrar themselves, they were met by the human mage Nominus Vlo, who escorted them before the elderlocks. There Tsuno pleaded for deliverance from the curse that had destroyed his family. The elderlocks refused to intervene directly. Instead, they revealed a prophecy.

They foretold that Tsunosoto Akazi himself would one day discover and administer the cure to the Qindrid Curse—but only after swearing his life to restoring the Balance by eradicating the umbran from Penthara. Another chosen soul, a stoneborne yet unknown to him, would share that destiny. Before Tsuno could reclaim his own people, he first had to save another nation from the corruption of the qindrid.

The revelation eclipsed every desire that had once driven him. No longer was his purpose merely redemption for his family or homeland. It had become a burden carried for the fate of all Penthara.

Leaving AeriAllyse imprisoned within the Dendrallthae, Tsuno ventured into Aggedon in search of the mysterious candidate foretold beside him. Though years passed without discovering the chosen stoneborne, he spent that time earning the confidence of the Aggedonians while quietly uncovering the identities, habits, and weaknesses of every Wyldenar umbran throughout the land.

When patience could delay him no longer, the Westwalker emerged. Under that infamous alias, Tsuno dispatched secret scrolls throughout the neighboring kingdoms, exposing every stronghold and defense of the Aggedonian umbran. Reluctant nations soon answered the call. What followed became the Second Grey War, during which countless qindrid lifemates were slain. In a matter of months, the Westwalker transformed from Aggedon's most trusted diplomat into its most hunted enemy.

Forced into hiding, Tsuno found sanctuary among the Wyldenar of Artopia, who honored his devotion to the Balance. Yet concealment alone could never fulfill his oath. The prophecy demanded allies as much as resolve, and there remained one man whose friendship might change the fate of the north: King Tytus Roth of Frostdale.

Granted an audience upon the king's coronation, Tsuno recounted his purpose and the greater war quietly unfolding beyond Barredom's borders. Tytus saw not a monster, but an opportunity to accomplish what generations of rulers had failed to achieve.

By royal decree, Tsuno became the first qindrid ever pardoned within Barredom, publicly honored as Friend of Frostdale and placed under the crown's protection. Though suspicion lingered among the people, none dared challenge the king's command.

Over the years that followed, Tsuno became one of Tytus's most trusted advisers. He guided Barredom through wars, brokered alliances with Artopia, exposed enemy movements, and helped lay the foundations for victories that reshaped the northern kingdoms. His greatest triumph came in securing the alliance that made possible the Battle for Northaven, though the victory demanded the life of King Tytus himself.

Before his death, however, the king ensured his son, Aerik Roth, would uphold the title of Friend of Frostdale, preserving Tsuno's place within the kingdom and allowing the Westwalker's lifequest to continue.

As the years passed, new visions came to Nominus from the elderlocks. They foresaw the return of the Neveril and the rise of a force capable of consuming the human kingdoms through deception rather than conquest alone. Though much of the prophecy remained veiled, the champions destined to oppose it did not.

Besides Tsuno and the still-unknown stoneborne candidate, two others were named: Khomo'Jhuvonus, the legendary Terollar king of the Glace Isles, and Ryleohk, the only surviving child of Lilealah and Agendwar. Nominus entrusted Tsuno with the khomo's original axe as a token of peace and instructed him to seek the pair.

With the aid of the Sylvanil Sentinel Order, Tsuno crossed the Bay of Trolls and began tracking the greatest hunter the north had ever known. Strength alone could never prevail against Khomo'Jhuvonus. Only patience.

For weeks Tsuno studied their movements until he discovered a ritual hunt the khomo and his adopted ward repeated every pentday among the glacial shallows. There he devised an elaborate snare that ensnared both hunters beneath the fractured ice. It was the only means by which he could secure an audience without bloodshed.

Rather than threaten them, Tsuno spoke of the Balance and the prophecy. He explained the roles each was destined to fulfill and offered Khomo'Jhuvonus his ancestral axe as proof of good faith. The Terollar listened in silence before accepting the charge laid before him. It was not fear that won his cooperation, but honor.

Before they parted, the khomo entrusted the axe to Ryleohk instead, charging the rogue to one day use it against the very parents who had abandoned him to death on the day of his spawning. Their farewell ended two decades of fosterhood, and Tsuno departed the Glace Isles with an unlikely companion who scarcely spoke a civilized tongue.

They remained for a time among the Wyldenar of Artopia, where Tsuno attempted to temper Ryleohk's feral nature while carrying out missions for the Balance. Though signs of the Neveril surfaced throughout Aggedon, their enemy never revealed itself.

Tsuno also renewed his alliance with King Aerik Roth, warning him of the prophecy while concealing Ryleohk's true origins. He omitted all mention of Khomo'Jhuvonus, instead fabricating a simpler tale that tied the rogue to Artopia. When Barredom later prepared an expedition against the Glace Isles, Tsuno persuaded the kingdom to abandon the campaign, insisting the Terollar were not their true enemy.

His goodwill was repaid with misfortune. Not long afterward, Khomo'Jhuvonus annihilated nearly an entire company of Eldenvale Rangers upon Aggedonian soil. Though Tsuno had played no part in the massacre, suspicion consumed Barredom. His protections as Friend of Frostdale were suspended, and the kingdom he had faithfully served closed its gates against him.

The following year proved no kinder. While in Artopia, Ryleohk discovered the lifetree of the progenitors responsible for Lilealah and Agendwar and, overcome by rage, attempted to cut it down. Such sacrilege demanded death under elvan law. Only the mercy of his grand-patriarch spared him, reducing the sentence to exile. Tsuno shared his companion's punishment, and together they departed Artopia with nowhere left to call ally.

They wandered the wild reaches of Ur Dynelenox through passing seasons, hunted by some, distrusted by most, until only one possible ally remained—the enigmatic Queen of the Grey.

Unlike the rival powers of Aggedon, her clans stood apart from the endless conflicts consuming the realm. She agreed to grant Tsuno an audience upon one condition: he and Ryleohk would slay the dreaded Witch of the Wyldewoods, whose existence continued to threaten her people.

Together they hunted the witch with the same calculated precision that had earned Tsuno the name Westwalker. When her head was delivered, the queen granted him one final boon, allowing him to bear the witch's head and return to King Aerik Roth as a gesture of reconciliation.

Barredom cautiously restored its trust, again employing Tsuno and Ryleohk as specialists for the dangerous missions no ordinary soldiers could survive. Time and again their cunning dismantled enemy strongholds, eliminated powerful clan leaders, and secured victories that conventional armies could never have achieved.

Yet despite decades of sacrifice, betrayal, and triumph, Tsuno's lifequest remained unfinished. The cure had not been found. The prophesied stoneborne candidate had yet to reveal themself. The Neveril still lingered in shadow.

Everything Tsuno had endured—every kingdom crossed, every ally gained or lost, every life taken in service to the Balance—had led only to this fellowship. And at long last, destiny had begun gathering the final pieces.

Tsuno finally snapped from his reminiscent trance, realizing Ryleohk had been staring at him for quite some time—his silent, brooding, singular associate.

"I feel I am close to home, my one friend," Tsuno whispered as he veered in his search to the invisible eastern skylines beyond, toward his own homeland.

He could sense in his friend's grey eyes that Ryleohk, too, knew the end was near. The age of Aggedon and its qindrid armies was dissolving into just another era of history.

A quarterstaff knocked three times against the tree's base, followed by a bird noise from one of the Boarneck men. Ryleohk and Tsuno peered down through the evergreen's intricately woven branches to view the seven mercenaries below. The Thurowood traps had been finished.

Ryleohk safely jumped down between the branches to land gracefully at the base of the colossal tree's trunk. Tsuno followed suit, innately employing his skyborne impower to drop as lightly as a leaf. Wyldenar elven and the skyborne qindrid were numb to nature's falls.

All his sky-blue eyes saw was Wraith and the two tools of death companioning it now. The unique white weapon and his hand crossbows lay against the tree base, yearning for priority usage, readied to soon take grey life. The history of his construction of Wraith came to mind, but he set it aside, done with reminiscing for the day.

The hand crossbows were each armed with a five-bolt clip on top, coated in poison from the slime that was excreted by the scales of the rare bluefin fish, found throughout Aggedon's lake lands. An injection from one of the bolts would induce an immediate fit of convulsions, followed by cardiac arrest, unless the victims were stoneborne; they were impowered with resilience to the full effects of poisons.

Wraith, on the other hand, was fitted with no such toxin-tipped bolts. Its outlandish magazine, placed in the center of the unique bow's design, was loaded with five long-bolts engineered for rapid release of the bowstring, without the need to pull a new one per shot. The fact that the projectiles were larger than a normal bolt but shorter and thicker than arrows also ensured that they could not be returned at him by enemy archers.

He grabbed the three repeater apparatuses and called for Nho. The hour for the reckoning of Two-Towns was fast approaching.

AERIK (II)

HEART OF THE SHADOW

Her panted breathing against his open lips injected air into his exhausted lungs. Her recurrent ecstatic moans did well to make him ignore the rapidity of his beating heart and the drench of euphoric sweat from his brow, dripping down his entire naked body. His eyes shifted habitually to peer through the curtain tears to his right, to gaze in a switch of fantasy at Henrick's twin-sister prostitutes.

But his focus shot right back up into her big brown eyes. She was staring through his soul like she loved him to the core and they were destined to be entwined together, matched in carnal connection. Aerik grasped her by the back of the neck, forcefully pushing her sliding body deeper onto him, and believed he loved her too. He may have all along. This was Sorene. And no amount of whores Henrick might have paid could steal his gaze from her virgin allure.

They had not even made it to the bed. On the chair beside it, Sorene rode him, kissing and screaming into his future plans, dashing through his scatter of raw emotions. He had never been pleasured by anyone like her, not by the professionals of the lower villages, nor by the paid exotics that came through with the seasonal fairs. She was made for him. Nothing could ever compare now.

As she forced him to climax on top, he pressed both palms around her face to embrace her in the deepest kiss he had ever given. They both whined in rapture, their mouths not leaving one another's until their breathing and moans had waned to a whisper.

I love you, Sorene. He didn't say it as she slowly lifted her shaking legs from straddling his waist upon the chair. She giggled and kissed him once more, fanning the perspiration glistening on her flesh in the candlelight, and pulling back her tangled raven-colored hair. *I think I will say it,* he mused with a confident grin, but the ruckus on the other side of the room from Henrick's sexual escapade fractured his resolve to be romantically sincere.

Sorene spoke first, however. "That was the best I've ever had, Aerik," she purred. "Why are you leaving me?" She performed a dramatic pout and placed her hands defiantly on both hips.

Best you've ever had? I thought you were a noble virgin, Sorene of House Perrimore. Aerik's surprised semblance said it all without him uttering a sound. Sorene, the Prize of Perrimore, she was called, and evidently, she was skilled in the erotic arts from experience beyond what aristocratic suitors were privy to. It made sense. He attempted to admit logic to battle his discontent.

But she wasn't done. "They do sound like they are having fun. You won't mind if I join, will you? I won't be seeing Henrick again most likely either, and I shall miss you both so dearly," Sorene pleaded with the same pathetic pucker.

She is truly serious? Aerik only looked to the floor, at his pile of clothes strewn about, shook his head, and laughed uncertainly. He couldn't make eye contact with the apparent succubus. He incredulously waved his hand at her in a shooing manner and impassively let out, "Farewell to you too, Sorene."

He sat there a moment longer, until the chill of the room settled over his bones once the heat of pleasure had fled his blood. Slowly he began to slip on his garments from the corner, detached from overthinking what had just transpired. Not just with Sorene but with everything that was bizarrely being introduced to him this new Dawning season of Kingfall. He may have achieved a position as a paladin aspirant, but he no longer desired any of it. All that he had yearned to ascertain had been revealed to be nothing short of a dark beacon in an obscure sky of false hopes.

He could hear his cousin's drained voice asking Aerik permission for the unexpected sex partner joining in. Henrick knew that Aerik had reserved feelings for Sorene. He chose to ignore it all and let his best friend's conscience play out its own moral course of action.

When Sorene's newly added moan and the harlot sisters' chuckling combined, Aerik discerned the verdict on his cousin's weak ethics concerning the flesh. It didn't matter now.

Thirteen rips in the curtain. Seventy-eight plank fixes on the floor. He inhaled deeply and closed his eyes. *One door, two sisters, three whores, four moles on the fake twin with the blonder hair, five lit candles, six drawers in the wardrobe, seven piercings on the brunette, eight candles altogether.* He exhaled his way back into sanity.

Aerik opened his eyes again, surveying the familiar room. Henrick and he had frequented it quite often when in the city main. By happenstance, they had procured it a year past, in private and independently of their esteemed families' knowledge. Monetary allowance and highborn influence had helped to dissuade a fugitive merchant of some sudden misfortune, and he was less than reluctant to sell his midtown abode in central Frostdale for a meager offer.

And ever since, the small city house had remained a playground away from home for the two boys. The bedroom upstairs they separated by the makeshift torn blanket of a curtain for intended privacy, but the dilapidated fabric had seen its fair share of drunken shenanigans since then. Paid harlots, gambling sessions, foreign drug experimentations from the Dominadom—it all went on. Intoxicated talk about all kinds of blasphemy against his faith in the Fives, and his failed belief in his own house, and even his kingdom's transgressions were all voiced. But only to Henrick. They had a bond of loyalty that could never be broken. How they had ever even believed they were worthy to join the righteous Paladin Order was beyond him.

But then he pondered everything he had just discovered at the end of the Trial of Truth. *Righteous? What have we gotten ourselves into, Henrick? Sworn to silence indefinitely now. The Paladin Order is more vile than all the plagues and poisons combined. The Pentagogue itself is the very breeding ground of all things evil as we know them.*

Sorene's familiar sexual pant and sounds came again, harder even than when she had been with him.

Nine. He searched in desperation to continue to count. He found it. There, in front of him all along. That dark beacon in the obscure sky of those false hopes. *Nine points on the star.*

He awkwardly looked at the spiked mace granted to him after the Trial of Truth, as if it were some enemy artifact unwelcome on the turf of his homeland. It had nine spikes in total, just as depicted on the Ampion flag.

Aerik had been educated that the dawnstar mace was intended to represent ten points, not just nine, with the weapon's haft as the last. The spike protruding from the top of the weapon and the very haft to wield it were meant to symbolize the shadow element as the beginning and end of all things. *Strange adaptation, being that Daynishmen are of tairan and fire descendancy, not of the shadow line whatsoever,* Aerik mused. He had even heard that the very Pentagogue temple itself was constructed in the spired form of an upright dawnstar, towering over the centralized capital of Az'Dayne. Such progressive architecture was far too profound for Aerik to comprehend.

He glared at his new weapon as if it were a single foe facing him for a duel in the room. Aerik reached to the accursed weapon and held it firmly in both palms, embracing his new, corrupted fate. He and his cousin both knew the course their path was leading them down. It was the same road their very fathers had allegedly ventured along, the one that cost Lord Lucas Blackendale his life and Tomas Brigannor his sight. The hushed hearsay whispered that their paternal peers had been conscripted into some clandestine scheme, betraying their role in their faith and country. He had ignored the unpopular gossips all throughout his past, but he could no longer now. Incidentally, he found himself at a crossroads between following his father's unfinished footsteps and joining his mother's naive crusade for hard justice on the losing side. *I sense darkness either way. We are in the Umbran Pledge now, Henrick. There is no turning back ...*

Aerik dwelled on the consequences of his newfound enlightenment and what he had seen behind the bookshelves at the Trial of Truth, and on the final answer given to him by the shadow knights.

He suddenly feared lingering over the unthinkable subject. The tormenting sound of Sorene and the two sisters fornicating in their uninvited orgy finally dissipated, just as his cousin's presence went mute alongside them. The flicker of the burning candles held more weight in faint audibility than any of the living in the chosen crude harem.

It is all over now. Accept it. Your family's survival is all that matters. Know how much I do love you, Mother and Brie. The north was about to be behind him, the region of all things shadow by element and lineage descendancies.

They would be on their way to the south soon enough. "To the south, then," he whispered to his dark weapon. "To the heart of the shadow itself."

ONDREW (VI)

ZSOLINDAL

Bizarre stairways warped in disorienting, mazelike patterns. The stone steps often defied the conventional directions of north, south, east, and west. Many routes also formed upside down and sideways, which no human could hope to navigate. Intricately sculpted dwellings of the natural element were situated throughout the desolate colony. Most of the large huts hung inverted, like large hives, while some had been erected upon the stair walls and level ground.

The same fur-covered humanoid skulked parallel to the knights as they ascended through the foreign city. The Skystone ape toted a broken spear shaft everywhere it appeared, regularly disappearing through some shadowed domicile and later reemerging in the entry of another. It was as if every Neveril home were linked to the others through a series of interconnected, hidden tunnels. Ondrew opted not to chance any scouts to explore that theory just yet.

While the persistent bestial spy from the beginning of their trek remained in sight, the knights spotted more than just the one ape as they delved into the vast ghost town. Fortunately, any sign of them being in troops by the hundreds had not proved true yet.

The day's march progressed through restless hours of pure paranoia. When exhaustion beckoned for full sleep, the trudge through the incalculable stairways only strengthened. Any moments of respite were taken briefly, with naps lasting only as long as another knight could eat his quick meal.

Stealth was a known protocol without having to be instructed aloud. Only one dared to prove his madness. A day in, several men back in line, Ondrew heard the strings of a familiar lute being plucked, and the entertainer's rapturous voice echoed in song.

You sir, there,
Here we are, the unfinished.
Do you hear me now?
Destiny's cry … say dare we try.

O'er here, my lord,
We've yet come so far.
Do you see me now?
Sun in my sky … oh, it is aye.

You sir, there,
Evermore, the unfinished.
Can you feel me yet?
Death's kiss, but why … is this goodbye?

O'er here, my lord,
We've yet long to go.
Can we share this taste?
Our fate to die … But no, it 'twas …
Just all … our little lie.

If it hadn't been such a mesmeric escape from the drudgery of the underrealm's venture, Ondrew knew he would have silenced the minstrel sooner. But whether there was more to the ode or not, Odemnar the Vellyan didn't allow another verse. "Keep that up, pretty man, and I'll put my spear through the skull of every Timberland here," the giant barbarian threatened.

Ondrew didn't hide the incredulous stare he cast on the bard for his inopportune timing in the dire setting. Sarin, the wily girl of the troupe, countered the Vellyan with annoyance in her tone. "Timberhand."

"Say what, wench?" Odemnar spun around to tower intimidatingly over the petite girl.

Kyson put his lute down as the march of the Norther Knights slowed into a halt to surround the rising agitators. Kyson sarcastically explained to the ignorant hillsman what Sarin had implied. "You said 'Timberland.' She was correcting you. What you meant to say was that you will put your spear through the skull of every Timberhand here." He picked his lute back up and began strumming it once again to the same tune while humming the tune instead.

Broc didn't wait for the Vellyan's hostile retort, stepping in between Kyson and Odemnar to simmer down the altercation. Broc's aim was peace, but his words, as always, were spiced with fire. "Be he daft, Drew? Someone rip the sod's tongue out!"

Odemnar's elder companion, Aramgar, seized the opportunity to reach for Kyson's instrument and attempt to wrench it from the bard's grasp. But the Timberhand was far too dexterous and vigilant. Kyson pulled his lute behind him, with his bow drawn in an instant, point-blank between Aramgar's eyes.

Aramgar was slower to the draw but didn't tarry in hesitation to raise his own weapon without a hint of panic. The robust Vellyan centered his massive arbalest crossbow back at his challenger, calling Kyson's bluff. Five other longbows targeted instantly the big man to match Aramgar's threat. The Timberhands were quick to prove their loyalty to their own.

Kyson's smile brimmed with manic glee. He lowered his own bow to shove his chest against the point of the bolt loaded on the arbalest, teasing his fate.

Ondrew's tolerance could stomach no more antagonism among his men. The audacious minstrel had to be checked. "Kyson, we are unwelcome here." He pointed to the consistent follower on the visible stair ledges beyond. "Those echoes will have carried to the entire troop by now. We cannot afford casualties or to be drawn into a fight."

"Hmm, that scout there?" Quick to counter an opinion, Kyson signaled to the known ape blatantly watching on the distant tread, just out of arrow range. "Or that beast there? Or that new one over there?" He pointed to one other atop one of the domiciles, and then to a third Skystone ape Ondrew had not even seen, crouched behind a small sculpture.

"I know twice less than two coppers about these things, but I would wager we set that alert the very moment everyone here decided it wise to march in steel down these tunnels. The beasts proved they already knew of us when they mutilated your two pathfinders."

Ondrew squinted in distaste at the man's insubordination. Kyson made it obvious he didn't quite feel the brotherhood his oath to the Norther Knights had committed him into. "*Our* pathfinders," Ondrew stressed to remind him. "You are one of us now. So are the Vellyans. We have no proof that these Skystones are vast in numbers, as suspected. Those may just be starving ravagers. But too much sound ..."

Kyson's unruly behavior was proving to be boundless with another intrusion into his peer's advice. "Prince, we are found. There will be a fight," Kyson candidly put. "And if my destiny is short-fated to being a snack for a bunch of ape-men in an abandoned elvan catacomb, then by the Fives, I am going to at least be eaten in a good mood to my own sound."

The disruptive minstrel produced no laughter with his sardonic repartee. Even his fellowmen retreated from his defense, putting their bows away and their shamed eyes to the floor.

Ondrew chose to end the pointless charade with one final lecture. "Prince? Norther Knight commander? King Ondrew Roth even one day, perchance? I pay no mind to what you entitle me, but as long as it is tantamount to any form of authoritative respect, I order you to silence, knight."

Kyson dithered in contemplative turmoil on whether to retaliate with another rebellious rebuttal, but instead, all the unpredictable Timberhand returned was an obedient nod and a clever grin, followed by silence. Ondrew expected at least one final quip, but none came. Kyson put his lute to his back and readied his bow for the enemy, falling into formation like the soldier he intermittently was.

Frostdale's motley unit advanced through the open, cavernous citadel, unimpeded by anything other than the same redundant watchers on the backdrops. The few inquisitive Skystone lurkers were not going anywhere, but Ondrew gave his men no aggressive objective of removing them.

The derelict Neveril settlement linked onward through the scaling of its labyrinthine steps. Giant, sinister nest-like structures pervaded the cavern-scape to serve as the elven's stone dormitories. Colossal spiked ceilings and abysmal shadowy pits rivaled one another in a passive competition in the foreboding panorama. A working aqueduct system networked throughout, originating from a crystalyte-lit waterfall on the ascending backdrop. The nature of the gems' radiance emanated down the entire cascade to give the appearance of glowing crimson waters.

The peregrine underground led the scenic expedition to an unambiguous courtyard in Zsolindal's central square. Rune-ornamented steps rose as high as the spacious cavern chamber allowed, ascending into the most arresting sight to be beheld throughout the city.

Ondrew spearheaded the Norther Knights and ceased the march before the great marvel at the base of its rise. His inquisitiveness about the mysterious elvan race teemed. It seemed his men shared his awed curiosity, not minding the recess.

"A temple?" Datron inquired in a hushed tone, unable to take his fixed gaze from the spectacle above him.

Ondrew had already been eyeing the alluring umbran for any answers before Datron broke the quiet.

Lilealah looked back on Ondrew, not Datron, when giving her response. "Elvan cultures have no temples. The Neveril are no different. This is a grove."

The stone steps just before the zenith of the rise became white as ice. The spherical sanctum itself was blanketed completely in a glacial element, shimmering with a breathtaking radiance over the empty plaza.

"Where lifetrees are grown and spiritroots connect?" Ondrew probed, hoping his elvan lore was correct.

Lilealah kept her voice hushed and wary when explaining. "Zsolindal was a rather brief civilization for the Neveril Empire, one bathed in strife and blood. It dates back less than three centuries. Their presence on this side of the north has been flushed out time and again, relentlessly dealing with the invasions from the Glace Isles. Khomo'Jhuvonus eventually dislodged them from their underrealm in Aggedon, slaying the three sons of the standing Neveril emperor upon his final victory. Savage as the Terollar are, however, they heed strictly the creed of the elvan Balance and honored the law not to touch the grove of Zsolindal. There have not been Neveril present here for over three generations. While no wardens remain to protect it, there still stand the living lifetrees of those elven birthed in Aggedon throughout the last two hundred years. These are sacred grounds. It is forbidden for humans to see or touch them."

Every man around her stayed as silent as the crypt itself. Ondrew battled between overwhelming curiosity and respect for the elvan ethos but needed clarification, almost asking her permission. "Are you implying that none of us may enter the grove?"

Lilealah stared straight into his soul, he felt, as she attempted to take the lead, never letting her gaze stray from his eyes. That was answer enough for him.

To maintain his dominance within the crew, he initiated the climb to the high sanctum, giving instruction to Broc and Black to escort Lilealah beside him, as the knight-errant entourage eagerly followed.

The summit of the rise came after an exhausting hike. *A Neveril grove.* Ondrew knew of no man alive who had experienced the prospect of a lifetree or its spiritroots. Stepping onto such hallowed ground felt as if he were stepping onto the Godslands themselves.

The decomposed corpse of a long-dead Skystone ape slumped against a frozen pillar of the entry corridor. Its hands were placed to cover its eyes, as if hiding the creature's sight from the forbidden. Orange powder stains painted the pinnacle of the final icy steps. Ondrew could see evidence of what had transpired even before Mathias pointed it out. Neveril glyphs tiled the ceiling above the loosened pressure plates. The non-native apes had done the Norther Knights a favor by triggering the firetears traps.

Ondrew cautiously took the first step inside the ghostly gallery of abandoned victims. An azure mist of pure cold saturated the air. The walls and ceiling of the globular structure were sheened with dense blue ice, illuminating the whole of the ethereal chamber.

Small, white-barked trees, approximately four men in height, ornamented the vast cave ceiling like alien stalactites, a bizarre spectacle to absorb as reality. Not a single lifetree stemmed from level ground, defying the laws of nature in the topside world. The armored skin of the phenomenal entities was tinted by a white husk, matching that of the Neveril that they spawned. Even their sharp, pine-like branches and leaves held the same tint, covering the roof in a tent of snow-colored needles.

The bases of the supernatural tree trunks were entangled in blood-red roots stretching across the frost-veiled surfaces. Some of them coiled around the main stalks of the trees, while others wormed outwardly, interwoven throughout the ceiling, which they were bedded into. The living veins of the upside-down lifetrees pulsated like a plethora of beating hearts.

Ondrew tried to account for each tree, seeing how many had survived the past Terollar onslaughts, long before he or his father had been born. Most of the Neveril lifetrees seemed obviously dead, likely nine of every ten. *There must be still over two score of these trees alive? And so the Norther Knights can now say they have seen a Neveril grove, and the last living lifetrees of the City of Ghosts. Pray the Fives we live to tell this tale.*

The true marvel behind the birthing of the elven and the exact phenomenon was an esoteric science to him, but being born of House Roth in Barredom, he had received the highest form of education on elven, more than any others his age growing up throughout Frostdale.

He knew that unspawned elven, still in their cocoons grown on their parents' lifetree, were known as saplings. And that, strangely enough, it was not required that a male and female become lifemates by elvan biology. An elvan might have two fathers or two mothers as their parents. Procreation attempts occurred only during certain seasons, dependent on the elven's descendancy, and so long as the two lifemates were within their lifetree's node—the aura emanating from two lifemates when next to their lifetree. *And evidently, the aura that surrounds umbran lifemates when next to one another, according to Lilealah's account.* Lastly, he was aware that a spiritroot was like an ethereal umbilical cord between the elvan and its lifetree, and it was invisible to all but the one it was connected to.

Ondrew's attention was stolen from the mystic landscape by something caught in the corner of his vision. He could see his own reflection in the mirror of frost surrounding him. While his men spread about to inspect the many other exotic aspects of the Neveril nursery, he was more interested in the simulacrum staring back at him, matching his every move. He walked up directly to the ice wall and had a glimpse of himself for the first time since he had left Castle Frostdale.

His soldier-cut brown hair and groomed beard were no longer spruced for elegance. He looked ten years older, ashy from the rocky debris of the cavernous trek, disheveled and browbeaten. His dark brown eyes gleamed on his face in some phantom image of himself. He considered the reflection a manifestation of what Zsolindal would do to him and his men if they could not escape its aura of death and loss soon enough.

Ondrew broke away to review what the rest of his men were indulging their fascinations with. Not a single elvan skeleton could be found—not of the Neveril nor any Terollar. Other than the lifetrees looming above their heads, the only remnant of past elvan existence in the prohibited lair was the accumulation of Neveril armaments piled into a shrine-like cache at the center of the grove. The sizable, deep-curved blades, shaped more like scythes than swords, seemed the most abundant of the weapons in the hoard of treasured artifacts. *These must have been what were wielded by the final sentinels that fell failing to defend this warren.*

Odemnar stepped to loom over the steel remains of one of the expired wardens. Ondrew could discern the barbarian's admiration with the dead guardian's unwieldly Neveril sword. The Vellyan reached down to filch the scythe-like blade but was sharply warned otherwise.

"Take nothing from the fallen," Lilealah prompted in an intimidating tone she had never used before.

Odemnar and the other potential pilferers snapped back from their motives to look upon the ominous umbran and warily backed away from any malignant intent. Ondrew studied the greed of some of his men, beaming in their eyes. Temptation was the bane of all virtues. Only half were disciplined soldiers. Others were fledgling knights or old nobles with a background in the defense of the court or royal army. And then there were strangers altogether to him, such as the Vellyans and Timberhands.

All had one single thing in common: none of them owned any lands, no longer belonging to any house names they could call on as their heritage. If they carried noble blood, it had been cast away for a greater cause. The Norther Knights were not mercenaries either. Ondrew had incidentally turned his loyal following into a band of destitute apostates in the eyes of Barredom.

He observed Datron trying to filch a piece of branch from one of the surviving lifetrees, pulling his knife from its sheath to amputate the prospective trophy. Ondrew trailed in favor of Lilealah. "And we do not take from the living either. The Norther Knights are neither grave robbers nor treasure chasers. We will not tarnish this forbidden sanctuary with our uninvited iniquities." His indisputable directive was followed by him taking his leave, exiting the grove to continue their mission.

His second, Broc, reiterated his objective. "Obey your leader! Fall out!"

The knights returned to their quest out of Zsolindal, through the winding path of the stone-stepped, urban underrealm. The bestial admirers that had shadowed the party the entire hike proved to be oddly absent after their descent from the grove. Not a single ape appeared for the remainder of the stair-bound expedition out of the elvan city.

Ondrew glanced at each of the Timberhands: Kyson, Sarin, Caldwell, Tarance, Jonthon, and Ryder. Of all the men in his radical contingent, if he were asked to guess which would attempt to thieve from the Neveril grove, he would have named any one of them with no hesitation. But none had attempted to acquire any of the oddities in the icy sanctum. The bards were an unpredictable addition of rebels, against anything even remotely anticipated.

The inconvenient web of Zsolindal's steps was not always so linear as to make for good ground that humans could traverse. Being that Neveril could walk walls and ceilings with no sense of gravity, they did not construct their roads for the expediency of the probable invader. The Norther Knights often had to veer off the beaten path in order to progress toward their destination out.

But finally, signs of the exit were unveiled as the intricate steps came to an end. Groans of fatigue were traded between the knights, and Ondrew allowed a moment of relief, extending the consent for hushed chatter once more. After their legs had had their rest and their guts their fill, Ondrew led the last stretch out of Zsolindal's stone cityscape. The cavern gradually narrowed, funneling the group close against the towering rock walls. High crags and spiraling pathways made up the face of the cavern corridor.

The tapered passageway curved into an even thinner channel. The group rounded the corner, with their umbran captive centered in tow, and there they uncovered the ploy. In front of them, all above, and slowly swarming the bluffs behind them was the army of Skystone apes.

Mathias hissed an obscenity. "These clever-devil fucks."

Just then, an evident chief of the brutish troop rushed forward in a frenzy. The resident alpha toted a large iron chain around its massive neck, like some fancy trinket. A torn cloak was tied awkwardly on its shoulder, like some prestigious badge. It stopped abruptly in a powdering stomp of rocky debris, slamming its fist to the ground and growling hysterically. Its large yellow fangs protruded as it howled.

The Skystone apes were at least half a foot taller than their black-furred southern cousins, the Brutongan gorillas. Covered in long white hair, thick like that of some shaggy sheepdog, their faces carried emotion and intelligence unseen in any other beasts Ondrew had come across. Beyond, a hundred pairs of eyes seethed with a hungry fury ready to be unleashed.

The apes' apparent chieftain rushed forward with an intimidating taunt, stopping again halfway between his troop and the knights to repeat his threatening howl. Ondrew and his vanguard carefully wedged in closer to prepare their shields against the inescapable onslaught. And just then a screeching twang let loose as a powerful crossbow bolt thudded deep into the heart of the agitated beast.

The alpha ape's heart exploded, and it went down in an instant. Aramgar stood poised with his emptied arbalest trained on his slain target. *Impromptu move, but wise, I hope. They should scatter without their alpha.*

But no such scattering commenced. Two other large Skystone apes hurtled forward to strip the dead dominant of its possessions. One donned the iron chain, while the other ripped the cloak free. A third beast, wielding a grove sentinel's two-handed scythe blade, joined the two at the forefront.

The plot to bully back and push through was not going optimistically. *Or perhaps we should run …*

HONORAH (V)

BLACKENDALE

Black curtains. Black bedding. Black rug. Black decor. Black wardrobe. Black stone. Even the dark wine in the dim candle radiance made it appear as a vintage concocted of pure shadow itself.

She took another sip from the nearly drained decanter, shaking her habitually overused chalice upon her lips and spilling the sweet-and-sour liquid down her chin.

For no reason whatsoever, a tear stumbled out of the corner of her right eye. She was feeling incredibly vulnerable and was finally able to excrete true signs of emotion and weakness—irreparable damage that none could ever witness from her. Not even her failing gods. *This room needs more darkness. None can see this.*

This was her personal chamber. This was her bright life outside of the grueling Frostdale Deeps and loathed council meetings. She was alone now, no consoling family, not a single friend, utterly alone, as always.

Her inebriated eyes swayed across the room to several particulars. Her naked bed sat cold, with nothing but an empty mattress, with the goose-down pillows lying in the corner atop the bundle of bear-pelt blankets. She hadn't been able to lie in her own bed since the day she was told those cold words from Smiles: "I will tell you how Lucas and Justan died trying to become one of them, one of the new qindrid, just like that eyeless heretic Tomas Brigannor."

Tomas ... Her brother-by-law might have been blind in the eyes but was far from sightless in the knowledge he withheld. He had refused to accept her demands for an audience since that session in the Troll Gardens, and even so, Norah knew that Tomas would never reveal a thing through conventional questioning. She would have to resort to more creative methods of extraction.

Another time. She stirred her half-filled goblet with her middle finger before taking the next taste. She slowly inspected the rest of her chamber as if it were her first time in some abode completely foreign.

Her closet chest was in such disarray, one might deduce a supernatural cyclone had made its way in, with open drawers and random apparel chaotically strewn about. She took note of the open balcony, with its dark drapes, across from her. The thin curtains were swaying toward her, dancing with the faint northern breeze, inviting her to come closer and play.

The embers in the glowing hearth to her left were dying, but the warmth still grazed her exposed calves through her loose gown, sending a shiver up through her spine.

Norah took another healthy sip of the wine, and there, out of the fringe of her eye, she saw the mirror. She was aghast to even take notice of it. In front of the bed, against the wall and beside the fireplace, it stayed, like a daring portal into the undesirable, yet it beckoned her presence too. She refused. For now.

She looked down to her caressing fingertips, to the lone thing she fondled beneath. *Hello, my lost love.*

She touched his face and wept some more. She had taken down the painting that was mounted above her headboard. Her eyes pooled as she studied the handsome depiction of Lucas but shifted to a sense of disgust when she perceived her own image beside him in the portrait. She falsely appeared as something pretty in the picture. *Tell me I am pretty now, Lucas. You are blind in the Godslands if you do.*

But she was happy in the painting. And she vividly remembered being so once upon a time, when the painting was drawn for them. Their first anniversary—Lucas had always been the romantic in the beginning. He paid high coin to the best in Barredom for the talent upon the framed canvas, though she couldn't for the life of her recall the name of the artist.

She owed the man an eternal debt. The painter had given her the only image of her foregone husband that she could still tangibly cling to next to deep-reaching memories inside her conflicted head.

I died with you that day. I was at such peace as a Blackendale. We Bayns are a miserable brood since Great-Grandfather passed. Bathed in hate, dried in death – look at us all now. I brought you this.

Her great-grandfather, Ondrew Bayn, was the last Bayn king of Barredom before House Roth usurped his rule, one hundred seven years ago. House Bayn, during its final reign, utilized the aid of mages from Mageholme to beat back the invading stoneborne that had conquered the city of Defiance and were encroaching on the northern Highlands. This became known as the Cold Caster War, in which the Umbra mages involved did play a crucial part in Barredom's victory over the qindrid occupying its homeland.

Following the triumph, Ondrew Bayn kept a strong alliance with the mages and allowed its citizens to trade and find sanctuary freely throughout his domain. This was a widely unpopular decree in the kingdom, which spread unrest faster than the ugliest of plagues.

House Roth, under King Thandon the Firstnamed, "the Revered," amassed an uprising to force House Bayn out of the throne, which succeeded, but he allowed the Bayns mercy in honor of Barredom's founder family line. The final rebellion battle that took place was titled the Siege of Castle Bayn.

Her great-grandfather had no male heirs during his reign as king. A remarriage truce was made one year after he stepped down from his royal seat, to one of Thandon Roth's daughters, despite his age of sixty-one. They did miraculously bear a son that very year, with whispered rumor that he must have been magically touched by the mages to do so at his age.

Ondrew Bayn passed at age seventy-nine, during the rule of King Thandon Roth the Secondnamed, "the Cold." A nationwide commemoration in her great-grandfather's name was called to honor and celebrate his life and rule. This respect further solidified the mending peace between the Roths and the Bayns.

Ondrew Bayn's son, Iveur Bayn, who was Norah's grandfather, was raised to the position of High Warden of Barredom during the ceremony – Lord of Castle Bayn, keeper over all prisoners, and commander of the dungeon guard throughout the kingdom.

And there her grandfather remained to this day, one hundred one years old, still in seeming health, but it would likely not be long until the Fives took him.

Norah's father, Gavan Bayn, the only son of Iveur, had sired her three older brothers and herself. She was born a mistake, her mother had admitted to her, ten years after her youngest brother, Justan. Lamentably, Norah held absolutely no memory of her father, as he died when she was just two years old.

He had met his end heroically, fighting the trolls as a soldier during the Invasion of Teralloe. Broderick, her oldest brother, was slain during the Troll Skirmishes at the fall of Trolltown. Her second brother, Tarian, fell during the same ongoing border war as Broderick, but defending the Trollbane Towers instead.

All to trolls … Father, Broderick, Tarian, Justan, Lucas. The Bayn curse. I am sorry, my love. Norah's tears freely pooled into drops over the painting beneath her mournful gaze. *I no longer want the name. Come back to me, when all was right.*

Barredish widow law decreed that one year after the husband's death, the widow must revert back to the house name of her maiden status. She would still retain rights to her former husband's estate properties and accumulated wealth, so long as their children were younger than age fifteen, but only their children would carry on the surname. And Ebrielle and Aerik were only at the ages of seven and six at Lucas's time of death.

My Blackendale hero … I was happy once, you know? Norah's eyes glossed over again as she petted his face on the canvas. *Tell me it isn't true, Lucas. Don't let them all lie to me.*

Her hands quivered as she bore the chalice back to her mouth and spilled the entire cup across the painting. Norah broke from her spell of intoxication and hastily began blotting up the wine soiling her most precious possession. The act only smeared it more into the fabric, staining her lover's face with a cloud of darkness.

She burst into rage and threw the painting against her headboard, cracking the frame into pieces on impact. She stormed over to the mirror to confront her worst enemy.

And there she was. A withered, broken vessel where once had stood a respectable, fair lady of the north. Her hair was no longer thick and yellow, but now the palest shade of blond, thinning throughout. Dark and puffy bags bulged below her eyes, with wrinkles like tiny bird's feet in the corners. And her eyes themselves … *You are darkness reborn, aren't you? You are as vile as the beasts below. To kill and understand the monster, one must become one.*

Norah's eyes plunged pure hatred into the reflection of themselves. Her mouth curled into a sinister snarl. But then it all went blank, back to the vacant shell of hollow humanity left within her soul.

Before she knew it, her feet were already advancing toward the balcony. The stone tile grew colder on her bare soles the further she pressed away from the hearth, but she defied its counsel to turn back. She found herself exposed, looking down from her high tower perch, across all of upper Frostdale.

The melting snows barely clung to the multitude of rooftops across the urban canopy, as a sure sign that the Sunder season was nigh underway. The full moon was particularly bright, illuminating in full color the night's terrain. The gables of the capital city were textured in the standard green slates of Barredom's universal conformity. The castle park was shining in reds and purples and yellows from the many species of flowers ornamenting its grounds. The popular Bendon's Pond, named after Bendon Roth, "the Bloodless," two kings prior, was spectacularly beautiful in the twilight as a still blanket of blue splendor in the middle of the township commons.

At least, she wanted it to be beautiful. But nothing was any longer. It all blended into the bland drabness of her miserable existence. *Torture. Procure. Butcher. Maybe eat, maybe sleep, maybe not. Repeat.* She told herself she was satisfied in her work. She beguiled herself over it all as often as she could, to maintain the momentum of yearning to still breathe. *My king, my queen, my people of Barredom have no more need of me – they shun me like some expired nuisance. My daughter hates me. My son hates me. My …*

Norah took her feet to the balcony's parapet and leaned over to look straight down. There protruded the flag of House Bayn, five floors down her personal tower. It pointed like a long spear, beckoning her to join it.

My husband betrayed me. But I forgive you, my love. She veered further over the stone barricade of the terrace. Her heels no longer touched the brick beneath them as her toes stretched her dangerously forward. The night breeze wrestled with her hair in a vicious tussle. Her eyes closed, and she felt her lips curve into a soft smile. Perhaps this was what she needed to feel ultimately content. *I am on my way to see you, Lucas. Goodbye, Brie and Aerik. I am sorry …* Norah felt her waist continue to bend, and her feet had left the floor.

A sudden knocking at the door forced her eyes to open and shoot back inside her chamber. Her feet had found level ground again. She waited a few seconds, believing the sound to be a figment of her imagination or a sign from the Fives to reconsider her decision. But the knocks came again.

Annoyed, she briskly stormed over to scold the intruder interrupting her final moment. She unlatched the bolt locks and flung open the door to stare the menace in the face.

It was an armored officer of the Deeps, Markus Ackhill, captain of the Forlorn. Norah had entirely forgotten, in her drunken escapade, what she had instructed the man to do—execute an important task for her earlier that very eve.

The look on her face clearly spelled out the question, *Well?* But no such query was voiced aloud.

"It is done," Markus proclaimed.

She had received a letter from High Chancellor Soro, firmly restricting her access to select trolls in captivity. It was said that they were the king's words, and that the elven would be brought in for a final public execution after the ceremony at the Hall of Final Light for the judgments wrought upon the qindrid prisoners.

She was expressly forbidden from visiting the trolls Zuulzin, Jrulthun, and Smiles, in obvious fear from the royal court that she would let her prejudice get the better of her control and have them slain during an interrogation session. Her peers were not misguided to presume such a probability. There was nothing more that she desired than exactly that.

But she wasn't done hurting the one who had hurt her the most, the one who had taken Lucas from her. Kind-Eyes needed to suffer in a way nothing in her torture garden could achieve.

She knew that when elven mated, they mated for life. Their kind was not possessed by the carnal desires that humans were infected with. As a general rule, once an elvan loved, it would be with only that one for the remainder of its long lifespan, never again becoming physical or emotional in such a way toward another.

And she knew the tale of Zuulzin all too well. How it was an outcast of its Glace Isles tribe, even exiled for a time, for its choice in a non-Terollar lifemate, seeking out the sentimental company of a human. How it had fallen for Carah Blackendale during its captivity by Vanson, the father of Lucas, and how she had helped the troll escape its bonds so they could elope together into hiding. The unspoken truth that everyone knew was that Carah loved the fiend back and hated her cruel husband, most likely staging the planned assassination of Vanson that occurred during the escape.

Zuulzin became the bane of the Blackendales that day, as it later took Lucas's own life as well in revenge for Lucas finding and reclaiming Carah, only to have her burned at the stake for being defiled by a troll. They publicly set the record that she had been kidnapped and raped, but no one behind closed doors told that story.

The only way to truly hurt the aging troll was to violate it back. Nothing in the way of knives or fire or wicked tools of her trade, but something much more poignant that would last the rest of its shortened life in its haunting memories.

She had ordered Captain Markus to bring Kind-Eyes to the largest brothel in Frostdale. She had paid high coin to the madam and all nine of her harlots to force themselves on the prisoner and give it an unwanted experience of the flesh. The guardsmen had ensured the safety of the women at the establishment by keeping the troll detained in wrist cuffs and a muzzle over its mouth.

Zuulzin had taken Norah's only lover from her. She would defame its sacred memory with its only lover by besmudging it with a plethora of new.

"Details, then? Did it fight back?"

"No, he didn't fight back," Markus explained. "He just stood there, looking at nothing but the wall for a long while. Then he just looked sad, as he always does, gazing at each whore, in pity almost, as they tried."

"What do you mean, as they tried?" she countered, confused, prepared to hear some disappointing news.

"They tried, Inquisitor, but …" The officer paused and looked at the ground submissively. "His body failed him. The troll does suffer the aging. Perhaps he just—"

"It's not the aging," she interrupted and shooed him with her hand. "You did as bidden. We are done here. Dismissed." Norah didn't wait to see the captain bow to her before she abruptly shut the door, back in solitude.

She was supposed to feel the sweet contentment of retribution after committing such a deplorable act against the troll enemy's honor, but she simply felt no such passion. Strangely enough, she just felt shame for the dying old thing. She realized she didn't need to torture it any longer—or torture herself. She simply wanted them all dead and gone, and to be done with it.

Perhaps then she could begin anew and reassume her marital surname as Norah Blackendale, and leave this malicious creature that had become Norah Bayn in the cold Deeps, where it belonged.

EBRIELLE (V)

SEEDEN'S DEN

A horn tankard slammed on the table, spewing black ale all over her hands. The startlement jolted her into spilling her own mug. "Brie! Back to me," Aerik scolded. "I thought we were having drinks together."

Out of her whimsical fantasies and back inside the tavern, she blinked herself away from her habitual detachment. The young minstrel in the corner, playing the mandolin slowly, shifted faces from Kyson to some other fair fellow, who was a complete stranger to her. A pair of female belly dancers crowned in red wigs and role-playing dresses shared the stage with the performer as he spun some tragic tale of two twins.

Ebrielle glimpsed around, surveying the unfamiliar atmosphere, grounding herself back from her recurrent musings. Unruly drunkards lined the bench tables, swapping battle brags—half probably total lies, and the other half likely tall-tale exaggerations, from her critique of their sheer obnoxiousness. Most of the men in the inn appeared to be has-been war veterans living in the past, or never-was aspirers falsifying their heroic deeds not done. The lowest-level harlots she had ever witnessed prowled the tables for open coin and easy prey. Some didn't even care enough to find a room for the poverty-stricken lot and accepted coppers for a quick fuck out in the open for perverted spectators to cheer on. Pickpockets bumped around the floor, and cheap cutthroats for hire curtained the corners. This place was a gutter for all manner of filth in the north. This was Seeden's

Den. And this would be her first and last time ever visiting it, she swore.

Her cousin Henrick, across from her, chimed in with his assent. "I swear by the Fives, I have never seen anyone daydream as much as you."

Ebrielle pulled the green hood of her cloak lower to keep her face obscured and puckered her lips in an agreeable lack of excuse. "I am so sorry."

Aerik slipped her a sly smile. "Thinking about that bard again, are you not?"

"Why, whomever do you mean?" she replied coyly, failing to hide a grin, but then shook her head. "No, it is more that I am trying not to think of the husband forced upon me by Mother."

"When do you meet him again? I hear he is really old," Henrick asked, attempting to get a rise out of her.

"I hear he is really rich," Ebrielle countered. "Lord Haelyn Rook, archon of the Silverlakes. Mother is to meet him at the greyborne executions at the Hall of Final Light. Evidently, seeing a qindrid is something he has always wanted to do."

Aerik took a healthy swig of his bitter beer and made a disgusted face. "And he is going to get his wish by watching them die? Sounds as atrocious as Mother. They shall get along fine."

"You will be leaving right behind us, then, Brie." Henrick seemed quite confused. "Remind us, why are we even here, doing this, then?"

"Indeed, sister. Show me what you've been fiddling with in your hand the whole time." Her brother hinted at her hidden wrist underneath the table. "I know that is what this is about. Tell us your great secret, and we will tell you ours."

Henrick shot Aerik an incredulous glare of severe concern, not concurring with that bargain. But Ebrielle was far too consumed by her own dilemma to dwell on her brother and cousin's plight.

Indeed, what am I doing here? Seeden's Den, of all places. The shady tavern house sat outside the city's southern gates, in lower Frostdale Village, notorious as the most popular haunt in the region for all manner of men of heinous and scandalous character. It was the most unlikely place three teenagers of noble birth should find themselves in the hours of the waxing night. But this was where she had been specifically instructed to go to meet her contact.

Ebrielle pulled the small open scroll she fondled in her palm and laid it bare across the table for Aerik and Henrick to read.

The Axes of the Sons, which you seek, are yours. Grant me a private audience, and I will give you the best thief in the north to do the deed on my coin. Meet me alone at Seeden's Den at twilight in two pents, on the third day.

A Hidden Hero among Hidden Foes

Ebrielle explained how she had come across the note. "This scroll was handed to me by a street urchin the moment I departed from the Grand Artificer's tower, when I visited to acquire the Chosen Troll's axes. Now is the day and hour instructed. This troll, Smiles, their ambassador in the captured war party, he presented me with the most curious trade, if I would bring these relics to him. I believe it in Barredom's best interest to follow through with his implied accord."

Aerik scrutinized her with suspicion as his eyes squinted over her, reading straight through his sister. "Mother does not know about this, does she?"

She looked utterly annoyed with her brother's insinuated chastisement. "You know that answer, Aerik. What would you have for my fate, then? While you two are off to become honored paladins of the greatest order in the Dominadom, I am being pawned off like prize cattle to a stranger almost twice as old as Father! Or at best, I am stuck in the Deeps with our lovely Royal Inquisitor as her shadowing pet everywhere she glooms," she huffed, stealing Aerik's mug to swill down the rest of his bitter ale in one go.

Aerik's visage immediately shifted to intentions of retaliation, but then, just as fast, it changed to a smirk as he shook his head at his stubborn sibling. He waved over a tavern wench that Henrick was blatantly stripping with his eyes and had the maiden refill their tankards before he countered.

"Well, what personal victory are you wishing out of this? You bring these axes to this troll envoy; what happens after? You expect Mother, or the warden, or the king or queen, will actually consent to his release with these fabled weapons? Brie, that is quite a stretch."

It did sound ridiculous when someone else said it aloud, she admitted to herself. "I do not know the steps of how to get it done. But

I do know, by all my faith in all the Fives, that I am doing the right thing. Mother and Father …" She paused, choking back a threat of tears and a lump in her throat before she proceeded. "Their grudges and their hate have been their undoing. They will not be mine. And they should not be our people's. Torture and death have never bullied trolls into peaceful terms. Perhaps a simple amount of compliance finally will. If I have a chance to bring armistice between the Glace Isles and us for good, now that the Chosen Troll is gone, I will do what is necessary."

She took another hearty guzzle from the hard ale, staring glossy-eyed at nothing in particular on the table, heavy in contemplation. "Whatever is necessary," she reconfirmed, more assured of herself. "All I know is what Smiles requested and what this scroll asked of me. Norah thinks me weak and naive." She sipped again in disdain, too bitter in her heightening intoxication to refer to her mother as family. "These others see my potential to get these affairs done with no prejudice."

"Well, the note clearly states to come alone. Whoever this agent is, they are likely not to appear so long as we are present beside you." Aerik stated the brusque logic. "But I am glad you weren't daft enough to try to dare into Seeden's Den without us either," he chuckled to counter himself.

Henrick tried to lighten the somber mood from grave banter back into something more positively memorable for the trio's last meeting in a long time. "Then I say I raise my drink to this Hidden Hero, and the true, not so hidden hero, Lady Ebrielle Blackendale, our Savior of the North, the new emissary of Frostdale!"

The two siblings couldn't withhold their smiles at the hopeful notion. They stared into each other's matching hazel eyes and envisioned better days to come. They downed their mugs at their encouraging cousin's toast and waited for the next fill to go again. Aerik was the next to raise his horn cup for the sentiment of pleasant farewells. "And I say to the Vist with these snows and the cold! Here's to flowers and fineries! And five fucks to our cursed north! Bring us a greener south!"

She disciplined herself to endure the impending long sip until they retired their mugs, but the knights-to-be were in no hurry to rush their final fill. Pride aside, Ebrielle knew her alcohol tolerance simply could not compete with the two sturdy boys. Her head was spinning, but her mind was still clear on one neglect.

Aerik had a "great secret" of his own, he had mentioned, one that Henrick made evident he was uncomfortable with voicing. Her selfishness in remaining engrossed in her own quandary had kept her from honoring the trade of compassion. She had to ask before the ale drowned her wits entirely. "Your turn now, Aerik. What troubles have you two discovered? You mentioned something."

Henrick looked around nervously at every patron near, as if any one of them could be some murderous enemy. She had never seen her cousin act with such paranoia. Aerik studied the tavern door instead, his hyperintuition homing in on something in particular. Her brother grabbed both of her palms, pulling her tiny hands toward him on the table, and stared in all grim seriousness into her frightened eyes. His voice was dark, ominous, and hushed. "Forget these axes, Brie. Get out of the north. Frostdale is no longer a place of allies."

Henrick rocked in his chair, nervously glancing about at every flickering shadow. Aerik's eyes shot back to the door of the tavern, then back to his sister. "These are dire times, with our enemies wearing the faces of our friends. Marry that archon and leave this place, I beg of you. I can say no more. It's too late."

Ebrielle sat agape, vexed by his foreboding tidings. *What did you two see? What has changed so quickly?* "Too late for what?"

"They are here now," Aerik simply warned. "Cowl down. Do not follow. I love you, sweet sister. Until we meet again in greener fields."

He jumped up from the table and briskly started for the exit, with Henrick directly behind him. Her cousin gave her a sad farewell nod just as the inn door swung open with a charge of paladins unexpectedly bursting in. Eight armored knights surrounded her brother and cousin in a menacing stance. One of them, under his helm, spoke something sternly to the two boys, but the minstrel's music and the tavern's ambiance was so loud she could not make out the words.

And just like that, Aerik and Henrick were escorted out of the inn, and she was left alone at her table in Seeden's Den. She panicked, still baffled at the scenario that had just transpired. Her focus caught the three empty tankards in front of her, and a sudden wave of sadness crashed over her. And then the sorrow became nerve-piercing apprehension.

Her ears picked up an unruly drunkard screaming at the same wench who had been serving them all evening. She heeded one of the stage dancers, threatening the inebriated array of debauchery pawing at her dress. Another man, missing half his teeth, threw his mug against the wall, smashing it into splinters, for no reason she could discern. Her peripheral vision picked it all up, but she wouldn't dare to look upon any one thing directly. Her cowl was now down so low she could only see the tabletop in front of her nose. She had to leave. This was a failure. *I am just Ebrielle Rook now, future widower of the dying old man of the Silverlakes.*

She stood up with both hands on her hood to ensure it remained low enough to conceal every feature on her fair face. The moment she turned to exit the tavern, her intoxication and impaired vision caused her to clumsily bump straight into a tall patron looming in front of her. "Sir! Apologies," she squeaked, not even braving a look up as she tried to elude the intrusion.

A gentle hand caught the front of her shoulder, stopping her, as he softly invited, "Sit back down, Lady Ebrielle Blackendale, daughter of the Royal Inquisitor."

This was him. Her contact. She did sit back down on the instant, and only then did she gamble to meet his gaze with hers.

"I know you," Ebrielle muttered in disbelief. He kept his hood low like hers, but his distinctive green eyes were inimitable. She could never have guessed it was he who had scribed the note, but suddenly she already felt more at ease, even though the man was a stranger to her except in the Frostdale court.

"High Chancellor Soro, yes, my lady, it is I."

"So you are this Hidden Hero, then? I just did not expect …" She trailed off, embarrassed over how to even address the lofty, intimidating man.

"One of my station," Soro guessed at her surprise. "It makes no matter. I know something no one else does. And you and I, we have aligned goals with these Terollar in our Deeps. I, too, want a truce. I am here to grant you a way to get the axes, but after I tell you how, I must tell you why."

"How, then? Your scroll mentions a thief."

"The bard coming on stage as we speak, behind me," Soro elaborated without turning his focus from Ebrielle. She noticed it was a girl, likely younger than herself. Her face would have been pretty if not for the burn scars on her brow and side of her face, along with her rather masculine spiky black hair. "Candrice—a servant of mine. The deed gets done during the executions at the Hall of Final Light. The whole town, including most of the city guard and Az'Dayne's royals, will be there. You will not be joining.

"You will take this elixir." Soro pulled out a tiny vial, large enough to hold maybe two drops of liquid. "It will make you appear sick with the sweats, which will be very fleeting, perhaps an hour or two. Your mother will relieve you of your duty, and you will be free to meet with my thief just outside the Deeps for the axes you seek. Candrice will find you."

Why me and not you? You have the highest power of the court and can get the axes without such a farce. Ebrielle's eyes must have been openly transparent to convey her thoughts as the chancellor deciphered clearly her uncertainties.

He narrowed his exotic green eyes at her with a reassuring elucidation. "It cannot be me that performs this. It must be you, Lady Ebrielle. The animosity between the Royal Inquisitor and myself is not undisclosed. She holds no more friends in the high court. Her favor with the king and queen is moot at best. And Az'Dayne has not made the transition easy on her. Her time on the Frostdale Council has an expiration date soon to pass. But it does not have to be so for her daughter. You are of the blood of House Bayn, the oldest line in Barredom, of the nation's original kings. And of the blood of House Blackendale, those that were the most reputable huntsmen in the country for generations. I am offering you a chance for elevation, to stop living under your mother's doomed shadow. You can object to the marriage proposed by this undesired Lord Rook, as by Dawning's end, there will be southern princes and younger, richer lords lining up at Frostdale's gates for your hand, if that is your desire."

This was her first exchange with High Chancellor Soro, and it was going nothing even remotely like the version she had observed from encounters with her mother present. With his chiseled features across his naturally smooth face and suave aptitude for wordplay, Ebrielle admitted to herself that it was quite easy for her to fall victim to the man's eloquence. "You spin a riveting sale, High Chancellor. I am listening. What happens to my mother, then, should I commit to this for you? For us?" She played along. As much as she had begrudged her mother for many years, her conscience could never settle with taking away the only remnants of dignity and prestige Norah still clung to.

"Lady Honorah Bayn will be appointed Keeper of Castle Bayn, a new title I will petition King Aerik to approve, which he will. Your great-grandfather Iveur, High Warden of Barredom, is on his last breaths. He is old and dying. Barredish property law is contradictory and diverse among different sovereigns, but I can promise you, within my power, she will maintain control over the prison complexes of Castle Bayn and the Frostdale capital, as well as the multitude of auxiliary dungeons throughout the kingdom. After General Randon's conquest of Two-Towns, and any further exploits through Aggedon, your mother will have her hands full with greyborne prisoners that will be more than enough to take her mind off the loss of her position as Royal Inquisitor, and she will be exempted from necessary Barredish politics, which she so detests."

Ebrielle knew her mother's pride would never forgive her if she entertained Soro's intentions, but her interest was piqued. She had to know more. "Indulge me, then, please," she countered with poise and decorum, sensing she may have the upper hand in this bargaining over her luck's sudden favorable turn. "All of this for me, and nothing for you? That doesn't seem very typical of the Soro I have heard so much about. How can this come to pass with Warden BrKaim after I have the axes? Will the Deeps even release Smiles with a court official's permit? The suspicion will be too great after. I may even be subject to accusations of treason."

"You will not," he refuted bluntly. Soro subtly set down his second offering on the table for her to grasp. "This is a signet ring of substitute station on the council's blessing. It resembles your mother's as Royal Inquisitor. I am hereby promoting you to Surrogate Inquisitor in her absence, to be announced officially in due time if you accept. No matter, however—you will have the Frostdale Council's blessing in this matter carried forth, and in fully sanctioned capacity. Warden BrKaim will have no choice but to comply with your mandate while everyone is absent at the judgments."

For someone afflicted with incessant imaginary delights, this night she was living through seemed more surreal than the far-fetched fancies that always beset her. "Okay, so I won't be branded a traitor of Frostdale with this blessing from the council, you say? But how do I manage an escort for Smiles's passage back to the Glace

Isles? Forgive my cynicism, High Chancellor, but the details of this master strategy are quite vague at best."

"Again, you will not" is all he repeated.

"I understand. You have assured me I would not be branded with treason, but how—?" Ebrielle attempted to ask, but she was abruptly interrupted for Soro to further elaborate.

"No. You will not be releasing Smiles. I never said that was part of the plan." Ebrielle shot a perplexed look at Soro, but he wasn't done clarifying. "I have strong knowledge to believe that this Terollar ambassador you have been speaking with is not who he seems to be. The Forwoken Order I am affiliated with is rich in the arcane secrets of the Terollar race."

"The mortali," Soro continued, "have never been recorded as being permitted into a war party outside of the Glace Isles, or other regions of explored Terollar territories. You are learned in what practice they specialize in for the tribesven, are you not?"

Ebrielle felt entirely confident she was educated on that subject of popular troll custom. "Yes. A mortali is a vocation appointed only by the khomo himself, and it is the highest rank among the tribesven, next to the alpha. They are sacred elders, generally said to be the oldest members alive, and they act as sage voices for the tribe. They are masters at the medicinal and alchemical arts—shamans, if you will. They are also the venerated groomers of the tribe. Trolls have the innate power to heal wounds and restore energy without a thought, so in turn, if they were to cut their hair, it, too, would immediately begin to heal back to its natural long length as if it had never been tampered with in their entire life. The mortali specialize in concocting some form of antihealing salve that keeps their hair in whatever class-rank trim the khomo has decreed for them."

Soro smiled widely, as if she were his apprentice passing an important trial. "And does your Smiles in the Deeps show the physical signs of what you might believe to be one of the eldest of the tribe on the Glace Isles? And was he not with the war party when mortali in their culture are forbidden to attend?"

Ebrielle thought quietly, knowing Soro had well deduced these answers preemptively. "What are saying?"

"I see that you know much about Terollar culture. But how much do you know about the Glace Isles king's history? There are archives a century old, from former Barredish prisoners who escaped their incarceration at the hands of these local Terollar, that particularize certain discoveries. The prominent one at hand being that these surviving captives of old witnessed the khomo of the isles performing the arts of the mortali himself, even teaching other shamans the practice. According to Honorah's reports, this *'Smiles'* self-entitled himself as Master of the Mortali."

Ebrielle's mind raced to process the hints that were fed to her. The High Chancellor wanted her to deduce the facts herself. He was testing her.

There were haunting portraits of the Glace Isles khomo, painted all throughout the Barredish and Aggedonian societies for generations. The variations sometimes deviated, but they all held true to one identifiable trademark. The khomo had a high-crest hairstyle—where the sides of one's head were shaved completely, but a long, crested strip was left to remain from the brow to the back of the head. Depictions she had seen of the khomo always seemingly exaggerated the dramatic length of his high-crest to be as tall as the length of his own head.

The khomo trained his mortali. He was specialized in the creation of the salve so that he could change his hairstyle or that of his tribesven at any given time. But ... Ebrielle voiced, "General Randon's report conveyed that it was indeed a troll with the khomo's high-crest that was seen executed by Jrulthun, his alpha. No other trolls on the Glace Isles have ever been allowed to wear this style. You are implying that one of his tribesven sacrificed himself? They switched hairstyles from the mortali practice as a ploy?"

"There is a term on the Glace Isles: *Vlaka'Rahsee*. It means 'a good death of one's choosing'. It is a common practice for a warrior to embrace this sacrifice for a greater good. Any tribesven would be honored for this duty if the khomo bestowed it upon them for the advance in the restoration of the Balance," Soro further educated.

"Do you comprehend what I am implying now?" Soro lowered his tone to a whisper and made it real. "I am saying that your *'Smiles'* is Khomo'Jhuvonus, and that you know it to be true, Lady Ebrielle."

Her chair involuntarily slid back rapidly from the table. It jolted into the adjacent bench and rammed her back against another's. A yowl of drunken curses from an old cripple ensued as she hastily scurried back to Soro's protection with her cowl so low she could now only see her own bosom and nothing else. Her hands blindly found the haven of the familiar table, and the chancellor grasped her sweaty palms firmly in his. She was too scared even to make eye contact, for fear of hearing any more hard facts she knew would unavoidably follow.

"This is how it all plays out, Lady Ebrielle. Listen carefully, and do not deviate." High Chancellor Soro uttered his scheme in imperative urgency. "I must attend the judgments at the Hall of Final Light. You will be the one to execute this for the kingdom. Credit will fall to the both of us when the deed is complete. After you have the axes, bear the signet ring, and get an audience with Warden BrKaim in the Frostdale Deeps. Tell him you have proof from me that the khomo of the Glace Isles yet lives and is among those in captivity. Give him this signed letter for validation." He presented his final gift across the table for her to employ in the upcoming scheme.

"As Surrogate Inquisitor, you will have the authority to command the prison guard. The warden will need to bring all reinforcements from the Deeps to the bridge for your protection and to keep the elven below in control. Once at the Forlorn, you can single out Smiles for extraction. Have this foul nemesis of Barredom detained alone in the warden's private cell, and prompt the guard to test and see if he is indeed the possessor of these weapons. I will leave early from the ceremony, making necessary appearances and ensuring that Norah is distracted from joining our victory here."

Soro beamed with confidence, as if he could taste the savory triumph of his elevated political status already. "Any further concerns or hesitations?"

"Oh, only a thousand," she muttered with anxiety.

The chancellor's feverish grin did nothing to bolster her trepid resolve. He endowed her with a conclusion of encouraging words instead. "I always remember and reward my friends. Your mother cannot be made aware of this, however. It is imperative that no one else knows of this. Can you swear this to me?"

"By the Five and Five, and my life, I swear to you," she sincerely promised, lost in the momentum of it all.

"Good. Lady Honorah Bayn will be treated fairly and justly with her new position at your family keep, to the east. Her current rank will diminish in the court as necessary, but her authority will be similar at Castle Bayn and more suited to her talents, but no less significant over time. You will gain lands and holdings of your own and be crowned with titles the heralds and nobles will make for your renown once this deed is performed to perfect fruition. You will no longer be the meek and quiet daughter of the fading Royal Inquisitor and the fallen captain of the Eldenvale Rangers." Soro paused as he constructed his ego-building crescendo.

"Instead, you will become titled Hero of Barredom, who personally confronted the khomo of the Glace Isles and brought an end to his malicious reign. Your name will ascend in precedence through every rescribed history book, and your children to come will shelter in your image as a champion of justice done.

"And ultimately …" Soro shifted his tone to one much more sympathetically inviting, as if he had researched her truest desires beforehand. He finalized his capable spiel with her heart's actual desire. "You will gain your freedom to marry whomever you choose."

Ebrielle had just taken notice, through the distraction of the exchange, that one of her hands was still interlocked with Soro's as he broke her concentration to reconnect her with her palpable surroundings. The young chancellor perched the top of her tender knuckles on his puckered lips for a kiss before releasing her hand.

As an involuntary wave of heat blushed over her at the unexpected gesture, it took her a moment to analyze his conceivable intent. *Did High Chancellor Soro just subtly propose for my hand after this is done? I do suppose he is not unpleasant to look upon. Not at all, actually. Though can he grow hair? I do hope he can grow hair. And he will need to remove those ridiculous gold rings piercing the top of his ears.* Ebrielle snapped herself from such shallow ponderings, back to the portentous account of what was presently being conveyed.

Her eyes wandered to the female bard on the stage in the corner as she assured him, "I will be there to meet your Candrice on the day of judgments on time. I want this more than anything else. I am forever in your debt, High Chancellor." Her hazel eyes fell upon Soro in a different light, as if he were the fair-faced savior she had never known she needed.

The tall, exotic man stood, towering over her still sitting. It seemed a whole minute passed as he evaluated her with his radiant green eyes before he concluded, "No. The north will be forever in *your* debt. See this through." And then he departed.

Ebrielle sat bewildered in an abundance of thoughts and scenarios she had never fathomed to entertain until just a moment ago, after the chancellor had dropped such profound insights upon her.

It wasn't until the door to the tavern shut behind Soro that she gathered she was again all alone, enveloped in the debauchery of Seeden's Den. Her feet found the exit to dim-lit streets before she realized she had even fled from the table.

She should have been nervous walking the disreputable streets of southern Frostdale during the peak of the twilight hours, but with each new step she took, she noticed all dread fading from her cold veins. The night's chill was gone, and she felt warm with poise. Her stride made her posture proud as she idly drew the hood down from her cloak to reveal who she was for all the ill-doers and lurking criminals to see.

She was the Hero of Barredom, the girl who had brought down Khomo'Jhuvonus, and she no longer knew fear.

ONDREW (VII)

INTO THE GROVE

"Into the grove!" Ondrew bellowed his desperate command for the tenth time. The group was now halfway up the massive Neveril-built stairway.

Six bows released alongside a powerful arbalest. Four beasts fell. The Timberhands and Aramgar, with their ranged deterrence, were proving respectable worth. Aramgar's heavy crossbow contraption was killing anything it connected with in one shot. And the half dozen Timberhands were in unison with placing three deadly arrows per ape, in the skull, neck, and heart, without missing a beat. Sometimes Kyson would even let loose a spare to close a single kill on his own. Nine to Kyson alone now, Ondrew noted.

Odemnar, Broc, and Black maintained a feeble vanguard as the Norther Knights backtracked up the steps. One intrepid ape dared his luck on a charge against the glaive-handling Vellyan. Odemnar took two massive palms to the face and a stone to his head but prevailed to cleave the hostile's jaw from its skull. He thundered some untranslatable curse at the beast and made an audacious charge toward the oncoming troop in a daunting suicide attempt.

An excess of the brutes came hurtling up on all routes, intending to flank and find weak points in the hold. Ondrew prayed against his men's recalcitrant tendencies, that they might just subdue any unruliness in their blood until the oncoming assault expired.

"The whole troop is coming, sire!" Datron blurted the obvious in panic.

"Not enough arrows for all this," Sarin yelped, her voice cracked down to a squeal. "Takin' two or three to bring one down!"

"Then aim better," Kyson stipulated, targeting true on one ape to drop it dead with one precise arrow to explode the heart. A thudding bolt from Aramgar followed in the closing beast next to Kyson's victim, taking it by the skull and down the steps to tumble several other aggressors over.

The knights reached the pinnacle of the grove. They swiftly scattered inward to their wooded sanctuary. "You will have just enough," Ondrew assured Sarin. He took his sword forward to yell directives to his men. "Norther Knights, shields in the front!"

Twenty-one familiar armored men beside him chanted, "Osh, osh, oshah!" raising their shields to the air, then slamming them to the stone, forming a defensive wall against the impending onslaught.

Ondrew looked behind him to Lilealah backing away in the center of the group, desperately scanning the chamber for any further proof of protection for her own safety. "Lilealah, stay to the rear of the grove, out of sight! Men, protect your charge!"

"Eldenvale Rangers, spears ready! Just behind them, in the middle!" Ondrew ordered to Mathias and his eleven hunters. "I want a bow between each spearman! Timberhands and Aramgar, get in file!"

The Eldenvale Rangers lined up behind the shield-wielding Norther Knights, spears readied, with the Timberhands and sizable crossbowman braced strategically between them, as told.

"Strength on the flanks! Odemnar to the left, Broc to the right." Ondrew instructed his two most capable melee soldiers. His burly second and the Vellyan split from their current stations to promptly do as bidden by their commander.

The first of the Skystone apes made it up to level ground, forming inside the Neveril grove. "Heed my command, and we prevail! This is not your fate, men!"

Ondrew's bellow was trailed by the immediate typical cheers of, "Osh, osh, oshah!" The Norther Knights assembled, as directed, in a C-shaped formation, with shields in front, spears and bows in back, and the strongest fighters on both ends.

The white-furred brutes swarmed in by the masses now, roaring bestial threats and taunting to bestow a brutal death upon the group. Obvious alphas of the troop began to scope out the weakest in the line.

"Tell the Godslands they can fucking wait! We'll see their shores another day!" Broc spat to the ground and smashed his sword against his shield, ready to murder.

Four apes flaunting weaponry, including the largest brute wielding the sentinel blade, bundled up to take their chances on the smallest in the shield line. *Datron ...*

The ape-men came in full, funneling straight into Datron. The dexterous swordsman jabbed two quick stabs into the eyes of the first attacker, sending it reeling away in agony. But its train slammed straight through the boy, pummeling him to the ground.

"Shields!" Ondrew thundered to the group, and the gap was closed. Two of the spearmen lifted the injured knight to recover his place in line.

The first wave bludgeoned the shield wall with heavy fists and crude weaponry. A few knights grunted in distress between the blows as their forearms broke within the straps. Willem had his entire shield stripped from his arm, brace and all, and took a huge hammering fist to the helm. The knight dropped unconscious on the instant but was pulled back from the line by Mathias in the rear.

"Spears!" Ondrew bayed out the order.

The armored wall instantly tapped the stone from its formation as the shield knights took to one knee, and the Eldenvale Rangers lunged forward to thrust a sharp death into the wave of immediate beasts. Several apes went down to the ground, but Tolbert's spear was seized straight out of his grasp and turned back on him in the upper thigh.

"Shields!"

The wall came back up, and with it, so did the second wave. The powerful savages slammed against the wooden defense, buckling the formation's right flank. Gerrick and Donal hit the floor, and one ape went charging through.

Panic stirred among the spearmen and archers not prepared for the beast, but Odemnar was quick to act. His polearm took the brute in the back, impaling it through the spine.

Donal, still prone, was snatched by the ankle and pulled into the chaos. His comrades nearest to him dropped their shields in an attempt to save him but failed at retrieving him, only further weakening the wall. Ondrew had to act promptly to save the Norther Knight.

"Loose!" Ondrew lowered his stance with his shield as he had done for the spearmen. His men followed his lead. The six Timberhands and Aramgar let loose their arrows on the aggressors over Donal. Three apes fell dead and one retreated, surprised and injured.

One beast threw a broken spear at Aramgar but badly missed. Aramgar rewound the crank on his slow arbalest, and a few of the Timberhands released yet another volley near Donal's oncoming assailants. Gerrick and Piper rushed to their friend's rescue and pulled him back to the security of the line.

"Spears!" Ondrew was not ready to seize his offense. The apemen seemed more shaken up from the retaliation than the shield defense. The rangers plunged their longspears into the nearest brutes. Ondrew thought he saw four more fall. One reeled, squealing from a spear tip to the eye, and sprinted in a furor from the grove.

Oakley's spear was stripped from him and broken in half by one beast. To the left flank, Broc was being beaten badly by two apes. He pushed his sword through the jaws of one, rendering it limp, but lost his blade, lodged in the animal's skull. The beast he was left with took Broc's own shield and started using it as a vicious weapon to pummel him against the chamber wall. Ondrew's resilient second wasn't out for the count. As the most indomitable soldier Ondrew had ever met, Broc retaliated by throwing a futile fist of his own back into the savage creature's face.

"Shields!"

The defense came back up. But what saved Broc was an arrow whizzing by his ear to nail the brute in the temple, spearing into its brain. Kyson was too opportunity-prone to wait for the order. Broc retracted his sword and stood stubbornly, ignoring his injuries, roaring at his enemy that he was back in the fight.

The third wave of monstrous beasts did not come. More swarmed into the chamber of the Neveril grove now. For the first time, they seemed to be evaluating the strategy and prowess of their enemy. Ondrew tallied forty-plus and still counting as their numbers grew. They were allowing a respite, but he would not take the reprieve when initiative was paramount.

Ondrew shouted an impromptu directive, as it was time to maintain a debilitating counteroffensive. "Loose!" And the Timberhands released their arrows once again.

Two daring beasts soared in a leap off the lowered shields of

Shaun and Kenton, adjacent to Ondrew. The first took one of Aramgar's bolts to the throat. The second one landed behind the ranks but seemed lost as to which target to assail. Ondrew didn't let its decision see fruition. He and several nearby knights plunged their swords into the back of its thick skull and hide several times until it went down, still.

"Spears!"

A mound of dead beasts was now hoarded at the Norther Knights' boots. Ondrew took a long step over the sprawl of corpses.

"Shields!"

And it was as if the cunning apes had learned what the command meant. The moment the shields went up was when came the next wave, and the largest one yet. The Skystones used the bodies of their fallen as the first step, then the tilted wall of the Norther Knights' shields as the second step to propel themselves over the line and up into the dead branches of the ceiling-rooted, white-barked lifetrees of the former Neveril. More than a decem apes made it into the otherworldly wooden stalactites.

This sudden turn of events was the first time Ondrew had felt a loss of calculated certainty. He would not lose one man to these lowly fiends. "Broc, Odemnar, Black, Mathias! The trees! Timberhands, free shots! Men, do not break the line!"

The Skystone apes that made it over the shields broke from their perches in the lifetrees to bull-rush in random directions toward the back of the postured line.

The dual-battle-axe-wielding Black Brigannor was the first to make contact with the foe. The mute fighter lodged the first axe beard into the top of one's skull and took his other axe to the side of its neck, spraying himself with blood from the dead animal.

Odemnar charged at a sprint with his glaive that took the next ape's life when he impaled the thing through the high torso, and the Vellyan kept pushing its limp body to the back of the grove in a manic battle frenzy.

Broc got caught in a match with two at once. He was holding his own, but none were going down.

Kyson and the Timberhands successfully felled two as they dropped from the trees, and Aramgar's arbalest took a third. But one of the beasts had hungry intent on the archers. It took flight in a leap and buckled Sarin to the ground. His initial grip on the feeble girl ripped half the hair out of her scalp as she helplessly squealed for her life underneath the savage.

Datron left the line out of permission and thrust four stabs into the back of the beast before it knew it had been struck. When it turned around to retaliate, the dexterous young knight ducked the oncoming blows, and he uppercutted his blade straight through the bottom of its jaw, ending the ape's assault and saving Sarin's life.

Ondrew evaluated the shield wall holding its defense and shouted a command to the Eldenvale Rangers before breaking away himself. "Spears!"

The Norther Knight leader spun away to assist his second in his vicious duel. Broc's skill and tenacity were unmatched by most, but these Skystone apes had a savagery and sheer strength that no human possessed. His friend was badly beaten, though the battle rage within the warrior would not hint at it.

Together Ondrew and Broc prevailed in precision versus raw power and cut the starving savages down in a fashion only long-term, practiced training partners could have mastered.

Ondrew glanced around, hastily analyzing the damage to his knights from the Skystone troop. The apes that had broken the line in the jump were all slain. Sarin remained on the ground, out of the match, along with a few of the rangers near Mathias. The hunter captain was freeing his spear from the chest of one beast, while another wounded spearman was tending to Denson, screaming in agony from having half his shoulder and bicep chewed off. *These poor beasts are just victims of hunger, and we are simply not easy prey. Fives, may they retreat and find food and peace and leave us be. This is needless killing,* he prayed with a futile pity for them.

The apes surpassed them in numbers fivefold but nonetheless had lost a healthy chunk of their troop since they instigated the assault on Barredom's wayward knights errant. Normal beasts would have fled. But Skystone apes were not normal beasts.

Ondrew saw the same signs of trepidation in the apes as he had in men when fear infected the spirit. The Five and Five were with him. His loyal, capable men were with him. Destiny was with him. Dread was now with the enemy. This time it was his turn to cheer the traditional mantra. "Osh, osh, oshah!"

Ondrew dropped his shield and charged forward, hacking and cleaving at every ape nearby. He took the nearest by surprise and injured it with a precise jab through the lung. His men shadowed his advance. The front line merged with the back line, and somehow the smaller defenders pushed the stronger brutes closer to the steps of the grove's exit.

The apes were running out of alphas to bolster their aggression. Yet another effort at a half-hearted attack did come. A half score of beasts came forward. One went completely berserk and knocked Godrey unconscious in a massive blow but was swiftly slain with a series of blades.

Ondrew would take no risks. The defense of his men trumped any need for resolute aggression. "Shields!"

This time no aggressors came. Only a few remained in the grove, while the rest sporadically backtracked down the steps. One injured ape howled in violent defiance. The creature's fearlessness seemed to rekindle a fire in the remainder of the hesitant horde. The bold howls were traded down the stairway, seeming to inspire the troop into a final full assault.

"Loose!" There would be no final assault. Arrows flew. Kyson ended the first ape that opened its mouth. "Loose!" The Timberhands were unloading their entire quivers now, while Aramgar tried to keep up. Mathias threw his spear like a javelin through the chest of one beast, swiftly retrieving it and returning it to the battle.

The Norther Knights surged toward the dregs, assailing the final remaining aggressors. Defeated shrieks echoed down the stairway and across the derelict colony beyond.

"We see you, Zsolindal!" Ondrew shouted at the entrance to the grove. He banged his sword to his shield, taunting any more foes into trying themselves. He then opened his arms wide, his blade and shield outstretched to the caverns. "The Norther Knights see you, and we do not hide!"

The apes in their entire troop were scurrying down the stairway now. Whimpers of agony and defeat reverberated down the stone surroundings, becoming less prominent as the ape-men scuttled away and hid.

A roar of triumph bellowed about the grove and steps wherever the scattered knights had placed themselves in the finale of the skirmish. Broc BrKomak walked up the steps to stand straight before his liege and held his sword out toward him in an honor salute. "To our prince! To the Prince of Barredom!"

The Norther Knights in unison, even the Vellyans and Timberhands, all followed in the same resonant chant. "Osh, osh, oshah! To the Prince of Barredom!"

Ondrew had never felt so proud of his position. There was no disorder in the chaos, only structured obedience to their esteemed commander. In retrospect, he mused that by Barredom turning its sovereignty over to the Az'Dayne Dominadom and influencing his decision to denounce his house name, he was now allowed this rare triumph with his honored men-at-arms. Without such, he may have just acquired his kingship by decree of bloodline alone, without earning anything through trial and worth. *It is through deeds like this that true heroes are forged,* he conjectured.

A familiar feminine hand came from behind and rested upon his shoulder. Lilealah made it evident that she believed in him too. Ondrew closed his eyes to soak in the moment, listening to the uproar of victorious cheers from his men. Zsolindal was almost over. And there indeed was light at the end of this tunnel.

HONORAH (VI)

THE HALL OF FINAL LIGHT

Norah looked to the skies for an answer to the day's end. The morning blue was blotched by a surplus of clouds, concealing the sun. The welcoming warmth of the approaching Sunder was present, however, battling with the brisk chill of the dawn's northern winds.

The procession's lengthy ride was going at the pace of a leisurely walk. The royal guard steered hundreds of spectators through the village outskirts of Frostdale, southbound through the hilled highway of the Cold Road. Villagers, castle citizens, and even Daynish outsiders joined in on the ritual march. Paladins and veritans and their aspirants who had passed the Trials approached from behind the masses.

Norah rode in the center as the keystone of the fervent parade. She had adorned herself with the full ceremonial garb that implied her station as Royal Inquisitor. She wore a black robe of fine cloth with the sigil of Frostdale embroidered on the back of her attached mantle. The cowl of her robe formed into a high point, making her appear over half a foot taller than she actually was, quite an imposing figure. The lower half of her face was masked by a veil, leaving only her dark eyes to be seen beneath her hood.

Behind her were five stoneborne and five greyborne prisoners, bound and surrounded by an escort of the royal guard. Their sentence to meet their sacrificial execution at the Hall of Final Light was underway.

She could hear the advancing trot of the paladin and veritan troop parallel to the prisoners' parade. Norah glanced back in hopes of catching her son riding through the ranks, daring to dream that she might at least get to say one final farewell to him.

The march was nearing the roadside estate of her brother-by-law, Tomas, where she assumed Aerik would at least want to say his piece to the uncle and aunt who had raised him. She caught a glimpse of them standing by the road, among the other curious villagers. And then, just as she had presumed, her son did emerge to make his way to the two.

Appearing effusively gallant in his new veneer, Aerik had been fitted in Daynish armor from his pauldrons and breastplate down to his plated boots. It wasn't the paladin ensemble his peers were wearing, and he was without a helm, but it was as knightly as Norah had ever seen him all the same.

He jumped off his charger to embrace the true guardians responsible for his upbringing. His Uncle Tomas and Aunt Elsa cried as they hugged their foster son. Henrick soon joined to give his parents his own farewell, and eventually, the two paladin aspirants remounted their horses to blend back into the march.

Norah's heart stopped for a beat as Aerik left Henrick's side and steered his steed toward her. The pure excitement of her smile was screened beneath her veil, but Norah's eager eyes quickly converted into an aloof disposition to guise her true emotions.

Riding beside her, Aerik stared at the side of her cowled head, undeterred by its onward gaze. "So, this is it," he candidly prodded.

Norah felt weak in her obstinacy. She dared not match his scrutiny. "It seems it is, Aerik," she replied.

"Well, then." Her son laughed bitterly, turning his attention away from her. "Farewell, Inquisitor."

Aerik kicked the side of his horse to steer it away from Norah, off to find his comrades. "Aerik, wait! No." He instantly broke her hard facade. She pulled her veil down. "I am not good at this. I have lost my touch," she humbly admitted in the sweetest tone she had heard uttered by her own mouth in years.

"You have lost more than your touch. You have lost your way, Norah."

Inquisitor. Norah. He knows I hate when he does not call me Mother.

In sincere remorse, she pleaded, aware of her unworthiness. "You know I love you. You and Brie."

Aerik acerbically scoffed, "We are tools for your end game. I am sure you do cherish all your little pawns."

It was not often Norah felt defeated in verbal combat. "Aerik, we cannot do this now. My sweet boy, I am eternally sorry, and I do hope I find my way back to you one day, and that you can forgive me," she implored tenderly. "I know I am undeserving."

She detected a tear swelling in her boy's eye, and his chin quivered when he kept to his intractability. "I have said my goodbyes, Mother. I have to go."

At least I received a "Mother" this time. Perhaps there is hope. "Aerik, just please promise me this. These paladins and veritans. Our king and queen, and Az'Dayne as a whole." Norah took a deep breath and shook her head, hoping he would listen to her advice. "Something is not right. I can see and feel it in my soul."

Aerik raised an eyebrow cynically. "For once, I think I may know more than you. But it is a little late for me now, and I am sworn to silence. You would be wise to follow after Ebrielle and leave this place."

Norah ignored her son's absurd advice to leave her position in Frostdale. "Sworn to silence? My son, since when did that stop me from learning what I want to know?" She insinuated her famed reputation and title, attempting a joke, but was clearly terrible at it.

Aerik just stared sadly toward the southern road. His tone was hushed and somber, his eyes never looking at her. "I fear I will never see the north again. And I think you should soon consider the same. Know that I do love you still, Mother."

And Aerik left that as his goodbye as he trotted away to merge with his faction, cantering past the growing rally. The last image of her son fused with the fade of armor ahead, galloping south for Az'Dayne, likely never to return to Barredom. *But I did not say goodbye ...*

She thought she might choke. Her breath was lost between her throat and her lungs. Her face felt red with fire, and her cheeks tightened as if she would turn to stone in a spit. The tears were there, building up inside her, unable to pour out. An overflow of emotion was preparing to combust within her.

She quickly pulled her veil back up to mask her detectable weakness. And that was it. It was over as fast as it had come. Her dark eyes returned to cold hollows of no sentiment. She allowed her face to petrify back into the sinister but regal version she was renowned for. And the morning ride carried on into the midday peak.

Norah had done this march half a hundred times. The public qindrid executions were a revered affair for the common folk. The grandeur of Mount Merridan consumed the attention of all as the judgment procession neared its destination.

Upon the rocky base of the small mountain, the epochal Hall of Final Light gradually came into view. Its enormous entryway had been erected as if it were built for gods and titans, a place where mortal men were forbidden to trespass. Massive stone blocks formed the frame, individually etched with several pictographs representing the five gods of the elements and the five goddesses of the seasons.

The hall itself was actually an intricate tunnel system through the stunted, conical mountain. The main rise sloped steeply upward, beginning from the mount's western base at the entrance from the road but ending in a spired ridge. The man-made corridors split in two directions, running parallel to each other, as soon as entry into Merridan was made.

A lone rider poised atop his white steed at the hill's entrance into the hall. His face seemed kind but aged beyond his years, weathered with experience. His hair and beard were ash-peppered black, showing signs of his senior years. He had obvious nobility in his veins, evident from his posturing and choice of fine attire.

His exquisite doublet was made of the finest bright green exotic cloths, while his gloves, boots, and even his cape were fashioned of multilayered strange leathers. He was adorned with more gold and emerald trinkets than she had ever witnessed upon a person in her entire life. And his anticipative gold-flecked eyes never left her stare as the vanguard of the parade marched into his vicinity.

The aristocratic stranger eagerly took his steed a few steps forward upon her approach. This foreigner was waiting for her, and she was certain of exactly who he was: the Tairancian she had been anticipating an introduction to. *I thought to meet him in the castle tonight, as our letters arranged.*

"Lord Rook?" Norah tentatively advanced, second-guessing her assumption of his identity.

Fortunately, her intuition proved sound. "Lady Bayn, the Royal Inquisitor. Long yearned!" Lord Rook beamed a disarming grin and bowed from his horse.

Norah returned an invisible smile underneath her veil. "How long have you been made to wait?"

The wealthy Silverlake magnate took his wandering gold eyes from her and peered to the steep slope of Condemnation's Climb, and then back to the confined qindrid behind her. "Oh, my whole life," he whispered distantly, as if under some entrancement spell.

Norah briefly speculated upon his intent and history, scrutinizing her daughter's future husband, as if it would help her gauge his soul for good or bad. "Come, ride with me to the highborn terrace, at the top. We may talk of your bride-to-be outside of letters." She reined her mare to lead forward.

Norah, Lord Rook, High Priest Ichael, and Soro pushed upward onto the hall's slope, known as Condemnation's Climb, while the royal guard encircled the qindrid just behind. The nobility shadowed in tow, while the lesser folk were ushered through the parallel side passages at the hall's base. The highborn and the common people were separated to observe the execution, the former from the summit's terrace, the latter from its nethermost focus of the drop.

Lord Rook snubbed the idea of the essential subject. "I know all I need to know to understand she is what I want. I meet her on the morrow still, no?"

"Absolutely, my lord. We can stall that subject until the pleasantries are in person, then," she reluctantly permitted. "What else interests you?"

Lord Rook looked behind him to the ten Aggedonians. "Why, them."

Norah matched his study of the shackled greyborne and stoneborne, paying less attention, as if they were just any random mix of the common-sight foe for her. She sighed. "Ah, yes. You wrote that you have always wanted to see the qin. May I present to you your first? These were Aggedo—"

Lord Rook interrupted. "They are not my first qindrid to see. They are simply the only greyborne and stoneborne I have ever seen."

"Oh?" She was a bit bemused in her regional demographics. "They have skyborne that have come through Tairancia and Az'Dayne? Where did you see them?" Norah only knew of qindrid in Aggedon and the northeastern countries, but never on the mainlands south of Barredom.

"I have never seen skyborne either," he replied.

"I do not understand your implication, I suppose. Qindrid come in three forms: both the skyborne and the stoneborne, and then the greyborne, if they are born of the qindrid breed that have lost both their umbran makers," Norah clarified. "I would be happy to educate you on the histories and culture if you so wish."

The lord of the Silverlakes considered the royal guard for a good moment, exempting from his gaze the captives. He nodded away, returning his eyes to Norah. "I do not understand, either. But it is real."

Does he see what I sense? Everything and everyone is off. Just as Smiles spoke of. Norah kept her inner assumptions to herself to hear what the archon would admit to. "What is that?"

"It is real that what I see around me is sometimes unreal," Lord Rook obscurely elaborated in a low voice. "Az'Dayne. Khalimia. Psaegora. Tairancia. And now Barredom. People are not who they seem to be."

Lord Haelyn Rook glared curiously upon one random sentry of the royal guard. He kept his eyes on him, even when Norah implored, "Enlighten me. I, too, feel this."

"Here is not the place," Lord Rook quietly warned. The elder aristocrat shot a suspicious glance at the noblemen behind the guard, and the ritual priest, Ichael, beside them. "Elsewhere, this evening, far away from any others. I will tell you all I know," he promised.

Norah was intrigued, keen to quicken the day's end and finish the sacrificial executions. "Indeed, please," she entreated in a soft tone, veering in her own certainties about every living entity near her.

Norah and Lord Rook finished the rest of the climb engaged in more pleasant banter over the vast differences between Barredom and Tairancia. The morbid topic of lost loved ones was exchanged briefly in shared sympathies just before the group arrived at the next plateaued tier of the colossal hall.

The royal guard conducted Lord Haelyn Rook and the other nobles through the side galleries that led to the spectator balconies, known as the highborn terrace. Norah was left alone with just the prisoners, Ichael, Soro, and the armored escort. She looked behind her and peered down the great Hall of Final Light. Condemnation's Climb was trimmed with hundreds of flaming lanterns down to the base—the last light the doomed at hand ever would see.

The procession continued on a short distance higher until the summit's end was met at an open stone-brick cliff. The group stood atop the eastern side of the small mountain, looking down the precipice.

Ten stalls served as designated guideways for the incarcerated qindrid. Between the fifth and sixth stall, a bedecked plank protruded over the vertical ridge. The escarpment below was efficiently carved out in a rectangular formation from the peak to the base. The highborn terrace loomed underneath, functioning as a balcony stadium for the privileged to witness close at hand the sermon of the high priest, while the lowest terrace was reserved for the commoners to directly participate in the activities of the macabre ceremony.

The royal guard diligently placed all ten qindrid in their individual stalls. Leg braces with shackled attachments on the thigh and calf were fastened to long black chains. Each Aggedonian was strapped in before the sacrificial rites could officially commence.

High Priest Ichael approached the ritual bridge overlooking the drop when the procedure was finished, and the royal guard returned to their delegated stations.

Norah stood firm on her high steed with an emotionless visage over the ill-fated. She vainly attempted to ignore the sight of Soro perched atop his horse, adjacent to her own in a symmetrical distance from each other in formation with Ichael. He was the only other member of the Frostdale Council permitted on the judgment terrace, and not present on the royal terrace with the others, among them the king and queen. It was the only time she had ever shared these sacred rites of damnation with another from the council, and she did not like it. She refused to allow the unwelcome wretch the pleasure of taking note that she registered his presence at all.

Her dark eyes sought out the fading fiery sphere burrowing into the horizon of the grey dusk that enveloped the bluff. As the sun descended, so did her gaze, down to the royal terrace, one tier below their own and across the chasm from the highborn terrace.

There sat King Aerik Roth and Queen Annison Roth on their stone thrones built into the royals' embellished balcony, with the Frostdale Council positioned in raised seats behind them. In front of them stood the imperial dominarchs, Vaximus Az'Ampion next to King Aerik, and Sriyah Hazhalah next to Queen Annison. The Az'Dayne Dominadom's high rulers leaned over the suspended terrace's rails and eagerly awaited commencement of the ritual. The day marked the first in history that any dominarchs had ever attended the Barredish executions at the Hall of Final Light.

Finally Norah peered to the bottommost visible region of the cylindrical death pit. Most of the limbo was meticulously carved into deep nothingness. Just even with the common terrace was the only level ground, with a substantial jut of rock left unmined yet excavated into a shallow gorge filled with fresh water. The prominent, grit-filled pond stood as the finality in the sacrificial execution of the last qindrid prisoners.

Each prisoner would suffer the wrath of the deities of the Five and Five at the hands of the country's highborn and lowborn alike and would be entwined in pairs for their similar fates. The innermost qindrid to Ichael's half bridge would find their doom with the tairan god and the goddess of the season of the Dawning, which they were now in. Outward, next to them, the two qindrid would be brought to justice by the god of fire and the goddess of the approaching Sunder season. Following, those in the middle would come to pay their respects to the god of the sky and the goddess of the Reaping months. Approaching the end, the god of shadow and goddess of the Umbra would get their sacrifice, just before the conclusion of the judgments with the persecution for those intended as an offering for the god of all water and the goddess of the cruel Torrent season.

Ichael stood over the plank-bridge, facing the chained qindrid, as he began their final rites in a small prayer to each god and goddess, asking the Five and Five to bless the citizens and soldiers of Barredom for the sacrifice of these heretics offered unto them.

The white-bearded old priest called out to the first god in the pantheon, the Lord of the Land, of all things tairan in element. Two guards stood near an intricate winch mechanism with a release wheel that connected to all ten chains strapped to the prisoners' lower bodies. As Ichael shouted reverences to the deity, the zealous patricians on the terrace of highborn followed in an outcry back to condemn the Aggedonian. When the ritual passage concluded, an acolyte pulled the lever on the first stall, and instantly the stoneborne fell through the retracted floor.

With only his lower body shackled to the bindings, the Aggedonian whipped to a halt and spun upside down to suspend him evenly between the terraces of the highborn and the royals. They gave the doomed qin a chance to vent his godless curses in his Norspeak tongue before Ichael gave the signal. The high priest dropped a lone rock down the vertical bluff to disappear into the darkness beyond, as far as sight could see.

As if they had all taken part in this execution rite a dozen times before, as many of them had, the Barredish aristocrats on the high-born terrace acted on cue. Each were prearmed with similar small rocks of their own. They released them in no particular order of violent chaos aimed to stone down the helpless target. Many more than half of the rocks missed their mark, but several connected all about his body and head. Grunts of pain echoed out from the qin, but he was stoneborne, with his skin naturally hardened to resist such bludgeoning attacks.

The priest allowed the nobles their fun until they tired of it, but as the rock pile was depleted, Ichael motioned to the guard at the winch. The stoneborne's chain was dropped to rapidly descend him into the stone floor at the bottom, breaking his neck with a swift crack.

The dead qindrid was then withdrawn back to the stall, where the guardsmen could undo the chains, and the corpse was discarded over the ledge to vanish into the blackness of the seemingly endless pit.

High Priest Ichael shifted to his next sacrifice in a prayer to the Lady of the Dawning, the goddess of the first season, which they were now in. The one marked for death was a greyborne. His stall was opposite that of the stoneborne that had just perished, nearest to the plank-bridge. The veneration continued, ending with the floor being retracted the same.

This chain's length, however, descended all the way to the common terrace. After Ichael gestured with his drop of the stone, it was the common folk's turn to contribute to the executions. The commoners made short work of the greyborne, as his skin wasn't naturally armored, like the stoneborne's, and their numbers were doubled, along with their sheer enmity.

Soro audaciously moved his horse directly to the other side of Norah's, just before Ichael began the third qindrid's execution. *You cannot move from your position during the judgments, you amateur.* She paid him zero regard, pretending he was a phantom that did not exist.

Ichael gave his blessings to the Lord of Fire next. The stoneborne two stalls from the right of the bridge was addressed during the priest's oration. The lower half of the qindrid's body was enveloped in a black, tar-like substance. As the stoneborne's hatch was released and his chain flung him down to the highborn level again, Ichael sequentially followed by tossing a lit torch down into the abyss.

The noblemen and women were prompted to the next choice of weapon granted to their condemning hands. A hundred fiery balls of pitch-dipped cloth were hurled over the ledge to aim at the pendulous captive. Only one needed to connect, but several did instead.

As the stoneborne wailed through his ear-splitting, agonizing fate, Soro took the diversion as a prospective moment to annoy her with the most bizarre remark. "Your daughter is quite the opportunist, you know? Bold and intelligent. You might be wise to reconsider pledging her off to a southern marriage so soon."

Fuck the Fives, is this impudent fool speaking during the judgments for? Norah looked around incredulously at the guardsmen, the acolytes, then High Priest Ichael, as if pleading for someone to strangle the source of her irritation on the spot, but none were paying attention to anything but the rites. *I have nothing to say to this jade-eyed outlander.*

The fourth qindrid was dropped as Ichael finished his worship sermon to the Lady of the Sunder, goddess of the second season. As the greyborne descended to the common terrace to receive the same incendiary punishment as the stoneborne before, and his death screams began, Soro spoke up again.

"As it turns out, she has the Axes of the Sons in her possession now. She plans to exploit a great secret that only she and I know of. Someone that yet lives, that all believed dead. Something that changes everything."

If her glare could cast fire and combust the head of the chancellor into a torch, she swore she would pray to the Lord of Fire aloud in the middle of the rites right then. But her dark eyes just carved into his strange green orbs and allowed the provoker to elaborate as she maintained her respects to the hallowed judgments.

"He was never slain by Jrulthun. You know of whom I speak," the chancellor whispered.

"Absurd," she spat back, rolling her skeptical eyes. "How could you possibly deduce this? And if so, why have you done nothing of it and told me only now?"

The next stoneborne was sermonized in piety shown for the Lord of the Sky. The doomed Aggedonian kept his gaze to the stone across the chasm, with his clear, gemlike eyes wide in silent prayer to his umbran maker.

High Chancellor Soro smirked at her as if she were some despised peer he had replaced and he had won some game of long-feuded competition. Keeping his tone low, he hushed, "Why, I did not need to tell you. I promoted Ebrielle to Surrogate Inquisitor. And oh, I discovered this quite some time ago but just needed the right time to execute it for my own sublime purposes, you see? Everything is falling into place, Norah, former inquisitor."

This is no game we play now, fool. This is my daughter's fate you gamble with, bringing her into your scheming. She felt so betrayed by her own blood. She wanted to scream over the whole judgment terrace to stop the ceremony entirely. Whatever was going on with Ichael and the sequence of the rites in front of her no longer mattered. She could only see her true enemy in front of her now. And his name was Soro. "You go too far with your threats. This is not the place. Be quick with this farce, and tell me who, then."

Soro was equipped to prolong toying with her swelling rage. *How could Brie be so daft as to trust this fiend?* The chancellor came out with it. "Smiles."

She knew that name would haunt her. And it all made sense to her that it could be that specific troll if there was any merit to Soro's horrific inferences.

"He is Khomo'Jhuvonus in the flesh." He muttered the forbidden name as if he held no fear toward the popular superstition. "He is very much alive and well."

Her heart hung in her throat, and she couldn't have uttered a word even if she had wanted to. A score of scenarios flashed through her head of all that allegation implied, that the archnemesis of Barredom was still in the secured custody of the Forlorn. She had every noteworthy troll adversary she could unravel in her grasp. *But Ebrielle …*

Soro audibly finished her pending dread for her. "Your daughter has been instructed to bring the Glace Isles king up from the Forlorn for extraction into Warden BrKaim's private chambers. There, they will test the axes to see if they are indeed those of legend, as he was known to be the only one to carry them. Your daughter has been a good little pet and will be duly rewarded when this is seen through."

He smugly grinned.

What have you done, Soro? Her visage no longer even held hostility, only grave fear of the many consequences that would likely occur if his little political ploy went awry in the troll's favor.

"If you hurry, Norah, you may be able to stop her, if all of this displeases you."

He didn't need to taunt her any longer. Her mare had already turned in a fervent race back to the Frostdale Deeps. She would accept the repercussions that would certainly ensue from her insult to the king for the premature departure, but Norah's intent obsessed over a single focus. *Khomo'Jhuvonus dies tonight.*

EBRIELLE (VI)

SURROGATE SURMISE

The final doors to the topmost tier of the Forlorn's winch lift were in sight. The warden fumbled with his keys to unlock the barred gate to the corridor that would be the final stretch. He sighed and shook his head in doubt, holding on to the document Ebrielle had presented to him, signed and sealed by High Chancellor Soro. The warden had taken the bait.

But that didn't mean he liked it. Warden BrKaim, with his mass escort of armed prison sentries, stood in front of the gate to face her. He narrowed his eyes, gripping tightly at the scroll. "Are you certain you did not misinterpret the High Chancellor?"

Ebrielle remained confident in her ploy and looked at the warden incredulously. "Even the Royal Inquisitor would know not to question the final voice of all law in Barredom, Warden. This is Soro's command, sanctioned by our very king."

He wasn't quite satisfied, regardless of the sealed letter. But he had brought her this far. She knew his stalling was only for his own conscience but wouldn't hold any weight toward denying her wishes. Ebrielle pushed past the hesitant prison master.

"It just seems that for something so critical, the Royal Inquisitor or High Chancellor, or even King Aerik himself, would deal with it personally." BrKaim trailed after her, pleading some logic.

"Personally and immediately," she concurred. "That is why they want him prepared for their arrival after the judgments. Instructions lead me to believe they will be here at any moment once the rites conclude," she lied, squeezing her palms around the thin leather bundle in her arms. She could feel the shape of the three legendary weapons, from blade to haft, even through the hide that protected her against the bloodrime poison. "The High Chancellor and my mother have agreed not to involve the king in an audience in the Deeps if such an implausible incrimination is not beforehand proved. That is where you and the dungeon guard come in."

Warden BrKaim rushed to regain his lead. He held out his arm in front of her, halfway down the corridor to the lift, hindering her gait once again. "Lady Ebrielle. May I speak candidly, with no discontent toward the High Chancellor's written command?"

Ebrielle squinted at the door, more annoyed than nervous about his tenacious impudence. She stripped him of the scroll. "You have already broken the seal, but perhaps you need be reminded to read properly—or maybe reminded of your lower station, Warden."

Ebrielle began reading the memorized scroll aloud even as BrKaim reopened it.

"'Through diligence and research, a most dire discovery has been brought to light. The Glace Isles king is in our custody in the Forlorn. His death was a ruse staged by his tribesven during General Roth's capture of the umbran. This enemy will be tried immediately after the qindrid judgments at the Hall of Final Light. Only the privy of the Frostdale Council have been made aware of his distinction.'

"'By the power vested in me, I invoke you, Lady Ebrielle Blackendale, as official Surrogate Inquisitor, to govern this on King Aerik's command. The living khomo is to be individually detained in the high cells, and the three Axes of the Sons are to be brought before him to validate his incrimination as the sovereign nemesis of Barredom.'"

Ebrielle pompously performed as she had witnessed her mother doing so often. "Signed by High Chancellor Soro of the Qaegons," she concluded arrogantly.

Warden BrKaim dryly grinned. "I did read it, Surrogate. We are to bring the alleged to the high cells outside my chamber and then present the relics before him. It says nothing of jeopardizing the safety of the one daughter of the Royal Inquisitor by allowing her into the Forlorn. Perhaps it is you that misinterprets your empowerment." He jabbed her with a rather condescending yet compelling rational debate. "I only exist for the ultimate security of the Deeps."

Ebrielle was not allowing the warden to take away her glory. She needed to fulfill this task she had committed to, attesting to her mother that she was more than just some rich nobleman's brood vessel. All the apprehension she had formerly had in confronting Khomo'Jhuvonus faded in the moment of her aggravation toward BrKaim's determined reluctance to let her pass, as her letter implied she was permitted to do. She would be respected. "You need my privy eyes to point out the accused, Warden."

Ebrielle stood in front of the door to the lift. Her nerves shook through her skin and teeth, causing a consistent shudder she could barely manage to mask. Her hands were clammy with an abundance of sweat, and her courage was rapidly diminishing. But she was almost there. She wasn't going to give the warden the satisfaction of detecting any weakness in her fortitude. She would follow through with her mission.

"Dungeon guard of the Frostdale Deeps!" *There must be almost one hundred of you*, she estimated through an impromptu count. "Your Surrogate Inquisitor dictates you open the door and prepare the lift for prisoner extraction." She sounded as close to the spawn of her mother as she ever had.

The door sentries behaved as bidden with no hesitation. Warden BrKaim stood beside her, his former stern look becoming softer, almost pleading. "Lady Ebrielle. I beseech you to simply step onto the bridge and indicate to me who the alleged is. After his detainment, you can await safely in my chamber."

Even though she had already inadvertently met the legendary monster and conversed with him face-to-face, Ebrielle well knew that this new introduction was about to be different. BrKaim's cautionary insight seemed wiser as each second passed. She took her first step out onto the ledge before the lift and then looked back at the warden, nodding her consent to his request.

Ebrielle walked out to the middle of the bridge, ever tentatively, terrified to inspect and see her childhood nightmare staring back at her. She closed her eyes, took a deep breath, and finally opened them with an exhalation and a searching gaze into the below.

The cylindrical dungeon of the Forlorn had a roof not high above Ebrielle's head, level with the ground that the Frostdale Deeps were based beneath. Two winch lifts had been constructed at different tiers in the dungeon: one near the base entrance to the Deeps, and the second on the opposite side, further down, with a ledge and door leading to the qindrid cells.

The Forlorn had been built vastly deep, comparable to an immeasurable well. Below the prisoner crossway, the bricked pit evolved into a cavernous abyss that led to nothing but a sharp demise of jagged rock at the bottom. The nethermost region, far below Frostdale, was known to end near a cistern of water that filtered in from the Otticus River, leading all the way under the Gahoanan Mountains and into the Bay of Trolls.

Echoes from the slightest of sounds reverberated throughout the vertical dungeon, as if any noisemaker were within direct proximity. She could hear the trolls shuffling and mumbling far beneath her; they may as well have been on the bridge, holding her hand.

Ebrielle examined the pile of congregated elven, all uncomfortably accrued in a small throng toward the far end of the crisscross-patterned footpath below. Many seemed cloistered below others, as if to hide their malignant intent. It seemed entirely irregular behavior, and questionably suspicious.

"Why are these trolls amassed in that corner? Has no guard thought this suspect enough to raise alarm to your captains?" she challenged fretfully, still searching for her fated adversary.

"I am the captain of the Forlorn, Surrogate. And these fiends have been at this behavior for three days. We have been instructed not to inspect below until the Royal Inquisitor has returned," a handsome, middle-aged prison officer declared. She still was not used to being referred to as an inquisitor herself by right.

One elvan emerged from the huddled horde, his blond hair spiked tall only down the middle to the back of his head, and shaved on all sides. It was as if he had anticipated the exact day of his disclosure and transformed his style back to the identifiable portrayal he was renowned for. *Smiles.* It was *him*—the Glace Isles king. *You are being entirely too confident and considerate, aren't you?*

He grinned at her, raising his hands innocuously away from his body, with his palms faced toward her. He stepped away from the assemblage and over to the ledge platform, awaiting his invitation to the top.

"Is this our accused, Surrogate?" Warden BrKaim asked with loathing thick in his tone.

Ebrielle closed her eyes once again, taking a deeper breath than before. When she reopened them, they were fueled with fury, with all fear buried behind her lifetime of inherited hate. "His name is Khomo'Jhuvonus."

"Drop the lift!" BrKaim shouted. "Troll, prepare for extract!"

The Forlorn captain signaled to the winch sentry, and the lift was lowered all the way to the checkered promenade of elvan prisoners. It seized its extension at the ledge in front of the indicted Chosen Troll.

Khomo'Jhuvonus stepped forth willingly. He maintained his perpetual stare and smirk at Ebrielle. The Chosen Troll's stance, with his innocently extended arms, never wavered as the chain to the lift wrapped around the winch system, hoisting the kingdom's archrival to her stage at the bridge.

She felt she would break from his overly smug leer at any second, but she had to hold strong to her fearless facade. Crossbowmen armed with sleep-poison bolts, specifically made for trolls, poised for the condemned elvan to come into range for command to put down. He was less than halfway up, but it felt like an eternity had passed in intolerable anticipation.

Something stole her attention below the lift, in the mysterious huddle on the stone crossway. The trolls all began to rapidly separate. One held a Terollar-crafted longbow, already nocked with an arrow for release.

The crossbowmen saw the ploy too late. One took an exceptionally large arrow through the chest, reeling dead over the bridge into the darkness of the gorge.

"Lady Ebrielle, leave now!" the warden screamed in dire entreaty.

More trolls began producing hidden bows, spears, throwing axes, and even melee weaponry. Some could now be seen with climbing spikes attached to their feet and hands. The enemies' bows were aimed and loosed in efficient, premeditated unison. Even with the elevation disadvantage, those with bows did not miss.

Several guardsmen fell to the unexpected arrows. "Sound the bells! Put every troll down!" BrKaim cried out for reinforcements with a return volley of his own, fiercely grabbing her shoulder, imploring her to retreat. The fear in his eyes was deeper than that of his squealing voice. "Call in the city watch!"

Ebrielle was petrified in a stupor of despair. Her mind had told her to flee even before the warden begged her, but her feet betrayed her. She couldn't take her mesmerized gape from him. Her impending doom.

His arms rose higher out from his sides. His confident smile was entirely charismatic, yet simultaneously intimidating. This was a seasoned architect in scheming that never erred and played everyone in his malevolent game.

The bundle of bloodrime weapons in her grasp began to quiver out of her control. The Axes of the Sons were acting as if they had a sentient yearning to return to their master. The weak leather wrap that contained them was becoming loose, and she was losing control. *But he promised he would not kill me ...*

She had never been subject to such imminent danger before, nor any real magnitude of duplicity. Even when Warden BrKaim's last words—"Lady Ebrielle, go now!"—shrieked in his hoarse voice, she still found her body frozen to fate's ultimate design.

Fear had left her. It all dissolved into a fusion of curiosity. She tried to turn to sprint, to warn, to live. She wanted to cry, to pray, to beg. She struggled against all broken will to at least ask the devil closing in if he had any honor toward his word of intending her no harm.

Ebrielle had no idea how they all could have managed to obtain weapons and climbing spikes to begin with. These were the same trolls that were originally detained in the Forlorn, with no hint of reinforcement from any outside help. Any troll who was hit by a bolt freely jumped into a suicide jaunt from the ledge, vanishing into the depths of the black void.

She could no longer hear the warden's screams. The chaos had overtaken her senses. She dared to hope even when nearly every last guard on the bridge had fallen to troll arrows.

Only a decem dungeon guards could manage at a time at the opening of the Forlorn, while the remaining were stuck shoving through the corridor prior, ruining their advantage. Ebrielle again dared to hope when the Forlorn captain dropped dead right before her. She trembled violently, nearly fainting as she watched BrKaim fall lifeless into the pit, crashing awkwardly onto the troll-filled ledges.

She dared to hope even when the three axes magically flew from her clutch to return to the grip of their rightful owner.

WESTWALKER (VII)

TWO-TOWNS

Eight horses lingered in a line at the southern fringe of the Thurowood. Each sled was harnessed behind the steeds, with a surplus of blast-salt kegs secured on them, blanketed in hide tarpaulins to veil the contents for an inconspicuous approach. All except for his, which was filled with imitation platinum ore for the ploy at hand.

Tsuno studied the saddled mercenaries beside him. Each man was now adorned with full Aggedonian garb, their faces concealed by boiled-leather helms, with their little exposed skin doused in ash paint to guise them as stoneborne. Their attire was the same as that of Tsuno's most recent qindrid victims, other than the upgrade of shortbows and small quivers across their backs. Their arrows were equipped with resin-soaked tow tied just below the head to provide prompt incendiary igniters. He had come to learn that six of the seven men Tristostopher had assigned to him were capable archers. The last was the man behind the powder's alchemy, Jonan Riveiros.

Tsuno poised upon a Utamian-bred horse. It was the first time he had mounted a steed other than Nho in decades. An incidental pang of guilt washed over him, as if he were betraying a lifetime friend with the act.

He looked back to Nho's melancholic stare at the tree line. Tsuno couldn't risk the mythical beast in the impending perils. His horse had as much renown as he did and would be recognized at first sight by any watcher on a tower, due to his famous long blond mane and the feathering around his hooves, as well as the notable black-and-white piebald pattern across his sheeny hide. And all that could be picked up by simple scrutiny from a distance, as the green glow in his eyes gave light to the telltale signs that he was no normal horse. Nho was what was known as an animayan, which was the outcome of another avenue certain elvan races could take when committing to the Taboo.

The elvan races of pure elemental descendancy were not subject to the persuasion or capacities of the Taboo, since they were unwavering entities of the true Balance. These stood as the Sylvanil of the tairan, the Ibyssai of the fire, the Shirenar of the sky, the Dendrar of the shadow, and the Oceanil of the water. However, each elvan race of the sublineages could enact the forbidden practices of the Taboo in a specific eligible path, depending on the elemental descendancy.

Those of mixed shadow descendancy could engage in the Taboo to become umbran. These included the Shiniryn and the Wyldenar, who were well recognized as having capitalized on such forbidden practices. The Neveril and the Lunaril were also theoretically candidates for such, but the occurrence was unreported.

Another path of the Taboo was the Animayan Transfusion. The act of becoming an animayan was a dual process of suicide for the elvan, and reincarnation. The elvan could self-sever their hunder, their wisp-like soul, leaving their mortal body to become nothing more than a dead husk, and could then possess any young beast, within a cycle of age, so long as the animal matched with their own descendancy. The elvan then lived symbiotically in the mind of the beast, with the elvan's soul interdependently transfused. By doing such, the animal would live exponentially longer than the norm for its species, and while it still held thoughts and actions of its own, the hunder of the dead elvan maintained its former life's memories and mental aptitude. As years passed, however, the hunder inside would eventually fade in its ability to produce such prior means of reasoning, and it would simply find itself in a state of peaceful nothingness within the creature's psyche toward the end of its life.

Tsuno remembered the day he had come across the Terollar Nhoenathor, and the melancholic state of depression he had been in over the fate of his raped and murdered lifemate. Tsuno had only known the elvan in the flesh for three days before Nhoenathor committed to the choice of Animayan Transfusion. Little did Tsuno know at the time that those few days were only the prologue of the next thirty-eight years they would spend as inseparable. Conjuring the details of that early introduction was a mental detour he could not afford to embark on in the present moment. Focus on the daunting task before them was eminently needed.

Tsuno gazed back at Nho, knowing the supernatural being could still comprehend the empathetic bond they had shared for so long. The animayan bobbed its head back and reluctantly retreated into the safety of the forest. *Don't go far, friend. We will reunite shortly.*

Tsuno adjusted the fur blanket lying over his lap, obscuring his recognizable wraithwood repeater bow, and checked his cloak to ensure his two handheld crossbows were concealed as well. He moved his arms in a circle, testing his flexibility, unused to the qindrid leather armor he had been costumed in.

He peered across the open field that served as a short expanse between the Thurowood and the gates of Two-Towns, and to the fortified Great Grey Wall to the immediate east. The wall had two prominent guard towers to pass in the field between, and atop the battlements of the city itself, he spied at least three more archer towers, not including those of the barbican over the main gates.

This is suicide ... "It is time," Tsuno said aloud. He placed Landron's helm on his head and nodded to the brave men next to him. "You all know your places and my signals," he reminded them.

Tsuno turned around to his own sled as Ryleohk climbed under the tarpaulin against the mound of pseudoplatinum at the rear of the sled. He was painted in dried blood across his neck and chest as a deception of a corpse, in case he was discovered. "Ryleohk," Tsuno started, "don't do anything—" he paused for a moment to think of how to describe his uncertainties "—you would ever normally do."

Ryleohk's surly grumble came from under the cover upon such advice, and Tsuno forced himself satisfied with that reply, spurring his new mount into a slow gait, leaving the defense of the Thurowood behind.

The powder specialist, Jonan, hurried to bring his horse beside Tsuno's. "If they send an escort out to meet us before we reach the gates ..." Jonan stammered nervously, second-guessing their strategy.

"Then we stick to the plan. You all remain silent. I speak. If that fails, we all rush the mine for detonation and cover. And most of us die," Tsuno finished bluntly. "We already covered this. It's a probable outcome," he wasn't hesitant to admit.

It wasn't enough. They had spent the last pentday going over every detail and bolstering each other's resolve against the futile possibility of success without casualty, yet now these seven Boarneck mercenaries were suddenly infected with the worst disease that could be wrought upon a man before a battle: fear.

"Everyone in?" he asked for his own assurance that no one was about to recoil from the plan. *Surely Tristose didn't send me cowards for the main breach of the gates.* "Do not forget to address me by Landron only. Now, say your stoneborne names to me, and we move out."

And one by one, beginning with Jonan, the qindrid-guised mercenaries all spoke their names from Landron's Lilealyte hunting party, from what Tsuno remembered from his study on them before he and Ryleohk had baited them under their counterambush.

"Michayle."

"Aldor."

"Timance."

"Eredis."

"Brom."

"Thuros."

"Yalen."

"No one speaks now but me," Tsuno commanded. And the eight sled-bearing horses commenced across the open snowy meadow.

This was not how Tsuno operated. The Westwalker brought his enemies into his traps. He did not bring his traps to his enemies. Every few minutes passing felt like an hour. They had barely moved.

The group was passing the first guard tower of the Great Grey Wall. He hoped the safe distance was just close enough to allow the greyborne sentries to spot their qindrid disguise, but far enough to safeguard them from any scrutiny of flaws in their ruse.

Five curious archers made their way to the crenellations of the tower's peak. Tsuno waved a known salute the Aggedonian soldiers used and was relieved to see the gesture returned to him promptly with respect by the sentries. He was uniformed in Landron's signature bounty-hunter garb, which obliged extreme esteem among the militia.

If they recognized him as Landron Thalbear, he knew he had their attention. Landron had almost as much prestige as the clan magnans themselves. He was reputed throughout western Aggedon to be an appointed professional for tracking down and removing problem targets with his small group, similar to how Northaven had used Tsuno as a subterfuge specialist.

The group gradually closed the distance between the first tower and the second. The horses marched in single file with the sleds in tow. The men behind him all did as bidden in required silence to fulfill the mission.

As they approached the last tower, five archers again appeared. One greyborne soldier rushed to the large bell hanging from the open parapet.

Don't do it. An archer seen wearing decorative spaulders, unlike the others, stepped between the nearest battlement for closer investigation of the intruders in the field below him. He shouted in the expected Norspeak Tsuno was well fluent in. "*Identify yourself!*"

Tsuno refrained from looking back at his command of men, conscious that they would misread it as a gesture of doubt. Instead, he stood proud with the same salute he had given the first tower. He shouted back in Norspeak, "*Landron Thalbear, Lilealyte and first hunter of Magnan Vaktus Thalbear, who has joined the Great Exodus!*"

The one sentry did not relent from his station near the bell, awaiting his officer's response. The tower officer finally did return the salute after a valid pause for inspection. "*Welcome back, then, Landron! Two-Towns offers you respite! What have we with you?*"

Tsuno could see the archers above, curiously ogling what spoils lay beneath the sled tarpaulins. This was a foreseen obstacle to overcome in the conscious strategy playing out. "*Ambush on a half score of Dish! Mining crew from Northaven! Sleds full of platinum ore to bring into the mine!*" He referred to the Barredish by the slang term used by Aggedonians. "*I would see Magnan Orlrick or Magnan Winthar if available inside, to discuss the ore and discovery of a new mine!*"

He was well refined on the political geography of which magnans ruled over specific Aggedonian regions or towns. He knew that even if one of the overlords of Two-Towns was available for an audience, they would likely make him wait hours for contact over something as trivial as extra ore during such a time of pending war. He just needed to be allowed inside the mine.

Take the bait. "*Good hunt! See you on the inside!*" the lead watchman shouted back with a final salute and threw a gesture to an underling to give notice to the barbican over the main gate.

The ordered archer ran up a short, winding flight of hidden steps to reach the tower's roof and began waving a blazing two-torch staff in the direction of the overseers of the gates of Two-Towns. The enormous wooden gate followed with a booming crack at being unbarred for opening to the homecoming party.

"That went smoothly," Jonan whispered, positioned directly behind Tsuno.

The skyborne didn't need to turn around to throw his voice behind him, ensuring his words carried to the ears of each man. "Stay with the plan" was all he warned.

Things were going smoothly. Too smoothly. They were nearing the main gates, already open for their explosive entrance. All they had to do was reach under the barbican's mining entrenchment and release the sleds. Probably two or three sleds' worth would do the trick to collapse the gate towers into rubble, according to Jonan's reckonings of the blast salt's potential.

The mine's entrance. I can hit each atop the towers and barbican from here. His sureness was more of a deterrent to his anxiety over the fact that they were also without the advantage of elevation and far outnumbered. And just then the scenario worsened as three greyborne guards approached from the city's entry. *Fuck the skies.* He blasphemed his very core descendancy's element.

"The escort party. Now what, Westwalker?" Jonan spluttered behind him, with downright terror thick in his quaking tone.

This time Tsuno did retort back to his lackey. "Do not call me that. Wait," he demanded sharply.

The imminent greeters trekked across the shallow snow with a fervent but amiable bearing. The one in the lead threw them a friendly wave and shouted something lost on the artless winds of the narrow valley. Fortunately, being skyborne, Tsuno could utilize his impower to discern the name being called as if no wind at all prevailed across the prairie vale.

The greyborne in the lead hollered a reception once again. "*Timance!*" The innocent Aggedonian beamed with a wide smile as if he intended to be reunited with a long-lost friend. *Fuck the skies ...*

The mercenary guised as Timance, Landron's lead archer, looked nervously to Tsuno for an expedited salvation from their looming dilemma. "What do I say?"

Even then, Tsuno could not offer an intelligent solution for his misfortune. The escort soldier came once more in his Norspeak tongue, more ardently expectant for a reply. *"Timance! It's Ermond, your cousin!"*

Even though Timance had been a stoneborne, it was possible for him to have a greyborne cousin. If both umbran lifemates died, then all of the specific qindrid they had turned would descend from their elemental abilities into a state of what was referred to as severed. They could again reproduce, as when they had been human, with other severed qindrid or greyborne. It was not unlikely that a sibling of Timance's parents was one of the severed or greyborne.

The Boarneck archer pleaded, "Westwalker. What is he saying?"

"Stop with the name. Lift your bow as a salute to him. He is your cousin," Tsuno hastily explained, gaining swift doubt in this daft group of foreigners he had been forced to die beside.

The Timance pretender did as bidden, being the only one with a true longbow for sake of the bounty archer's guise, obliging the qindrid to hold his arms out as if he meant for his cousin to dismount and embrace him.

Tsuno had to act on his authority quickly. *"You may reunite with blood once we are inside the mine. It has been a long ride, and we are ready to discard our tow,"* Tsuno shouted demandingly in a deep-toned Norspeak dialect. It sounded like a fair but harsh term, he realized, but he hoped the guardsmen accepted it.

The greyborne did not look pleased by such a precondition. To Tsuno's dismay, Ermond audaciously advanced against his authoritative behest. *This is going to end badly.* Tsuno had to keep Ermond's focus away from the one he believed was Timance.

"What have we here?" Ermond pestered, moving dangerously closer, now pointing at the intentional peek of the platinum facade on Tsuno's sled.

Ryleohk growled low, and Tsuno's eyes instantly shot the hidden elvan a cold warning, as if he could shut him up with a penetrating glare. *"I need you to notify the magnans of our return, for an audience about this bounty."*

Still the impudent greyborne didn't concede. He only yielded his pace forward and ventured a disgruntled grimace at the one he thought was Landron. Then he turned his gaze on Timance. *"A lot of horses, cousin. Since when do we Aggedonians condone riding these beasts of the Dish?"*

None of these steeds are even Barredom-bred, you ignorant ... Tsuno dismissed his annoyed thoughts and elaborated as arrogantly as he believed Landron might. "*Since First Hunter Landron Thalbear comes bearing these sleds to carry his prized haul. These horses are a gift for the magnans,*" he countered, annoyed.

Ermond shook his head at Timance, as if condemning his cousin for the company he kept. The bold greyborne took a glimpse at the false ore and went to remove the entire tarpaulin from Tsuno's sled, openly revealing the ruse of the dead Wyldenar on the back of the sled.

Ermond and his two guardsmen's eyes went wide in curiosity as they started to approach even closer. But Tsuno spoke first. "*A prize from our hunt. It is who you think it is. Trailing the rogue was how we found the mine. I intend to collect my bounty for him as well.*"

Ermond flanked Tsuno, keeping a cautious distance between him and the horse, appearing to hope for a better view of the sled's contents. He looked back at his fake cousin with a squint of growing suspicion.

"*Enough dallying. Inform the magnans we will await them in the mines. Qin, move out,*" Tsuno commanded.

But Ermond held a hand up in defiance. "*There are just a few issues I have, Landron. One, I don't answer to Lilealytes. If you haven't been made aware, your umbran has been captured by Northaven, it seems. And the rest of your army is long gone to Caelduym, or wherever your Great Exodus stole them to.*"

Does this fool have a death wish for himself?

Ermond persisted in his open doubts. "*Two, I have been ordered to inspect everything, you see.*" Ermond's scrutiny fixated again on the ploy of the dead elvan, and then he looked directly into Tsuno's blue eyes, shuffling nervously for the first time. Tsuno's own hands fidgeted with Wraith underneath the blanket in his lap as Ermond turned to address the greyborne behind him, struggling to maintain complete composure. "*Signal for more of the militia to escort our honored bounty hunter inside.*"

A dreaded familiar noise whistled past Tsuno's ear. The Terollar throwing axe found itself in the middle of Ermond's skull, splitting his face in half.

Fuck the skies ...

Tsuno spun around hard in his saddle, incidentally jerking his mount in confusion. Ryleohk was past everyone in the blink of an eye, even as Tsuno realized the mantle in his lap had fallen to the ground.

Ryleohk seized his axe from Ermond's skull and took it to the nearest greyborne, in the side of the neck, before the next qindrid could react to his doom. The third clansman took flight in a sprint back to the safety of the gates. But he was not as quick as the Wyldenar's axe, which buried itself in his back. Ryleohk had taken out all three qindrid in a matter of seconds.

"*Westwalker!*" A booming accusation came from the side guard tower. The officer turned to pick up a large hammer and reared back to clang it against the tower bell to raise the alarm.

Fuck the cursed skies ... And you are the first to die ...

Tsuno aimed Wraith to release a practiced deadly shot that planted a bolt through the officer's chest.

"To the mine! Now!" Tsuno shouted his desperate order to the Boarnecks behind him. He kicked his horse into full speed with the heavy sled in tow.

The mercenaries all acted on the do-or-die impulse and followed in the wake of the Westwalker's reckless ride. Tsuno caught a peripheral glance at arrows being launched by the remaining archers in the side tower. He turned back to watch one of the Boarneck men being unsaddled by the blow of a shaft plunging through his lungs, falling dead to the snow.

An arrow flew at Ryleohk, stopping right before his feet. The dexterous elvan zigzagged in a nimble pattern back and forth, gliding freely on top of the snowy field as he sprinted in the direction of the tower.

And just then the bell was rung, three dings. More aggressors appeared with curious looks and readied bows in the barbican above the main gate. The men's Aggedonian soldier attire had offered them enough subterfuge to keep the gate sentries hesitant, assessing what all the fuss was about.

Their attention seemed more focused on the obvious enemy in the form of the charging Wyldenar directing his course toward the side tower. Several archers took aim to stop the elvan in his tracks.

Tsuno knew he could easily reach the mine entry in time with the offered distraction of his friend. The archers were completely oblivious to the threat below. He could blow the wall safely, at the high risk of watching his only trusted ally die. Today was not the day Ryleohk would die.

Tsuno pulled hard on the reins, stopping his steed in his tracks, while the other mercenaries rode past him. Tsuno aimed his wraith-wood bow carefully at the barbican's sentries while their attention was diverted by Ryleohk. One of their arrows flew to the rogue. But only one. The unfamiliar warhorse stood still just long enough for him to rapidly release five shots.

Three fell dead, and one ducked out of battle from a bolt to the shoulder. More archers appeared between the battlements, all seen between the spiked ramparts to be lighting their arrows on fire with flaming oil at their feet before letting loose their next volley. Tsuno swiftly loaded five more long-bolts into his clip extension and glanced to Ryleohk to ensure he remained unscathed.

Arrows rained down toward the lithe killer. His weaving scuttle to the Great Grey Wall was proving flawlessly effective. Ryleohk didn't slow a beat when he neared the impossible stone-brick climb. His feet switched from gliding on the surface of the level meadow to a full, unimpeded dash up the vertical ascent. The Wyldenar's boots found the melt of Dawning snow streaming down the wall from the tower parapet. He ran on an unfeasible path to the tower's top, sprinting freely on the snow-slicked surface as if it were a paved highway.

A loud series of booms discharged in front of him, stealing the attention from all else. He watched one sled blow short of its destination, chain-reacting with another, instantly disintegrating the two men and their bomb-loaded sleds. The impact of the shock wave and heat tossed his horse into a frenzy, bucking him clear of the saddle.

His back landed as softly as a feather, as if he had only dropped a finger's width from the ground. His slow-fall skyborne impower was active at all times. Alarm and instinct brought him immediately back to his feet, Wraith in hand. His ears were ringing. His borrowed mount was fleeing in the opposite direction to the fray with the sled and all still attached.

Ryleohk was atop the side tower now, tossing one archer over the wall, embedding his axe in the head of another and throwing it at the last sentry before the qin could even nock an arrow. Ryleohk had unmanned the side tower as fast as he had climbed it.

Jonan and two other mercenaries successfully made it to the entrenchment under the gatehouse. With the bells rung, several Aggedonians littered about, dead, and the premature series of explosions, the alarm of sabotage was screaming an assault on the city's outer bailey.

Jonan fled from the excavation entry toward the safety of the Thurowood tree line. *Where are you going? You left the other two men in the mine? Someone has to detonate the charges …*

Tsuno caught a glimpse of Ryleohk throwing qindrid from the wall through crenellations as he massacred any unaware greyborne he encountered on his run. The rogue eventually ended his slaughter and took a fearless leap back to the snowy battlefield, unharmed.

Tsuno needed to finish this. If none of the blast salt was ignited at the mine, then all would be a failure. Three men were dead, with Ryleohk and himself likely soon following. Jonan was now in retreat, two others confirmed still in the mine, and the seventh mercenary had been strangely absent during the fray. Countless men of Randon's army and the Boarneck Cavaliers were waiting for their signal.

To get to the three sleds in the entrenched mining access, he had to get closer. Skyborne were far enhanced with speed in their steps, and the wind naturally came to aid his desperate chase to beat his foe into the mine. Tsuno took off in a sprint to close the gap between life and death, at a pace faster than he had ever run.

Greyborne militia were swarming now. Most went into the tunnel below the barbican, but a good many had another intruder in mind. He had been seen.

Tsuno threw Wraith behind his back to equip both handheld crossbows, which he kept at his waist. These greyborne would feel the instant lethality of the bluefin poison that coated the bolt heads. Dually armed, he unloaded both repeater weapons on the immediate hostiles. He dropped both small crossbows in favor of Wraith once again as he swiftly pressed through the threshold of the mine's entryway.

There he saw the two mercenaries, both fighting their own futile battles. The Aldor-aliased Boarneck was frantically trying to free the harness that hitched the sled to his horse. Each of the three sleds filled with blast salt had been strategically placed, according to the plan, against the separate wooden beams that held up the excavation tunnel, directly underneath the main wall of Two-Towns. The Timance-guised archer was playing hero, launching arrow after arrow at any qindrid that dared into his vicinity. Several greyborne lay dead around his sled, even with several visible injuries and an arrow protruding from the Boarneck's thigh.

A punctual javelin speared through the chest of the courageous bowman, ending his trial of bravery. It was now just the two of them. There were still at least five greyborne in the mine, and many more pouring out from the bailey above, soon to join. As the last Boarneck was surrounded by the group inside, he seemed to give up on getting out of the scenario alive.

Tsuno stood at the mine's entry, looking at each sled and then back to the mercenary. A shout came behind him of "Westwalker!" letting him know that time was of the essence to execute the action.

He nodded to the Boarneck, and the archer returned the solemn gesture, understanding what the cue meant. Together the skyborne and mercenary lit their next shots on fire and aimed for a different sled each. He could hear a swarm of the enemy not far behind him, charging to make a trophy of his head on a spike.

But they would not reach him. His fiery bolt connected true with one of the kegs, just as he saw his human companion's sacrifice with an arrow strike the adjacent sled.

Tsuno turned to flee the impending wrath of the blast salt and inevitable collapse above him, seeing the small mob of greyborne foes rounding the barbican's corner to claim his life. He succeeded in taking a decem strides out before the boom took him in the back. He could feel the immense blaze that swept away the lives of those behind him so quickly, they couldn't even manage a scream at the pain.

He wasn't sure if he had a string of hair or any skin left underneath his garb. It all went numb in the sweltering blaze. But he was sure of one thing: his feet had left the ground some several seconds back, and he was being propelled uncontrollably through the air.

His eyes went blind from the sting of heat, and his ears went deaf from the incendiary burst. His head spun into dizziness, and then it all went black. But it didn't matter. Tsuno embraced the peace for which he was long overdue.

HONORAH (VII)

TIME TO MEET THE KING

Norah trampled into the stable house of the Frostdale Deeps. Her strenuous ride had stolen her breath, dizzy in a sweat of anxiety, as she urgently tethered her horse in a frantic fumble. She must have called out to the stable hands a dozen times for assistance, but none came to her beckoning. She didn't have time to dwell on the punishment she warranted to exact on the man once her hasty priority was settled.

Norah flung the heavy dungeon doors open and hastened for the warden's chamber. This was the hour she would expose the Chosen Troll in the flesh. The khomo would stare her in the eye as it was condemned before the high seats of Barredom. It would know that it was Lady Honorah Bayn, the Royal Inquisitor, widow of Lord Lucas Blackendale, who had brought about its doom. It and all its minions would feel her wrath as they writhed through the most excruciating execution she had yet to devise in her twisted imagination.

Something seemed amiss, though. Not a single watchman was in station or in sight. The corridors were empty, as were the cells where prisoners formerly resided. The lamps upon the wall were dead on their mounted sills, leaving the halls ever more ghastly black the further she delved into the Deeps.

She didn't like the eerie feeling of imminent dread growing inside her. "Ebrielle! Warden BrKaim!" Norah desperately demanded at the top of her lungs.

No answer.

What is this madness? She reached high upon the wall to feel for the next sconce, and once it was found, she stole her source of light from its shelf. Norah fired up the tinderbox attached to the lamp and swiftly jogged to where Soro had indicated her daughter might be. Her feet found their way through the high cells to the warden's chamber.

"Ebrielle! BrKaim?" No sign of anything. Empty.

Norah felt her heart taking on an unfamiliar reaction. She detected the shadows cast from the flame in her hand, quivering in a rapid dance on the chamber wall. She looked down at her grip to see it trembling violently. Her windpipe felt as if it were collapsing, making breathing difficult, and her cheeks suddenly bore a sensation of being gauntly skeletal, as if her face were swallowing itself whole and committing to death. This was an entirely forgotten sensation she had not felt in a long time.

She was nervous. She was scared. "Brie? Guards! Brie, answer!" Norah screamed, pleading for a solution to the nightmarish, bizarre mystery settling in. She needed a response or to wake up soon.

Norah took her free, shaking hand and palmed her wrist in a futile attempt to assuage the unintentional shudder holding the lantern. She bolstered her courage to try other alleys of the dungeon for answers to explain the unrealities around her. She stormed over to reopen the door of the missing prison keeper's private room and choose a new path for inspection.

She was relieved when she saw the massive feral elvan directly in front of the door, anticipating her. Over seven feet tall, covered in fresh green war paint, its long dreadlocks kempt for battle, and a huge Terollar spear in hand, Jrulthun diabolically smirked down at her. *At least none of this is real. I knew I was dreaming ...* Jrulthun, the alpha, was safely in the Forlorn, impossible to escape.

Her body went still, and she felt calm, knowing it was all just a silly nightmare. *None of this is real ...*

When his guttural accent grunted, attempting the Civil tongue, "Time t' meet da king," she knew it simply wasn't true. And that gave her peace of mind to finish her surreal hallucination.

Even as the enormous troll grabbed her throat, lifting her from the ground, and all life began to flow from her body, she believed she might have smiled in that moment of alleviating serenity. It was all just a bad dream. She just needed to wake up.

ONDREW (VIII)

OSH, OSH, OSHAH!

As the final stretch of the tunnel's egress to the outside drew closer, the cave walls echoed a shared aura of reverberating jubilance. Festive laughter, combined with the Timberhands' elated instrumentals, saturated the subterranean hall. Ondrew was a proud commander. His formerly insubordinate coalition had fused together into a disciplined array of capable soldiers when put to their first test in synchronized battle. Even their boots were married in accord as the tread forward sounded to a percussion-matched march.

Ondrew took the lead with Lilealah by his side, temporarily relieved of her bonds. He looked over to the impossibly beautiful umbran and smiled, and she smiled back.

His eyes were more focused on his joyous men behind him than scoping out the steps ahead. He found himself turning often to spy each of the social cliques, now all intermingled, with no sense of division among the new unity.

He saw Sarin punch Datron on his wounded shoulder from behind, but when the boy-knight spun to confront his unprovoked assailant, he was only met with a firm and awkward kiss on the mouth. She thanked him for saving her life in the fight against the Skystone apes and promised to repay him properly. Ondrew imagined Sarin as when he had first met the lone female in his fraternity. Not the prettiest, with her one lazy eye and thin lips, but appealing in the face to a fair degree, at least before Zsolindal had taken ahold of half the hair on her head and beat her in grit on the brutal journey.

Nearby, the massive Vellyan Odemnar carried two Timberhands, one in each arm. Ryder and Caldwell squirmed to get free, while Aramgar and two other Timberhands, both Jonthon and Tarance, nonchalantly trekked behind them, bursting into amused tears at their friends' folly in antagonizing the half-giant in jest.

Mathias was talking to the mute battle hero Black about the recent fight and delving into old topics that only the two veterans were old enough to remember.

Broc BrKomak's voice could be heard over the whole lot. Ondrew's second boisterously coached Donal, Oakley, and Tolbert on their transgressions in the skirmish and how to better avoid them in the inevitable fights to come. The men were making light of the situation, too victorious in mood to let the surly knight steal their moment. They kept cracking jokes at Broc to get his tough exterior to break, and each time they got him to grin, they would all chuckle, only stimulating him to pretend more seriousness and vehemence once again.

The group held no more enmity. No more family feuds or cultural indifferences or bitter prejudices. They were a perfectly polished version of all he had hoped to cultivate at this juncture. *These are my Norther Knights.*

And then there was Kyson. The bard walked by himself, not far behind Ondrew, away from the others. Even the way the man self-confidently took each stride was caked in pure charisma. Ondrew often found himself envious of the fostered lowborn. Maybe if he carried Kyson's amount of magnetism, Frostdale and Ondrew's own parents would not have discarded him to the cold, like trash for the wolves to consume. The archer was staring back at him with his amber southlander eyes. Kyson grinned at his leader and bowed a sincere respect, still moving forward.

Ondrew nodded back. *You are a curious one, Kyson Greene. I cannot sort you out. But there is more to you than even you know, I wager.* He turned back to speak an opinion to Lilealah, but suddenly something cut him off.

Kyson's voice. The soft introduction to "The Anthem of Frostdale" resounded from the minstrel's lips. His crescendo into the chorus shut the whole group down into silence as the uphill hike proceeded. *You may very well be a wizard.*

He did not even use his lute, only his voice. His ability to stir heavy hearts and hush small armies was spellbinding. Ondrew had never seen a true mage perform, but as far as he was concerned, this was real magic, just as the bard had boasted on the boat before entering Zsolindal. As Kyson rounded to the repetitive verses of the ode non-native to him, the other Timberhands slowly joined in. And then more of the contingent of Norther Knights chimed in. Even the two Vellyans began to hum in harmony to the hymn. Eventually, the whole lot was participating in the regional psalm behind Kyson.

Ondrew let the anthem finish three times over, taking in every word of his country's sacred song. As they finished the last verse, he stopped in his tracks in all seriousness and shot his hand to his sword hilt. The group were prompted to a halt and mimicked his defensive maneuver. He looked at each of them in the eye in the dead stillness. Slowly, a good-humored smirk crept onto his face as he could play the ploy no longer. He reached into the satchel at his side to pull the remaining Utamian Sweetmint out into the open. Ondrew uncapped the bottle and took a healthy swig of the milky alcohol, then held up two more flasks for the group to view.

"Osh, osh, oshah!" The Norther Knights cantillated the signature verse and bellowed out a hearty laugh. He tossed the bottles directly back to Kyson for him to partake and pass along the line to let everyone in on the reward of revelry.

The Osh Mantra was a phrase composed by the ancestral Barredish highborn warriors. Even though it implied to the ignorant a simpleton's cheer, it was far more complex in symbolism than barbaric gibberish. In the ancient Agge tongue, now referred to only as Oldspeak, and hardly learned or uttered by either the modern Barredish or qindrid Aggedonians, the word *osh* meant "to persevere." While the term *oshenosh* translated as "to persevere against all odds," over time the word was simplified to just *osh, osh*, meaning the same thing. In the near-forgotten Oldspeak, the derivative *oshah* was to be construed as "to persevere again, continuously." And so, as the earliest Barredish champions intended of the mantra's deciphering, the chanted phrase "Osh, osh, oshah!" should have been interpreted as "Persevere against all odds again and again, as long as one lives."

The march recommenced with the fresh victory's celebration. His attention again settled on the umbran gazing back at him. She was the one to speak first. "You did well by them, Prince."

He was getting used to that word from her and his men. But he could not lose sight of modest realities. "They did right by themselves. That fight was all they needed. I did nothing but yell a few commands."

"You will make quite the humble and honorable hero when this is done." She shook her head, seeming to disapprove of his approach.

"When this is done." Ondrew skeptically repeated the phrase she had just used. "We are all yet far from being heroes. The true tests will come upon the open fields, when we have the greys to contend with."

Lilealah shot him a random familiar question. "Do you trust me?"

"This is the second time you have asked this. My answer is the same." *Why do you ask this, umbran? What do you have planned to warrant doubt?*

Lilealah did not respond. She just stared ahead now with empty black orbs, impossible to read. He yearned to get to know the clandestine master of his enemy that he was ironically sentenced to protect. "Do I trust the nemesis of my forefathers and countrymen, current and long past? Do I trust the one surviving turner of the Transcendence that swept through and conquered what is now western Aggedon? Do I trust an elvan that subjected herself to thousands upon thousands of seduced humans in front of her lifemate, participating in whatever details of the sensual ritual, as is forbidden for me to know? Do I trust that?"

The temptress glared through him, unperturbed by his cynical implications concerning her malicious motives. His eyes caught her perfectly pouty lips and were swallowed whole by her dark orbs, as if they were void-like heavens promising everlasting peace.

Ondrew shook himself free of the misplaced moment of lust and fixed his gaze ahead again. "I have given you my answer about trust at the guildhall in Defiance. It has not changed." He shut the topic down. He seized the opportunity instead to better educate himself on her history. "If I may know more of you, though? I would ask about your lover and how he passed."

"Oh, so on to lighter subjects, then," she sarcastically chuckled before emphasizing her harsh opinion on the next word. "*Passed*, you say? That is a pleasant term for it. Agendwar was butchered by Khomo'Jhuvonus."

Lilealah went on to explain. "He was my lifemate. But he had not been my lover since the beginning, and nor had I been his. Not since our first ritual of the qindrid Transcendence. It all changed then between us. When we made the choice to become umbran together, we knew that bond would die. We eventually just became at one with a duty to our cause above all else."

"Forgive my lore of the elven, then. I was taught that lifemates were timeless lovers unto death among your kind." Ondrew felt utterly ignorant admitting this aloud.

"An umbran is as much an elvan as a qindrid is still a human," Lilealah softly chastised. Fully aware of her grey skin, the same hue as the qindrid enemy, and her pointed ears slanted flat and outward from her head, the sharp fangs, and long black nails, matched to her all-ebon orbs, Ondrew berated himself for classifying her as still elvan whatsoever. It was obvious she barely clung to any remnant of that heritage digressed from ages ago. "If that answer does not suffice, then yes, most elven do love their lifemates timelessly. But it is not uncommon to find love again in another once the lifemate is gone to the Beyond, or to the dust of nothingness in an umbran's case."

Ondrew permitted that to marinate in his mind, that once Lilealah died, there would be no hopeful afterlife for her. Umbran and pure qindrid, such as the skyborne and stoneborne, forsook their place in the great Beyond or Godslands, choosing the boon of a near-ageless mortal existence on Penthara, all for selling their soul to the shadow element to be forgotten and utterly gone to the darkness once their life ended. For the elven devoted to the Balance, or humans fervent in their regional theologies, choosing such a heretical curse was unfathomable. But as for the less pious or the altogether unbelieving, they seemed ideal candidates for undergoing the Transcendence.

Seeing as how Ondrew was engrossed in his musing, Lilealah purred on. "I see the way you look at me. Is there a reason you ask?"

He purposely shot an obvious glance at the exposed cleavage of her healthy bust, up to her slender neckline, and then to her lips. "I look at you the same way all men look at you, umbran," he lied rather crudely.

She read straight through his bluff, as if she were some savant inside his moral mind. "Lilealah," she corrected, underlining her name for him to say. "And no. No, you do not."

Lilealah turned the subject on him. "And what of the only son of the king, and former heir to the kingdom of Barredom? How many lucky maidens have been graced with the love of the handsome Prince Ondrew Roth?"

That aroused a laugh from Ondrew. "Love has been an elusive prey even for former princes, it would seem. It is a concept lost on me more than ever now. Alas, even my own mother and my own father …" He trailed off in bittersweet reminiscing.

"I enjoy learning of you. Please continue," she implored in all sincerity.

Ondrew gritted his teeth and exhaled in frustration before venting his tale of unexplained recent discord between his parents. "I was told my mother, the queen, returned to Frostdale before I departed for Defiance. I have not seen her in over two years. She was sent away for an illness to be cured by the gifted of Mageholme. I was not allowed to visit her, nor was even my own father. We thought she may be dead."

Ondrew shook his head. "But she came back. In high health, they say, better than before. The mages did their deed. But she did not feel it fitting to see her son off before he was cast away to perils deeper in the bowels of Aggedon than any Barredish has ventured before. I received not one letter of her wanting an audience as I took this quest, and her knowing the grave risk I am enduring for a country that turned its back on me.

"And my father," he continued, diverting to the king. "I no longer even know him. He is a stranger in a house that was once my own to share. He was a just man, someone who cherished his wife above all else, someone who loved his son dearly, someone who worshipped his country and believed in its strength. King Aerik Roth would never have bowed in subservience to this unsolicited Dominadom, or even an Aggedonian invasion. He would have fought honorably unto defeat or victory, and included his son in it. It all makes little sense, the world warped and stripped before me.

"So, no. It is paralleled with my history that I know little to nothing of the concepts of love. And I imagine neither do they." He turned side-on to point back at each of his Norther Knights as he referenced them. "Broc BrKomak, rightful yharl of Mount Komak, protector of our western harbors and war hero during our last invasion of Vellyon. Mathias Oreville, scarred victor of numerous troll encounters and commander of the famous Eldenvale Rangers, survivor of the deadly confrontation with the Chosen Troll. Black Brigannor, the legend, the only Barredish ever to escape the Fourteen, at the cost of his voice for that slit across his throat, with a higher qindrid death count than any alive today in our ranks. I could keep naming each of their commendable exploits, down to the Vellyans and Timberhands. But each of them was born as someone, of blood of a house that meant something to their country, but now are all nameless and shunned outlaws like myself, all for holding dear the creeds we were raised by."

Ondrew finally went silent. The umbran, even in all her imbued wisdom, appeared to clearly be at a loss on how to reply to such a heavy burden of caged anguish unable to be unleashed. "My heart feels for your plight, yours and your knights'. I do not know how else to respond to ease your woes."

"There is no response. There is only blind trust at this point. So, let us continue onward. My mood should not be so dour in this moment." His tone became quieter and more docile as he finished the rant.

"Ondrew." She had rarely ever called him by his actual name. He was already several steps ahead of her now, choosing solitude in the lead, but his focus stole back to her beckoning. "Before all is done, know that I will give you peace in enlightenment on the many uncertainties that usher your sorrows," Lilealah vowed.

Of course, she is learned in more than I will ever be privy to. She is the ancient enemy of my people, yet evidently in secret council with the Frostdale royals. He inwardly cursed the paradox. Before he realized it, his expedited pace had taken him far away from his troop.

He needed the serenity, devoid of the echoes of his men's mirth and removed from the tantalizing sorceress. He numbed himself against any memory concerning the bloodline from which he had been excommunicated. It was just the dark cave hall and him now, alone in the mutual brooding of their shared solemnity in being forsaken.

But then, abruptly, around the tunnel bend, it struck him. The first glimpse of sun seen in a countless number of days skulked from the underrealm's up-winding path. Ondrew stopped in his tracks at the glorious tease of Zsolindal's exit shortly ahead, with the Norther Knights just over fifty yards behind.

"We have light!" Ondrew bellowed out behind him, unable to see the group with the twisting cavern egress.

"Five by Five fucks, we made it!" exclaimed the tiny voice that could belong to none other than Sarin.

A period of silence resonated, as if the whole lot were staring at the girl for using such blasphemous profanity, but then a hearty guffaw burst out, and Broc's voice concurred. "Five by Five fucks, we did!"

"Norther Knights! Destiny speaks! Redemption for your houses in the histories to come is just ahead! Join with me!" Ondrew inspired the unseen entourage.

"To the rightful king of Barredom!" Kyson shouted.

The rest chimed in like a thunderous choir. "To the rightful king of Barredom! Osh, osh, oshah!"

That was all he needed to precipitate motion from his own boots. His feet took to an anxious jog as the tunnel straightened out on the ascent. He could now smell the evergreens of the wilderness close by. He could feel the comforting chill of the northern gale invading the cave. His ears picked up on every sound of the advancing horizon: the birds, the wind through the trees, a rock falling.

It was all so mesmerizing. His stride was motivated to hasten to be the first to taste Aggedon's splendor. As the sun's brightness blinded his unadjusted eyes, he closed his lids to empower his other senses to take control. It was as if his feet already knew the way.

Suddenly, the foulest sound he could dare to imagine interrupted his eager pace into a petrified standstill. He could not commit his light-blinded focus to the culprit of the click beneath his boot, so instead, he gazed behind him to the halting approach of the confounded retinue.

"Prince." Lilealah's sweet tone reached out, horrified disbelief across her visage.

"Drew, no." Broc stared in denial at the ground beneath Ondrew.

Mathias whispered the truth that everyone in the vicinity had already deduced but was too afraid to confirm. "Firetears ..."

Finally, Ondrew braved facing his predicament. He found the minute holes piercing the cave wall on either side of him. The initial trauma of confusion and denial transformed into sheer fear, with a prayerful look into the many hollow eyes of the lifeless rock staring back at him. *Not like this*, he begged of his gods.

"Sire, don't move! I'll go outside and fetch a rock, and we can—" Datron blurted in a hopeful epiphany, but Ondrew fast interjected.

"No. The plate is the size of my boot."

"Pah! The fuck, then, Drew?" Broc burst into a fit. "Ye're just gonna give it up t' the Godslands then?"

"You will lead them well, Broc. I have brought each of you this far. You all know the way from here." His tone simmered melancholically. He was unable to look at any of the disappointed faces of his knights.

"Who says we lose our prince today?" Broc roared to the group around him, challenging any to answer wrongly. "Mathias, Black, cloak up! Knights, stay back! We rush an' take him off! Drew, wrap yer cloak round yer head!"

Ondrew countered by drawing his sword, pointing it at his aspiring rescuers. "You will do no such thing. I already cost us the Shaw brothers. I will lose no more men on my watch."

"Then I guess that damned sword holds nary a threat then, eh? I be not losin' no man on m' watch neither, specially not m' fuckin' sire!" Broc was a good man—his best man. It was a commendable tribute for him to try. His second was not going to back down.

Ondrew found himself mortified, unprepared to die. He felt his body slump and quiver uncontrollably, all of his ambition decimated, with nothing but a wave of overwhelming flashbacks and future images that would never come to pass bombarding his mind. He expected that death might find him on this peril-filled endeavor, but not in such an undistinguished manner. *Such an inglorious, unheroic exit for the former heir of Barredom. Fives, I beseech you, have I upset you also?* He felt as betrayed by his deities as he had been by his parents.

But destiny had spoken. This was where it ended. His purpose was to bring the Norther Knights together, the last true descendants of the old Barredish bloodlines, and escort them to the surface of central Aggedon, to end the timeless war between the qindrid and the humans for good.

Broc was still shouting, but Ondrew was sure his sense of hearing no longer had the capacity to listen. In his final moment, he did look at each of them, at each bold face of every Norther Knight, as not just Broc and Mathias and Black but all of them, the Vellyans and Timberhands included, wrapped their cloaks around their heads to prepare to save their prince or die with him. It was a beautiful sight. *They are ready.*

"To persevere against all odds again and again, as long as one lives." He whispered the meaning behind their customary mantra. He then looked above to glare down his apparent assassin face-to-face, the Neveril runes that staged his murder.

His focus caught their valiant charge out of his blurred peripheral vision. They would never make it in time. He made sure of it.

This time he shouted it. "Osh, osh, oshah!"

He lifted his foot from the trap plate, and the orange cloud enveloped the world he knew in a fatal embrace.

WESTWALKER (VIII)

STEP INTO THE DEMISE

Tsuno woke to a whimsical reality following his plight from the blast-salt explosion. His body felt as if it were hovering over the snows, drifting backward across the blanket of frost between Two-Towns and the Thurowood. His corpse must have still been somewhere close to the wall, and this was his spirit retreating to wherever the lost souls of skyborne went.

He knew his soul was tainted and would not admit him into an afterlife with his ancestors in the Godslands. He would never share the heavens with his son or grandchildren to come. He had severed that deal with his gods long ago, when he chose a life as a qindrid.

Tsuno gazed deep across the fading fields to the enkindled debris and devouring red flames of the disintegrated Two-Towns barbican. Fiery flakes littered the air above, coupled with smoke and ash. The main wall had been successfully demolished by the three sleds that made it into place. He attempted to lift himself higher off the ground, toward the clouds, for a better view, but a sudden pang flared down his neck and into his back. *But the dead feel no pain.* The realization shook him from the stupor of the impact.

Tsuno could see his feet now, covered in familiar timeworn boots. His sleeping legs reposed comfortably against the sled beneath him. His hand involuntarily lifted to see if he had indeed succumbed to the life of a ghost or if he still contained some remnant of control over his corporeal self. *I am alive.*

The riveting epiphany jolted him back into tangible cognizance.

He had felt at peace, being so for as long as he was still dead. But now he again felt the emotions that coincided with living. Combat awareness united with disorderly unease coursed through his veins.

Resolving that all agony was best snubbed, Tsuno drove his throbbing neck to roll back his head, just enough to behold the source of the momentum that had stolen him away from the impending peril.

He was not surprised to see the heroic culprit. His savage elvan companion heaved and huffed at the reins of the sled, with no horses in sight. Ryleohk glided effortlessly over the snows, yet the weight of Tsuno and the sled seemed to be sapping the rogue's stamina.

He instinctively called out behind him, more so to see if he could hear his own voice, to solidify his new theory of resurrection, than for any futile expectation of getting a reply. "Ryleohk? Wait!"

Why he would demand his wise guardian wait made no sense as he heard the absurdity spew from his mouth. Even as he did, Tsuno surveyed the gang of promised wrath charging through the bright red fires at the city wall.

Ash-haired soldiers with smoke-hued skin by the hundreds. The greyborne militia came pouring out of the breach in hordes. Northern qindrid never utilized horses, unlike the eastern breed from the Sho'Lon region, where Tsuno was from.

The throng of qindrid took off in a charge toward the only two enemies in sight. The greyborne were midway across the field now. He considered saying a vain prayer to AeriAllyse, his one umbran maker still alive, whom he had betrayed, or to his long-forsaken deities, knowing he was more likely to be cast a curse than blessed with a miracle. Instead, he changed his faith to the only thing he did still believe in—Ryleohk.

Tsuno looked up to the sky, through the thin canopy of the tree line of the Thurowood, where the Wyldenar parked the sled. A greedy murder of crows salivated overhead, awaiting their due feast. His gaze went to the amassing enemy funneling out of the riven town gates, and then behind him through the trap-lined forest and the canopy above. A subtle smoky tinge of possibly two dozen campfire clouds leaked into the skyline, just enough to fuel the Two-Towns reinforcements' command toward suspicion of a small demolition vanguard, rather than the truth of two thousand mounted mercenaries strategically sited in various positions. *Tristostopher's bait.* The

Boarneck Cavaliers were in place in the vicinity.

The company captain likely had a large contingent of his men in place along the west of Loch Karlohr's northern shore, to act as a flank, while the remainder were scheduled, in safe placement in the Thurowood, for the second signal, to release the final traps. The plan was still on.

As the ride brusquely adjourned, before Tsuno could look up, Ryleohk already had him standing upright. Battle rage injected an invigorating grit back into his blood and bones, resolving his motivation to endure. Wraith was slammed into his chest. Tsuno was still confused as to where his missing hand crossbows had been dropped, but the Wyldenar commanded his attention with a set of unexpected choice words.

"You are survivalist," Ryleohk sputtered in broken Civil tongue with a hint of Trollspeak, exercising a line Tsuno was oft known to use when describing himself. It was the first time Ryleohk had spoken to him in as long as he could recall. Tsuno had come to simply accept that maybe the Wyldenar was far too gone into his deteriorating feral state to still communicate in known dialects, as was the norm for the aging affliction of all rogue-elven.

Tsuno looked into the fierce, tenacious eyes of the rogue-Wyldenar. Grey through the skin, the hair, the eyes, the heart—a neutral but raw hunter. Ryleohk was a silent killer born into death.

The flat-eared elvan pushed the bow deeper into Tsuno's chest, almost tripping him over, and snarled, "Go survive!"

Tsuno glanced at each premarked tree on the Thurowood's perimeter and noticed two of them had been triggered. He recollected the absent mercenary and Jonan, who had gone missing in the chaos. His eyes scoured the woodland grounds for Nho, but there was no sign of his beloved horse.

He took one final look at the accruing militia mob, soon to be at his feet, and replaced Wraith in its strap around his back. Ryleohk disappeared into the world of branches and piney verdure above.

His right hand gripped the knife handle at his belt. His left quickly slipped into a fastened leather glove, which clutched a whittled bar secured by two pulley ropes that hung from a bough high above. He trained a wicked sneer on the hostiles before him, now within a spear's throw ahead.

"*Step into the demise*," he taunted with his signature death line in their Norspeak tongue, using his impower to throw his voice into the wind like a phantom elemental whisper upon the ears of each one.

Javelins flew, but they were too late to catch their mark. Tsuno cut one of the ropes on the pulley, and his other hand went to the handle as he shot vertically up the tree to its thickest branch. The pulley stopped only for a second due to the vibration of the halted momentum. Tsuno swung himself forward to push his feet off the main trunk of the tree and felt the rope catch the pulley for the slanted descent backward.

He couldn't help but smile as he looked down upon hundreds of muddled faces. The qindrid aggressors watched their prey, high above, recoiling away from them along a zip-line contraption far beyond their mechanical comprehension. They were in the great gauntlet now.

As their full pursuit came through, Tsuno watched safely from above. The Two-Towns vanguard fell to the first of his crippling gambits. A series of large hidden caltrops had been laid out to slow the immediate pursuit and scatter the horde into a more cautious approach. Several qin went to their knees with large shaved-bone barbs impaling their boots, tripping the sprint of the militia's unison into a fumbling anarchy.

This was an intended ruse. As anticipated, the pursuit avoided all manner of underbrush, only stepping into the forest-floor clearings, where there were no caltrops, and injurious trapfalls were ready and waiting. The screams of agony made Tsuno's eyes narrow as he felt his persona becoming the alter ego they all cursed. And the curses did come.

"Westwalker!" His alias was shouted as if it were the vilest profanity one could give to a fellow qindrid. He heard the name over and over, followed by a tirade of other Norspeak obscenities. He had predicted the unseasoned Two-Towns substitute soldiers would react to their north gate's demolishment in a rather brash and unrehearsed act of fury. And his logic was proved valid.

He could see them bleeding now as their comrades attempted to pull the multitude of victims from the hidden ankle traps. Everything was falling into line. The Two-Towns militiamen were no longer in a hurry as they began to guardedly choose their steps. This led the majority into a tapered path, onto a series of logs conjoined over a shallow concealed trench.

Rows of qin entered the bridge points now, skeptical but progressing. Some relented in caution, while others still persisted to aid injured fellowmen. As long as Tristostopher was at the rendezvous in a short time, Tsuno deemed his trap mastery a success in bringing the city militia outside of their comfort zone, ultimately serving Barredom with more greyborne captives than they had ever held in custody, once the conquest of Two-Towns was over.

The zip line's altitude gradually ebbed toward the ground, just as his peripheral vision picked up on the one thing that could make it all go awry. *The deserter.* The Boarneck mercenary who had fled from the explosion breach stumbled along, with an obvious broken leg, parallel to the bridge, scrambling frantically away from the oncoming hostiles. He must have fallen from his zip line somehow from not strapping his arm in properly.

Several qindrid leaped from the bridge in pursuit of their nearest source for bloodshed. The man wailed, piteously imploring a prisoner's mercy, but found none. All he was granted was a score of hungry blades. The largest greyborne clansman who struck sawed through his neck, roaring while holding the dead man's head menacingly toward Tsuno.

Tsuno half expected a camouflaged, axe-wielding phantom to come down and avenge the dead Boarneck, but Ryleohk never came. All that did come was more of the militiamen leaving the bridge, discovering they could disperse into the woods now, free of traps. The one coward Tristostopher had consigned to him may very well have cost him his life.

Tsuno could see the small landing glade now, and the crossbow tower he had designed. He needed his reinforcements from the Boarneck Cavaliers. Too many of the Aggedonians had strayed from the trap path.

While still suspended from the pulley system, he twisted himself to face forward just before the drop, prompting his slow-fall impower to gracefully reunite him with level ground. He landed just in front of the elaborate turret contraption he had had the Boarneck mercenaries assist him in the construction of, but that was for the final stand.

Tsuno rushed to the tinder pile trailing a powder line leading under the log bridge. His fingers earnestly picked up the flint firestriker to spark the flame and detonate the main trap. A hissing crackle snaked its way from Tsuno's feet as the blast salt burned away in a chase to its purpose underneath the hapless bridge.

He was beyond reluctant to ever see another explosion again after his last encounter, but he boldly prepared himself to face at least one more nonetheless. Tsuno squinted his narrow eyes and gritted his teeth to embrace the inevitable boom.

And the succession of booms did come. Wooden shards and bright red flames flew into the disintegrated canopy above. Slivers of the combusted logs alongside severed bone and limbs married into a macabre scene as a spray of blood coated every tree in the vicinity.

Tsuno found himself on one knee with his eyes closed to shield them from the red glow. When he opened them to rise again, he found it not so easy. A spear of splintered log was lanced straight through his left calf. He didn't have time to dwell on the pain.

Several qindrid were approaching with rage in their determined eyes now that they could see their palpable nemesis in the flesh, the mastermind behind their comrades' annihilation. *I do not die in the north.* He bolstered his confidence with Nominus Vlo's prophecy about his destiny undone.

Tsuno defied his injury and stood anyway. He had to get up the turret tower. He hastily limped up the steps of the small fortification. It had never been precalculated that he would be manning this defensive position alone, but hard fate had spoken nonetheless. This was a thing of his design. This was an engineering feat of the demise. And this was the final stand.

Twenty high-powered crossbows, nocked with bluefin bolts, were mounted on swivel devices, enabling the user of the weapons to aim anywhere below them in a semicircular radius, freely moving to target up or down, and all within that half sphere of ensured death.

And the body count was augmented by numbers again as the foolish tried their luck on the Westwalker. His skyborne speed allowed him to dexterously spin and set from bow to bow to bow, aiming and killing. After each click, a qin fell dead.

One greyborne attempted to rush in on him unawares from the rear, near the steps, but found himself ensnared in a net, lifting him into the trees. Ashy smoke shrouded the vast foliage, high and low, obscuring anything beyond forty feet away. His ears picked up the wails of the wounded and the cries of the dying. He could also hear the reckless charge of the brave and the vengeful.

A new berserker rushed up the steps with his sword held above his head and his mouth open, bellowing some wild death shriek. Tsuno had a choice to put a bolt from Wraith through him, or through the stealthy Aggedonian who appeared on his left flank, crawling over the tower in a similar assassination attempt.

A familiar shrill flew through the air as an axe cleaved through the side of the first assailant's head, cracking it open like a split melon. Tsuno took his repeater bow to the qin breaching the side of the small siege defense and placed a shot through the greyborne's forehead. By the time he looked back to Ryleohk's kill, the axe was gone, and the elvan was back in hiding.

Four more came to claim their victory trophy, each in different directions. The first of the wave took another net trap into the trees, being wrapped in a fading scream out of the fight. The following aggressor made only a single step before the axe of an unseen specter hacked into the greyborne's collarbone. The third took a precise crossbow bolt to the throat.

But the fourth had more success. Tsuno saw out of the side of his eye the javelin that was let fly. He turned to dodge just as it clipped the swivel crossbow he garrisoned, but the spear shaft ricocheted to broadside him across his face. The momentum of the weapon planted him prone on the deck. Tsuno rushed to pull Wraith back for a draw on the clansman rushing up the steps, but the attacker was already there, slamming a mace against the upper limb of his bow. Tsuno went to pull his knife, but the burly clansman beat him in a fully charged tackle to the ground.

The Aggedonian promptly stood to crush Tsuno's skull with his mace, but he wasn't as quick as his haste-enhanced foe. The greyborne was left with a stab through the boot, a deft spinning sweep that planted him on his back, and a knife through the throat that ended the swift challenge. Tsuno took no pause in rapidly returning to his feet, snap-flipping forward with his wraithwood bow aimed to slay.

Another greyborne appeared up the steps, promising a repeat round with no break between. But as fast as he rose for the new fight, the qin fell lifeless back down the steps. His head was cleanly cleaved off at the neck by the Wyldenar's axe.

Ryleohk guarded the stairway, allowing Tsuno to refocus on the onslaught in front of him. He aimed Wraith at each advancing foe from the militia and released a fatal long-bolt volley on four more advancing qin that cleared the smoke. With his bolt clip depleted, he set the bow down to man another turret.

More silhouettes appeared through the thinning cloud, and still no sign of Tristostopher. Tsuno spun on every advancing fleshly shadow as it appeared from the cindery veil that encased his small arena. All who dared upon him died to swift expertise from the last of the turret crossbows, until the litter of fresh dead was so high, the corpses were piled in sporadically placed mounds.

Tsuno looked down to the side of his ribs at some mystery wound he had just now taken note of. An unseen projectile from the enemy had obviously clipped him in his fury. He could hear Ryleohk finishing off another qin at the base of the turret fort's steps. The crossbows and Wraith were now empty of bolts, and he had no time to load more.

The fire fog was near above their heads now, and he could finally see the full advance of the Two-Towns retaliation. One other that came forward caught another net snare. As the hostiles came in full, Tsuno had no other cards left to play but one. He had memorized exactly where he had plotted every single trap. And he knew precisely where he needed to step next.

Tsuno took Wraith and performed an impossibly far leap that only a skyborne could manage. His feet hit the shifting carpet of broken conifer leaves and cluttered green cones. It all swirled in an instant to give way to the net beneath them as the complexity of rope webbed over him to take his body high above the enemy. He felt the wrath of the log fragment behind his shin as the snare came to an abrupt jolt at the tree's high juncture, where the trap had been tied.

The last of the net snares caught one more greyborne. But then the remaining horde gradually gathered underneath. Some prodded forward in a skeptical scatter in the direction of the campfires just ahead. Others remained focused on ways to release their netted brethren, which included getting him down into their grasp. It wouldn't take long to figure it all out.

Tsuno's senses espied two sudden godsends above and below: the sight of Ryleohk camouflaged motionlessly on the branch across from him, and the thunder of thousands of hooves underway.

Tristostopher's belated horsemen swarmed into the wooded terrain, hewing straight through the befuddled enemy. The disadvantaged were instantly overpowered by a sweep of Boarneck-bearing steeds that filtered into every gulley and glade throughout the expanse of the southern Thurowood. Tsuno could only imagine what the fields outside the Two-Towns north wall looked like by now, with the barrage of mounted mercenaries flowing in. Tristostopher himself likely rode the lead into the panicked city.

He watched the flawless massacre below, swaying, uncomfortably tangled, in his own trap. Drips of blood trickled from his injuries, sprinkling droplets onto the fray below. He thought to yell for aid but didn't. Instead, he surveyed the others webbed in similar circumstances beside him in the treetops. None of them seemed to be paying attention to him, perhaps unmindful of the fact that it was the Westwalker with whom they shared their ensnarement.

A spell of wooziness washed over him, almost taking him back into the blackness, but the presence of his friend nearby strengthened his resolve to stay awake a bit longer.

Ryleohk majestically balanced on the bough that held Tsuno's net in suspension. The look the Wyldenar gave him was something terrifying and new. He had seen rage in the elvan's eyes time and again. He had stared into the cold indifference of the killer's grey orbs. But this look was different. This was a visage of sadness—of apology almost.

"Friend," he sputtered, clinging to consciousness despite the pain and blood loss. "A little help?"

The taciturn hunter just stared with a face etched with the same request for forgiveness of premeditated conclusions. Tsuno was unaccustomed to this trait in the rogue.

The Wyldenar approached softly and put a hand on the net. Tsuno enclosed his friend's palm with his own and bluntly asked, "Ryleohk, where are you going?"

Ryleohk pulled his hand free and slowly backed away down the high tree branch, turning away.

Tsuno shouted incredulously after the rogue-elvan. "Like this, then?"

"*She is near. I sense it,*" Ryleohk ambiguously worded in his more familiarized Terollar tongue. The Wyldenar didn't even need to explain for Tsuno to understand that "she" was in reference to Lilealah, Ryleohk's traitorous matriarch, who had brought him into the world and tried to take him out of it on the same day.

"Then I will join you." It was a plead more than a statement, but he responded back in the Civil language.

"No. You will stay with the humans. Like you always do. It will never get done." Ryleohk glared at Tsuno with some form of resentment before his semblance shifted to softness once more, with a somber tone. *"You must save your people and others' people before you return home to family. But I must kill my family before I ever have a home."*

Tsuno didn't know what to say to that tragic fact, so Ryleohk finished it for him. *"Survive. We will meet again, my grey brother."* He cited a title no elven used.

And just like that, Ryleohk left him. Tsuno watched the rogue-elvan slip through the boughs and fade into the Thurowood thicket, out of sight.

His family. His horse. His one friend. Despite the masses of alleged allies below, he felt thrust into the dread of solitary abandonment. "Brother," Tsuno whispered back, after Ryleohk was gone. "But you are my only family now."

Tsuno looked below to the frenzied scuttle of Tristostopher's sadistic troop. The darkness invited him to rest, but the numbness of fresh seclusion took over, inducing a feeling of new fear. The north's nefarious trapmaster was at their mercy.

HONORAH (VIII)

THE FORLORN

Norah woke from her dream to find herself still deep inside her worst nightmare. Her wrists and ankles were bound, stretched outward on the saltire she was strung to. She perched upon an acquainted apparatus, misplaced in the middle of the Forlorn crossway. Shackled to a pentacrux, she was encircled by her troll prisoners in all directions. Each was impossibly armed with the foreign weaponry of their homeland. Norah desperately looked each foe in the face, searching for familiarity to exploit a stratagem out of her macabre dilemma.

Strangely, among them was the recognizable qindrid that had maimed himself during the truth-tonic ploy. *Oenayus*. She recalled the greyborne's referenced name. They must have rescued him from the infirmary, proving the theory that the clansmen of the Akaydis Coast were indeed in league with the Glace Isles elven.

The mighty Jrulthun stood in front of her, as tall as the pentacrux itself. A sinister grin was spread across its expression of promised pure malevolence. The savage troll snarled and stepped aside for the mastermind to come into view.

And there it was, in all its glory—Khomo'Jhuvonus, the Chosen Troll, king of the Glace Isles. Its signature high-crest was now ornamented with a green stripe that ran lengthwise through its hair, painted with the familiar dyes of the Glazjhendun. Its face was decorated with two golden teardrops beneath the corner of its left eye. The paint over its right eye was shaped like a blazing jade halo enveloping that side of its face. It remained seated upon BrKaim's high wooden chair, apparently stolen from the warden's chamber.

The three bloodrime axes it had been so persistent in asking for were soundly resting across its lap. Each of the axes was diverse in design, but they were identical in the material they had been forged with. Norah had never seen bloodrime shaped into such fascinating specimens of Terollar weaponcraft; she had only seen clusters of it in the Grand Artificer's laboratory. She thought their icy skin looked more like frozen bone fragments in an anarchic improvisation, fashioned into random shapes of promised death. Red veins were smothered beneath the rime and squirmed like pulsating snakes over certain surface areas. These were weapons fit only for the vilest, wickedest fiend in the realm.

And then it smiled that eerie jester-like grin and winked at her the same way she had, as a signature vow of pain and malevolence to come.

"So glad you could join us in time," it enunciated casually in the Civil, aristocratically free of any Terollar accent. "Today is a very special day for me. Do you know what makes this day so special? Today is the day I look my enemy in the eye and deliver justice to the north." Its words mimicked her exact introduction upon her first session with them in the Troll Gardens. The fiend proved it was an admirer of irony when it repeated another of her lines from the original encounter. "I have a guest I brought just for you."

The elven behind the khomo's chair separated to reveal an even worse reality than she could have imagined. This horror could get no crueler. Her daughter, with her arms roped behind her back, was pushed forward beside the monster who had orchestrated the evil affair.

"Ebrielle!" Norah cried as her heart jolted from her body and her face imploded into tears of repentance.

Khomo'Jhuvonus interrupted the reunion, piping up coolly as it leaned back in the seat with its green eyes focused on the weapons resting over its legs. "Oh, I found my axes, by the way." The troll's fingers tenderly stroked them as if it were caressing a litter of beloved pets. "Your daughter was too kind in returning them."

"Oh, Ebrielle, you stupid, stupid girl! What have you done, child?" Norah screamed pointlessly at her ill-fated daughter.

Ebrielle's tears streamed down in a sudden gush, matching

Norah's own, and she collapsed to the ground as her quaking legs gave way. "Mother, I'm so scared!"

"Let her be! Take me as a ransom! Send her to do your bidding!" Norah tried, with all her distinctive strength and resolve crushed away. "King Aerik Roth will pay any demands for his Royal Inquisitor! I have worth. She does not!"

Ebrielle trembled into a fit of sobs. The troll ignored Norah's pleas, remaining fixated on the long-lost axes.

She beseeched him again, attempting to calm her shaky voice to the best of her fleeting ability. "Please! Supplies? Peace? An enemy dead? Tell me what it is you want." Norah demanded a reply.

This time her troll interrogator did look up, squinting in disgust. "Interesting. I remember you saying you do not make bargains with trolls, just before you knifed my tongue out. Again. And again. And again. And more times. It has always been you that has insulted me."

Norah was still too in shock over the vivid strangeness of the dreamlike scenario. Her disoriented focus floated to the elven all around her, painted and dressed for war. "How did you manage this? How did you all arm yourselves?"

"My only fear was that if your cunning reputation proceeded you, you would already have deduced the obvious and put an immediate end to this plausible outcome before you. But I must say, your remarkable lack of astuteness has been rather dissatisfying. We of the Glace Isles have always rendered the shrewd Lady Bayn of the Deeps as far more formidable," the Chosen Troll patronized her.

She was immune to verbal provocations in her present state. This was the game she played with all her prisoners. Did it really think to goad her the same with such feeble efforts on her misguided foresight to even anticipate this improbable scheme? She ignored the troll's taunting and let it enjoy itself talking some more. "The cache of arms was placed in the caverns beneath your Forlorn months ago, by allies I have incorporated all throughout Frostdale."

Barredish allying in secret with trolls? Since when did the Godslands catch fire and the sun freeze over? This is seditious absurdity. She refused to believe in such a failing infrastructure in her homeland from all angles: the Dominadom, the mysterious change in select highborn, and now apparently those troll allied as well.

The khomo further expounded. "We heal in these natural settings. The fall does not kill. One by one, each day, the Glazjhendun traded who made the jump to retrieve the weapons. It has long been known you keep your Terollar prisoners in this Forlorn. A folly on your end you should fix soon, after I allow you to live today," it concluded with a surprising tease.

Norah's tears had ceased. She stared skeptically at her tormentor. "I live today?" She dared hope. "*She* lives?"

Khomo'Jhuvonus shot her a disarming grin. "I made her a promise. She lives, as does her choice for one other. Fortunately for you, if you comply with my requests, I will go on my way. You will ensure my exit is unfollowed. And that was your last question for now." The Chosen Troll stood and strolled up to her cross. Its eyes seemed sincere. This was an entity of legend that did not have to lie to get what it wanted. "I will take the role of the inquisitor now, Honorah Bayn."

Somehow she could not match her nemesis's unapproachable scowl. Her attention faded to the side, somewhere into the blackness of the depths below. "Ask," she whispered acquiescently.

"Who am I?" The simple but obvious inquiry came.

"Khomo'Jhuvonus." She tentatively defied convention to utter the forbidden name aloud.

"Do you know the truth about your dead husband?"

Why does it always resort back to this? Norah's demeanor was fueled by her known ire at the troll's audacity to bring up such a sensitive matter. She hollowly glared into the nothingness of the abyss, refusing to answer.

The Chosen Troll continued anyway for her. "Allow me to elaborate. He was no hero of his people. He was like the rest of them: frightened and defeated from being enlightened about a greater enemy consuming all of Penthara from the inside out. Like your Annison Roth. Like your new Frostdale Council. Like so many within your breaking country's nobility. Barredom, Az'Dayne, and Khalimia all suffer from the Qindrid Curse, albeit in a different guise from what consumes openly in Aggedon, Caelduym, and Sho'Lon."

Norah's mind drifted from the room, the way she imagined her victims must have often attempted during her grueling sessions of similar methods. The troll sought to break her. It needed to feel the negative emotion rising under her skin. But she was now numb. Her ears were no longer present. Norah and her daughter were far from this place, safe from any future harm Barredom could bring.

"Lord Lucas Blackendale aspired, for him and his men of the

Eldenvale Rangers, to what was granted to your fair queen. But alas, they are Barredish, like you, and she is of a Daynish bloodline. They were not eligible for the new type of Transcendence, which only the Neveril can offer—not being of the correct descendancy. He was given a choice instead: to join what I have discovered is known as the Umbran Pledge, or to have his family and men murdered. The whole of the Eldenvale Rangers were given this same threat. And this is how I found them," the voice came again, finding her wherever she failed to escape to. She was back on the pentacrux, looking down upon her archenemy.

"Stop." Norah's eyes were glazed with dried tears, and her heart was empty, but her tone was severe.

But she was in no position to make demands of her tormentor. The Chosen Troll arrogantly sneered in triumph, knowing she would be crushed in any further attempts at persuading her cognizance from the room. "I allowed two to live, even knowing they had already committed to this Umbran Pledge. Once sworn in by the Neveril, there is no recourse. Your blind brother-by-law, Tomas Brigannor, and Mathias Oreville, now of the eschewed Norther Knights, are in league with this clandestine enemy that infects your country's capital like a festering pestilence spreading from its urban organs."

"Yet you let them live," she pondered aloud. "Why?"

"Do you always kill your little prisoners before baiting and catching the true enemy that is the architect behind it all? I think you believe you are patient, Norah, but it is clear that you are not," the Glace Isles king criticized again. "Sometimes you should let the fearful pawns live, to send them back into the web and discover where the spider lies in shadow. My nest of busy bees is high above these spiders' webs, watching and playing, intermingled in this multilayered disarray of plotting upon subplotting that you call home.

"I know them all now," Khomo'Jhuvonus claimed with conviction. "All the big, bad spiders, down to all the little mice, and the vermin in between." The troll legend casually stroked Ebrielle's hair while she sat and sobbed irrepressibly, all the while staring down its trophy captive. Norah could not match its unapproachable green-eyed gaze. "And I am going to tell you all my great secrets, Lady Bayn."

"What then? What am I to do for you, for you to keep me alive? Am I another pawn in the webs for your spies to watch as it all unravels into chaos? Am I to meet these troll-friendly conspirators? And what of this other race of qindrid that are not skyborne or stone-borne, or the greys without umbran? What do the long-gone Neveril care of human politics, north or south?" She knew she was unleashing every question there could be, even after the troll had warned her she would be granted no more. Somehow the curiosity had made her temporarily lose sight of her immediate fears from her dire situation.

"Tsk, tsk, always the inquisitor, it would seem." The khomo beamed a wide grin like it had been known to do when the Forlorn guardsmen had dubbed it Smiles. "I forgive you. We do not have much time." It glanced to the top of the well-like oubliette dungeon, as if expecting undesirable company at any moment. "I will answer each before I take my leave."

Ebrielle was a trembling fit on her knees, her eyes transfixed by the besmudged bricks beneath her, unable to meet her mother's apologetic regard or any of the barbaric elvan horrors that encircled her. *Oh, my poor, silly girl, why did I bring you into this with me?*

"What will Lady Bayn do for the khomo of the Glace Isles? Why—" it paused to accentuate the last part of its answer with deep satisfaction "—I will allow you to become one of the revered troll-friendly conspirators, of course! I would make you a liaison of the Glazjhendun, to together liberate the realm from all qindrid and umbran, to unveil and eliminate their affiliates, and to stop any other aberrations that oppose the Balance."

What a disgusting notion. A friend of trolls? Myself and Khomo'Jhuvonus allied in conjoined efforts to save the north? Fives wake me now from this ludicrous hell, I beg of you! Norah's wide brown eyes defined how her reasoning vexed her.

The long-hushed rumors of Lucas's downfall were coming to appalling validation. The suspected truth of Tomas Brigannor's condemning allegiance. The bizarre shifts in political standpoints among the majority of the influential upper court. The absolute slaughter of the entire guard in the Frostdale Deeps. The reality that the Chosen Troll was indeed still alive and had engineered this perfectly executed position. Her daughter's grim crisis staring her in the face. The insinuation of her son joining the binding cult of an expanding enemy like one never known before. And hints of a new type of qindrid with a powerful elvan affiliation she knew little about.

"To collude with the trolls? I am sure it will result in great amity.

Such an honor you grant me." She cursed her own impulsive idiocy the second the sarcastic words escaped her mouth.

"That tongue of yours again," the khomo threatened with a wicked sneer, "always esteemed as your greatest tool, though it proves more to be your principal flaw."

Her eyes sank impassively, as if permitting the grim tidings to proceed. "You will not meet the Glace Isles collaborators. They will meet you. But I will tell you who they are. And I will tell you that you will not like it." The troll took entirely too long a pause before clarifying for her anxiety to contain itself. "You have met High Chancellor Soro, haven't you?"

Impossible ... Any other name could have been uttered, and she might have been able to swallow the betrayal of even a loyal friend better than this unseen scenario. *First, you trolls? Now, I am intended to conspire against my country's royal wishes with the most contemptible man in the history of the court?* It all made sense now though, with Soro's antagonizing antics at the Hall of Final Light, and the fact that he had restricted her from any further torture sessions on the trolls. Norah's neck hung in defeat, hoping that maybe the collapse of her heavy head might snap it into eternal peace.

"Soro and the Forwoken are not what they seem either. I played my game back on the kingdom that is playing it on the rest of the realm. The monks of the Qaegons all have something in common. Green eyes, tall stature, chopped ears—Soro decorates his in gold rings, while the monks veil themselves with fitted masks and hoods to hide the maiming that the mortali have visited upon them. They keep their ears and hair guised for a reason. They are as Terollar as the Glazjhendun of my isles, elvan to the core, with not a single trace of a human bloodline. And your Barredish highborn under Yharl Seagram Bloodmont of Whalestown are all part of it, raising Soro at an early age to rise within the Frostdale ranks."

Norah rebelled to hold faith in her deceptive ears even more than her cheating eyes now. *This is all some dark hallucination from troll magic. This mortali, or one of its shamans, has cast some sorcery on my mind.* "None of this can be true." She violently shook her head in disbelief. "Fives wake me now."

"But you are more awake than you have ever been, Lady Bayn, and your gods are nowhere near. Only me. Only us," Khomo'Jhuvonus said plainly, beaming its same dramatic grin. "Soro, born as

Sorovronus, is my grandson. He is of the blood of my youngest daughter. He was my recent contingency plan to keep you in check, and closely monitor you, should there had been any hint that you would shift from typical torture to execution on my tribesven of the Glazjhendun. But your repute proved true, as anticipated, and we felt confident that death and mercy would play no part in what you considered retribution.

"We made adaptations before the deal for his rise was schemed with the Yharl of Whalestown, shortly after we subjugated the harbor's nobility as peacefully and quietly as we could. House Bloodmont was offered peaceful reign over the crab and fish catch, along with the whale hunt south of the Glace Isles. We further offered a tribute of the spoils looted from our Aggedonian exploits. The yharl fast became the richest and most influential in your country, thanks to us. We even allowed it to be him that pretended to discover the Forwoken monastery in the Qaegons. He introduced the Terollar monks into the fold of your high court, as Sorovronus was elegantly maneuvered up the ladder of Frostdale's favor."

"Soro … the Forwoken … all trolls." She was far from her bindings in the Forlorn, no longer tied to the cross. Ebrielle wasn't present. The Terollar elven were all illusions, and the vessel that feigned speaking as her nemesis was nothing more than a specter of her drugged imagination. She was under some concoction of outlandish elixirs, no doubt. *Where was I last?* She could no longer recall.

"You asked one other question. The most important one of all." The phantom troll tried to invade her dream once more.

She languidly inclined her head, facing her oppressor with a grunt of debility. *I can no longer remember.* "The Neveril?" She did remember, through her spinning state of delirium. *Is this what my victims feel, then? The troll has yet to even draw blood from me …*

"The Neveril are still here. They are all around, from the north to the south, as well as in half the human nations in the east. Only the greater powers of the west survive their inevitable infiltration—the kingdom of Vellyon, the Utamian Exchange of Goldgarden, and of course, the Thrench Empire. And perhaps the southeast Tongan territories. Now, as to what they created …" He paused to ensure he had her undivided lucid attention.

He? Why am I humanizing this wretch? They are all "it." It, it, it … Norah ground her teeth as a surge of fortitude flooded through her veins, coercing her body to poise as straight as she could muster on the pentacrux tormenting her bloodless limbs. She was weaker than she thought. She had never endured such tests of her physical tenacity before. Flaccid in fatigue once more, Norah realized the toll that the Deeps had taken upon her over the wilting years. Her overzealous appetite in her cruel work, the lack of true sleep and nourishment since Lucas's death, and her general dispassion for life had crippled her overall vitality into a state of atrophy.

"What do I call them? How do I find them? The Neveril and their qindrid among us," she pleaded, ready for answers if this was indeed no bad dream she could awaken from.

"You will not see the Neveril. Ever. They are the puppet masters behind it all." He educated her on the hard truth. "Any elvan of the mixed shadow lineage can enter the Taboo to become umbran. History only reports on the Shiniryn and Wyldenar, but the Neveril indeed did, all in secret. They became umbran by the numbers and were embraced in their society instead of shunned. The Neveril, these elven of fire and shadow descendancy combined, brought the wrath of a whole new race on the realm. While the skyborne and stoneborne took their nations in full through open domination, acquiring many enemies and suffering countless wars, this infiltration by the Neveril has been much subtler, with no such opposition," he ardently tutored.

"The Neveril qindrid in question are much more formidable." The verbose troll continued to expound upon the true crisis at hand. "They can be as silent as a lifeless night. They walk walls and ceilings like the ground under your feet. They pay no heed to the harmful effects of smoke and fire, and cannot burn. Their kind has such an impower that allows them to take on the form of those they study. It is not fast, not all at once, but a slow molding of those they choose to shift into. Masters of their race are more efficient than others, learning more forms and shaping themselves more quickly. They can take on faces, bodies, voices, and even modify heights and weights to some degree." Khomo'Jhuvonus paused, forcing her chin with his firm hand to an elevation where she was coerced to come face-to-face with him. "This is the end of all human civilization. The age of something new and sinister—the era of the neverborne."

"The neverborne." The abhorrent word came out of her cotton mouth like a curse filled with bile, though she had never heard the term before. "How long have you known? What am I to do?"

"Sorovronus," he said it again. This time she listened. "You will not be in contact with me. Only the High Chancellor. Your instructions are very clear. You are to free Aerik Roth from his captivity and save Barredom."

Norah was entirely confused, sure that she must be waning from the debilitation once again. "King Aerik? But he is safe in his quarters, in seclusion."

The words sounded as ignorant in her head as they did when she said them aloud. It did not take the khomo to confirm the disconcerting realization of her shameful gullibility. "Come now, after all I have just told you? The King Aerik you see hiding behind closed doors at the court is an imposter, a neverborne infidel not yet ready to introduce himself to the public, as your actual sovereign is being remarkably reluctant in undisclosed captivity. Queen Annison, as predicted, is among the turned enemy and is one of them. There were no mages involved in her recovery. Only the promise of immortality through the Neveril."

Norah was not sure she could handle any more revelations of her world's undoing on this queer day. Everything she had come to know was morphing into an impossible backward reality. *My enemies are my allies, and my country's nobility, with the king and queen, are my …* Her thoughts could not conclude. She felt that her eyes were no longer glossy from the former impulsive swell of tears. They now just felt dry and red and wide and mad. But she held no lingering fury for the trolls. The indignation within her was now in a comically ironic acceptance of her life's circumstances in general. She did not hate any particular race or individual in the moment. She only loathed one entity—her life.

"How do I even find King Aerik then?"

"You are going to do a great many feats this coming season of the Sunder. Know that you will free your king, saving Barredom from the Dominadom's grasp. You will kill your queen and this imposter king. The current Frostdale Council will fall. And you will never again harm another Terollar of the Glace Isles, ensuring that Barredom ceases hostilities against us indefinitely. Again, Sorovronus will show and tell you the details. We are running out of time," the khomo confidently directed, leaving no room for noncompliance.

"Kill the queen? Kill the false king? Me? Convince Barredom to make peace with trolls?" She couldn't help but burst into a hysterical laugh. It was all too surreal a mocking parody of her entire life's standards.

"Do you have any further questions before we begin?" The smile disappeared from the khomo's face, and his demeanor instantly switched to dispassion.

Norah felt as if only her head remained alive in her entire body now. She was sure if they were to torture her by limb or gut, she would feel nothing with the numbness. Only one answer remained ambiguous. "Ebrielle? You will let her go?"

"You have my vow of it," he assured her. And somehow, even though she did not trust or know this nemesis, that phrase gave her peace of mind. But then he elaborated. "But there are just a few final things."

"Damn the Fives with you, troll. Be done with it," she profaned against her better judgment, out of sheer fret.

"You see, it's just that." Khomo'Jhuvonus shook his head in disappointment, smirking as his green-dyed high-crest waved about. "That tongue. We do not seem to have need of it. I only need your political influence, Lady Bayn, and your assurance as long as you are alive. I think Soro can do the talking for the both of you, do you not?" His huge, sinister smile returned. There was no way out of this fate, she realized.

The Chosen Troll winked at her and nodded back to his aged son, Zuulzin, who brought over a pair of tongs and a prepared hot, sharp knife. How many times had she cut out the khomo's tongue under his alias as Smiles? She wasn't sure she had even kept count. Norah's mouth puckered in protest against the unimaginable anguish she was about to suffer. "You had me for a moment. You are good. You are indeed still the monster of the stories."

"Still with that tongue again. It just has no place in the plan, Lady Bayn. I simply only need you alive. You understand." Khomo'Jhuvonus feigned a frown of compassion. "But I do not need you getting yourself killed. And I do not need you telling anyone how we escaped. It would not be very 'troll-like' of me to leave you completely intact, now, would it?"

Ebrielle protested. "No! Please! Please!"

"Ebrielle! Look away!" Norah stared at her daughter, holding back the choke of absolute fear bloating inside her throat. Her unyielding pride excused her from matching the judgment stares of the troll audience, or the disconcertingly morose visage of Kind-Eyes briskly walking toward her.

Zuulzin shoved a tight piece of torn cloth inside both of her nostrils, suppressing her ability to breathe by any means other than through her mouth. She tried to squirm and hold out as long as she could, but time fast expired. She took a heavy gasp for air and closed her eyes to embrace the nightmare. And that was when she felt the tongs go in.

"A tongue for a tongue," Khomo'Jhuvonus growled in the guttural Terollar dialect as she tasted the searing heat of the sharp knife Zuulzin pushed into her mouth. Norah's gurgled screams were muffled by those of her own daughter, who refused to look away from the grisly display. Zuulzin pulled away with her bleeding tongue, there set in the tongs within his grip. She watched the aged elvan toss it underneath her suspended feet, like it were a piece of rejected fat to feed the hounds. Norah tried to curse at the beast, but she no longer had that ability. All that came was an unrecognizable cry of pain.

"Good," came the voice of Khomo'Jhuvonus, taking control of the vast chamber once more. "Almost finished now. I am sorry you do not heal as fast as we do. In fact, you never will. Just as Zuulzin never will after Lucas destroyed his chance for a lifetree." His words were harsh and entirely spiced with premeditated malice.

Norah felt increasingly dizzy, suspecting she may take to the darkness soon. Only the dread of the outcome for her daughter reinforced her resolve to persevere in a conscious state of mind. Her head was suddenly ten times as heavy, and Ebrielle was fading into the image of a distant cloud.

His voice came again. "You will do as bidden. And your daughter will be returned to you, unharmed and untouched." Her vision was swiftly becoming a blur as she strived to maintain consciousness. The implications of what that meant had not even fully registered.

She could perceive each troll, one by one, jumping from the Forlorn's footpaths into the chasm below, all seemingly suicidal leaps. It was a bizarre act to witness. Oenayus, the lone greyborne, proceeded to take his leave by a rope that hung off the ledge. Only the khomo, Jrulthun, and Zuulzin remained with Ebrielle and her.

Norah's final failing sight idled on her sweet, innocent daughter, kneeling in front of her. She and Ebrielle would survive.

Khomo'Jhuvonus whispered, "I leave you now. I have a strange feeling I can trust that you will not pursue me."

Zuulzin followed up his father's concluding speech by climbing down a rope descending into the chasm. Khomo'Jhuvonus took his axes and shadowed his son out of sight into the darkness below.

"I'm sorry! I am so sorry! Mother, please forgive me!" Ebrielle begged through a hysteria of sobbing, slowly finding her feet to walk toward her maimed mother.

A massive opaque silhouette loomed over Ebrielle's tiny frame. *Jrulthun.* She had forgotten he hadn't taken the jump to join the others yet. His deep, raucous tone came in his own language, which both she and her daughter fluently understood. *"The khomo extends his gratitude for this new pact of trust. You can now think of me as her caretaker. Do as the khomo bids."*

A surge of rage brought Norah back around, seeing her daughter's desperate face clearly now. Norah ineffectively kicked and thrashed against her bindings, just as Ebrielle turned herself to futilely fight against the mammoth of a troll before he threw her helplessly over his shoulder.

It was the last thing she heard. *Do as the khomo bids.* That and her daughter's lurid screams echoed down the abyss as Jrulthun descended into the nothingness below. Norah slipped deeper into her nightmare, and as the resounding voice of her doomed child dissipated into an evanescent whisper, Norah allowed the inviting black void to consume her.

ONDREW (IX)

THE UNFINISHED

It was a particularly beautiful morning. In all fact, it had never been so beautiful. It was his last sunrise. The Dawning's death in the Cycle of Kingfall, before the first furrow toward the Sunder, the cyclical evolution of the tairan season transitioning into the fire months. Yellowish golds on orangish reds eclipsed the wooded landscape below the crag that would serve as Ondrew's final respite.

Long-lost warmth spotlighted his bearded face. His watery eyes carefully absorbed the serenity of the heavenly horizon deep into the country of an ancient enemy that would now serve as his destined tomb. The jagged canopy of the evergreen Wyldewoods against the sharp ridges of Ur Dynelenox did not seem at all so menacing, unlike what he had envisioned.

His senses were enhanced, more astute than before. He caught a glimpse of a mountain bear and her two cubs, down the rocky pass as she escorted them to safety in whatever daily journey they were on. A flock of singing ravens chased and chattered over the tall pines, soaring like a fluttering silhouette against the contrast of the divine cloudscape. And a floral smell suggested something quite pleasant just over the bluff's steep drop. This was not a place of evil. This was simply another northern home to many innocents: the beasts and birds, and the greyborne born into the blight, with no choice in the matter.

Ondrew sat with his back to a flat boulder, his legs outstretched before him and his sword sprawled across his lap. His helm and shield and pack had been discarded. The subtle pain shooting through his veins endorsed the understanding that he still had more time before the numbness of the lethal poison took hold.

"Sire." Broc's bass-pitched voice slipped through his distracted musing. His second's tone came out more saddened than he recalled ever hearing from the typically boisterous knight. "This goodbye, then?"

Ondrew's thoughts were in a thousand places at once. Regrets and reminiscences of his past, and fears for the future of his men and kingdom. He held on to love and hate, fondness and bitterness, fair memories and failed aspirations, in every aspect of his unanticipated shortened life.

He had almost forgotten that Broc, Black, and Mathias were still beside him on the open ridge. *And Lilealah. I see you too. How could any man not see you?* His lazy focus perused the voluptuous umbran, from her feet to her beautiful face, standing just beside him.

"They are yours now, Captain BrKomak. This is for you." Ondrew handed over the rolled map of Aggedon and the route's drawn details to the wyrmway. He had already elaborated to his senior knights on all that he had been made aware of, and on what he expected to survive henceforth as the legacy of the Norther Knights. Now would be the true test for his men. And they would have to finish the great quest without him.

"I will save you all a seat beside me in the Godslands. I'll have the mead waiting at a feast for our reunion. Farewell to the best men I've ever known."

Black Brigannor bowed stoically, keeping eye contact with his liege as he took his leave. Mathias Oreville put a sympathetic palm on Ondrew's shoulder and held it for several seconds before turning to rejoin the others at the cave mouth. And Broc knelt to one knee and cradled him in a mutual grasp of respect around the forearm. "I'll be bringin' the mead meself, Drew. Been m' life's honor t' be beside ye in this. Any last thing I can do?"

Ondrew had already settled how it he wanted it to end. He didn't have the luxury to ponder otherwise. "Tell the bard to come see me. I would hear a song and talk with the umbran alone before—"

Broc abruptly stood up and bowed, not needing him to finish the dire implications of the rest of the request. Only Lilealah and Ondrew remained on the cliff for a short period.

He knew she would have something to say after hearing his entreaty for a private audience. "You wish to spend your final moments with me and not your friends?" she purred, seeming surprised.

"Are you not also a friend now?" he countered. He tossed her a lethargic grin before she could muster a defense. He still had his wit, but he could feel it in his infected blood that he no longer had his energy. The toxin coursing through his body was taking its toll.

Kyson approached before the two could engage any deeper. The minstrel humbly but awkwardly stepped forward and knelt low. The charismatic southlander announced himself. "I am at your life's service, Your Highness. You wished for me?"

Ondrew thought on the bard's ironic proclamation and couldn't help but afford him a heartfelt smile. "Kyson, I am certain by the blood of the Fives I never wished for you, yet I am graced with you nonetheless."

The usually jocular Timberhand appeared not to know how to retort to that. Instead, he just aimed his head down to the stones beneath his feet, like a submissive dog.

"You have been quite the fortuitous savior I believe the Norther Knights were in need of all along." Ondrew beamed in a sincere twist of admiration.

Kyson's gold-flecked amber eyes found their way back to Ondrew's, but the man's semblance was sheerly taken aback in astonishment. "Savior, my lord? I attest to many vain titles in jest, but this one far exceeds my merit. Such a compliment from you, however, is not taken lightly, I assure you."

For an uneducated foster raised by forest villagers, the archer was sophisticated in his vocabulary, and his enunciations were an odd mixture of dual accents, the Daynish and Tairancian combined, as if he had been raised in separate tutoring from the other Timberhands. With the right exquisite garb, the performer of obvious Daynish-Khalimishe lineage could easily pass for a Dominadom aristocrat, and none would blink an eye in doubt of it.

A sudden run of liquid streamed from his left nostril onto the top of his mustache and lips. Ondrew caught and wiped it on instinct with his fingers. *Red still. But the bleeding has begun.* "I don't have much time. I need two things from you, Kyson 'Southland' Greene."

Kyson poised obediently, readied to comply with any possible appeal. "The first?"

"Yharl Broc BrKomak is now delegated captain of the Norther Knights. Followed by Mathias Oreville, then Black Brigannor, to Pyper Bloodmont, to Kenton Lockehart, and so forth down the line. These men are Barredish highborn. Former yharls or renowned war heroes. But they lack what you have in charisma. And you carry it like a natural aura."

Kyson prodded to be enlightened on his unfamiliar gift. "Indulge me, then, please."

"Your mere presence commands absolute attention. Your skills in battle demand respect. Great men and hard warriors fall silent when you speak. You cast spells on the minds and hearts of all around you. You say you are born of unlearned birth, fostered and trained by simple villagers. I say you are the most naive wise person I've met. Kyson, you're as royal as a Roth in Frostdale, and you just don't know it yet."

Clearly, the southlander was confounded again about how to respond to such a flattering assessment. Thus, he said nothing as Ondrew finished his point. "Broc is a strong and capable commander, but the men will need a true leader. Not one so formally announced. But a beacon of unbending hope. The Norther Knights need you more than ever now."

Kyson returned a heartwarming smile. "I will uphold your esteemed standards as a badge of honor for all my days to come. This I vow to you."

"My second," Ondrew started, but his nose bled again out of the same nostril. He tried to stop it once more, but the trickle came freely now. *Still red.* He sighed in relief. "I would hear your song one last time."

"My song, my lord?" Kyson inquired, seemingly confused about which particular one was requested.

"The one you always sing. I would finally hear how it ends," he clarified.

"Ah, that one is unfinished. But certainly, your wish is my pleasure." The bard gracefully bowed and backed away a bit as he coolly handled his lute in place.

You, sir, there,
Here we are, the unfinished.
Do you hear me now?

Destiny's cry … say dare we try.

O'er here, my lord,
We've yet come so far.
Do you see me now?
Sun in my sky … oh, it is aye.

You sir, there,
Evermore, the unfinished
Can you feel me yet?
Death's kiss, but why … is this goodbye?

O'er here, my lord,
We've yet long to go.
Can we share this taste?
Our fate to die … But no, it 'twas …
Just all … our little lie.

Because we are …
Oh my, sir, Lord, yes, we are …
Evermore, we are
Yet the unfinished.

Ondrew played the verses of Kyson's ode over in his head, deciphering the connotations of the obscure lyrics. "'The Unfinished,'" Ondrew whispered.

Kyson politely attempted to correct him. "Well, no, my lord, that is not the name of the song. I simply meant that it is not yet fini—"

"'The Unfinished,'" Ondrew interjected a little more loudly. "I like it. I think it is about us. The Norther Knights." He drifted away in a fleeting daydream as he felt the bleeding once again, this time from the right nostril as well.

Kyson's only rebuttal was a concerned semblance of tear-checked sadness, guised behind a soft grin. "I will keep playing for you. Do you have any final advice to offer me?"

"Yes," Ondrew admitted as he glanced back to the entrance to the cave back to Zsolindal. "Watch your step." He couldn't help but chuckle for making light of his fatal situation.

Kyson evidently wasn't comfortable with someone else stealing the comedic role, or he genuinely refused to adhere any amusement to the tragedy. "I bid you a safe journey to the Fives, Your Highness." The bard bowed his head as he took his farewell to the crag's edge and faced the Wyldewoods below.

His enchanting melody began again. And that was when she sat beside him, her back to the stone like his, with her fingers interlaced with his own. The exotic enemy's sensual touch felt strange, but he welcomed it.

"Any moment now." Ondrew could barely hear his own voice. Liquid was pooling in his ears, muffling the sound of all life. His focus basked in the rising sun.

"I must apprise you of a fact first," she confessed.

He did not question in response: the act of even breathing was proving to be an exhausting trial for his weakening body. His eyes found hers as the umbran came on again. "I want you to know about your father."

He did not expect that. Pending news about the king shot a sting through his chest, pounding through his lungs. His grip unconsciously tightened around hers. But still it was her turn to speak. "Your true father, Aerik Roth, is being held as a prisoner in secret, far from the court of Frostdale. The man who poses as the king of Barredom, who has shunned all audiences, is something else entirely."

His fingers forwent her own. His mouth was open, and he could taste the iron on his bloody tongue. *Who are you, witch? How deep does your reach go?* His words remained stuck behind his awestruck gaze.

Her black orbs fixated on him, undeterred. "I tell you all of this so that, as you die, you are aware that your true father, the one who did not betray you, does still love his son and his kingdom. And he would not relent to the Dominadom's heavy hand. So he was forced, as they put a plague on your mother. It was all a strategy, you see. The only cure offered for Queen Annison was to undertake the Transcendence. The queen was never even brought to Mageholme. She was already weak-willed and festered in disloyalty to your father. It was not hard to break her. She took to the turn and is now one of the new qindrid, just like the majority of the Frostdale Council and Daynish dignitaries in place."

He could feel the drip coming out of his ears now. He was almost glad for it. The blood tried to mute the most appalling scenario he could possibly imagine about his kingdom. *Father, I am so sorry I am failing you. It was much better when I thought you only hated me.*

"They are called the neverborne, shapeshifters who are impowered through the descendancies of fire and shadow. They are the qindrid product of the Neveril umbran, to whom the entire realm of Penthara has been oblivious for decades. And they are everywhere now: the puppet masters of the Az'Dayne Dominadom, your precious Barredom, and many regions between."

The level of treachery she was confessing to was far too paramount for Ondrew to fully assimilate. His scowl said it all as he commanded his arms up to strangle her on the spot, but his fingers never even twitched. Everything around him was betraying him, even his own body. "Why you? What role do your stoneborne play beside this new foe in this apocalypse to come?"

"As I told you in the beginning, the Thrench Ashenwave is the only true enemy of the elvan race as a whole, as their empire continually grows and swallows all. A treaty has been made among all qindrid nations now to unite against the common monster breaching the eastern shores. The Great Exodus has brought my army to join with the Caelduyan and Sho Kung skyborne, with the aid of the Neveril Empire. House Emmonost, which leads the Ashenwave, has never met resistance like it will from our stance. I have an arrangement that Barredom and Aggedon will be mine once I have allowed your country to believe it was conquering the north from our retreat. The neverborne rulers in place will turn your people from the inside out and remove those who do not comply with the Umbran Pledge," she explained of the sinister master plot.

"What of my men, then? The Norther Knights." He wheezed to barely talk now, but his concern for them exceeded all else. "What was our fate all along?"

"They will have a choice at the end. They will be offered the chance to become qindrid, based on their descendancy. Kyson is the only one eligible to become neverborne, while the other archers and your Norther Knights can take the Transcendence to stoneborne from the umbran who still remain at Aepox. The Vellyans cannot be turned. But it is no matter. Those two, along with Mathias Oreville, your Eldenvale Ranger captain, have already been a part of the Umbran Pledge for some time now and will do the bidding of the binding oath. Alternatively, if your knights do not partake in the ritual to transcend, they, too, can take the irrevocable pledge. If they refuse, I give you my word that I will be merciful and make their deaths quick."

She leaned over to embrace his lips in a deep kiss that he was too paralyzed to refuse. His neck slighted him, unable to turn away. His teeth ground behind, and his eyes glowered in fury.

"You are a hero for this, Ondrew Roth. I will ensure it is known. I did so wish to reward you," Lilealah purred in futile seduction. She stood from her perch and left him to die alone, with just him and the bard on the bluff.

Somehow the Fives blessed him with one last ounce of defiance of the toxin's paralysis. His hand shot up to his nose and ears to wipe away the drain of fluid streaming down his face. It was thick and orange now, and he felt it out of the corner of his mouth. A swell of tears formed in his eyes as his focus stood still over the fiery-red-haired bard. *No, not yet ...*

Kyson ended his tune timely, looking back to his dying liege. Their lamenting eyes locked as if they were one and the same on that instant. "Evermore the unfinished. Save us all, friend," Ondrew muttered on his own deaf ears, trusting his words to resonate aloud.

He could feel a burn on his cheeks from a piercing cold breeze married with the sun's ascending warmth. And that was when it happened, as an orange tear fell from his eye.

AERIK (III)

TO GREENER FIELDS

The trample of hooves trespassed upon the northernmost pinnacle of the Utamian Thoroughfare by the thousands. Horses lined the southbound road in dual lines of symmetry for countless fields, with the paladin aspirants' contingent amid the procession. The snow-coated soil evolved from a commingle of waning whites to a gradual greener life as the encroachment of Az'Dayne's finest traversed the lands out of Barredom.

Aerik strode in a synchronized gallop beside Henrick, diverged from the disarray of an irregular march. They were a practiced duo, playing a game of conformity against bedlam's burden. They could not be undone as Blackendale and Brigannor, bloodlines of the ever-esteemed Barredish royal houses.

He caught the glimpse of his perturbed cousin in his peripheral vision. Henrick was damned by the same knowledge as he was but could not voice it aloud. Aerik skeptically surveyed the three young initiates in his vicinity, vaguely familiar from seeing them around Frostdale.

His focus then homed in on the Daynishman directly in front of him as he trailed in his wake. *A spellblade on your right hip. It's seen many uses. Daynish by blood. The best swordsman among all that I've seen. Where do you hail from, deadly stranger? Something is amiss with your intent.* Aerik had just picked up that the man's left glove was custom-made to be shorter in the fingers, as each digit seemed to be missing the ends where his nails would have been. From knuckle to the first and second phalanges, but the third had apparently been severed from his index down to his small finger. His light-brown hair was long and wavy, tucked underneath the back of his helm. He realized he had never seen the killer's face.

The victor of the Melee impossibly seemed to register the scrutiny and peered back to interrupt the evaluation.

"Do not provoke his attention," his cousin warned.

His eyes shot back to Henrick, worried about the irrefutable decision they had made. "Say it," Aerik demanded quietly.

"Fives or no, we are right royally fucked in all of this," Henrick spat candidly.

"Keep hushed," Aerik warned, paranoid as his gaze instinctively glanced back at the Daynishman, no longer paying them any heed.

"This is the entrance to the end, Aerik. My pa warned me some. I did not want to say it, but now ..." Henrick didn't need to finish saying the known revelation. His cousin had been told and shown the same thing as a conclusion for the Trial of Truth, as no doubt they all had. The paladins, the veritans, and so many others already, they were all no longer human. Turned into qindrid like never before seen nor read about. They were living in a realm of doppelgängers. And it was too late now. They had already been brought into the light. They were now a part of the growing sect of secret-keepers and plot-pushers. To try to escape now would mean a quick and sure death.

But Aerik knew he could not become one of the new qindrid, even if they tried to make him undergo the ritual. These were the Neveril involved, elven of shadow and fire descendancy, like the one he had seen in the library at the end of the Trial of Truth. Only humans of correlated descendancy could be turned—the Psages, the Daynish, or the Khalimishe. Barredish, like him and Henrick, were only susceptible to becoming stoneborne, through the Wyldenar umbran.

But all paladins are neverborne? We were never going to become paladins, Aerik dismally realized. *What have they devised for us?* He had just registered that his heart was beating faster than the hooves of all the southern army. Henrick's sweaty brow mimicked his own inner fears. They had to escape before reaching the capital.

Aerik pressed his steed next to Henrick's and muttered just audibly enough for his friend to hear. "You know what we have to do."

"Your fates have already been decided," came a stranger's voice. The spellblade's white mare had delayed, striding adjacent to their own now. The foreigner had finally spoken. "You needn't encumber yourselves with the burden of worry."

His face was covered by a helm that fitted more like a mask. Iron in the front but just a strap for the back, the armor wrapped around half his head. The eye slits were downturned in sadness, as was the indent of the mouth, while only the nostrils were cut out for breathing. His words were muffled behind the mask.

"What do you know?" Aerik implored.

"What do I know?" the enigmatic champion teased. "Oh, only everything there is. Only all that matters."

"What can we do to stop it, then?" Henrick beseeched of the man, as if praying to a divine itself.

"Barturon Chandoss, though they think me to be Nikayle de'Queur," was all he replied.

The two were confused by the juggling of subjects. Aerik spoke up for both of them. "Why hide your house for being Chandoss? Nikayle, or Barturon, may we call you friend? Is there no way to elude this curse underway?"

"Aerik Blackendale and Henrick Brigannor—two rich boys inspired to be knightly aspirants, both of famed but doomed northern fathers. And now these two rich boys have been shown the light that is the shadow, the truth that is the falseness, the face of a friend that is the guise of a foe. You both are drowning and wish a way to the surface. But there is no more surface, you see. There is only darkness now. You must simply learn to breathe within it. The two rich boys did not listen well when 'twas revealed their fates have already been decided," Barturon riddled in his odd dance of words.

The two cousins looked to each other for answers to the peculiar fellow's riddles. Henrick's paranoia was voiced first. "What happens to us, then? Do we die? Tell me that much."

Henrick, a large and stalwart boy, whom Aerik had never known to be afraid of anything, was visibly quivering in fear. Aerik attempted to at least decipher some of the conundrum the spellblade was hinting at. "We are too deep in this game. They will force us to become part of some pact to fulfill their behest. There can be only total subservience with no hope of escape."

"Oh, but there is. And I will only offer it once. You will know when. I advise you take it. And you can both know one more token. Neither of you are going to Az'Dayne," Barturon dispassionately promised.

The spellblade's horse abruptly skipped back to his place in the march. Aerik and Henrick decided not to exchange any more feedback on the conspiratorial matter, surrounded, as they were, by duplicitous strangers and complex layers of sedition.

Spellblade was both the name given to the magical weapons and the wielders of such. The sword in Barturon's possession was bound to him, and only him, for the entirety of his life. Only certain generations in the specific house bloodlines could be awarded the blade's acceptance. The sentient sword always chose its owner for a reason, infused with an elvan's hunder to bring it to life during its forging, keeping the memories and skill sets of all its masters.

Aerik had never seen a true spellblade in Barredom, as they were nothing but fabled tales of the southern realms, but all boys growing up in Frostdale had heard the fanciful legends.

The appearance of the sword was just as he had always envisioned it: elaborate gold and elvan bone in the hilt and guard, an impossibly exquisite emerald for the pommel, and enchanted unbreakable glass for the blade. It was said that when a spellblade invoked the magic stored within, absorbed from killing mages and consuming one of their powers, the transparent blade would glow green with specific runes, depending on the conjured spell.

Aerik couldn't avert his eyes from the sheathed perfection upon Baturon's hip. *One hundred thirty-six men ahead,* his nervous scrupulosity counted to break away from his fixation. *Seventy-two brown, fifty-seven black, four white, three mixed.* He tallied the colors of the horses now. He tried not to dwell on the gravity of his impending grim-lit future, likely to be short-lived if he did not choose wisely.

He grievously found himself engulfed by a world-dominating throng of shape-shifting qindrid, or those unturned yet sworn to their cause, and moreover, now alongside some voluntarily placed insurgent alluding to threats on his fate. Aerik tried to think of the few positives of the subtle environs in his vicinity but could identify only one bittersweet find.

The snows were melted from the highway, and the grass nearby was green in abundance. The season of the Sunder and the climate of the south were swiftly proceeding. But he only yearned for one thing now: the fastest route back to the comfortable cold whites of Frostdale. The only place he knew he could ever call home.

EBRIELLE (VII)

LITTLE MOUSE

The hard faints had come and gone. Hauled like paltry luggage across a monster's back, most of the descent through the Forlorn and out of the Merridan Caverns had been a haze of surreal denials between lapses of time-eluding blackouts. The burning rub of the rope down, the stabbing catch of jagged cave rock, the sound of the shallow subterranean river being trampled and defiled – none of it had registered as tangible truths.

She was a zombie living in a shell of what had once been her living body. She could no longer talk and dared not futilely fight back, since the ability to fear or anger had long fled her crippled mind. The state of narcolepsy she had been cornered into was a blissful stupor, and she was either too timid or too inept to seek her way out. But she did not care. She simply no longer cared about anything. The Five and Five had already prescribed her this absurdity, and her efforts to escape would be in vain against the divine design of her cruel deities.

The sign of something strangely human brought her to again. It was a fleet of fishing ships, built small and dexterous for narrow water channels, not the kind to withstand substantial sea voyages.

The flags atop the single masts were familiar to her. *Seagram Bloodmont, Yharl of Whalestown.* The boats were armed with Forwoken monks and manned by Whalestown fishermen. The Terollar elven were segregated aboard and dispersed into the stock holds belowdecks, where the fresh catch was meant to be stored. But there would be no fish or crabs on this run, only trolls intent on being set free, as bargained.

And who would contend to taunt the wrath of the legend that was Khomo'Jhuvonus? Evidently, none. Puppets of House Bloodmont smuggled her and the most favored of the Glazjhendun, including the khomo, aboard. Muffled words of allied respect were traded between the Whalestown captain and the elvan mastermind before all were shuffled below to the secret hold behind a wall of empty seafood crates.

It was just the khomo, Jrulthun, Zuulzin, and six of his elite on board with her. The others had been dispersed onto other boats. No sounds were spoken. And finally the shift of the Otticus River's current could be felt.

The fishermen's ships were moving now. And she knew her direction from here. They would voyage to Whalestown in a surreptitious escape, then embark on seaworthy vessels into the Bay of Trolls for the khomo to reunite with his prepared army on the Glace Isles, no doubt. For whatever was in his plan thereafter, she could only fathom a score or more of violent possibilities.

Ebrielle slumped, bound and timid, numb but aware of doom on all sides. The stout stench of the maltreated, barbaric fugitives refused to let her slip back into a comatose trance.

Ebrielle had just come to the realization that in all her life, she had never even visited Whalestown. She gazed on Khomo'Jhuvonus with no distress, her heavy head swaying in subjected disorientation still, and she smiled involuntarily up at him. *So tall. Each of you. Thank you for all the travels you will afford me that I could never have done alone.* She could have sworn she reached out to touch the savage sovereign but noted in a second take that apparently she hadn't moved at all, aside from the careen of her body against the shifting waters.

She was entering full dementia. The infection of hysteria was deep in her veins now, disallowing sane decisions. She supposed she might uncharacteristically act out an impulse from building mania any moment, surely spelling her doom. Instead, she just found herself staring upward and wide-eyed into the all-knowing green eyes of her towering captor.

The unbearable silence lasted at least two lifetimes, she believed she counted. She strained her ears to the creaking decks above, pretending she heard the voices of the men conversing and the river running. The elven enveloping her were trained in supreme stealth, and not even a hint of breath sounded from their still lips. They put themselves in a trancelike reverie, as if some deity of time had frozen them for inspection.

A tiny mouse scurried from around a crate and darted in panic throughout the maze of the Terollars' feet and her own. The starving creature's dismay was dramatized like a miniature solo performance when it scuttled through each empty container, searching for just one morsel of positivity to consume. The feeble young rodent squeaked in fruitless distress, cursing the world for an unfair hand, to no avail, for its fate to survive and adapt or to wither and die.

As the little mouse scampered into the far corner and just solemnly lay down, doing absolutely nothing, her empathy for the poor thing impacted her as hard as a lance through the heart. Ebrielle felt compassionate tears running down her face on both sides.

"Shh, shh now, poor little mouse," came a whisper in the Civil tongue by Khomo'Jhuvonus. "Round and round the maze you try, but why? So exhausting. So defeating. Left hungry, alone, and lost in the end. Why be a mouse, some say, scavenging at the scraps of those you hide from your entire life, when you can manage more powerfully as a rat and take what is yours by right, through cunning or might?"

Ebrielle said nothing to the allegory, still infatuated with the animal version of her own state, quivering and famished in the shadows.

"But the rat is even more despised than the mouse. So neither is a cure. And so many never learn this. But you must evolve into who you were meant to be. Even if your kind told you that you could only become either mouse or rat. My kind told me this, and I said no to it. Shunned, discarded, hated, and there were even attempts on my life. But I said no to those too. I became a different kind of beast. And I taught others the same."

His metaphoric words struck restored fortitude into her absconded essence. The tears suddenly ceased. She felt warmth in her flesh again. Her eyes once again secured the ability to blink as her formerly distressed semblance relaxed.

Khomo'Jhuvonus nodded to Jrulthun. The look he shot his alpha was as if the two had trained for years in proficient communion with each other, though she knew their affiliation throughout legendary conquests reached back more than a century, maybe even two. No human generation, next to qindrid, could claim that measure of extended warfare camaraderie.

The massive troll who guarded her then performed the most grotesquely startling action. Jrulthun inserted his thumb into his open mouth and clamped his teeth down like a guillotine blade, severing it bone and flesh. The brutish fiend of an elvan didn't even wince in pain, clearly practiced in countless cycles of limb loss and endured torture.

He handed the bloody appendage to his khomo. The Glace Isles king fingered it as if it were a delectable treat to evaluate before devouring whole. He then cautiously approached the petrified critter in the corner and gently offered the meal to it. The tiny thing changed its look from fear to ecstatic glee and took the hearty reward with hardly a hesitation.

It ate in peace, gobbling at the meaty thumb, glancing up appreciatively every few bites at the generous provider. She felt calm then. Savage as it was, as it always likely would be among the Terollar breed, it was a noble deed.

She looked upon Khomo'Jhuvonus for the first time in two separate lights. There was the one he was known for, the monster he was feared as, the being who had maimed her mother and had her father butchered, who had slain his own sons and subtly ordered his henchman to bite his very thumb off, openly accounting for the deaths of thousands of Barredish. And then there was the one he actually may have been all along, the finder of innocents and savior of the lost and hungry. The protector of mice and slayer of rats. The evolved among his condemned and complicated ilk. Perhaps he never had been the evil enemy of Barredom and Aggedon.

The little mouse stared at the menacing ensemble for a second before whisking away into the shadows at the far side of the stores. It was full in gut for now, and the good deed had been done.

"A lesson, then? Let yourself never again be caught in the futile maze. Evolve between the path of mice and rats. Let me show you the way." The khomo put a reassuring, amicable hand on her shoulder, and his strange embrace felt nothing but fatherly, like some destined guide of her mentorship into final freedom.

My troll captor, the country's most hated foe, is my new sage to heed? Her illogical thoughts coerced an unsure look at the ground, and she shook her head in doubt. But her words vocalized the utter opposite to the northern nemesis. "Then teach me," she muttered in all sincerity.

"First, little mouse, let us start by never giving me reason to call you that again," Khomo'Jhuvonus chuckled as he began with the rest of his enlightenment. There was a long voyage to go.

EXCERPT

BOOK 2

SPELLBLADE

PROLOGUE

The fetid trudge through the combined sewers of the largest metropolis on all of Penthara led through undeniably the most putrid zone in the realm. Goldgarden, the City of a Thousand Canals, the Untouchable All-Touching, the Capital of Commerce, the Isle of Innovation—the list of its world-renowned titles went on and on. And yet the last place a person would want to be was in its foul-smelling and often dangerous bowels, known as the Flush, beneath the overpopulated streets. But this was not an unfamiliar place. This was all familiar territory for Xalo the pit gladiator in the underworld of illegal slave trade.

His wrists had been tethered tight behind his back, bound by a thick rope, while his ankles were shackled and chained together. Disarmed but unharmed, he stood surrounded by his eager ushers, each nervous but ready to discard his company for good.

He glanced over the decem men in the escort party. All were dirty creatures of the poorest crime syndicate in the entire cityscape—a gang of miscreants known as the Copper Jacks, who controlled all of Copper's Side. They dressed in mismatched leather scraps with random tears in the fabric patched over with cloth rags of browns or yellows. Their hair and beards looked like they had never discovered the mysterious arts of the somehow elusive abundance of city barbers. Each of them carried their crude weaponry in hand, including butchers' blades, fishing knives, makeshift spears, and spiked clubs. And these were the alleged elite of their clique, vicious killers proven in their crafts of murder and mayhem.

Their underboss, Atrick, stood several paces from Xalo, in front of the lot. His blond beard was trimmed, and his hair was cropped short, spiked up. His studded black leather vestments were an obvious testament to quality and price. And he was the only one in the group wielding an actual sword—in fact, two swords. The one sheathed at his right hip was none other than Xalo's famed spellblade.

The word *spellblade* had a twofold definition. Both the magically sentient sword and its chosen wielder bound to it were termed spellblade.

Every spellblade sword ever made had been forged at the same time and devised of the same shape, all crafted by the same smiths in Elothia long ago.

The ambiguous components used in forging such relics were said to be taken straight from the Vist and fabricated in Spellspire, the ancient capital of Elothia. With a single-edged, slightly curved blade, it was expressly designed for swift slashing precision. The magic swords were known for their enchanted glass blades, unnaturally sharper than any metal and more indestructible than diamond. The guard was oval-shaped and gold-coated. The most sinister piece on the weapon, however, was its hilt, made from an elvan's spine. A spellblade's pommel was capped with a signature brilliant emerald of the most flawless cut, which, of all the gems on Penthara, had been proven to have certain arcane capacities.

The swords had originally been made for the purpose of hunting down and exterminating mages. The final requisite in the making of a spellblade sword was its infusion with the essence of some rare entity beyond Xalo's knowledge. But he was aware that it was this special binding that enchanted the weapon to sense nearby humans born with the faculty to become mages. Weaker, untrained spellblade wielders were often caught in a form of possession by the sentient blade they were bound to, and they could easily lose control and attack a mage potential not of their own accord. Xalo, though, was not a weak or untrained spellblade.

Furthermore, if a spellblade killed a mage by the sword, they could absorb the mage's signature spell, which would be inscribed as a glyph on the glass blade, representing the spell's correspondent season, from which it pulled power. The wielder of the sword could then invoke these particular spells, and the power to cast the same spell again was replenished quite quickly if the sentient sword felt a sense of trusting synergy with its wielder.

All Xalo had to do was touch the glyph on the sword and whisper the name of the mage from whom he had stripped the spell. The glyph, along with the edge of the glass blade, would then glow a bright green—the color of raw magic—the same as the halo around his right eye, which would shine when revealing the blade from its bone scabbard.

A spellblade also imbued the wielder with martial weapon mastery, honed by each of its former chosen wielders. It kept a fraction of their essences inside the emerald pommel, which acted as a form of phylactery. The current wielder from the lineage could engage in combat with an identical form to those before. The sentient swords only bound themselves to those in the same lineage who were eligible to wield it. The blade might not always choose one in the next generation—sometimes the one following, or even further down the line. The rationale for why the swords picked whom they did, when they did, had become a fruitless debate.

Xalo had the embedded swordmastery of four of his ancestors locked within him through the power of the spellblade, along with seven spells he had acquired from the seven mages who had met their untimely ends at the edge of his sentient weapon. Each of their names was now a part of him: the two Dawning mages Qandor and Bellarae, the two Sunder mages Lichael and Yhondar, and the three Reaping mages Jezzerac, Herovocus, and Anasian.

He had come a long way since his upbringing in the Jaden Flats, a plateau territory against the Abellagen Ridge, which divided the country of Az'Eloth from Tairancia along the Triune River. His nomadic tribe had suffered the calamity of the Daynish forces encroaching on his now-crumbled former nation. He counted himself as one of the lucky ones to have made it out alive as a child from the massacre. Being a slave in Az'Dayne and eventually in Goldgarden, after being sold by one master after another, was the only life Xalo had ever known.

As an adult, he had earned a reputation as the deadliest pit gladiator throughout all of Goldgarden. The difference between a pit gladiator and a free gladiator was all in the name. Free gladiators were just that: free. They were popular citizens in organized public duels, fighting for prize and prestige for themselves. Death matches were always prohibited. But the inglorious life of a pit gladiator was never free—perhaps just more privileged than an average slave. Their masters might reward them with fine meals and whores after a win, and they held their own quarters within the estates, but they had no liberty to leave or roam the city without chaperone from an assigned custodian. And their illegal secret matches were often to the death.

Xalo had been forced to duel hard criminals, mage fugitives, elvan vagabonds, and even trained beasts. Oftentimes the pit masters would attempt to cheat the odds of his wagered fate by experimenting with more than one opponent against him, but such finagling thus far had found them failing at every attempt.

Slavery was indeed strongly prohibited in the region, but this was also a city called Goldgarden, where coin could buy turned eyes and hushed lips. It was a metropolitan hub of the most modernized entrepreneurs and upstarts from any social class in the realm, a place of opportunity where the poorest thug could become a street king by night and where the influential might transition day by day. Goldgarden was a city-nation, a world of its own, away from the outside political matters and wars across Penthara and even its own country of Utamia. As a paradise for urbanites, the city stood as a land of opportunity for the cunning, the strong, and those with the gift of the golden gab. The great city was a haven for new beginnings, so long as one had the stomach for it.

It was also a place known for utilizing its nation's elemental descendancy for novel inventions rather than religious reverence. With the Utamians being of the tairan and water cross-descendancy, the citizens of the metropolis were generally a conglomeration of the most innovative minds in building complex aqueducts and the most massive sewer system on Penthara. They furthermore utilized Torrent mages during their season to purify badwater, as they called it—contaminated, of the sea, and of the sewage flow—into fairwater, able to be consumed or used for bathing.

The urgent push through the underground channels rushed Xalo and his ushers to their destination point, where the group of thugs impatiently waited for their buyers to rendezvous with them. It had been several hours, after passing a labyrinth of corners and bridge planks, before the elaborate network of brick tunnels had delivered them to their intended terminus at a crossway.

The water from the storm drains and inventive sanitation system, along with the flow of liquidized waste, had been shut off at this point by sluice gates. All the walkways around could be accessed. It was the driest area Xalo had seen on the trek.

On a concrete corner ledge, a man higher than where he and the

Copper Jacks were filtering in from, was a ladder attached to the wall, which led back to the streets. Next to the ladder was a symbol painted in yellow over the brick for engineers to better navigate the Flush. Xalo knew what each of the symbols meant. This one marked their location in Goldgarden, directly below the end of the East Basin, in the Midway.

On the elevated area stood five armed mercenaries. Each bore a signature necklace with two punctured wild boar tusks as its ornament. They were each clothed in boiled leathers, and four handled longspears with broad heads. The fifth, their obvious leader, with a boar's head engraved on the spaulder over his right shoulder, held a two-handed scimitar and was marred by burn scars across his bald head.

Xalo couldn't refrain from unleashing his dry wit to antagonize. "My fellows, you truly shouldn't have." He feigned admiration, devoid of expression on his face. "I say, your hospitality is the topic of legends. I did not expect to walk the golden carpets themselves."

Xalo never smiled or smirked, or sneered or frowned. He always had the same plain look with his narrow brown eyes, heavy with a lifetime of distributing death. He kept a clean-shaven face that contoured his angular jawline and gaunt cheeks. His blond hair was worn in Elothian warrior fashion, slicked back and tied up in a topknot but razored to the skin around the sides of his head. There was no denying his ethnicity in a single glance, having a similar easterner look to the Sho'Lonese and Oriyans.

His armor tattoo, which covered his entire right arm and the same side of his chest, was a trophy earned for being deemed an elite Goldgarden gladiator, with over fifty victories. There were but few others that shared the same brand of prestige in the city's underworld. But the symbolic mark was currently covered in an oversized shirt fit for a prisoner, rather than his preferred garb, suited to agility.

As anticipated, Atrick seemed to get irritated and piped up. "Always got somethin' to say. Like a starvin' jester with bad jokes. The only fuckin' clown I know that doesn't smile." Atrick didn't even turn around or motion with his fingers.

But Xalo knew his worth to his buyers. And he knew each of these men he was in the custody of, as he had spent the last few years in their despicable company. "It pains me to learn that my time has to expire with the generous Copper King. Serving in such a prestigious outfit has been an honor fit for royals."

A couple of the men spat. A few more cursed him. Atrick just continued with attempted professionalism. He was the most experienced combatant in the group, and definitely the hardest. But Xalo knew he had a weakness in his temper if tested.

"Took long enough," the burn-scarred mercenary simply said.

Atrick answered for his gang as his henchmen and Xalo filed in from the sewer walkway to organize themselves in the dry cistern beneath. "Xalo, your employer is now Oldan Boldandgold, boss of the Boarneck Company. Meet your new custodian, Gastion."

"Thus far I've only been introduced to cutthroats and slave-driving docklords," Xalo replied cynically, hoping to get a rise. "Remind me to thank you also, Atrick, for being such a merciful custodian yourself these past few years."

And that did it. Atrick swung around and neared as close as he dared. "Xalo, you're weak. Ya always have been. Ya never won't be. Ya can't even lift a cheese knife without gettin' sick from betrayin' that bond between ya an' that blade you're cursed to. You're just a skinny fuckin' cornered cow that we all keep milkin' in the dens. An' that's your life, ya see? Till your employers decide you're worth more to be butchered than milked."

Xalo's facial expression still didn't change. It never did. "Never been the cow, Atrick." *I am the caged bull.* "I've never been the cornered cow ..."

"Gastion, apologies an' greetings." Atrick swiftly shifted back to business. "Got orders for a change of plan on his account. Had to send a separate crew to get those papers delivered to your guild, as requested."

"Yeah, yeah, we heard the deal," Gastion retorted. "All o' youse are just more o' a shamfucked lot is all, but we ain't here to size our cocks today."

"'Kay then," Atrick replied, obviously annoyed, seemingly ready to break as always. "We ain't here to bump on horse fuckers and pig stickers either. Down to blood and gold." As he walked behind Xalo, Atrick condescended to release his frustration by shoving him forward. "As promised, Xalo the Zero, Champion of the Underover, Blood of the First Spellblade, Copper's Killer, Magebane, the Ear Collector, the Eloth—"

"The Elothian Element. Yes, we know all his aliases. Needless grandiosity. The sale is already—" Xalo's new employer's custodian attempted to shun the upsell but was cut off by Xalo himself.

"That's Elothian Elephant. Not Element."

"What in the Fives," was all that Gastion could counter with, clearly dumbfounded by a slave backtalking.

"Elephants. They are from Elothia, my homeland. The strongest beasts in the realm, known for utilizing one extra-strong limb."

Xalo saw that he was getting no response and only wide-eyed looks, so he continued to explain. "Like a spellblade?"

Still no response came from either group.

"Hunted and endangered now, like the elephants?"

Only more stares were shot due to the insolence of his audacity.

"You still don't get the reference," Xalo said, nodding to Atrick and Gastion. "Okay, continue."

Atrick shook his head in seeming embarrassment for representing him. "Let's get this over with."

Gastion simply snarled, "Let's."

"Here's his blade," Atrick proclaimed, walking up the steps to release the dangerous weapon into the new caretaker's possession. "Don't let him get near it, or ya all know the end. We'll take the other half of the coin now for the deal. The reins are yours, horse lords."

"Ear Collector?" Xalo interrupted, and all stopped to take full notice of him again. "Never actually collected an ear as a trophy. That is just manipulative flair to declare I've slain many elven. Wise for street hype, I agree, though all of those kills were forced. I actually prefer their lot over ours."

And just then another voice chimed in, feminine and foreign. "Pleased to hear Xalo holds no bad blood with the elvan race, as the chattering urchins like to whisper otherwise."

She came into the light, entering from the tunnel opposite the one used by the Copper Jacks. "Scarless" was hissed in fear by the mouths of each thug near Xalo, referencing the most popular nickname by which she was revered.

"But what if there is a higher bid than the Boarnecks can offer?" Scarless teased, with her own three menacing companions striding in beside her.

Scarless was a Terollar elvan, one of a race commonly slandered by being vulgarly referred to as trolls. If one lived in Goldgarden, one would undoubtedly have heard of her. Rumored to be the youngest daughter of the king of the Glace Isles, she was a rare find in the metropolis realm of humankind, even though the city was known to harbor almost all the races of Penthara.

She was taller than an average man, probably just over six feet, built strong and muscular, but still feminine. Her skin was fair and without a single blemish or scar, as all Terollar were known to regenerate from any injury quite rapidly. Her piercing light-green eyes were the distinctive trait of all her ilk. Her blond hair was most eccentric, Xalo thought, shaved short, almost to the scalp, around the sides of her head, with precise lines razored to the skin and the top grown out excessively long in a mane of thick-braided tails that almost touched the backs of her knees. She had the youthful looks of a woman in her midtwenties, but Xalo and everyone else knew this to be an elvan facade, since most could attest to her having been around for nearly a century by recorded accounts—such were the blessings of the slow-aging race. Her stern but beautiful face was savagely painted, as were her companions'. They each had a different way to depict a particular dead white tree upon a black background.

Scarless wasn't dressed in much for her disruption of the trade meet, fitted in leather pants dyed to a dark green, tucked into cheap, mundane black boots that matched her gloves. A thin white shirt with ruffled cuffs and loose laces down her bosom adorned her torso, as if she had no care in the world for protection from an impending fight.

She was armed with a spear like none Xalo had ever seen. It was altogether alien to look upon. The Terollar weapon was entirely made up of the same otherworldly material, from its haft to its guard to its blade point. The singular substance appeared to consist of small, metallicized frost shards layered over one another. A red veinlike network was incorporated throughout the white spear, pulsating underneath, between, and over the material of the weapon's construction in no set pattern. Xalo thought spellblades to be the most exotically beautiful weapons that had ever existed in the realm, but he had never seen one of these before. Yet one couldn't necessarily classify it as beautiful. It was instead terrifyingly outlandish and mesmerizing. He judged a person's choice of weapons before he even analyzed the shape of their body or took note of their face. It was the gladiator ingrained in him.

None had thus far come to learn the full story of why Scarless was here, so far from home. But once she had arrived in Goldgarden, she had swiftly climbed the ranks of the underworld, risen to become the most feared crime overlord in the vast city. Few to no gangs would ever dare oppose her as of late. Almost none, that was, but for the Boarneck Company, which was still establishing itself on the island metropolis.

"Why're ya getting involved in this, Scarless?" Atrick demanded. "Ya had your chances to bid, and yet ya always avoid the buys. The deal's done with Oldan of the Boarneck Company. Ya can't compete with him."

Scarless made her purpose for the intrusion simple for them. "Not here to make a deal with the Boarnecks. Nor with the Copper King. My bid is for Xalo alone."

TO BE CONTINUED …

NOTE FROM THE AUTHOR

Thank you for taking the time to read *Kingfall*, the first book in *The Neverborne Series*! There are other books in the series currently published as well if you wish to continue the journey with *Spellblade* and *Greyfire*.

Spellblade is the second novel, but not a sequel. It is a simultaneous story transpiring at the exact timeline of *Kingfall*, with a different set of POV character in the south. By the end of *Spellblade* the plotlines of those characters will impact the plotlines of the *Kingfall* POV characters. *Greyfire*, the third novel, will pick back up directly after *Kingfall* with the characters you are familiar with now.

As an independently published fantasy author, your review is critical to my aspired growth and credibility. If you enjoyed *Kingfall* it would mean the world to me if you could take a small moment to leave a fair review on Amazon or Goodreads!

If you wish to follow more updates about my future novels, or would enjoy watching other video content please feel free to follow me on TikTok. I even have full pronunciation guides for my character names and unique words, and have videos that go into thorough detail on my magic system and world of Penthara.

TikTok Handle: @author_ezekieleversand

APPENDIX

Human Elemental Descendancies

Tairancians: Tairan descendancy. West central Penthara.
- (Modern) Tan or fair skin, brown eyes, blond or brown hair.
- (Indigenous) Tan skin, brown eyes, dark brown hair.

Khalimishe: Fire descendancy. South central Penthara.
- (Modern) Brown skin, amber eyes, red or black hair. Southern look.
  (Indigenous) Brown skin, red eyes, red hair. Southern look.

Sho'Lonese: Sky descendancy. Eastern Penthara.
- (Modern) Pale skin, light blue eyes, blond hair. Eastern look.
- (Indigenous) Pale skin, grey eyes, blond hair. Eastern look.
- (Skyborne) Grey skin, light blue eyes, white hair. Eastern look.

Vhall: Shadow descendancy. Northern Penthara in recluse.
- Black skin, grey eyes, no hair. Endangered race. *(Eight feet tall)*

Thrench: Water descendancy. Western islands and eastern Penthara.
- Brown skin, blue eyes, black hair. Islander look.

Daynish: Tairan and fire descendancy. South central Penthara.
- Tan or fair skin, amber or brown eyes, blond, brown, or red hair.

Elothians: Tairan and sky descendancy. South central Penthara.
- Pale skin, light brown eyes, blond hair. Eastern look.

Aggeans: Tairan and shadow descendancy. Northern Penthara.
- (Barredish) Fair skin, brown eyes, blond, brown, or black hair.
- (Aggedonian Stoneborne) Grey skin, crystalline eyes, no hair.

Utamians: Tairan and water descendancy. West central Penthara.
- Any natural color skin, any natural color eyes, any natural color hair.

Tongans: Fire and sky descendancy. South eastern Penthara.
- Black skin, brown eyes, red hair. Islander look. *(Over six feet tall)*

Psages: Fire and shadow descendancy. West central Penthara.
- Brown skin, red eyes, no hair. *(Five feet tall)*

Behemons: Fire and water descendancy. Southern islands.
- Brown skin, brown or blue eyes, black hair. Southern look.

Caelduyans: Sky and shadow descendancy. North eastern Penthara.
- (Skyborne) - Grey skin, light blue eyes, white hair.

Oriyans: Sky and water descendancy. East and west Vist-based isle.
- Tan skin, blue eyes, black hair. Eastern look.

Vellyans: Shadow and water descendancy. North western Penthara.
- Brown skin, blue eyes, black hair. *(Seven feet tall average)*

The above height descriptions are for the average adult human male, five feet ten inches. On Penthara the average adult human female is six inches shorter than the males.

Elvan Elemental Descendancies

Sylvanil: Tairan descendancy. North western Penthara and all groves.
- Brown skin, luminous yellow eyes, gold hair. *(Eight feet tall)*

Ibyssai: Fire descendancy. Race extinct.
- Reddish skin, luminous red eyes, vibrant red hair. *(Five feet tall)*

Shirenar: Sky descendancy. Eastern Penthara.
- White skin, luminous silver eyes, silver hair. *(Over six feet tall)*

Dendrar: Shadow descendancy. Northern Penthara.
- Black skin, dark grey eyes, black shadowy hair. *(Four feet tall)*

Oceanil: Water descendancy. Western Penthara oceans underwater.
- Pale scaly skin, luminous blue eyes, blue hair. *(Seven feet tall)*

Zandaryn: Tairan and fire descendancy. South central Penthara.
- Tan skin, orange eyes, yellow or orange hair.

Terollar: Tairan and sky descendancy. Northern Penthara.
- Fair skin, green eyes, blond hair. *(Seven feet tall)*

Wyldenar: Tairan and shadow descendancy. Northern Penthara.
- Tan skin, controlled color eyes, controlled color hair.

Tortharan: Tairan and water descendancy. Race extinct.
- Brown skin, green eyes, green hair.

Solaril: Fire and sky descendancy. South eastern Penthara.
- Tan skin, pink eyes, females pink hair, men vibrant red hair.

Neveril: Fire and shadow descendancy. Subterranean Penthara.
- White skin, red eyes, no hair. *(Five feet tall)*

Forlore: Fire and water descendancy. Race extinct.
- Light-brown skin, purple eyes, purple hair.

Shiniryn: Sky and shadow descendancy. Eastern Penthara.
- Fair skin, silver eyes, intermixed silver and black hair.

Vistaryl: Sky and water descendancy. Vist in recluse.
- Pale skin, light-blue eyes, light-blue hair. Endangered race.

Lunaril: Shadow and water descendancy. North western isle.
- Black skin, dark-blue eyes, dark-blue hair. *(Over six feet tall)*

The above height descriptions are for the average adult elvan male, six feet. On Penthara the average adult elvan female is one foot shorter than the males.

Elvan Impowers

Terollar — *tairan and sky descendancy*
Passive Impowers: Regeneration (in outside elements). Tirelessness. Blooding (progressive adrenaline rush, can cause heart attack). Hair continuously grows back to the longest state it can be.
Resistances: Electricity. Poison, drugs, alcohol (due to regeneration).

Wyldenar — *tairan and shadow descendancy*
Passive Impowers: Tairan-bending (tairan terrain bends in their favor in immediate vicinity). Shadow-bending (cold terrain and shadows bend in their favor in immediate vicinity). Can change hair and eye color at will. Animal affinity. Become deathly ill outside of nature.
Resistances: Poison. Cold. Disease.

Neveril — *fire and shadow descendancy*
Passive Impowers: Wall-walking (walk on walls and ceilings as if on level ground). Darkvision (light-blinded). Crystalyte communion (can communicate with anyone touching them through psionics). Silent movement.
Resistances: Cold. Disease. Fire. Heat. Smoke.

Shiniryn — *sky and shadow descendancy*
Passive Impowers: Enhanced running speed (twice that of humans). Enhanced endurance (twice that of humans). Wind-walking (glide on air as if walking on it). Wind affinity. Slow-fall. Sun-sickness.
Resistances: Cold. Disease.

Zandaryn — *tairan and fire descendancy*
Passive Impowers: *to be discovered …*
Resistances: *to be discovered …*

Solaril – *fire and sky descendancy*
Passive Impowers: *to be discovered …*
Resistances: *to be discovered …*

Vistaryl
Passive Impowers: *to be discovered …*
Resistances: *to be discovered …*

Lunaril
Passive Impowers: *to be discovered …*
Resistances: *to be discovered …*

Sylvanil
Passive Impowers: *to be discovered …*
Resistances: *to be discovered …*
Immunity: *to be discovered …*

Shirenar
Passive Impowers: *to be discovered …*
Resistances: *to be discovered …*
Immunity: *to be discovered …*

Dendrar
Passive Impowers: *to be discovered …*
Resistances: *to be discovered …*
Immunity: *to be discovered …*

Oceanil
Passive Impowers: *to be discovered …*
Resistances: *to be discovered …*
Immunity: *to be discovered …*

Qindrid and Umbran Impowers

Stoneborne – *tairan and shadow*
Maker: Wyldenar umbran
Passive Impowers: Hardened skin. Enhanced strength. Cannot be harmed from falling. Sleeplessness. Cannot produce offspring. Agelessness. Darkvision.
Resistances: Cold. Poison. Acid. Drugs/herbal side effects.
Immunities: Disease.

Skyborne – *sky and shadow*
Maker: Shiniryn umbran
Passive Impowers: Enhanced speed. Slowfall. Throw voice in the wind. Wind affinity. Sleeplessness. Cannot produce offspring. Agelessness. Darkvision.
Resistances: Cold. Electricity.
Immunities: Disease.

Neverborne – *fire and shadow*
Maker: Neveril umbran
Passive Impowers: Shapeshifting. Wall-walking. Silent movement. Sleeplessness. Cannot produce offspring. Agelessness. Darkvision.
Resistances: Cold. Fire. Heat. Smoke.
Immunities: Disease.

Greyborne – *any shadow*
Maker: Qindrid with no umbran or born from other greyborne.
Passive Impowers: Sleeplessness. Darkvision.
Resistances: Cold.
Immunities: Disease.

Umbran– *shadow dominant, in addition to their elvan descendancy*
Elvan Subrace: Wyldenar (tairan), Shiniryn (sky), Neveril (fire).
Passive Impowers: Those of their elvan subrace. Cerebration. Node aura. Qindrid transcendence. Sleeplessness. Darkvision.
Resistances: Those of their elvan subrace.
Immunities: Disease. Cold.

Geography of Penthara

(LEFT / WEST SIDE OF MAP)

Starfell - Lunaril homeland. Thrench-ruled.
Depyreoshlinyoq - Oceanil underwater homeland.
Vellyon - Vellyan Kingdom homeland.
Oriyen - Oriyan homeland between the Vist.
Tortharus Isles - Thrench-ruled; formerly Tortharan.
Vistyzus - Thrench-ruled; formerly Vistaryl.
Throng - Thrench Empire homeland.
The Sisters - Pirate isles. Formerly Daynish-ruled.
Forlornedian Isles - Thrench-ruled; formerly Forlore.
Behemon Isles - Behemon homeland. Thrench-ruled.
Artopia - Wyldenar occupied. Sentinel Order capital.
The Dendrallthae - Dendrar secret homeland.
Aggedon - Aggedonian qindrid clan country.
Nrathe - Former Vhall homeland. Desolate ruins.
Glace Isles - Terollar battle outposts loyal to a khomo.
Barredom - Barredish Kingdom homeland.
Zsolindal - Former Neveril northern sect. Abandoned.
Undawned Lands - Unclaimed barbarian territories.
Mageholme - Sanctuary region for the hunder-touched.
The Insurmounts - Psage mountainous homeland.
Psage Coast - Psage Trade Union territory.
The Tairanheart - No-man's-land of many territory lords.
The Tenwoods - Village colonies ruled by Psage seers.
The Sevenmoors - Governed by seven witches.
Utamia - Utamian homeland. Land of free states.
Goldgarden - Realm's largest city, ruled by secret seats.
The Silverlakes - Free region lorded over by an archon.
Tairancia - Territories split between Az'Dayne and natives.
Az'Dayne - Daynish homeland. Dominadom capital.
Savatarm - Neutral province trade hub for the west coast.
Khalimia - Khalimishe Queendom. Daynish-ruled.

Geography of Penthara

(RIGHT / EAST SIDE OF MAP)

Umbralle - Vhall retreat location after the fall of Nrathe.
Skystone Isles - Raider isles and land of intelligent beasts.
Tundura - Wyldenar homeland of scattered tribes.
Teralloe - Terollar homeland of scattered tribes.
Caelduym - Caelduyan homeland. Skyborne country.
Helderak - Coalition of Terollar, Neveril, and Shiniryn.
Cabernus - Neveril surface army. Access to Caldwuera.
Caldwuera - Neveril capital of eastern underrealm.
Blood Beach - Terollar and Thrench disputed region.
Ghost Isles - Neveril underrealm highway.
Kol'Kolar - Shiniryn homeland of scattered tribes.
Julkunda - New Throng, Thrench-ruled; formerly elven exiles.
Xai Lon - Sho'Lonese free states of greyborne majority.
Sho Kung - Sho'Lonese skyborne kingdom.
Sho Jan - Sho'Lonese human empire of the old ways.
The Westway - Sho'Lonese and Oriyan tradeway.
The Shirene - Shirenar homeland. Vistaryl refugees.
Brutonga - Tongan homeland of scattered tribes.
Majamn - Tongan kingdom of fanatics and mages.
The Sacreds - Tongan ritual isles.
Arastarianar - Solaril homeland.
Solfeiel - Solaril exile and dungeon isle.
Old Elothia - Ruins of a nation. Destroyed by Neveril.
Az'Eloth - Elothian homeland and union. Daynish ruled.
Zandabar - Zandaryn homeland, mostly Daynish allied.
Wroth - Zandaryn extremists against human rule.
Zshunthavia - Zandaryn and Solaril trade hub.
Sundorion Isles - Unsettled beastlands; formerly Ibyssai.
Az'Elvenyah - Neveril underrealm beneath Az'Eloth.
The Netherall - New underrealm created by Dawning mages.

Powers & Organizations

The Ashenwave - the infamous armada of the Thrench Empire known for bringing the Tortharan, Forlore, and Ibyssai elvan races into absolute extinction, subjugating the Lunaril of Starfell, and conquering the Vistaryl elvan to cross over the Vist from the west to the east to establish New Throng out of Julkunda.

Az'Dayne Dominadom - the largest land nation on Penthara, overseen by Dominarchs Vaximus Az'Ampion and Sriyah Hazhalah. It consists of many countries with former kings and lords under its vast rule: Az'Dayne, North Khalimia, Az'Eloth, Tairancia, Barredom, and former kingdoms of the Tairanheart.

Boarneck Cavaliers - the mercenary faction of horsemen in the Boarneck Company, led by Tristostopher Boldandgold.

Clan Thalbear - the stoneborne clan that once ruled Thalvoska and the territory around Loch Vosk and Loch Thal before former King Tytus Roth's invasion took place that established Northaven.

Clan Tytalon - the stoneborne clan that rule the capital of Aggedon in Aepox and the Tytalon Forest.

Eldenvale Rangers - a group of specialists bent on eliminating Terollar threats originally formed by Vanson Blackendale, now captained by Mathias Oreville.

Elderlocks - a circle of Dendrar elvan seers residing in the Dendrallthae who use seerstones and other divination methods to project favorable paths of the realm's future.

Forwoken - an order of mysterious monks from the Qaegons in Barredom who swear an oath to remain silent and covered, governed by High Chancellor Soro as sentries for the Barredish royal houses ever since the Az'Dayne Dominadom's local rule.

Glazjhendun - the exclusively elite war party of the Glace Isles, under the command of Khomo'Jhuvonus.

Great Exodus - the mass movement of Aggedonian qindrid started by the Wyldenar umbran, Lilealah, to evacuate their homeland through wyrmways to reach Caelduym with the purpose of aiding the skybornes' imminent war with the Thrench Ashenwave.

Greene House - an orphanage in the village of Whitewood in the Tenwoods known to foster children free from bias.

Hroganyn's Horde - an assemblage of allied greyborne clans that want nothing to do with Aggedon's war against Barredom, nor any foreign politics, amassed in the northernmost plains of the country, loosely governed by the Queen of the Grey.

Kingdom of Barredom - northern kingdom under the sovereignty of the Az'Dayne Dominadom, overseen by King Aerik Roth and Queen Annison Roth.

Lilealytes - the greyborne and stoneborne loyalists of the umbran Lilealah who support the Great Exodus.

Neveril Empire - the largest power on all of Penthara. It governs not only the Neveril elven but secretly many other nations.

Norther Knights - a group of formerly highborn Barredish men, founded by former Prince Ondrew Roth, who have denounced their lands and titles in rebellion against the new sovereign rule of the Az'Dayne Dominadom over their homeland.

Oathemic Cabal - the organization of assassins not aligned with the Pentagogue or Dominadom. It mainly consists of absolved mages, spellblades, and stealth-trained killers who perform assassination contracts to protect the integrity of Az'Dayne and its people.

Paladin Order - the faction of the Pentagogue specifically for paladins, overseen by the Imperial Patriarch.

Pentagogue - the theocratic power that dictates all matters of the law for the Az'Dayne Dominadom. It consists of paladins as the enforcers and veritans as the magistrates.

The Reluctants - the greyborne clans and qindrid people of Aggedon who refuse to leave their homes or surrender to Barredom's advancement on their land; not aligning with the Great Exodus, Hroganyn's Horde, or Clan Tytalon.

Saiyenai - a monastery of fosterling boys and men in Xai Lon, thoroughly trained in survival and combat tactics, who were once indifferent to the civil rivalries in the Sho'Lon countries, but eventually succumbed to the pressure of Sho Kung to take on the skyborne qindrid Transcendence.

Sho'Lon Empire - an eastern country of people from the sky descendancy who were the first to fall under the Qindrid Curse and became a divided nation between the humans of the old ways in Sho Jan versus the skyborne and greyborne of Sho Kung.

Sylvanil Sentinel Order - the timeless guardians for the sacred groves of the majority of the elvan races, also acting as a faction of zealous wardens, who seek out capable opposition to defend against those who would disrupt the creed of the Balance.

Thrench Empire - a sea nation ruled by Emperor Djediheth Emmonost. It is notorious for its history in conquering and annihilating territory occupied by the elvan races, and it consists of many territories in the west and now the east: Throng, Starfell, the Tortharus Isles, the Forlornedian Isles, the Behemon Isles, the Sundorion Isles, Vistyzus, Julkunda, and Blood Beach.

Timberhands - a small band of six minstrel orphans from the village of Whitewood out of the Tenwoods who have grown to become capable archers and hunters, offering their services for the greater good around the northern region.

Umbran Pledge - an oathbound network of those in the Know of the Neveril Empire's presence and of the neverborne scheme to take over the human power nations.

Veritan Order - the faction of the Pentagogue specifically for veritans, overseen by the Imperial Matriarch.

The Pentharam System

TIME

Day – Twenty-five hours.
Furrow – Intermittent day between seasons.
Pentday / Pent – Five days.
First-Day – First day of a pent.
Second-Day – Second day of a pent.
Third-Day – Third day of a pent.
Fourth-Day – Fourth day of a pent.
Fifth-Day – Fifth day of a pent.
Month – Five pents, or twenty-five days.
Season – Five months, or twenty-five pents, which is one hundred twenty-five days.
Year – Fifteen months, or three seasons and their following furrows, which is three hundred seventy-eight days.
Cycle – Five seasons and their following furrows, or six hundred thirty days, or one and two-thirds years.
Generation – Twenty-five years.

Dawning – First season, tairan element, gold as color.
(translation is most relative to Spring)
Sunder – Second season, fire element, red as color.
(translation is most relative to Summer)
Reaping – Third season, sky element, white as color.
(translation is most relative to Autumn)
Umbra – Fourth season, shadow element, black as color.
(translation is most relative to Winter)
Torrent – Fifth season, water element, blue as color.

Word Glossary

Agge - the outdated, rarely used, language of the Aggeans.

archon - a territory leader that has been granted entitlement by their sovereign to lord over a state within their country.

the aging - a condition suffered by an elvan who has had their lifetree destroyed, causing them to age at an accelerated rate depending on how old they are.

animayan - elven who have chosen the path of the Taboo to have their wisp reincarnated in an eligible newborn animal aligning with their descendancy, keeping the majority of their intellect and memory.

aspirant - the title of a paladin or veritan knight in their initiate stage.

Balance - the universal elvan creed based upon the belief in absolute neutrality in all aspects of life and the elements.

Beyond - the afterlife for all hunder, acting as a symbiotic conglomeration of spiritual entities that exist on another plane of existence within the Vist.

blast salt - an explosive compound made of white granules that disintegrate most materials immediately in a red flame.

the Blooding - a Terollar impower that initiates after being in combat, and particularly accumulates through being wounded, which essentially is a progressively regenerating adrenaline rush.

bloodrime - a poisonous parasite that tends to feed on lifetrees in its native region of Teralloe. It is known for being carefully extracted for the purpose of being crafted into weaponry that returns to its wielder that acts as its host of the lifetree they were bound to.

bluefin - a deadly poison from select fish in Aggedon that causes heart failure upon impact of the exposed skin.

bornday - an individual's birthday.

cerebration - an impower afforded to all umbran which allows them to see and hear through any qindrid they have turned as a vessel of surveillance, also discovering their precise location, but by invoking such the umbran is left vulnerable and immobile, allowing all of the qindrid they have turned and the children they have spawned to know of the umbran's location as well.

Civil - the common language taught to and understood by almost every culture on Penthara.

commandant - a rank under a general, typically acting as a commander over a significant fortification or part of an army.

cross-descendancy - elemental lineage of two elements.

crystalyte - a mineral that is typically radiant red in color, but does manifest in other variations. It glows bright if put within an atmosphere of lethal conditions, due to poison or lack of air, or if any living being not of a specific elemental descendancy correlated to the gem's color come within close proximity.

dawnstar mace - (translate to Morningstar mace description)
decem - a unit of measurement used for ten of anything
descendancy - the specific elemental lineage of a human or elvan, which defines their race, eligibility for certain transcendences, and impowers at birth if they are elvan.
Dominadom - a vanity term for a nation considering themselves larger than an empire, such as with Az'Dayne, ruled by dominarchs.
dominarch - a ruler of a Dominadom above all others.
dreambloom - a lethal poison from a plant in the Sho'Lon region that causes an instant comatose state followed by heart failure. (Also refer to as Yoshira's Mercy).
ebonice - a phenomenon of black ice that cannot melt that rarely occurs in the north during the Umbra season.
ferahn - a large carnivore hybrid resembling between a wild cat and a wolf that can naturally camouflage its fur coat to hunt.
firetears - a lethal Neveril poison of orange mist that rapidly destroys the body's sensory organs within if inhaled.
Five and Five - the popular human religion that adheres to the worship of the five gods of the elements and the five goddesses of the seasons.
ghost - derogatory slang for a Neveril elvan.
ghostgrass - a white weed native in subterranean regions that reverberates sound amongst the connected ghostgrass.
Godslands - the concept of the levels of afterlife in the Five and Five religion, believed to exist in the deepest areas of the natural elements on Penthara that no mortal can reach.
grove - a protected sanctuary of elvan lifetrees.
hunder - an elvan's soul, connected to their spiritroot.
impower - a special inborn or acquired supernatural power with some elemental influence.
the In-Between - a mirror plane of existence, only visible to the naked eye in the Vist, that entities such as hunder, wisps, and spiritroots exist in.
khomo - a Terollar elvan term for a Chosen of their race, recognized and honored by the Sylvanil Sentinel Order, often bestowed with the same respects as a king.
lifemate - an elvan's permanently bound partner through conjunction of each other's lifetree. An elvan can only reproduce with a lifemate, and never again with another.
lifequest - a calling an individual considers as their life's destiny, whether chosen for it by others, or by coming upon the aspired quest by personal enlightenment.
lifetree - what an elvan is born from, spawned from a cocoon of their parents. The elvan is bound to their lifetree, which determines their life span and elemental connection to their impowers.
mage - a hunder-touched human, bound to a single season and interrelated element, who has been interfused with wisps, acquiring the supernatu-

ral faculty to cast magic; gaining more impowers as they advance in tiers.

magnan – an Aggedonian chieftain that owns a town or castle.

masque – a mask that symbolizes one's status or family in Az'Dayne.

matriarch – a female parent in elvan culture.

mortali – a revered elder in Terollar culture who acts as a shaman, a sage, and the specialized groomer for assigned hairstyles within their specific tribe.

node – the aura surrounding two elvan lifemates when they are within the vicinity of their lifetree, which allows them the ability to procreate during certain times. For umbran, their node gradually comes into existence the longer they stay in one locale, enhanced even further when with their lifemate. Umbran can utilize the node to enthrall humans of eligible descendancies.

Norspeak – the language of Aggedonians.

paladin – the knighted male enforcers of the Pentagogue's law in the Az'Dayne Dominadom.

patriarch – a male parent in elvan culture.

pentacrux – a saltire crucifix.

qindrid – a human who has been turned by two umbran lifemates into an altered state with acquired elemental impowers, mentally linked to their creators' agelessness. All qindrid have grey skin, cannot sleep, are immune to disease, and are resistant to the cold.

qindrid (greyborne) – a severed qindrid whose umbran creators are no longer alive, but they can reproduce with other greyborne. Offspring of such qindrid are also greyborne. Characteristics include grey skin, hair, eyes, and nails, disease immunity, an inability to sleep, and resistance to cold.

qindrid (neverborne) – a qindrid turned by two Neveril umbran, with certain impowers of the fire element. Characteristics include grey skin, red hair, black eyes and nails, infertility, an inability to sleep, shape-shifting, silent movement, wall-walking, immunity to disease and burns, and resistance to cold and smoke.

qindrid (stoneborne) – a qindrid turned by two Wyldenar umbran, with certain additional impowers of the tairan element. Characteristics include grey skin, hairlessness, diamond-colored eyes and nails, infertility, an inability to sleep, armored skin, enhanced strength, immunity to disease, acid, and falls, and resistance to poison and cold.

qindrid (skyborne) – a qindrid turned by two Shiniryn umbran, with certain additional impowers of the sky element. Characteristics include grey skin, wind-affected white hair, light-blue eyes, white nails, infertility, an inability to sleep, the ability to throw their voice, slow-fall, enhanced speed, immunity to disease and wind, and resistance to cold and lightning.

rogue-elvan – the offspring of umbran lifemates, with grey features in skin, hair, and eyes, with downturned ears, gradually succumbing to bestial tendencies as they mature until they become fully feral.

sapling – an unspawned elvan still in the cocoon of their parents' lifetree before they are born.

score – a unit of measurement used for twenty-five of anything

shadow – the element that represents a combination of cold, disease, and darkness on Penthara.

Skystone ape – a native beast of the north taller than jungle gorillas that tend to be far superior in intelligence than other animals, and are known to even arm themselves with clothing and weapons.

spellblade – a sentient sword with an enchanted glass blade bound to specific individuals within a bloodline, that has been magically forged to absorb spells from mages that are slain by it, and to allow the wielder to channel the martial abilities of the prior wielders.

spellblade – the chosen bound wielder of a spellblade sword.

spellforging – the uncompromising craft of breaking down wisps into components that can be interfused within items to imbue them with specific magical properties.

spiritroot – an elvan's invisible, ethereal umbilical cord between their hunder and their lifetree that once severed will cause irreversible adverse effects.

Starfell steel – a forged metal utilized in Thrench weaponry.

Taboo – an irrevocable transformation elven of cross-descendancy can take, depending on their race (examples includes the Path of the Umbran and the Path of the Animayan, among others to be discovered).

tairan – the element that represents earth on Penthara in both natural or manufactured forms.

Transcendence – the process of one's transformed evolution from their natural aesthetics and capacities to acquire supernatural impowers, such as in the circumstance of becoming qindrid or a mage for humans, or umbran or animayan for elven, to name a few.

tribesvan/tribesven – elvan members of a tribe.

troll – derogatory slang for a Terollar elvan.

Trollspeak – a Terollar elvan derivative of the Civil tongue with a strong guttural inflection and mixed language.

truth tonic – a potion that induces a subject a willing desire to talk with no inhibitions, eliminating the concept of fear and lying.

umbran – an elvan of cross-shadow descendancy who has chosen the path of the Taboo to transcend with the shadow element, undergoing great physical change with altered impowers. They acquire the ability of cerebration, can carry their node with them as an aura, and can transcend eligible humans into qindrid.

veritan – the female magistrates of the Pentagogue's law in the Az'Dayne Dominadom.

the Vist - the mystical prime meridian of Penthara, narrower in the east, west, and south than in the north. It has the appearance of a green mist with geonomalies of unified hunder throughout its vast ethereal composition.

wisp - an elvan's soul that has left its mortal body and can roam freely. It is invisible, invulnerable, and incorporeal to most.

westwalker - slang for a Sho'Lonese or Oriyan human.

wraithwood - a white timber from the Sho'Lon countries that is used in weapons crafts due to its weight and pliability.

writ - an assassin's contract from the Oathemic Cabal, typically endorsed by both Az'Dayne and the guild.

wyrefire - regenerative candles made of a wick and wax harvested in Teralloe from insects that have borrowed the impower from the native Terollar elvan.

wyrmway - an elemental portal between two regions that opens during between seasons that only umbran or qindrid may enter.

yharl - a northern chieftain that is independent or answers only to the country's sovereign.

ABOUT THE AUTHOR

Ezekiel was born in Southeast Texas, and now resides in Houston after the global pandemic brought him back home from his exploits living in Las Vegas where he first published Kingfall. He is happily married to his beautiful wife Stephanie, his biggest supporter and best friend. He has been an avid lover of the fantasy and science fiction genre since he was a child. Telling the saga of the Neverborne Series and sharing the world of Penthara are his greatest passions in life.

www.ingramcontent.com/pod-product-compliance
Lightning Source LLC
Chambersburg PA
CBHW030626310726
48979CB00003B/903

* 9 7 8 1 7 3 4 2 7 3 7 2 4 *